THE UNKINDEST TIDE

**DAW Books presents the finest in urban fantasy
from Seanan McGuire:**

The October Daye Novels:
ROSEMARY AND RUE

A LOCAL HABITATION

AN ARTIFICIAL NIGHT

LATE ECLIPSES

ONE SALT SEA

ASHES OF HONOR

CHIMES AT MIDNIGHT

THE WINTER LONG

A RED-ROSE CHAIN

ONCE BROKEN FAITH

THE BRIGHTEST FELL

NIGHT AND SILENCE

THE UNKINDEST TIDE

The InCryptid Novels:
DISCOUNT ARMAGEDDON

MIDNIGHT BLUE-LIGHT SPECIAL

HALF-OFF RAGNAROK

POCKET APOCALYPSE

CHAOS CHOREOGRAPHY

MAGIC FOR NOTHING

TRICKS FOR FREE

THAT AIN'T WITCHCRAFT

IMAGINARY NUMBERS*

The Ghost Roads:
SPARROW HILL ROAD

THE GIRL IN THE GREEN SILK GOWN

*Coming soon from DAW Books

SEANAN McGUIRE

THE UNKINDEST TIDE

AN OCTOBER DAYE NOVEL

DAW BOOKS, INC.

DONALD A. WOLLHEIM, FOUNDER

1745 Broadway, New York, NY 10019

ELIZABETH R. WOLLHEIM
SHEILA E. GILBERT
PUBLISHERS
www.dawbooks.com

First Printing, September 2019
1 2 3 4 5 6 7 8 9

DAW TRADEMARK REGISTERED
U.S. PAT. AND TM. OFF. AND FOREIGN COUNTRIES
—MARCA REGISTRADA
HECHO EN U.S.A.

PRINTED IN THE U.S.A.

For Amy.
My mermaid.

ACKNOWLEDGMENTS:

Sometimes I am genuinely astonished that we've been able to get this far. This book marks the thirteenth of Toby's full-length adventures, and the tenth anniversary of my being allowed to introduce her to the world. To those of you who've been with me since the beginning: thank you. I don't feel like I'm being in the least disingenuous when I say that I couldn't possibly have done this without you. To those of you who are just joining us: thank you, and welcome. I think we're going to have a wonderful time together.

Every time I sit down to write one of these, I feel like "well, that's it, I'm out of people to thank," and then I pause for a moment and realize that there will always be people to thank, because the world keeps on turning, and people continue to be amazing and supportive and essential. So here are my thanks to the people who've kept me standing through the writing of *The Unkindest Tide*. Thanks to the Machete Squad, who keep me from falling flat on my face when I don't have to; to the entire team at DAW Books, where tolerance meets baffled amusement and everyone wins; and to the Penguin-Random House convention team, whose booths have provided me with safe harbors when the crowds got to be too much for me. All these people have kept me going when I wasn't sure I could.

Thank you to Vixy, who keeps me from drowning in my own ineptitude for paperwork; to my dearest, dazzling Amy, who keeps her fiddle at the ready; the Forgotten Gods RPG group, who are possibly the most civilized D&D game I've ever been involved with; Shawn, for being my off-site brain; Brooke, for being cheerfully prepared to tell me when I'm being stupid; Kayleigh, for being one of the purest sources of joy in this world; and to all the people who have sent me pictures of their cats when asked to do so. Thanks to Amy Mebberson, for reasons she knows very well indeed, and to Carla Speed McNeil, for blowing my mind on a regular basis. Thanks to Margaret, for enthusiasm, and to Whitney, for strapping on a pair of skates and trying to break some bones.

Sheila Gilbert remains the best editor this series could possibly have had, keeping these plates spinning with grace and solemnity. Joshua Starr continues to answer the phone when I call, and has learned to roll with whatever ridiculous things I say. Diana Fox is my personal superhero (everyone should have one), and Chris McGrath continues to take the images we suggest to him and turn them into magic. Finally, thank you to my pit crew: Christopher Mangum, Tara O'Shea, and Kate Secor.

Elsie is much larger now, and still made mostly of wasps. She's doing well, as are Thomas and Megara.

My soundtrack while writing *The Unkindest Tide* consisted mostly of *Hadestown*, by Anais Mitchell (still), the soundtracks to *Heathers: the Musical* and *Mean Girls: the Musical*, *Instar*, by Nancy Kerr, endless live concert recordings of the Counting Crows, and all the Annwn I have on my hard drive. Any errors in this book are entirely my own. The errors that aren't here are the ones that all these people helped me fix.

Come on. It's time to set sail. The horizon is waiting.

OCTOBER DAYE PRONUNCIATION GUIDE
THROUGH *THE UNKINDEST TIDE*

All pronunciations are given strictly phonetically. This only covers races explicitly named in the first thirteen books.

Because much of this book takes place in open waters, this pronunciation guide has been divided by land and sea. Some of the sea fae have appeared in earlier books.

LAND FAE:

Aes Sidhe: *eys shee*. Plural is "Aes Sidhe."
Afanc: *ah-fank*. Plural is "Afanc."
Bannick: *ban-nick*. Plural is "Bannicks."
Banshee: *ban-shee*. Plural is "Banshees."
Barghest: *bar-guy-st*. Plural is "Barghests."
Barrow Wight: *bar-row white*. Plural is "Barrow Wights."
Blodynbryd: *blow-din-brid*. Plural is "Blodynbryds."
Cait Sidhe: *kay-th shee*. Plural is "Cait Sidhe."
Candela: *can-dee-la*. Plural is "Candela."
Coblynau: *cob-lee-now*. Plural is "Coblynau."
Cu Sidhe: *coo shee*. Plural is "Cu Sidhe."
Daoine Sidhe: *doon-ya shee*. Plural is "Daoine Sidhe," diminutive is "Daoine."
Djinn: *jin*. Plural is "Djinn."
Dóchas Sidhe: *doe-sh-as shee*. Plural is "Dóchas Sidhe."
Ellyllon: *el-lee-lawn*. Plural is "Ellyllons."
Folletti: *foe-let-tea*. Plural is "Folletti."

Gean-Cannah: *gee-ann can-na*. Plural is "Gean-Cannah."
Glastig: *glass-tig*. Plural is "Glastigs."
Gwragen: *guh-war-a-gen*. Plural is "Gwargen."
Hamadryad: *ha-ma-dry-add*. Plural is "Hamadryads."
Kitsune: *kit-soon-nay*. Plural is "Kitsune."
Lamia: *lay-me-a*. Plural is "Lamia."
Manticore: *man-tee-core*. Plural is "Manticores."
Nixie: *nix-ee*. Plural is "Nixen."
Peri: *pear-ee*. Plural is "Peri."
Piskie: *piss-key*. Plural is "Piskies.'
Pixie: *pix-ee*. Plural is "Pixies."
Puca: *puh-ca*. Plural is "Pucas."
Satyr: *say-tur*. Plural is "Satyrs."
Shyi Shuai: *shh-yee shh-why*. Plural is "Shyi Shuai."
Silene: *sigh-lean*. Plural is "Silene."
Swanmay: *swan-may*. Plural is "Swanmays."
Tuatha de Dannan: *tootha day danan*. Plural is "Tuatha de Dannan," diminutive is "Tuatha."
Tylwyth Teg: *till-with teeg*. Plural is "Tylwyth Teg," diminutive is "Tylwyth."
Urisk: *you-risk*. Plural is "Urisk."

SEA FAE:

Annwn: *ah-noon*. No plural exists.
Asrai: *as-rye*. Plural is "Asrai."
Cephali: *she-fall-li*. Plural is "Cephali."
Cetace: *sea-tay-see*. Plural is "Cetacea."
Hippocampus: *hip-po-cam-pus*. Plural is "Hippocampi."
Kelpie: *kel-pee*. Plural is "Kelpies."
The Luidaeg: *the lou-sha-k*. No plural exists
Merrow: *meh-row*. Plural is "Merrow."
Naiad: *nigh-add*. Plural is "Naiads."
Nixie: *nix-ee*. Plural is "Nixen."
Roane: *row-n*. Plural is "Roane."
Selkie: *sell-key*. Plural is "Selkies."
Undine: *un-deen*. Plural is "Undine."

KINGDOMS OF THE WESTLANDS

Kingdom of
Frozen Winds

Kingdom of
Warm Skies

Kingdom of
Evergreen

Kingdom of
Leucothea

Kingdom of
Silences

Kingdom of
Starfall

Battle of
Silences

Kingdom
of the Mists

Kingdom of
Painted Skies

Kingdom on the
Golden Shore

Kingdom
of Angels

Kingdom
of Copper

Priscilla Spencer

ONE

March 8th, 2014

What's the unkindest tide?
> —William Shakespeare, *Two Gentlemen of Verona*.

SOME PEOPLE BELIEVE the rise of the cell phone—and the associated rise of the cell phone camera—must have been a boon for the private detective. After all, when your camera isn't just handheld, but is also attached to a personal communication device, it seems like it should be easier to surreptitiously photograph people doing things they aren't supposed to do. Like cheating on their spouses, or money laundering, or trying to violate the terms of their custody agreements. All those charming, frustrating little ways that people like to break the rules, captured for the courts with a single press of a button. No fuss, no muss, no need to get anything developed. Swell, right?

Not so much. The trouble is, cell phone cameras have a long way to go before they'll match the capabilities of a good zoom lens or long-distance rig, much less exceed them—and that's where I have a problem. I still need my good lenses, but the more ubiquitous cell phones become, the more your classic camera stands out to the curious bystander. I used to be able to wander around with my trusty Canon slung around my neck and be confident that anyone who saw me would take me for a tourist. Not anymore. These days, people *notice*. People *talk*.

Some days I wind up taking lots of pictures of flowers and graffiti and showing them to anyone who seems too interested. It deflects suspicion, and it's surprisingly soothing, even if I'm not going to get a gallery show any time soon. More often, I use some of my precious magic to hide my camera behind a veil of illusion. It makes me look like some sort of bizarre mime whenever I take a picture, but somehow, this is *less* obviously weird, at least in San Francisco.

Humans are strange.

I'd been following a man around the city with my veiled camera for three days, trying to get pictures of him meeting with a group of "investors" who were planning to use underhanded means to buy shares in his company. I didn't fully understand why they didn't just call their stockbrokers, but the man who'd hired me was the first man's business partner, and he was paying me well for my time and expertise. I don't question the check, as long as it cashes.

I used to be a more or less full-time private detective. These days, knight errantry eats up a lot of time, leaving me with curtailed work hours. Knight errantry also doesn't pay, not when you're talking cash money, and I'd jumped at the chance to pad my bank account back to something resembling normal. I have a lot of mouths to feed at home, and that doesn't even go into the cost of veterinary cat food for my two geriatric Siamese.

My patience had paid off. Patience so often does. After three days, several near misses, and two false positions, it had all come together in a photo opportunity so perfect that I'd checked to make sure it wasn't being staged. I'd captured the pictures my client wanted without being seen by my target, and had dropped off the film in exchange for a lovely check, complete with hefty bonus. Not too bad for half a week's work.

Depositing the check had been quick and easy and best of all, gave me an excuse to pick up burritos from my favorite taqueria. The scent of them filled the car, making me drive a little faster. Burritos are best when they're hot, and I wanted to get these home to my family before they had a chance to cool.

Home. Family. Two words I used to think would never apply to me again, which just goes to show how much things can change. Sometimes they even change for the better.

My name is October Daye. I'm a changeling, which is a fancy way of saying "one of my parents was human, and one of them wasn't." It sounds simple. It's not. Being a changeling means never really knowing where you belong. It means always feeling like you're standing on the outside of two worlds, unable to commit to being a part of either one, equally unable to walk away.

It's even more complicated in my case. I was raised thinking I was half Daoine Sidhe on my mother's side, making me a descendant of Titania. Well, it turns out my mother, Amandine the Liar, is actually the daughter of Oberon himself. She's Firstborn, and I'm . . .

I'm not *completely* new, but I'm not all that old, either. There are only three of my kind of fae in all of Faerie. We're called the Dóchas Sidhe. I'm still trying to figure out exactly what that means.

To add another fun little wrinkle, my mother's mother is a human woman, Janet Carter. Yes, that Janet, the one whose interference with Maeve's final Ride led to the Winter Queen's disappearance and changed the course of Faerie forever. So that's something fun for me to live with. Janet is still alive, by the way. She married my ex-fiancé after I disappeared for fourteen years. My daughter Gillian calls her "Mom."

My family tree has a lot of thorns, and a tendency to draw blood.

Being a changeling usually also means living on the fringes of Faerie's political structure, since the fact that we're mortal is seen as a sign of weakness. Again, things are different for me. Duke Sylvester Torquill of Shadowed Hills stepped in as my protector and patron while I was still a child. Thanks to him, when I got tired of living on the streets with the rest of the changeling kids, I had someone to back me up and take care of me. Under his protection, and after I'd discovered a new knowe for the then-Queen of the Mists, I'd been able to study for and eventually achieve my knighthood—something that was almost unthinkable for a changeling, even one with my bloodline.

Being a knight gave me a place in the Courts. It was a low place, sure, and many people regarded it as scarcely better than being treated like a particularly clever pet, but it had been enough to give me something to hold onto. I'm surprisingly difficult to shake once I have something to hold onto.

I started as a knight, became a knight errant—sort of a fancy way of saying "odd jobs person for the fae courts of the San Francisco Bay area"—deposed an illegitimate monarch, and helped the true ruler of the Mists claim her family's throne. It was a lot of work, and resulted in my being named a hero of the realm, which is sort of like being a knight errant, only more so. Heroes of the realm protect people.

And I have people to protect. Somewhere along the way, despite everything, I found my people. I have a squire. I have a Fetch. I have a man I love, who wants to marry me. I have a family, and they were all waiting for me to get home with dinner.

I drove a little faster.

The past three months hadn't been perfect, but they'd been surprisingly peaceful, despite presenting their own unique challenges. Gillian—who had been born a thin-blooded changeling and then turned completely human in order to save her from a painful, elf-shot-induced death—was finally part of Faerie. I'd been resigned to the possibility that I'd never see my daughter again, that one day I'd have to add her grave to the list of those I visited regularly, decking them with rosemary and rue.

Only it hadn't worked out that way. One of my old enemies, the false Queen of the Mists, had arranged for the kidnapping of my only child, and had nearly killed her by jamming an arrow dipped in elf-shot into her shoulder. Elf-shot is always fatal to humans. Gilly should have died. Gilly *would* have died if Tybalt hadn't reached her before the poison could stop her heart. He'd carried her onto the Shadow Roads, which are only accessible to the Cait Sidhe, and from there to the Luidaeg, the sea witch of legend, and my mother's sister.

Like I said, my family is complicated.

The Luidaeg had been able to give Gillian a chance to survive. She'd draped my daughter in a Selkie's skin, chasing the mortality from her bones for at least a hundred years. Most Selkies don't keep their skins that long, but in Gilly's case . . .

The elf-shot would linger in her system for a century. That's what elf-shot was designed to do. It puts purebloods to sleep, and it keeps them that way until the world changes around them, becoming something alien and strange. If Gilly set her sealskin aside before the poison faded, she would die. Her humanity was the price of staying alive. It was seeing her father, her friends, everyone she'd ever cared about grow old and die while she continued on. She'd chosen to be human when I gave her the Changeling's Choice, and then the false Queen and the Luidaeg had taken that away from her, one out of malice and one out of mercy, and I had to wonder whether she'd ever forgive any of us.

I haven't spoken to her since the day she woke up and realized her life had changed forever. I promised to give her whatever space she needed, to let her be the one to come to me. But really, I don't know what to say. "I'm sorry I saved your life" is a lie. So is "It's better to be fae." And "I didn't want this for you" just might be the biggest lie of all. Of course, I wanted this—or something like it. She's my daughter. I want her with me.

But I'm not the mother she reaches for when she's scared, or lost, or lonely. That honor goes to my own grandmother, Janet Carter, who stepped in and raised my child when Faerie conspired to take me away from her for fourteen years.

Sometimes I hate my biological family. Maybe that's why I've worked so hard to build myself a new one.

It was simultaneously late enough and early enough that traffic was light. The Market District was closed for the evening, sending its burden of businesspeople and their support staff scurrying back to their safe, secure homes, while the bars and clubs downtown had yet to hit their full swing. I passed Dolores Park and pulled into the driveway of my old Victorian-style house in nearly record time. The kitchen lights were on. I turned off the car, opened the door, and was accosted by the sound of classic rock blasting through the open window. May was singing along as Journey asserted the need to continue to believe. May, like me, can't carry a tune in a bucket. The effect was surprisingly charming. It said "you're safe here." It said "nothing is currently wrong."

It said "welcome home."

Since there were people home, the wards weren't set; all I needed to get inside was my key. I stepped into the warm, bright kitchen, where my Fetch was dancing in front of the counter as she mixed a bowl of cookie dough. She turned and grinned at me.

"I hope you got extra burritos," she said. "We have extra mouths in residence."

I raised an eyebrow. "How many?"

"Dean and Raj."

I raised the other eyebrow. "Raj got away for the evening?"

May nodded. "Uh-huh. Gin told him part of kingship is being able to delegate every once in a while, so he's our problem until midnight. That's why I'm baking cookies. They're working that poor boy to the *bone*."

"That poor boy is going to be King of Cats; he signed up for this." I swiped a fingerful of cookie dough as I headed for the hall. May laughed and hit me with her mixing spoon, getting more dough on my wrist. I grinned and kept walking, sticking my wrist in my mouth to suck off the sugary goodness.

As my Fetch—technically retired, since Amandine broke the connection between us when she changed the balance of my blood to save my life—May and I used to be identical. Now, years and quests and changes later, we still look like sisters, but we're not twins anymore. Her face is the one I had when she was called into existence, soft and round and human in ways my own face has forgotten. Her eyes are a pale, misty gray, and her hair is the no-color brown that drives a thousand salon appointments, a color she's constantly at war with, covering it in streaks of blue and green and purple and, most recently, flaming orange. It makes her happy, and I like it when she's happy. After all, she's my sister in every way that counts.

Her live-in girlfriend, Jazz, was in the dining room, sitting at the table and clipping coupons out of an advertising circular. She tensed and looked up at the sound of my footsteps, golden eyes briefly widening before she relaxed and offered me a somewhat weary smile. "Hey, Toby," she said. "Need me to move?"

"Up to you." I held up the bag of burritos. "As soon as I crinkle the foil, we're going to have an invasion of teenage boys. Salsa may fly. Your coupons could get royally wrecked."

"Yes, but I'll have salsa, so I'll live."

I watched her gather her coupons as I set my bag down and unpacked its contents. Fortunately for my ability to eat my own dinner, I *always* make it a point to pick up a couple of extra burritos these days. My house contains between one and four teenagers at any given moment in time—more if Chelsea's over and has decided she needs one or more of Mitch and Stacy's daughters to save her from being outnumbered by the boys. If there's one thing fae and mortal teens absolutely have in common, it's the ability to eat more than should be physically possible. I once found Quentin absently gnawing on a stick of butter while he was doing his homework. It would be terrifying, if it wasn't so impressive.

Jazz is a Raven-maid, one of the few types of diurnal fae. She and May make it work, mostly by spending their mornings and evenings together, then each doing other things while the other is asleep. For Jazz, "other things" usually means running her small secondhand store in Berkeley, on the other side of the Bay. Recently, though . . .

Recently, it's mostly meant staying in the house with the doors and windows closed, steadfastly refusing to look outside and see the birds in flight. My mother broke something deep inside Jazz when she kidnapped her from what should have been the safety of her own home. It had been part of an effort to blackmail me into bringing back her eldest daughter, my missing sister, August. As usual, Amandine hadn't cared who might get hurt, as long as she got her way.

She'd gotten her way. August had come home. And a lot of people had gotten hurt, including Jazz, who might never be okay again.

The smell of musk and pennyroyal tickled my nose a split second before arms slid around my waist from behind, pulling me against the solid form of a man only a few inches taller than I was. Tybalt buried his face in my hair, murmuring, "I was just thinking the house was surprisingly devoid of chaos, given its current occupants, and then you walked in the door."

"Well, I do live here," I said, continuing to lay food out on the table. "Plus I brought food, so this is about to be a battleground."

Tybalt laughed, breath warm against my ear, and didn't let me go.

Tybalt. My friend, who was never really my enemy, even when I'd believed him to be; my lover; my betrothed; and another victim of my mother's petty determination to have her eldest daughter back, no matter how many people were collateral damage. Tybalt had been King of Dreaming Cats long before he'd been foolish enough to get involved with me. Now, thanks to my mother, he'd stepped away from his throne, allowing the daughter of an old friend to stand regent in his stead while he tried to put himself back together. Cait Sidhe choose their rulers based on raw strength and the ability to protect the Court. By admitting he was too damaged to rule, even for a short time, Tybalt might have lost his throne forever.

I'd never considered myself a person worth losing a throne for, but Tybalt thought I was, and I've learned not to argue with him about that sort of thing. Instead, I was doing my best to live up to what he saw when he looked at me. That seemed better for both of us. Healthier.

Footsteps thundered in the hall behind us. Tybalt laughed again, drawing me even closer.

"Prepare yourself," he said, and the teenage wave descended.

Quentin Sollys, my sworn squire, who also happened to be the Crown Prince of the Westlands—meaning he'll be High King of the fae kingdoms of North America one day—ducked past me to grab the burrito with the "Q" on the side, tossing me a jaunty wave before he snatched the entire bag of tortilla chips and took off running.

Raj was close behind him, taking one of the unmarked burritos and two containers of salsa before chasing after Quentin and the chips. At least he slowed down long enough to offer a quick, distracted wave, which was honestly more than I'd been expecting. I grinned, leaning against Tybalt.

"Try not to get salsa on the ceiling this time, okay?" I called after Raj. "My hearth magic isn't good enough to deal with tomato juice on plaster."

"No, but May's is!" Raj shouted back, and was gone.

Dean was the last of our resident teenagers to reach the table. He hesitated, looking at the three remaining unmarked burritos.

Normally, we take a hands-off approach to feeding the teen swarm—leave the food unattended and they'll take care of themselves. I stand in loco parentis for Quentin in many ways, but I'm not his mother, and as long as he doesn't starve or get scurvy, I've done my job.

Dean, though . . . sometimes it's necessary to intervene a little with him. He's the Count of Goldengreen, not technically a teenager anymore—he's a year older than Quentin, who turned nineteen on his last birthday—and raised in the Undersea by his Merrow mother and Daoine Sidhe father. Dean isn't the youngest Count I've ever heard of, although he's one of the youngest without a Regent to massage his decrees into something more palatable for the local nobles. His reign has been—quite literally—sink or swim, since he started it with no idea how things were done in the land Courts, and was given his position almost entirely to prevent a war.

But he's done okay. His seneschal, Marcia, who was my seneschal when I was Countess of Goldengreen, has worked hard to steer him away from the nastier dangers of his position, and Goldengreen has always been mostly a show County, consisting of a knowe and a household and not much more. He doesn't have land to protect or official duties to perform.

He also, from the way he was looking at those burritos, didn't have much of an idea of how to deal with cylinders of food wrapped in nicely concealing layers of foil. I smiled, trying to seem encouraging rather than mocking.

"The narrowest one is vegetarian, the fattest one is chicken and rice, and the one in the middle is steak," I said.

He shot me a startled look which quickly turned thankful. "Quentin says I need to eat more mortal food, since there's going to come a time when Marcia is unavailable and I'm starving," he said. "That doesn't make it easy to understand the way they label things. Or don't label them, as the case may be."

"Well, I'd take the chicken and rice, since that's sort of a good starting point for the whole concept of 'the Mission Burrito.' Quentin has pork and way too many bell peppers, and Raj took the chicken supreme. Get them to give you bites, figure out what you think you might like, and I'll add your order to the list."

Surprise melted into genuine delight. "You'd be willing to do that?"

"Sure." I shrugged. "You're pretty much part of the family. We feed the family."

His smile was heartbreakingly bright. He grabbed the burrito I'd indicated and hurried after the others, back to Quentin's room and whatever terrifying mischief three boys with noble titles and the anticipation of the weight of the world on their shoulders could get up to. As a rule, I don't ask, and they don't tell me. It's safer that way.

With the teenage stampede finally out of the way, Tybalt removed his arms from around my waist and went to claim his own burrito. "I trust your evening's work went well? I think I like it when you do human detective things. You come home to me not having bled on anything at all, and it's delightfully novel."

"It also pays for these burritos, which is a nice change."

Tybalt sniffed. "Money is no concern."

"It is when you don't want to use fairy gold on the nice man at the taqueria." I'd been there once with Simon, my stepfather. He had charmed the counterman with his breezy manner and fluency in Spanish. I still got asked about him when I went to order food. It was nice, in a way, to deal with someone whose only impressions of Simon were positive ones.

Simon Torquill has been married to my mother since long before I was born, even if I didn't learn that fun fact until comparatively recently. He was, for a long time, my biggest bogeyman: the man who transformed me into a fish, abandoned me in a pond, and caused me to lose my entire mortal life. He'd taken everything I'd ever thought I wanted away with a single casual spell, and as far as I'd been able to tell, he hadn't lost a minute of sleep over it. I had been nothing to him. Just one more inconsequential changeling.

Only later I'd learned that he'd done it to protect me from a much bigger threat: his liege lady, Evening Winterrose, more accurately known as Eira Rosynhwyr, Firstborn of the Daoine Sidhe. I'd learned a lot of things too late for them to do either one of us any good, and now Simon was lost again, captive of his own inner demons, bound by a bargain he'd made with the Luidaeg to save his biological child.

I was going to find a way to save him. I was. I was just going to focus on saving the people closest to me first. You can't bandage someone else's wounds while you're bleeding to death from your own. It never works out the way you want it to.

Tybalt gave me a wounded look. I would have called it making puppy-dog eyes if he weren't literally a cat. "No," he said. "Money is no object. October, do you honestly think me such a churl that I would intend to live in your home in perpetuity, eat at your table, and not provide for you or your household in even a small capacity?"

"It never came up." I picked up my own burrito—basically everything I could convince them to encase in a single flexible tortilla—and produced the second bag of chips from beneath the table before plopping myself down in a chair.

"I've brought groceries," he protested.

"Yes, and I didn't ask about where they came from, because if you were enchanting some poor clerk into letting you shoplift, I didn't want to know." The fae attitude toward property can be, well, flexible, especially when the property in question is in the hands of humans. Purebloods mostly don't steal from each other unless they've got an army behind them. Everyone else is fair game.

"You used to work at Safeway, right?" asked Jazz.

I nodded. "I did, before May showed up and started helping cover the rent. That's when we were in the old apartment." The timeline there was skewed and simplified, but it was close enough to accurate. Sometimes things have to be condensed if they're going to make sense.

That's the history of Faerie in a nutshell, really. When you're talking about people who live for literal centuries, entire dynasties can wind up shortened to a sentence tucked away in a paragraph about how nice the flowers look when the spring returns. Legends are true. History is a lie. Everything old comes around and becomes new again, and people who've witnessed linguistic and continental drift firsthand are standing right there to give their opinion on it.

"I bought the groceries," said Tybalt, sounding only faintly offended. "I bought them with legitimate human currency, and did not rob anyone to get it."

I blinked at him. "How did you—?"

"I arrived in the Mists over a century ago, when there was no indication that this small, provincial kingdom would become such a hotbed of activity," said Tybalt. "I was in Pines before that, living among the mortals with my Anne."

"Oh." Anne, his first wife, had been a human woman. She died in childbirth sometime in the early 1900s. The local fae courts had been unwilling to step in and help her or their child.

It was because of that reluctance that Tybalt had disliked changelings for so long. A changeling took his wife away, even if it hadn't been intentional or malicious. I'd known things between us were never going to be the same when he'd finally broken down and told me about Anne. That was when he'd let his grudges go. That was when he'd admitted that he loved me.

Life is never simple. I'd say "when Faerie is involved," but I don't think I need to. Life is never simple, period. All we can do is hang on and hope for the best.

He smiled, finally picking up his own burrito: chicken, pork, beef, cheese, and sour cream. "Anne was quite annoyed when I took things from local merchants without proper payment, and I'll admit, I had a bit of a prior inclination toward paying, born of my time in the Londinium theater. It's better to pay people for the things they make, assuming you want them to keep working. I've never been inclined toward learning a mortal trade, but I did odd jobs enough to keep her fed and healthy, and I learned your banking system well enough to acquit myself."

I blinked at him slowly. "Tybalt. You didn't understand what a *car* was until I started making you ride in one. You'd never been on a *bus* before."

"Neither of those things is a requirement of banking, little fish. Money has many uses, and not all of them are related to transportation."

"I don't . . ." I pinched the bridge of my nose. "I don't know what to do with this. You have money?"

"Yes."

"How *much* money?"

"Sufficient that I can pay for groceries when I wish to, and I'll expect you to allow me to do so." He took a hearty bite of his burrito, chewed, swallowed, and added, "I am a part of this family. I will contribute, like it or no, and I will do so in ways that do not involve your bedroom."

A harsh cawing sound rang out from the end of the table. I whipped around, nearly dropping my burrito. Tybalt flinched, unable to quite control the momentary flash of panic in his eyes. Then we both froze, staring.

Jazz was laughing.

May raced into the room, face pale and eyes wide, clearly ready to jump into battle against whatever was hurting her girlfriend. Then she froze as well, pressing one hand to her mouth. Jazz kept laughing, leaning back in her seat and tucking her hands behind her head, seemingly helpless against her own amusement.

"Honey?" asked May. "Are you all right?"

Jazz shook her head, still laughing.

I found my voice, tucked away in a corner where I hadn't been able to reach it before. "I think she's going to be okay," I said. "I think . . . I think maybe we're all going to be okay."

May laughed once, and if there was a hint of a sob tucked inside the sound, none of us was going to point it out. She rushed to Jazz's side, putting her arms around the other woman, and they held each other while they laughed, and for the first time since Amandine had shown up at my door, I started to feel like maybe things were getting back to normal. We were safe. We were home. We were together, and we were going to be okay.

Tybalt smiled at me across the table as he picked up his burrito. I smiled back, and everything was exactly the way it was supposed to be. Finally, *finally*, everything was right.

TWO

THE HOUSE WAS QUIET by ten o'clock. The boys were in Quentin's room with the door closed. I should probably have been concerned about them getting into trouble, but I was honestly too relieved to know where they were to care. May's chocolate chip cookies had been baked and devoured, and May herself had gone upstairs, dragging Jazz by the wrist. They, too, had closed their bedroom door, and I felt like I'd be even less welcome in that particular room.

The remains of dinner had been cleaned up and either put in the refrigerator or thrown away; there weren't even any dishes to deal with. Tybalt and I took advantage of the rare lull to curl up on the couch and put on a BBC production of *The Tempest*. Not that we were paying any attention to it. There's nothing like Shakespeare to blunt the sounds of impending hanky-panky, or current heavy petting.

Tybalt had one hand under my shirt, cupping the curve of my right breast, while he tangled his other hand in my hair, tying knots that would take me hours with a hairbrush to untangle. I wasn't complaining. I was too busy trying to mold myself against him, making it easier for him to reach any part of my body that caught his fancy. Living in a house with three other full-time residents and an endlessly shifting cast of visitors has taught me to take my pleasures where I can find them, and at the moment, I was *very* focused on finding them.

It didn't hurt that Tybalt is possibly the most beautiful man I've ever been lucky enough to set my eyes on. Some of the Daoine Sidhe could beat him for pure prettiness—prettiness is sort of what the Daoine Sidhe do—but personal tastes have something to say when it comes to attraction, and Tybalt is so perfectly suited to my tastes that he might as well have been tailor-made to keep me happy.

He's lean, like the predator he is. Before we started sleeping together, I'd mostly seen him tense, defending his territory, his people, or me. I'd never realized he was capable of the complete, seemingly boneless relaxation of a housecat who feels genuinely safe. A truly relaxed Tybalt is a creature of pure, hedonistic softness, with the occasional flash of very welcome hardness.

Without a disguise to make him seem human, his fae origins are written plainly in the bones of his face, in the green, striated color of his eyes, and in the black stripes that paint a tabby pattern through his brown hair. His ears are pointed, his incisors are a bit too sharp, and his pupils are ovals that widen and narrow according to the light. He's powerful enough to keep the more animal aspects of his fae nature from peeking through when he doesn't want them to: unlike some Cait Sidhe, he doesn't have to walk around with a tail.

Of course, there are some animal aspects I don't object to. Tybalt buried his face against my neck, nipping at my skin with those pointed incisors, and I squeaked, making no effort to pull away. He took that as the invitation it was and bit harder, making a small growling noise.

The doorbell rang.

We both stopped what we were doing, Tybalt letting go of my hair and pulling back enough to blink at me, startled and visibly unhappy.

"Were you expecting someone?" he asked.

I shook my head. "No, and my phone isn't set to silent. Arden or Etienne would have texted." As Queen in the Mists, Arden Windermere is officially in charge of telling me when it's time to go out and do hero stuff. As Sylvester's seneschal, Etienne is usually the one who contacts me when my actual liege lord needs me.

Most purebloods aren't comfortable with modern technology. It moves too fast for them. Arden spent a century hiding in the human world, and Etienne has a human wife and a human-schooled daughter. Both of them prefer texting to calling, since I ask fewer questions when they just send me my assignment.

"Did Quentin order pizza?"

"If he did, he didn't warn me, and I'm probably paying for it. So if he did, I'm going to skin him," I said.

The doorbell rang again.

I pushed myself off Tybalt's lap with a groan, tugging my shirt into place before grabbing a handful of shadows and weaving them into a quick if clunky human disguise. Etienne would have been so disappointed in me. He liked elegant spells, and this wasn't that. It relied more on making people not want to look at the sharp tips of my ears or the inhuman paleness of my eyes than on replacing those things with believably human facsimiles.

My irritation at the interruption made the process easier than it would have been otherwise. Titania is the mother of illusions, the font from which all flower magic springs, and she's no ancestor of mine. Anything that relies on flowers has never come easily for me. Anger, on the other hand, gives my magic a pretty substantial boost. And boy, was I pissed.

Being a hero means people interrupt me, but that still didn't make it okay for someone to be ringing my doorbell uninvited at ten o'clock at night when my fiancé was finally feeling frisky. My sex life had taken a massive hit since Amandine decided to come knocking, and I was going to be grumpy about interruptions for quite some time to come.

"If it's your mother at the door, or your sister, or any member of your extended family, I am grabbing you by the scruff of the neck and hauling you into the shadows before they have time to do more than sneer," said Tybalt darkly, getting off the couch and following me down the hall.

"Be my guest," I said, and opened the door.

The woman on the front step looked at me blandly. "Took you long enough," she said.

I didn't say anything.

She looked like she was somewhere in her late teens, like she'd come to join Quentin's impromptu slumber party because it was more fun than hanging around watching Shakespeare with the boring adults. Her hair was thick, dark, and curly, gathered into twin pigtails that hung over her shoulders and tangled around the straps of her overalls. They were tied off with strips of what looked like electrical tape. Sometimes I wonder how she ever manages to take her hair down without screaming. And then I remember that she's so much older and more powerful than I am that she could easily swat me like a bug, and I keep my idle questions to myself.

She was wearing overalls, an old white tank top, and battered tennis shoes. The ghosts of old acne scars clung to her cheeks and forehead; her eyes were a murky, lake-bottom blue. She looked about as much like a powerful, unstoppable sea witch as I did, which was to say, she didn't look like one at all.

"Trick or treat," she said mildly. "Let me in."

"It's March, not October," I said, and stepped to the side to let her pass.

She stepped into the hall, accompanied by the smell of wind blowing across the open ocean. "Some people will tell you Halloween is every day if you have the right attitude," she said, flicking her fingers. The door slammed shut. Smirking, she ran her eyes first over me and then over Tybalt, taking in all the little signs of dishevelment that our hurried illusions hadn't been able to conceal. "Am I interrupting something?"

"If I say 'yes,' will you leave?" I asked, folding my arms. Tybalt made a small sound, although whether of amusement or dismay, I couldn't quite tell.

To be fair, most people don't talk back to the Luidaeg. She's the eldest of Maeve's remaining children, with so many centuries behind her that I'm not sure even she remembers—or cares—how old she actually is. Like most of her siblings, her power outstrips that of her descendants like a hurricane outstrips a zephyr, in both strength and flexibility. She can do things the rest of Faerie can only dream of.

Or have nightmares about. I've had more than a few nightmares about the things the Luidaeg thinks are good ideas.

"No," said the Luidaeg. She took another look around the hall. "Who else is here? I know it's not just you."

I wanted to ask her *how* she knew. I knew, of course, but that's thanks to a kind of tracking that seems to be unique to the Dóchas Sidhe. I can follow the scent of someone's magic almost to the ends of the Earth. If I breathed in deeply enough, I could identify every person in my house, from May's cotton candy and ashes to Dean's less familiar but increasingly well-loved eucalyptus and wet rock. No two people have precisely the same magical signature. Even if they possess some common element, such as roses or heather, there's always something about it that's unique.

"Tybalt, obviously," I said. "May and Jazz are in their room. Quentin's in *his* room, with Raj and Dean."

The Luidaeg nodded. "Good. Good. You can let your lady Fetch enjoy her evening; I doubt her Raven-maid particularly wants to see me."

"No," I admitted. "Jazz isn't a big fan of the Firstborn right now."

"That's going to make your wedding fun." The Luidaeg cast a measuring, narrow-eyed look at Tybalt. "I assume I *am* invited."

"We would no more dream of refusing you an invitation than we would of dancing naked through a storm of glass," said Tybalt smoothly.

"Unless that was your way of asking whether the wedding's still on," I said. "It is. Cake and everything. We just need to figure out when the Mists can spare us both."

"So next century; got it," said the Luidaeg. Her expression sobered. "Fetch your boys."

"Which ones?" I asked.

"All of them. This is relevant to all of them."

Tybalt and I exchanged a glance before he stepped around me and offered the Luidaeg a shallow bow. "Shall I show you to the dining room? We have a few burritos and some salsa left from our dinner, and I would be delighted to fetch them for your consideration."

"Sounds good," said the Luidaeg. She swung her attention back to me. "Be quick. I have things to do tonight."

"That's ominous," I said, and started for the stairs. When the Luidaeg says it's time to hurry, I hurry. Anything else could be taken as an insult, and while I don't actually think she'd hurt me on a whim, it's better to be safe than sorry.

I met the Luidaeg when I was investigating the supposed murder of Evening Winterrose, her half-sister and—as it turns out—her direst enemy. It would have been nice to know that at the time. It would have been even nicer to know that Evening wasn't dead but in hiding, healing and planning to come back and ruin absolutely everyone's night. Too bad Evening has never been particularly interested in being *nice*.

That's when I *met* the Luidaeg, but I've known about her since I was a child. She's the bogeyman fae parents use to threaten their children, the terrifying sea witch who will spirit them away to where the bad kids go if they don't eat their vegetables or practice their illusions or make their beds. Out of all Faerie's monsters, she's painted as the one with the sharpest teeth, the cruelest claws. I suspect that's more of Evening's work, because while the Luidaeg can be harsh, she's rarely cruel. Her gifts come with a cost. That doesn't make them evil. It just makes them expensive.

The upstairs hall was even quieter than the living room. I sniffed, detecting traces of multiple silencing spells. May and Jazz are usually considerate about that sort of thing. Quentin is less considerate than acting in self-defense, since I have a tendency to come to bed late, loud, and somewhat clumsy.

His bedroom door was closed. I knocked. There was no reply. I knocked again before I realized that if the silencing spell was good enough, no noise could get in *or* out. That's the trouble with magic. It's useful, but it isn't always easy to adapt to mundane uses.

In some ways, the fact that the people living with me felt comfortable enough to use silencing spells on their bedrooms was incredibly flattering. They knew that if something went wrong, Tybalt and I would step in—and if I really needed them, I'd call. Not even silencing spells can stop a cellular signal from getting through.

With that in mind, I pulled out my phone and selected Quentin's name from my contact list. It was already ringing as I raised it to my ear. I waited.

There was a beep. "Hello?"

"Why is there a silencing spell on your room so strong that you can't hear me knocking?"

"Um." I heard more than guilt in Quentin's pause: I heard loud explosions, and the sound of Dean whooping with delight.

I pinched the bridge of my nose. "You're playing video games with Chelsea again, aren't you?"

"Raj has the best reflexes of anyone we know! He could go competitive if he weren't—" Quentin caught himself and stopped mid-sentence.

"If he weren't expected to take the throne soon; I know," I said. "You're going to have to tell Chelsea you're sorry, but it's time to log off. The Luidaeg is here. She wants to talk to all three of you."

There was a long pause before Quentin asked warily, "Really?"

Smart boy. "Really," I said. "I think Tybalt's feeding her our dinner leftovers. Get downstairs as soon as you can."

I ended the call and turned away, hesitating only long enough to glance one more time at May's door, shake my head, and keep walking. May has a lot of my memories. She has a lot of my regrets. What she *doesn't* have, thankfully, is my personality: she looked at the things that made me who I am and interpreted them in a whole new light, weighing them against the memories she'd brought with her from her previous existence as one of the night-haunts and deciding that what mattered wasn't heroism, it was home.

She's my sister—the only one I'm willing to acknowledge. And what she needed, right now, was to spend time with her girl-friend, who was finally remembering how to laugh, and not get dragged into some wildly dangerous quest. I'd tell her what was going on before I did anything as serious as leaving the house, but for right now?

She deserved to rest.

Tybalt and the Luidaeg were in the dining room. She had claimed both leftover burritos, split them open, and created a half-horrifying, half-aspirational plate of pseudo-nachos by dumping their contents on the remaining chips. She was seated at the head of the table and munching steadily away, as focused as if she hadn't eaten since the last time San Francisco burned to the ground.

"I don't think some of those flavors are supposed to go together," I said, moving to stand next to Tybalt. He was leaning against the wall by the china hutch, which was really more of a "random mail and things we didn't care about enough to put properly away" hutch, keeping a careful eye on the Luidaeg.

"All flavors go together if you're willing," said the Luidaeg matter-of-factly. "Didn't you go to fetch the boys?"

"They'll be right down." I settled against the wall, folding my arms. "I'm guessing this isn't a social call."

"What was your first clue?" asked the Luidaeg.

"The part where you asked me to fetch the boys. Also the part where you don't usually just drop by for no reason. Is something wrong?"

"You could say that." She laughed, and the sound was mirthless, hollow; it was the rattle of bones across the bottom of the endless sea, and there was nothing in it that remembered what it was to forgive. "Something's been wrong for a long, long time, and it's finally time to make it right again, or as right as it can be. I'm not sure there's any real fixing what's been broken."

Dread coiled in the pit of my stomach. "I—" I began, and stopped, catching myself before I could ask the question. If she wanted me to wait for Quentin and the others, I would wait. No matter how difficult it was, no matter how much I wanted to know *now*. I owed her that much, after everything she'd done for me and mine.

The Luidaeg shot me a quick, thankful look and returned to her nachos, working her way through them with the single-minded focus of a woman who didn't know when she was going to eat again. I'm not sure the Firstborn—any of the Firstborn—actually need to eat; the rules for killing them are specific and complicated and don't include "starvation." But that doesn't mean they can't enjoy being comfortable, and there's something about a full stomach that's a comfort for almost everyone.

Tybalt shifted to stand closer to me. I bumped my shoulder against his, but didn't lean. This felt like hero business, and while I might resent both the title and the responsibility, it deserved to be taken seriously.

Footsteps cautiously descended the stairs. Only two sets, which meant Raj was unnerved enough about the interruption in his gaming time to have gone into full silent Cait Sidhe mode. Like Tybalt, he only makes noise when he wants to. Tybalt and I looked toward the hall.

The Luidaeg kept eating nachos.

"Toby?" Quentin was the first to appear in the doorway. He spotted the Luidaeg and shifted his focus to her, offering a small wave and an even smaller grin. "Hi, Luidaeg."

"Hi, yourself," she said, pushing her plate aside. "Come give me a hug before shit gets serious. You haven't been visiting enough recently."

"Sorry," he said, moving to do as he was told. "Between my lessons and Toby's hero stuff and hanging out with Dean, there hasn't been time for visiting old people."

There was a sharp intake of breath. If I turned, I knew I'd see Dean Lorden, absolutely horrified by the flippant way his boyfriend was talking to the Luidaeg.

If I'm comfortable with her, Quentin adores her. She was never his childhood monster. For him, she's always been a friend of the family, someone who helps as much as her admittedly restrictive geasa allow. That's my fault. I'm the one who introduced them, however accidentally, and also the one who kept dragging him into her presence. But it's been good for both of them, and I'm not sorry. There will always be a thin edge of fear in my dealings with the Luidaeg. Quentin doesn't have that. With Quentin, she can almost be normal.

Dean, on the other hand, grew up in the Undersea, where the stories of the Luidaeg are less "scary sea witch" and more "unstoppable force of nature." She's the last of the oceanic Firstborn known to be alive and active, and she hasn't been a part of the Undersea in centuries, not since Evening Winterrose arranged for the slaughter of the Roane. They were the Luidaeg's descendant race. She still hasn't recovered from their loss.

Like I said earlier, there's a lot of history around here, and sometimes it doesn't summarize very well.

The Luidaeg ruffled Quentin's hair before letting him go. "This old person could cause a tsunami to take out this entire city if she feels neglected enough, so have some respect," she said.

"The worst thing about that sentence is that it's true," I said dryly. The Luidaeg never lies. She can't. She can talk around things, she can deflect, she can even try answering a question that hasn't actually been asked, but she can't *lie*. I took a quick look around, noting Dean in the doorway and Raj a few feet away, watching the Luidaeg with unblinking eyes. I turned back to her. "We're all here. What do you want?"

"Are you sure?" She gestured to her nachos. "I could eat the rest of these. We could talk about things. The weather, maybe. I understand some people like to talk about the weather."

"Luidaeg." I pinched the bridge of my nose. "You didn't come here to eat nachos. Please. What's going on?"

"It's time. That's what's going on." She leaned back in her chair, closing her eyes and tilting her face toward the ceiling, like this would be easier if she didn't have to look at us while she explained it. "I made a promise—an ultimatum, more like—and now I need to keep it."

My stomach sank. I knew exactly what she was talking about, and yet I still wanted to hear her say it. Maybe if she said it, it would turn out to be something different. Maybe.

Probably not.

"What do you mean?" I asked, and was proud when my voice didn't shake.

The Luidaeg waved a hand, like she was brushing away a scrap of cobweb. "We have to deal with the Selkies. Almost three years ago, I told Elizabeth Ryan she had a year to notify the clans, and after that, their bill would come due. I didn't specify a date. I could have, I suppose, but if I had, I would have needed to stick to it or pay the price, and honestly, I didn't feel like taking that sort of risk."

"What bill?" asked Quentin. He glanced at me, confusion and curiosity in his face. "I wasn't there when you went to see the Selkies, remember? I don't know what you're talking about."

My stomach sank even lower. "Luidaeg . . ."

"No. They need to know, because everyone in this room is going to be touched by this, whether or not they're directly involved." She sat up and opened her eyes, rising from her seat so she could turn and address all of us at the same time.

Her eyes had shifted colors while they were closed, going from deep blue to pure black, a darkness that filled them completely from side to side. She had no pupils, no irises, no sclera. Just drowning darkness, as deep and pitiless as the sea itself.

"I am Antigone of Albany, known as the Luidaeg, the sea witch, and by other names, as they've suited those who would speak of me," she said. "I am the daughter of Maeve and the mother of the Roane, who kept the storms, who saw the future in the tangled tides. They were beautiful, my children, and they were innocent of the great, slow, terrible war fought between my siblings and I, for we had sworn, all of us, to keep it between ourselves. We hated, how we hated, but even in our hatred, we knew this was not their fight."

She paused, tilting her face toward the ceiling as she took a deep breath. When she spoke again, her voice was softer, if no less formal.

"People wonder sometimes why my father, who was never fond of dictating our lives and ways, set down the Law. He thought, you see, even until the day he left us, that we'd eventually find our way to peace without intervention, as he'd done before us. He was an . . . idealistic man, my father, and I hope he still is, because that's a rare gift. Even rare gifts can cause pain, when improperly used. Some of my brothers and sisters had children with teeth and claws, who were equipped to defend themselves. Others had children who could melt into the water or fade into the sky. And I had the Roane, and they were sweet, and kind, and even seeing the future couldn't convince them to be anything else. My father made the Law to protect the Roane and others like them from the cruel hands of Titania's brood, who would have slain all the children of Maeve purely to make their mother smile."

Another pause. She kept staring at the ceiling. A single tear escaped her eye, running down her cheek. It left a shimmering trail behind it, gleaming like mother-of-pearl. "One of my sisters hated me for reasons that had nothing to do with my children, and she hated my children because they saw the future and refused to share it with her. So one night, she put knives in the hands of people who saw Faerie as a land to plunder, and she told those people that if they slaughtered the Roane, they would find the secrets of immortality in the flensed skins of my sons and daughters, and their sons and daughters, all the way down to the babes in their cradles. My sister looked at my descendants and saw them as sacrifices. And then she saw them sacrificed. Not all, but enough. Enough to take a thriving race to near extinction in a single night. Enough to break my heart forever."

Dean was the first of the boys to realize what the slaughter of the Roane actually meant. He swayed in the doorway, horror and sudden nausea written in the lines of his face. Good. The others would get there, and they were good boys; they had a strong sense of right and wrong. I had faith that their reactions would mirror his.

"The children of the killers woke up the next morning—they woke *up*, when my children were never going to wake up again, when I was still ignorant of what had happened—and found their parents dripping with blood, wearing raw, freshly-flensed sealskins around their necks and shouting about immortality. They were going to live forever, they said. They were going to be powerful and unstoppable, just like the fae." The Luidaeg's lips curved in a cynical expression that could have been a smile, maybe, in another life, on another face. On her, it was the betrayed look of someone infinitely younger, infinitely softer, than the sea witch we knew and somewhat reluctantly loved.

"I guess it never occurred to them that if the fae were all that powerful and unstoppable, their knives wouldn't have been enough to slit my children's throats." She shrugged, almost shuddered, like she was shaking the memory away. "The children of those killers rose up against their parents, because they knew that when I heard what had happened, my wrath would be swift and absolute. They were thinking of *their* children. They killed their parents to try to appease me, so that some of them might be spared."

"Were they?" asked Quentin. His voice was very small, and very young. He sounded like the dandelion-haired boy he'd been when we first met, and not the almost-man that he'd grown into since then.

The Luidaeg lowered her head and looked at him, and there was kindness in her eyes that would have shocked most of Faerie. Not for the first time, I marveled at how such a legendary monster had become such an integral part of our strange and broken family.

"Yes, and no," she said. "I'm not my sister. I don't kill children. If we handed down the sins of the parents without consideration for circumstances, we'd never have parents or children again, because all the babies would be dead in their cradles, unable to learn. But I punished them. I had to. For the sake of the Roane who were still alive, for the sake of all the other descendants of Maeve . . . and yes, for the sake of my own children, whose bloodied bodies sank to the bottom of the sea to be rocked to their rest before I could get to them."

"The Selkies," said Raj.

The Luidaeg nodded. "The Selkies," she confirmed. "Their skins—didn't you ever wonder where they came from? Who had to be flensed to put such power into a pelt?"

"I think I'm going to be sick," murmured Dean.

"The first Selkies were the ones who brought the skins of my children back to me," said the Luidaeg. "They had blood on their hands, but they weren't the ones to shed it, and they said they were sorry. They said they'd do anything to assuage my wrath. So I made them my own. I draped them in sealskin and set them to the sea. I made them fae and less than fae in the same breath, because *their* children were still human, still mortal, and if they didn't want to suffer the way I'd suffered, they knew they would have to pass those skins along. Conditional immortality. The first generation of Selkies thought they could stand the pain. They couldn't. They've been passing the skins along ever since, sacrificing the sea for the sake of their children over and over again, always waiting for the day when

I would come and tell them their time was up, their penance was paid, and now it was time for them to settle the final bill."

"Meaning what?" asked Quentin.

"Meaning a daughter of Amandine's line has finally stepped up to do her damn job," said the Luidaeg. She turned to face me, and her eyes remained as dark as drowning. "Meaning I didn't give them time because I *wanted* to. I did it because I didn't have a choice. A hope chest wasn't enough. My own father's blood magic might not have been enough, even assuming he'd be willing to intervene on my behalf—and I couldn't count on that. I was already half-broken. I was already halfway to becoming the monster my sister wanted me to be. But they saw the future. The Roane saw the future. They saw *you*."

The blood rushed out of my head, leaving me faint, and incredibly grateful for Tybalt's closeness. He must have felt me wobble, because he slipped an arm around my waist, holding me upright.

"Oh," I said. "Is that all?"

The Luidaeg smiled, very slightly. "Liar's daughter, come to turn back the tide. That's what they called you. You're a living hope chest. You have the blood magic I've been waiting for. Oh, it could have been August—could even have been your mother—but neither of them stepped up. So it's on you. I have what I need to finish this. I told Liz to spread the word, and then I tried to wait until you'd gotten comfortable with what you had the potential to become. I really did."

"I know," I said. "You can't lie."

"I can't," she agreed. "But three years ago I told Liz the Selkies had a year, and I'm pushing the limits of that statement. You're ready. You're strong enough. I need to act, or I'm going to make a liar of myself. The consequences of that would be . . . bad."

"How bad?" asked Quentin.

"Bad enough," said the Luidaeg, eyes still on me. "You know what happens now."

I sighed deeply. "Yeah. I do."

The Luidaeg lifted an eyebrow. "You're not going to argue? Try to run? Any of that bullshit?"

"No. Even if I thought I could get away with it—and I know enough to know that I can't—I wouldn't do that to you." I looked at her as levelly as I could. "This is your family. You deserve to stop mourning for them. Go ahead and say it."

"Very well, then." The Luidaeg took a deep breath. The air around us slowed until it became perfectly still, like the air right before some terrible storm rolls in. It grew colder and full of static at the same time, crackling around us, heavy with the memory of lightning. The Luidaeg never took her eyes off me.

"Sir October Christine Daye, Knight of Lost Words, daughter of Amandine the Liar, sworn in service to Duke Sylvester Torquill of Shadowed Hills, hero of the realm in the Mists, there are debts between us," she said, and her voice was cold and hollow, and filled with ancient echoes. "Do you deny this?"

"I don't," I said.

Tybalt said nothing.

"I would have them settled," she said. "I would see you free of me."

"For five minutes, tops," muttered Quentin.

The Luidaeg shot him a look that was somewhere between amused and annoyed before she focused on me again. "Do you accept my right to demand repayment of your debts?"

"I do," I said.

"Then in two months' time, when Moving Day arrives, you will come with me to the Duchy of Ships, and we will finally put paid to the debts that lie between us. By the tide and the tempest, it is said; by the water and the wave, it shall be done."

A pulse seemed to flow through the room, striking us all, making the hair on my arms stand on end. Then it was gone, taking the chill and the electric charge in the air with it. I shivered, allowing myself to lean against Tybalt, keeping my eyes on the Luidaeg.

"That sounded fancy, but what did it *mean*?" I asked.

The Luidaeg looked suddenly weary. "It means on May first, you and I and whoever your Queen Windermere decides ought to be present will get on a boat and sail to the Duchy of Ships, where all the Selkies in the world will be gathering to have their skins permanently bound to their bodies. We're bringing back the Roane, Toby. After all this time and all these deaths, we're bringing back the Roane."

"Right," I said slowly. "That."

"You knew this was coming," said the Luidaeg. "You were there when I told Liz the bill was coming due."

"Yes, but . . . I sort of forgot a little?" I ran a hand through my hair. "It was always something that was *going* to happen, something in the future. Not something happening now."

"It's still something happening in the future. It's just that the future has a date on it." The Luidaeg turned to Dean. "Tell your mother the sea witch is calling in the Selkies' debt. She may or may not know what that means, but she'll want to be there, since it's going to be happening in her waters."

"I've never even heard of the Duchy of Ships," protested Dean, awe apparently forgotten in the face of his confusion. That, or my general air of disrespect was rubbing off on him. Sweet Titania, I hoped not. "How can it be in my mother's waters if I've never heard of it?"

"Ask your mother," said the Luidaeg, not unkindly. "I'll send word to the Queen in the Mists. It's an old protocol, but I suppose this as good a time to observe it as ever."

"Which protocol?" I asked.

Surprisingly, it was Tybalt who answered. "When one of the Firstborn performs a major working within a royal protectorate, it is considered only polite that they should warn the local regents, to prevent accidental interference in their business. It was most commonly used when Rides were to be declared."

The Luidaeg nodded. "And this is a sort of Ride, if you cock your head and squint. So I'll handle telling your queen, and spare you trying to explain it to her without spilling secrets that aren't yours to tell. The origin of the Selkies has always been kept quiet, for their sake as much as for my own. My sister doesn't get the satisfaction of knowing that people feel sorry for me because of what happened to my kids." She glanced back to me. "You're taking this better than I expected. I'm proud of you."

I frowned. "What's that supposed to mean?"

Slowly, the Luidaeg blinked. Then, in a careful tone, she asked, "You haven't put together what this means yet, have you?"

"Apparently not," I said. "Why would I—"

And I stopped.

Gillian—my daughter, my baby girl, born one-quarter Dóchas Sidhe, turned human by my own hand, turned Selkie to save her life—was wearing one of the stolen skins of the Luidaeg's children, and she couldn't take it off for a hundred years, or she would die. The Luidaeg was preparing to use me to offer a choice to all the other Selkies: they could be permanently bound to their skins, making them Roane, fae forever, and shutting their mortal families on the other side of an impassable chasm, or they could pass those skins on and die human, letting their children secure an eternity in the sea.

Gillian wasn't going to have that choice. Time after time, Gillian's choices had been taken away from her, and while I'd never done it to her on purpose, I had always, over and over again, been the architect of her loss. If she wanted to live, she would have to change one more time, from Selkie to Roane . . . and this time, there'd be no going back.

The Luidaeg nodded gravely. "There," she said, and there was no satisfaction in her tone. "You finally get it. I'm going to let you decide what you want to tell her, and—Toby? This may not mean much yet, but I'm genuinely sorry we didn't take care of this sooner, so you wouldn't have to tell her at all."

Part of me wanted to say not to be silly; if we'd taken care of this sooner, before the false Queen of the Mists had stabbed Gillian with elf-shot and left us with no choice but to turn her fae to save her life, there wouldn't have been a Selkie skin to tie around my daughter's shoulders. She would have died, and something inside of me would have broken beyond repair.

The rest of me wanted to scream and keep screaming, possibly forever.

The Luidaeg offered me a small, sad smile as she picked up her plate of nachos. "And with that, I think it's time for me to go," she said. "Nice seeing you all; I'm sure I'll see many of you on May first. Quentin, visit me more, or you're going to find something unpleasant in your bed one morning."

"Okay, Luidaeg," he said.

She walked out of the dining room. A moment later, I heard the front door open and close. I leaned against Tybalt, closing my eyes.

"Well, damn," I said, and that seemed to summarize the situation perfectly, because no one said anything else. We just stood there, a small, silent cluster, and waited for the world to start making sense again.

We were going to be waiting for a while.

THREE

THIS IS THE TROUBLE with time. No matter how much you think you have, it always passes faster than you expect. The Luidaeg had come to me at the beginning of March to tell me I had a job to do on Moving Day. We had all looked at the calendar, me included; had looked at the almost two months between the ask and the action, and thought we'd have plenty of time to deal with things.

There's no such thing as "plenty of time." We'd sliced those two months up and devoured them one piece at a time, spending their precious hours on shopping and cleaning, doing odd jobs for Arden and dodging uncomfortable questions from everyone who knew enough about my debts to the Luidaeg to ask them.

Only May, oddly enough, didn't have any questions. Only May had looked away when I tried, haltingly, to explain what was going to happen, and said, in a subdued tone, "Well, it's about time this came to an end. I hope you don't mind if I don't come with you. I don't like being in open waters."

I could have pressed the subject. I chose not to. We all have our secrets, and if May currently has more secrets from me than I have from her, I'm sure that will change with time. Our shared memories end at the moment of her transformation from night-haunt into Fetch. Gradually, they'll become less and less of who I am now, and I think we'll both be happier if we're in the habit of letting each other hold our tongues by then.

Arden had been somewhat less sanguine about the situation.

Arden had, in fact, spent most of an evening shouting at me. Surreally, that had been an almost comforting reaction. Arden Windermere, daughter of Gilad Windermere, rightful Queen in the Mists, had been denied her throne for more than a century by Evening Winterrose and the imposter Queen. When I'd first convinced her to take up her birthright, Arden had been fairly sure she'd never be able to live up to her family name, much less do her job correctly.

Watching her berate me for being willing to take orders from one of the Firstborn, I was fairly sure Arden was going to be fine. She was learning the limits of her responsibility. She had her brother back, and while Nolan wasn't ready to formally take up his position as her heir, just having him around had already proven to be a steadying, stabilizing influence on her.

Going with the Luidaeg to the Duchy of Ships wasn't the sort of thing that ought to be life-threatening—although Quentin was happy to remind me that I could make a trip to the movies life-threatening when I really *tried*—but even if something went wrong and we all wound up lost at sea for a year, Arden would be able to keep going without me. She didn't need a hero. She had a household, and a demesne, and she was going to be okay.

I was trying not to think too much about that whole "lost at sea" possibility. I don't like water. As in, "I take showers, not baths, and the one time Tybalt offered to take me to the hot tubs for a romantic evening, I damn near had a panic attack." I blame it on spending fourteen years as a fish, since I certainly didn't have any issues with water *before* that happened.

Sadly, knowing where trauma comes from doesn't magically heal it. Only time and effort can do that. The fact that I was even able to consider getting on a boat said a lot about how much I'd recovered since that initial injury; as long as I didn't drown or something, this trip would probably help me to recover even more.

Days ticked by, and plans were made as we inched toward Moving Day. May first had a lot of power and significance once, back in the days of the Three. There was a time when they'd formed a stable triad, keeping Faerie safe and secure. But something had changed. Whatever it was had happened early on, before changelings existed, before the Firstborn had children of their own, and it had resulted in Oberon splitting his time between two very different Courts. That was when the Divided Courts earned their name. Starting with their split, on May first, Oberon would kiss Maeve good-bye and return to Titania's bower. On November first, he'd repeat the trip in reverse.

Of course, that all ended when the Three disappeared. Moving Day has been symbolic for centuries. The smaller inhabitants of Faerie, the pixies and the bogeys and the so-called "monsters," still respected Moving Days. Even the ones who didn't necessarily pack up and go would at least rearrange their nests and shift their belongings in symbolic recognition. The larger fae, however, the ones who liked to pretend we didn't miss the Three, or that we hadn't been affected by the dwindling of the First in their absence, mostly ignore the significance of the holidays. They've been reduced to excuses for feasts and grand celebrations in the modern world, Beltane Balls and Samhain revels, and no one really talks about what those days originally meant, to us or to anyone.

I don't have many fond memories of my mother these days. I never had a lot of them, but the more I learn about her, the more even the good ones wind up tainted as I realize what she was to me. Still, I remember her waking me early on Moving Days, with scones and jam and bowls of berries in sweet cream. I remember her taking me around the tower grounds, telling the stories of travel, the migratory fae, the way we used to wander the worlds, until one by one, our Firstborn put down roots and wove themselves a homeland. Sometimes we'd go to watch the pixies in flight, but we'd always wind up inside, and spend the bulk of the day cleaning everything we could reach before moving our beds from one side of the room to the other, symbolically renewing the spaces where we lived, making them seem new again.

Those had been good days. Maybe the best days, as I measured the interactions between my mother and me. I lay in my bed three days before the end of April, Tybalt snuggled against me, his breath slow and even and peaceful, and wondered whether whatever the Luidaeg had planned for us was going to result in ruining those last few happy memories of my mother.

If I don't have a lot of fond memories of my mother, I have even fewer illusions about her. Most of them died a long time ago, and I can't say I was necessarily sorry to see them go. But it would be nice to still believe she had occasionally cared about me, even if it was only in the way a farmer cares about the dog who herds the sheep back into their barn at the end of the day. Maybe I'd never been anything more than useful to her. Given how much I *did* know, I wanted that to be enough. Oberon's eyes, I wanted that to be enough.

My elderly Siamese cats, Cagney and Lacy, were curled up on my pillow, keeping me solidly between them and Tybalt. They liked having him around in much the way I imagined they would have liked having a tame lion around: a larger predator that wasn't interested in eating *them* kept them at least a little bit safer, but that was no real guarantee that tomorrow, the lion wouldn't decide it wanted a meal of domesticated feline. They were technically subjects of the Court of Cats—all cats belong to the Court of Cats—but they weren't fae, and they couldn't reason with him the way a fae cat would have.

Cagney purred and pressed herself against my head. Lacey did the same. I closed my eyes, trying to convince myself I could go back to sleep. It didn't work. I'd gone to bed shortly after dawn, and while it had only been about seven hours, part of me was all too aware that midnight was approaching fast. Once the clock struck twelve . . .

We didn't have any carriages to turn back into pumpkins, but there were going to be some uncomfortable transformations all the same. Nothing was going to stop them now, short of another kidnapping or murder, and I wasn't actually sure either of those would be enough to get me out of this. The Luidaeg had been waiting centuries for the chance to avenge her children. She wasn't going to let something that someone else could handle force her to wait any longer.

"I know you're awake, little fish," said Tybalt softly. "Would you like to discuss what's troubling you, or would you prefer to play at slumber?"

I winced. "How long have you been awake?"

"Not long," said Tybalt. He ran a hand across my hair. The cats made small grumbling noises and got up, prowling down to settle at the foot of the bed, well away from any potential activity.

"Are you lying?" I rolled onto my side, so we were almost nose-to-nose.

Tybalt smiled. "Small untruths between lovers are not necessarily lies; sometimes they can be considered a form of kindness."

I considered this and sighed. "Right. Kindness. I'm . . . I'm all right, I think. This is a good thing. We're bringing back the Roane.

We could use a little prophecy in our lives right now. Maybe if we hadn't lost them, we wouldn't have been caught flat-footed when Janet broke Maeve's last Ride, and things wouldn't be so messed up."

"Ah, but if not for Janet, your mother would never have been born, and if not for your mother, *you* would never have been born, and perhaps I am a selfish man, but I prefer a world that has you in it." He leaned closer, until his nose actually touched mine. "Must I begin quoting sweet William before you'll believe me?"

"How did I wind up falling in love with such a nerd?" I asked.

He smirked. "Luck."

I laughed. "Right. Luck. Luck, and bleeding all over you way too many times for comfort, and a lot of other unpleasantness, but we'll roll with the one that doesn't ruin the upholstery." I sobered, looking at him. "Don't you wonder, sometimes, what it would have been like if we hadn't lost them? If, I don't know, Janet had broken the Ride but not so badly that Maeve . . . well, that whatever happened to Maeve happened? Maybe things would be better."

"Or perhaps you would never have been born because your mother would have been treated as a proper Firstborn princess, regardless of her maternity, and never encountered a human man, nor deigned to let him touch her." Tybalt ran a hand almost reverently down my cheek. "I am younger than the loss of the Three, but older than you."

"Very aware, and just human enough that it sort of creeps me out if I think about it too hard, so if we could not talk about your age in bed, that would be awesome," I muttered.

Tybalt laughed, once, sharply. "Oh, October, I look forward to the day when there are so many centuries between us that the existence of the years I spent without you is no longer of any importance or concern."

"That day is not today," I said.

"Indeed." He stroked my cheek again. "When I was a boy, quests to find our missing King and Queens were common. A good way of burning off extra, unwanted heirs, on the chance that your bed was blessed enough to get them. Too many good fae were lost, and not only from the Divided Courts, for with the loss of the Three, the surviving Firstborn began to go as well, and we were not as settled in the idea of ruling ourselves then as we are now."

I blinked. "What do you mean?"

"I mean there has never been a High King of Cats, but once,

men such as my father would have been unable to run their Courts as petty dictatorships. Malvic himself would have stepped in and stopped the cruelties, and he would have been allowed to do so, because we were in the habit of obedience. Our Firstborn, when they walked the world, did so as judge and jury—and while they may have kept us kinder with one another, they also kept us as children. We never learned the ways of self-control, for there was no need to do so."

"Huh," I said. "Evening must have *loved* that."

"Given her descendants, I'd suppose she still does." He offered a small smile as he sat up. "Now that you're well and truly distracted, are you prepared to tell me what's actually bothering you, or shall I dredge up more ancient history and pretend it passes for pillow talk?"

"Bastard." I swatted him in the arm as I sat up.

His laughter was sincere, and enough to melt away a bit more of the tension in my shoulders and back. If Tybalt was laughing, the world couldn't be *that* bad. "My father took no wife, and I never met my mother. He bought me from her when I was but a kitten, and my eyes not yet opened. My sister went back when she was older, after I was King in my own right, but it was too late; the woman who bore us had already stopped her dancing."

Meaning, in the often complicated parlance of the pureblooded fae, that she'd died. I blinked once, trying to decide whether saying I was sorry would be appropriate. He didn't seem upset, and there was no way of knowing how many centuries ago this had happened. Not without asking, and that would take us even farther down the path of "things I really would prefer not to discuss in the bedroom, thanks" than we'd already gone.

Pushing the covers back, I swung my feet to the floor and looked at my knees as I said, "I'm out of time. I have to go see Gilly today, and I'm not ready. I was . . ." I hesitated. Admitting this felt like cowardice; lying to Tybalt after everything he'd been through at my mother's hands felt even worse. "I know she's been going to see Elizabeth Ryan to learn how to be a better Selkie, and I guess I was hoping Liz would let something slip about what was coming. I mean, it would make sense, right? For her teacher to be the one who told her."

"And not her still semi-estranged mother. I can understand that." Tybalt shifted positions, settling next to me and rubbing my back with one hand, forming small, concentric circles. I was never going to get tired of the way he wanted to be always touching me, taking the social grooming of cats and extending it in a form my bipedal mind could easily comprehend. "But you *are* her mother, October. Whether she's mortal, fae, or in the middle, you're the one who bore her, and you never intended to give her up. That means something. That means you have a responsibility to her, and she a responsibility to you. If you come to her with information, she should listen."

I took a deep, shaky breath, leaning into his hand. "Will you go with me?" I asked. "To tell her she's going to have to choose whether she wants to die or lose her humanity forever?"

"Certainly, I will." He pressed a kiss to my temple. "But you're better equipped for this conversation than you think you are, my love. You've *faced* this choice, and you chose survival. She'll choose the same. She may not care much for your company at the moment. She's still your daughter, and that makes her a fighter."

"I hope so." I got up. "No time like the present, I guess."

Selkies, like seals, are largely diurnal. It was a problem back when Connor and I were dating. Connor O'Dell had been a Selkie diplomat, assigned to the Court of Shadowed Hills back when assigning diplomats to the Queen's Court had been a waste of time and resources. He'd been good at his job, so good that he'd eventually wound up married to Sylvester's daughter as part of a carefully orchestrated political alliance. We'd become lovers after the marriage ended—and very nearly before, a fact that I wasn't entirely proud of.

He'd died saving Gillian's life, and while the skin she wore had never belonged to him, sometimes I felt as if it had. Lose one Selkie, gain another. That's the way things had always worked for them. And I was going to be part of bringing that to an end. Their whole social structure, their way of life . . . it was about to die. I might not be the hand that killed it, but I was the weapon that hand was wielding.

Selkies were diurnal. Were Roane? Was Gillian about to find herself separated from her humanity for the rest of her long, long life, unable to keep her eyes open in the middle of the day, leaving her human father wondering what had changed?

Sometimes I felt like the person I really needed to apologize to was Cliff. He'd loved me once. He'd been a good man—still was, according to Gillian and Janet, who had never found themselves banished from the walled city of his heart—and he'd loved me, and what did he have to show for it? An ex-lover he thought of as a deadbeat, a daughter who couldn't tell him why she was pulling away, and a wife who'd been lying to him since the day they met.

I grabbed clothes without paying attention to what they were, yanking them on and pulling my hair into a rough ponytail. It's not that I don't care how I look. It's more that I've learned that the more attention I pay to my appearance, the more likely I am to wind up ruining something I actually like when I get covered in blood. Again. At least the blood is usually my own. I'm not sure why that's better, but it is.

Tybalt remained on the bed, watching me dress. Finally, he yawned and asked, "Am I permitted to be your boyfriend on this visit, or must I play the acquaintance if your former swain is present?"

"I'm hoping Cliff will be at work this time of day, but even if he's not, you can be my fiancé," I said.

Tybalt blinked. "Really?" He sounded pleased.

Too pleased. I nodded firmly. "Really. I'm going to marry you. Cliff moved on a long time ago, and if he doesn't like hearing that I've done the same, I don't think I actually care."

"You are an endless delight," he said, and stood, retrieving his own trousers from the floor. He hummed to himself as he pulled them on. The smell of musk and pennyroyal gathered in the air, twining around him until my Cait Sidhe lover was gone, replaced by a human man who looked very much like him, even down to the delighted twinkle in his green eyes. He was wearing a T-shirt with Shakespeare's face on the front, and his trousers had gone from linen to denim, but I would still have been able to recognize him in a crowd.

"No shoes?" I asked, amused.

"My own shoes can pass for mortal, and I refuse to appear before your ex-lover looking like the sort of man who wears *sneakers*," he said. There was a faint, arrogant sneer in his voice, and I'd never been so happy to hear someone being a snob.

There was a time, immediately after his abduction, when I'd thought Tybalt's arrogance might have been broken forever. There had *also* been a time, much earlier in our acquaintance, when I would have considered that a good thing.

Not anymore. He was my arrogant, smug, gloriously pointed King of Cats, and I wouldn't want him any other way.

I found my own shoes while he dealt with his, strapped my silver knife to my belt, and grabbed a double handful of shadows, chanting, "Ride a black pony to Banbury Cross, to see a fine lady upon a white horse. With rings on her fingers and bells on her toes, she shall have music wherever she goes."

The magic gathered and burst around me, drifting to floor level and leaving me garbed in a human disguise of my own, one that made me look like the woman who'd been Cliff's lover and Gillian's mother, brown-haired and blue-eyed and blissfully ordinary, unaware of the dangers ahead of her. Sometimes I miss being that woman, who never knew what she was capable of, who had never *needed* to know. She'd been ignorant in the most merciful of ways.

I looked at Tybalt, who was smiling at my transformation with simple affection, and thought I liked who I'd grown into being a whole lot better. But that didn't mean I couldn't feel sorry for the way the other me had ended.

"Are you ready?" he asked, stepping toward me with his hands extended, like he was going to escort me to a cotillion.

"I was going to drive," I protested.

He snorted. "Please. And look for parking in this mess of a city? Allow me the privilege of saving us both the time."

"You're too good at getting your own way," I said, and slid my hands into his.

Tybalt's smile was a knife drawn in a darkened room. "I'm a cat," he said, and stepped backward into the shadows, pulling me with him.

All Cait Sidhe have access to the Shadow Roads, the secret corridors and connections drawn between the dark places of the world. As a King of Cats, Tybalt's connection and control are better than most. He's strong enough to take passengers with him—which, at least in the last few years, has usually meant me.

It's cold on the Shadow Roads. It's cold and it's dark and it's airless, at least for me, because they can tell I don't belong there. Like all the truly ancient passages through Faerie, like the knowes, the Shadow Roads are at least a little bit aware, and they can reject the things that shouldn't cross their borders. Tybalt always comes out of the shadows chilly but not wheezing, and not covered in sheets of ice the way I do.

Well. Not always. There have been a few incidents where, for one reason or another, I was unable to run beside him and he had to carry me through the darkness, putting a heart-stopping strain on his system. With as often as both of us seem to wind up dead, we should really get a frequent-flier card for the underworld.

As long as there isn't time for the night-haunts to be called for either one of us, I guess we'll be okay.

He ran through the darkness, his hand tight around mine, and I ran beside him, closing my eyes to keep them from freezing, trusting him to know the way. Just the fact of that trust made the shadows feel warmer, although I still wasn't going to risk trying to breathe there. No matter how much I learned to follow my lover through the dark, I would never be welcome enough for the roads to grant me oxygen.

When we stepped out of the shadows on the other end, the brightness and warmth of the mortal world was a shock. I pulled my hand out of Tybalt's and staggered away, gasping, to catch myself against the nearest wall. Ice had glued my eyelashes together, but I trusted him not to have dropped us in the middle of a street or something.

Faerie survives because humanity doesn't know we exist. We have magic, sure; some fae could take out dozens, even hundreds of humans before they were overrun. But we don't have the numbers, and our vulnerability to pure iron means humanity will always have the upper hand when we're standing on their home ground. There are very few fae left in the former Kingdom of Oak and Ash, which consists of most of the land around the mortal city of New York. Once the iron makes it into the water, we're done.

Tybalt is savvy enough to have gone this long without getting caught. So I took the time I needed to catch my breath, and when the ice melted enough to let me open my eyes, I turned to find him watching me with undisguised fondness that seemed strange only due to his currently human appearance.

"Where are we?" I asked. I was barely wheezing at all, and I was proud of that.

"Service alley about two blocks from your ex-boyfriend's house," he said. "The owner of the liquor store," he indicated a door set into the brick wall in front of us, "keeps swearing he's going to install security cameras, and keeps putting it off due to the expense. I'm sure that will change when he gets robbed again, and we'll need to find a different path to visit this neighborhood, but the cats will keep me apprised."

"Even when you're not their King anymore?"

For a moment, Tybalt looked conflicted, unhappy and hopeful at the same time. Then he nodded and said, "Raj will rule them, but they will still respect my place as one of the Cait Sidhe, even as they respect his. I'll know where it's safe to travel."

I had a lot of questions, like what he meant when he said Raj would rule "them" and not "us," but for the moment, it seemed safer to let things slide. Tybalt was working hard enough to be okay with the changes in his life. They were necessary changes—he'd stepped down and allowed a regent to guard his throne for him because he needed the time to heal, not because I'd asked him to—but they were still an adjustment. For both of us.

"Come on," I said, and motioned for him to follow me out of the alley. Looking relieved, he did.

San Francisco is an old city, which means it's not as segmented as modern cities always seem to me. Small convenience stores and blocks of retail offerings are tucked into otherwise residential neighborhoods, making it possible for people to do most of what they need to do entirely on foot. That's a good thing, considering how bad the parking situation is. I fully expect someone to get murdered over a good parking place one of these days, and go off to prison utterly content, as long as someone else stays behind to feed the meter.

Turning left, we climbed the short hill between us and the nearest of those residential streets. The shops dropped away, replaced by the tidy, pressed-together houses that had been all the rage after the Victorians but before the condos. The house Cliff shared with Gillian and Janet—whose real name he still didn't know—wasn't far.

His car wasn't parked in the driveway. I felt bad about how relieved that made me. Still, the last thing I needed to add to an already-uncomfortable afternoon was trying to talk freely with my human ex-boyfriend sitting in the room.

Tybalt flashed me a quick, understanding smile. "It will be all right," he said.

"It'll be something," I said as I climbed the steps and rang the doorbell.

Seconds ticked by, enough of them that I was considering whether it might be a good idea to ring again, before I heard footsteps on the other side. I took a deep breath. No matter who opened that door, they were family, and that meant that they were complicated.

"Coming!" The voice was Janet's. I didn't relax.

Janet Carter—currently known as "Miranda Marks," thanks to both her assumed name and her marriage to Cliff—is human. Totally, completely, perfectly human. She's also more than five hundred years old, thanks to a curse flung by Maeve after her Ride was broken. Janet won't age or die, through natural or unnatural means, until Maeve returns and allows her to do so. And since we don't know whether Maeve is ever going to come back, well . . . .

She could be around for a long, long time. She's too human for Faerie, and too fae-touched to be comfortable as a part of humanity. Maybe it makes me a bad person, but in a way, I'm glad. She took my daughter away from me, and she did it on purpose, discouraging Gillian from reaching out, believing I was just another careless fae parent who didn't want or deserve her partially-mortal child. Janet and I have reconciled some of our differences. We've had to, for Gilly's sake. That doesn't mean I've forgiven her completely, or that I'll ever be able to..

The door swung open, revealing a woman with the healthy tan of a gardener and buttercup-blonde hair drawn back in a complicated braid. She was wearing a lace sundress, and she looked like she could have stepped off the cover of a magazine advertising the latest in holistic health care, or maybe the newest trends in early childhood education.

She blinked once. "October?" she asked, in a startled, wary tone. Her accent was pure California, but I could hear the shores of Scotland lurking beneath it, like her roots were unable to resist the magnetic pull of her own blood. She's my grandmother. Parts of her will always know me, whether she wants them to or not.

When I first saw her, Cliff's new wife, the woman who swept in while I was absent due to Simon's spell, the woman who won when I didn't even know that we were competing, I'd thought she looked too much like me for comfort, like Cliff had a type he couldn't get away from. There were similarities in the shape of our eyes, the length of our fingers, even the curve of our hips. Her coloring was more saturated than my own—Dóchas Sidhe always look faintly bleached, if my sister and I are anything to go by—but it was easy enough to draw a line from her to me, from me to her. Learning we were actually related had almost been a relief, except for all the ways in which it wasn't.

"Yeah," I said. "Can we come in?"

Janet glanced warily at Tybalt. "Your friend is . . . ?"

"Fiancé," said Tybalt. "We've met, in passing. You may call me 'Rand' if it suits you to do so, or you may call me nothing at all if that suits your sensibilities better. I'll be accompanying my lady either way."

Janet's wary glance turned into a blink, and then a look of dawning comprehension. "I see. Well, I suppose you'd best both come inside. I can put a pot of coffee on if you'd like something to drink."

"That's all right," I said, stepping into the front hall and stepping to the side so that Tybalt could do the same. "Caffeine doesn't do anything for me anymore, so coffee's just bitter and frustrating."

"That's not fair," said Janet. "Caffeine is one of the true wonders of the modern age."

"What do you consider to be the others?" asked Tybalt.

Janet shrugged. "The Internet. Telephones. Vaccinations. McDonald's. Fast food in general. I assume this isn't a social call?"

I wanted to ask more about that whole "McDonald's" thing, but this wasn't the time. I shook my head. "Not a social call, no. Is Gillian home? I need to speak to both of you."

Janet went very still, like she thought I might forget she was there if she just waited long enough. There was a long, silent pause. Finally, in a softer voice, she said, "May I ask why?"

"I'm not here to hurt her or to take her away from you," I said. "Please. Can you get her?"

"I don't know if I want you talking to her right now," said Janet. "She's in a delicate place. She doesn't need to be confused."

"I'm afraid I don't have a choice," I said. "I waited as long as I could, but time's short, and we need to talk before things go any further."

"It's all right, Mom," said a new voice. Janet and I turned in sudden unison, and there was Gillian, standing on the stairs with one hand on the banister, watching us. My heart leapt and sank in the same moment, the way it always did when I saw my daughter's face.

She was so beautiful, and still so mortal in many ways; being a Selkie hadn't changed the underlying softness of her bone structure, or stolen the riotous curls from her dark brown, almost black hair. Out of all Janet's descendants, she was the only one who didn't seem to have purchased her color from the "washed-out and pale" bin at the discount store. She was wearing sweatpants and a UC Berkeley sweatshirt, and she had never been lovelier.

Then she took a step toward us, and the air around her glittered, the way it always did when someone was wearing a disguise intended to let them pass for human. My heart sank again, this time with no accompanying uplift. She wasn't human anymore. She couldn't even wear her own face in her own home, not without alerting her father to the fact that something had changed, for good.

Gillian smiled when she saw the look on my face. It wasn't a kind smile. "Liz has been teaching me," she said, and snapped her fingers. The illusion around her fell away, leaving the smell of flowering fennel and primroses behind. It wasn't the scent her magic would have had if she'd stayed Dóchas Sidhe, but it was close, so close. I breathed in deeply, memorizing the unique signature of her magic, before looking at her without her masks for the first time in months.

She still looked essentially like herself, only . . . different. Her eyes were so dark they verged on black, irises and pupils blending seamlessly. Silver streaks ran through her curls, echoing the color of the seal's pelt tied around her shoulders. Her ears were dully pointed, not as sharp as mine or Tybalt's, but distinctly inhuman. She held up one hand, spreading her fingers to show me the webbing that extended to the first knuckles.

"Daddy won't be home for a few hours," she said. "I don't like being disguised all the time. It makes my ears itch."

Again, that strange fluttering in my chest. "Illusions make me feel the same way," I said.

"Huh." Gillian finished coming down the stairs, looking first at me, and then at Tybalt. "If I'm not going to wear a mask, you shouldn't either."

"As my lady wishes," said Tybalt, and let his illusion go.

To her credit, Gillian barely flinched when Tybalt's human disguise wisped away and revealed him for what he really was. She turned to me.

"Your turn."

I swallowed my sigh and flicked my fingers, willing the spell to break and disperse. I hate recasting my illusions when I don't have to. My magic is stronger than it used to be, thanks to the shifted balance of my blood, but illusions still don't come easy to me, and casting too many will leave me with a headache even my rapid healing can't get rid of. I can heal a broken bone in minutes and bring myself back from the dead, and I still can't cure migraines. Sometimes the world is just unfair.

Gillian tilted her head, studying me, and finally said, "If you'd looked like this when you came back five years ago, I might have believed you were really my mother. This is how you always looked in my dreams. Mom?"

"Yes, sweetheart?" said Janet, before I could open my mouth.

Gillian's smile was earnest and sincere, and so quick it broke my heart a little, because she had never been talking to me. "Can we go to the kitchen? I want to have time to put my face back on if Daddy comes home early."

"Of course," said Janet, and put her arm around Gillian's shoulders, guiding our involuntarily shared daughter away from the stairs, away from the windows through which a passing human might happen to see her, and into the room that belonged, more than anything, to Janet herself.

It was impossible to look at Gillian's choice of venues and not see it, however unintentionally, as yet another signal that Janet was her *real* mother. Janet was the one who'd been there when she lost her baby teeth, when she learned how to ride a bike, for her first day of kindergarten and her last day of high school. I might have given birth to her, but I hadn't raised her, and I still didn't know whether she was ever going to be able to forgive me.

The kitchen was decorated in early kitchen witch. The window garden was lush with herbs and flowering plants; there was even a tomato bush that had somehow been coaxed into bristling with early fruit, each one golden orange and perfect, like a tiny sun. I eyed the plants warily, relaxing as I saw that certain herbs and simples had vanished since our last visit.

"I cleared out the plants that were inherently harmful to the fae," said Janet, following my gaze and guessing the reasons for it. "It seemed unkind to ward my own daughter's home against her."

"Stepdaughter, if you please," said a voice, and for a horrifying moment, I thought it was mine. Then I realized Janet was looking at Tybalt. Relief washed over me. For once, I'd managed to keep my mouth shut.

"I don't think this is any of your concern," said Janet stiffly.

"Actually, he's right, Mom," said Gillian. Both Janet and I turned to her. Janet looked crushed. I didn't know what to feel. My heart was beating too hard and too fast, making my head spin. "You're my mom, but she's my mother. We can't pretend she isn't. We *shouldn't* pretend she isn't. Not with . . . everything." Her gesture encompassed her entire body, starting with the sealskin tied around her shoulders.

Janet's face fell. "Sweetie, you don't have to let her in if you don't want to."

I cleared my throat. "Okay, great as it is to go over this again, because I'm not tired of being stabbed in the chest just yet, I did come here for a reason. Gillian, honey, we need to talk."

"Why do parents always use food names when they're talking to their kids? I'm legally an adult, and you still treat me like a dessert topping." Gillian folded her arms. "Is this about whatever has Ms. Ryan so spooked? Because I've been waiting for someone to get around to telling me what's going on."

I should probably have felt guilty. All I felt in that moment was relief. Gilly knew this was coming; had been waiting, in fact, for someone to get it over with. I was actually doing her a favor for a change. "It is, yeah," I said. I glanced to Janet and Tybalt before asking, "Has someone explained to you where Selkie skins come from?"

Gillian nodded. "Mass murder, very sad, and it's why I'm not allowed to tell any of the other Selkies that their 'Cousin Annie' is secretly the actual sea witch from *The Little Mermaid*. I'm hanging out with Ursula on the regular, and I can't even tell the other fairies about it."

Something in the way she said "fairies" told me she was still spelling it wrong in the privacy of her own mind. She was adjusting to the idea that her world was different now, and she was probably going to be adjusting for a long time yet to come. If it had been up to me, I would have given her as much time as she needed. She was a Selkie now, fae and immortal, and she didn't share my tendency to run headlong into danger at the slightest provocation. We had time.

Except for the part where we didn't, because she wasn't going to be a Selkie for long. The time of Selkies was ending. "All right," I said carefully. "Well, the reason Selkie skins work the way they do—you can't flense fae at random and expect to become a skinshifter; skinshifters are rare, and the other kinds don't require anyone to die—"

"There are other kinds?" interrupted Gillian.

I nodded quickly. "Raven-maids and Swanmays. Well, and Raven-men. Swanmays are descended from a woman named Aoife, and they're hatched with their skins wrapped around them like cauls. Raven-maids and -men are descended from Aiofe's sister, Aine. They're not a part of this. Their ancestors didn't wipe out someone else's descendant line to give them access to the skies. You know . . . the Luidaeg told you, right?"

"I'm wearing her daughter's skin around my shoulders," said Gillian. She reached up to touch it, seemingly unaware of the gesture. "Yeah. I know she was their mother."

"She was also their grandmother, and in some cases, their great-grandmother." There had to be something about the presence of a descendant line's Firstborn that increased fertility, at least for the first few generations. The numbers didn't make sense otherwise. And that, like the topic of the other skinshifters, was currently beside the point. "The Luidaeg enchanted the skins of her slain descendants so that they would continue to hold the Roane bloodline until such time as she could make things right again."

I could see the moment when Janet understood what was going on. Her eyes widened, ever so fractionally, and the skin around her mouth tightened, like she was biting back some inappropriate exclamation. Instead, she drew herself up to her full height and took a half-step forward, putting herself, however subtly, between Gillian and me.

"No," she said. Her voice was ice and iron, foreboding, unwilling to let anything pass. "I refuse. I don't care. Send your sea witch to me directly, and I'll say the same to her. She'll not do this to my daughter."

"October's daughter," said Tybalt.

"My *own person*," snapped Gillian, and stepped around Janet, scowling. "I get that you're all older than I am, and you all know more about this 'traditions and dangers of Faerie' bullshit, but I'm standing right here, and I'm a grownup, whether you like it or not. What are you *talking* about?"

I took a deep breath. "The Luidaeg enchanted the skins of her dead descendants, so they would remain technically alive until such time as the Roane could be resurrected as a people. Not the individuals themselves—they're long since lost—but the Roane. They're a piece of Faerie that we've lost. The Luidaeg wants to bring them back."

"You may be getting more of the individuals than you think you are," muttered Gillian.

"What's that?" asked Janet, voice sharp.

"Nothing, Mom," said Gillian. She turned to look at me, seal-dark eyes wide and solemn. "If I'm following you—which isn't easy, since you seem bound and determined to talk your way around the problem as much as possible—you're saying the reason Liz has been drinking even more than usual and won't talk to me is because the sea witch is about to make all the Selkies go bye-bye, and replace them—us—with the Roane. Is that basically it?"

"Yes." I nodded. "You know I'm a different kind of fae than you are. I'm Dóchas Sidhe, and we're blood-workers. The Luidaeg is going to use my magic to bind the Selkies into their skins and transform them back into the Roane. I don't know exactly how it's going to work. But we're going to have to travel to a place called the Duchy of Ships, where the Selkies who intend to keep their skins will be gathering, and I'll cast whatever spell she wants me to cast, because I owe her a debt. Several debts. I don't have a choice here."

"Who intend to *keep* their skins," said Janet hurriedly. "That means some of them will set them aside."

"Probably," I said. "Selkie culture is centered on the idea that eventually, most fae parents will choose to become mortal in order to give the magic to their children. When there's only one skin, only one person can wear it. I'm sure some of the current Selkies will choose to set their skins aside for the sake of the ones who would have been their heirs in a few years."

"But Gillian can't do the same." There was a note of bitterness in Janet's voice, like we could have found another solution somehow, if we'd only cared enough to try. "You and your sea witch saw to that."

It was Gillian who shook her head and put her hand over Janet's, saying quietly, "No, Mom. It wasn't like that. The sea witch made me into a Selkie to save my life, because the stuff I was shot with—"

"Elf-shot," I supplied.

Gillian nodded very slightly as she continued. "The elf-shot is going to be in my blood for a hundred years. I have to be fae or I'll die, because elf-shot kills humans. If I give away the skin, I'll die."

"There must have been another way," said Janet.

"If the Luidaeg said there wasn't, there wasn't," I said. "She can't lie. I don't mean 'doesn't lie,' or 'tries not to lie,' I mean literally *can't*. Titania put the whammy on her the same way Maeve put the whammy on you. You can't die, the Luidaeg can't lie."

"Meaning you get to take your daughter back." Janet had stopped making any effort to conceal the brittle fury in her voice. I wasn't sure whether to be flattered or annoyed about that.

I did know one thing: much as I wanted to dislike her for everything she'd done, both to me and to Faerie, I felt bad for her. She looked at me like a mother whose heart was in the process of breaking, and that was exactly what she was, even if the child she was currently claiming was technically my own. Janet was in pain. Some of it was her own fault, but isn't that always the way when things are hurting? It wasn't like she was suffering for fun.

"No," said Gillian firmly. Janet turned back to her. I . . . didn't. I had some idea of what was going to come next, and I didn't want to see it.

"No," said Gillian again. "I'm not a toy that passes from hand to hand. She doesn't get to 'take' me just because I have to change again. The only way you'd lose me is if I died, and since I'm not going to do that, you're just going to have to get over this. Toby?"

"Yeah?" I asked roughly. Hearing her tell Janet "no" was more satisfying than I wanted it to be. It wasn't as heartbreaking as hearing her tell Janet that she wasn't going to lose her. No matter what, Janet Carter was always going to be my little girl's mother in so many ways.

"Tell me where to be and I'll be there."

I took a deep breath. "I'll send a friend of mine to pick you up at midnight tomorrow. As soon as the clock ticks over into May, he'll be waiting for you. I'm sorry, but Janet can't come. She's too human, and we can't tell people who she really is."

"I understand," said Gillian, and I could tell from her tone that she didn't. And it didn't matter because I'd done what I'd come here to do. We were all going to have to live with it.

"Great," I said. "I'll see you tomorrow. Janet, I appreciate your hospitality. We'll be going now." I turned to Tybalt, offering him my hands. He nodded once, immediately grasping my intent, and tangled his fingers through mine, pulling me into the shadows, leaving the warm, well-lit kitchen behind.

I didn't start crying until we emerged back into my bedroom. He put his arms around me and held me until the tears stopped and the ice had melted from my hair, and neither of us said anything because there was nothing left to say.

FOUR

STACY WATCHED ME THROUGH the driver's side window of my car, one hand resting on the wheel. "You sure you've got everything?" she asked.

I nodded, hoisting my backpack as if she would somehow be able to see and approve of its contents. "I even packed a toothbrush."

"Good." She nodded her approval. "You know May will never let me hear the end of it if I don't make sure you're keeping up with your dental health."

"That's May. Really concerned about my flossing." I tried to keep my tone light. I thought I almost managed it.

Jazz was in no condition to go on another wild adventure, even if this one had been directly relevant to her—Selkies and Ravenmaids are both skinshifters, but that's where the relationship ends. Air and sea have never been as close as they could have been. With Jazz staying home, May was staying as well, preferring not to leave her girlfriend alone. Much as I wished things had been different, it was good to know someone would be at the house to feed the cats and Spike, none of whom did well when expected to fend for themselves.

"Are *you* okay?" Stacy studied me, making no effort to conceal her concern. "This is a lot. If it wouldn't mean certain death, I'd give the sea witch a piece of my mind for putting this on you."

"It's my job, Stacy."

She shook her head. "It shouldn't have to be."

Stacy Brown has been one of my best friends since we were both kids living in the Summerlands and trying to figure out what the world had to offer to a pair of clumsy changelings with no magic to speak of. We ran through the halls of Shadowed Hills together, we got into trouble together, and when the time came, we left for the human world together, off to seek our fortunes in the land of our mortal ancestors.

We'd both been swept up by the machinations of a man named Devin, who had run a sort of thieves' den-slash-orphanage for changeling kids. He'd called it "Home," and it had been one for both of us, at least for a while. At least until Stacy had found her true love and slipped away, off to settle down in a small house in Colma and raise her ever-increasing brood of changeling children. I'd been—I was—an adopted aunt to her children, and she was still one of my best friends because sometimes, when you're lucky, the good things don't have to change.

"Hero of the realm, remember?" I offered a crooked smile before hooking a thumb toward the rest of my party, gathered on the edge of the pier and waiting for the next stage of our journey to begin. "Besides, I have these assholes to keep me out of the water. I'll be fine."

"I wish you didn't have to go."

"So do I. I appreciate you being willing to drive us. With Danny picking up Gillian, we needed a ride."

Stacy's mouth made a funny twisting motion. "I still say he could have fit you all in his cab."

"We're spending the next however long in the middle of the ocean together. We'll have plenty of time to talk. Now get out of here before the Luidaeg shows up and decides you're coming with us."

"Open roads," Stacy said.

"Kind fires," I replied, and stepped back, letting her pull away from the curb. I stayed where I was, watching the taillights dwindle as she rolled down the street. Then she turned a corner and was gone, and I finally turned back to my boys.

As my squire, part of Quentin's job is accompanying me when I do stupid shit; it's a learning experience. Most of what he's learning is how to get blood out of his clothes, but hey, at least it's educational. There'd been no chance of my leaving him behind. As for Tybalt, normally his duties to the Court of Cats would have necessitated him remaining in San Francisco, no matter how much he disliked the idea. With Ginevra holding his throne, he could do as he liked, and what he liked was keeping me out of trouble.

Two more figures walked up to the pair. Quentin promptly swept the taller into a hug. I hesitated before approaching the now larger group.

"Dean?" I blinked as the second figure came more clearly into view. "*Marcia*?"

"Hi," she said, with a quick wave of her free hand. She was hauling a suitcase that looked nearly as big as she was.

Quentin loosened his grip on his boyfriend enough for the other boy to lean around and offer me a sheepish smile. "Hello, Sir Daye," he said. "Did Quentin not tell you we were coming?"

"Not in so many words, although I suppose I should have guessed about you, at least," I said. "Is your mom meeting us there?"

Dean nodded. "She says it's important to make a good entrance."

"She would." Dean's mother, Dianda Lorden, was the Duchess of Saltmist, the nearest and largest Undersea demesne. It made sense for her to be present. It also made sense for Dean, as someone raised in the Undersea and now holding a title on the land, to be there.

I gave Quentin a sidelong look. His cheeks flushed red.

"I'm still your squire," he said. "I don't stop doing my job just because my boyfriend's here."

"Uh-huh."

"*Your* boyfriend is always around, and you do your job!"

"She also puts herself constantly into mortal danger, which is why I *need* to be 'always around,' as you so quaintly put it," said Tybalt. "Do you intend to distress your knight, your parents, and now your swain by putting yourself constantly into mortal danger?"

Quentin swallowed hard. "No, sir."

"Good."

I elbowed Tybalt lightly in the arm. "Don't scare my squire."

He grinned, showing far too many teeth, and said nothing.

"You're a little more of a surprise," I said, turning to Marcia.

She tossed her hair, which was long, blonde, and perpetually tangled, like it was considering an uprising against the tyranny of hairbrushes. "I'm *always* surprising."

Marcia was Dean's seneschal, which was part of my surprise. Normally, if he wasn't in the knowe, she was, keeping things functioning in the absence of her liege. The rest of my surprise had more to do with *what* Marcia was than who. She was a changeling, but only technically, and needed faerie ointment to see our world properly. Under normal circumstances, she would never even have been offered the Changeling's Choice.

I honestly had no idea how Marcia's past had led her here, to a moon-washed pier at midnight, preparing to sail for a place that technically shouldn't exist. We'd met when she was serving as a handmaid in the Japanese Tea Gardens, sworn to an Undine named Lily. After Oleander de Merelands arranged Lily's death, Marcia had switched her fealty to me and Goldengreen. I'd given my title to Dean, and she'd stayed with him, making sure he was prepared for the challenges of leadership on land.

"There is that," I agreed.

She smiled, bright and blithe and unconcerned, moonlight glinting off the rings of faerie ointment around her eyes. "I like adventures," she said. "This is going to be an adventure. Besides, Count Clueless here," she indicated Dean, who wrinkled his nose at her, "needs someone to make sure he wears the right things and uses the right fork. He's come a long way, but he's not attending this soiree as a member of the Undersea, he's doing it as the Count of Goldengreen. That makes a difference."

"I do much the same for my knight," said Quentin. Marcia and Tybalt both laughed, and we were fine. This was a good group of people. Together, we could handle whatever the Luidaeg—and the Undersea—wanted to throw our way.

A brief, companionable silence fell, finally broken by the sound of footsteps from the street. Tybalt and I exchanged a glance before the whole group turned, silently waiting to see whether it was something we'd need to worry about.

In a way, it both was and wasn't. The Luidaeg stepped out of the fog, followed by a woman whose orange hair and eyes could never have let her pass for human, even without the wings. They were large and filmy, colored like stained glass windows bent on representing the whole of the harvest. Her face lit up when she saw us—not as literally as it would have when we'd first met—and she ran over, bare feet slapping against the wood of the pier, to throw her arms around my neck and spin me around.

"We're having an adventure, aren't we?" she asked. The question was clearly rhetorical, since she was cutting off most of my air supply. "Out to sea! Out to see the mermaids and the mermans and all the rest! Oh, this is an adventure bigger than any I thought I'd be having, and that's for certain!"

"Hi, Poppy," I wheezed, and patted her on the shoulder in the vain hope that it would be enough to make her let go. "What are you doing here?"

"Right now, she's acting as my apprentice. If she ever wants to have a way to pay me to send her home, she'll need to make herself useful. This seemed like the sort of place where she could find useful things to do." The Luidaeg shrugged. "And I didn't want to leave her in my apartment. She has a nasty tendency to touch things, and she could get seriously hurt."

"What about Officer Thornton?" asked Quentin.

Officer Thornton was a human policeman who had been accidentally swept into Annwn for a while, and was currently recovering at the Luidaeg's place. Mortal minds aren't meant for the deeper realms of Faerie. It was anybody's guess whether he was ever going to wake up, and what condition his mind would be in if and when it finally happened.

The Luidaeg shrugged again. "He's not going to wake up while we're gone."

Poppy loosened her grip on me, pulling back and beaming. "It's going to be grand."

"Sure," I said, stepping away before she could grab me again.

Poppy is Aes Sidhe—as far as I know, the only Aes Sidhe left. They died out centuries ago. Turns out, they don't have a First-born: they're made when pixies give up their inherent magic in exchange for something bigger and more complicated. Poppy gave her magic so the Luidaeg could wake Simon Torquill from an enchanted sleep. Now Simon was out there somewhere, doing Maeve-knows-what, while Poppy was stuck in a size that wasn't natural for her, living with the Luidaeg because she didn't have anywhere else to go.

No matter how good your intentions are, there's always the possibility that someone is going to get hurt. Someone innocent, who didn't do anything to deserve it. Poppy was a clear illustration of that unfortunate reality.

The Luidaeg looked at our group, a frown growing on her lips. "Where's your daughter?" she asked.

"She's coming," I said.

She eyed me suspiciously. "Are you sure?"

"I sent Danny to pick her up. She's coming."

"She knows she has to come alone?"

"She knows."

The Luidaeg opened her mouth like she was going to say something. Then she caught herself, closed it, and shook her head.

I wanted to tell her not to cast aspersions on Gillian. I couldn't. I didn't know Gillian well enough to know whether she was the kind of person who kept her word. Maybe she was halfway to Canada by now, passport in her hand and bag over her shoulder, unwilling to take the step that would commit her to Faerie forever.

The Luidaeg, meanwhile, had found another target. "What are you doing here?" she asked Marcia, more curious than cruel. "Where we're going . . . if something happens, you'll be a long way from human medical care."

"Don't worry about me," said Marcia. It was impossible to tell whether she was being brave and talking to the sea witch like it wasn't a big deal, or whether she simply didn't know what she was doing. I hoped for the former. If she didn't know, someone would eventually tell her, and once that happened . . . .

There were very few things I could think of that would make being in the middle of the ocean even *less* fun. Trying to talk Marcia down from a panic attack while we were there was on the list.

Blithely, Marcia continued, "I've been in Faerie for so long that I wouldn't know what to do with a human hospital, and I'm sure the Undersea has healers. They have such a warlike culture, there's no way they could survive without someone to set their bones."

"A lot of them don't survive," said Dean glumly, looking at the water. "A lot of people think of Saltmist as this provincial little nowhere, because the land Courts are so strong here that the Undersea has never really wanted to force the issue of coastal and surface territory. We—I mean, they—maintain a presence. There has to be some reminder that the Undersea isn't to be trifled with. But in the deep waters, where land's just a legend . . . a lot of people don't survive."

"The ocean is not and has never been a toy," said the Luidaeg. Dean cast her a nervous glance. She ignored it. "Forget that at your peril."

"What are we calling you?" I asked.

She looked at me levelly. "Whatever you want. The time for pretty illusions is over."

Understanding washed over me. I swallowed my gasp. She wouldn't have appreciated it. The Luidaeg's gaze didn't waver. Her eyes were deep blue, drowning blue, like the entire ocean had somehow flowed into them and been trapped there.

The Luidaeg hated the Selkies for what they represented to her and to her family, but she loved them at the same time, because the Selkies had continued, through the long march of years, to treat her like a person. She *existed* in their eyes, as she existed in so few others. She was their Cousin Annie, and being Cousin Annie had been her escape from the pressure of being the sea witch. And now she was giving that away.

The smell of crushed blackberry flowers broke me out of my introspection. I turned to see a portal open in the air, disgorging a tall, dark-haired man with mismatched eyes, and—

"Cassandra!" I rushed over and swept my honorary niece into an embrace before I could think better of it, lifting her off her feet. She laughed and slung her arms around my shoulders, hugging me back. "I didn't think you were coming!"

"Yeah, well, Her Highness didn't want her brother traveling alone." Cassandra let go long enough to hook a thumb toward Nolan, who bore her uncouth pointing with a stoically tolerant expression.

The Luidaeg didn't look nearly so calm. "I wasn't aware Queen Windermere was intending to send a contingent," she said frostily.

"Aunt Birdie, put me down," murmured Cassandra. I did as I was told. She took a step toward the Luidaeg before sinking into a picture-perfect curtsy, head bowed, neck an elegant, vulnerable line. "I beg your forgiveness, Luidaeg. My liege intended no offense."

"Sometimes I *really* miss the old forms," muttered the Luidaeg. "You should have come to me with a raw salmon in your hands, its gills still heaving, and been apologizing before you were even close enough to look at me. You might as well stand up. You've already insulted me as much as you're going to."

Cassandra straightened. She wasn't wearing a human disguise, but she didn't need one as much as some of us; she could have passed for human in the right light, as long as no one looked closely enough to realize that her hair wasn't dyed. It grew in a natural gradient, blonde at the crown of her head tapering into black at its tips. Her ears were dully pointed, topped with tufts of hair in the same gradient, like she was some sort of humanoid lynx.

I've known her since she was born. She's Mitch and Stacy's eldest daughter, and I'm not thrilled about the part where she's somehow ended up as Arden's seneschal.

"My sister Karen sends her regards," said Cassandra. "She told me to say that she's been practicing her dream-walking just like you told her to, and you should be nice to me because I'm her favorite sister."

The Luidaeg actually looked amused at that. "Did she, now? Well, I guess I have to listen. It wouldn't do to piss off the only oneiromancer we have on hand." She turned to Nolan. "You, on the other hand, were distinctly not invited to this party. What are you doing here, Prince Windermere? Don't you know what happens to nobles who sail too far from familiar shores?"

"I stand as diplomatic emissary for my sister, Queen Arden Windermere in the Mists, long may she rule in peace and in plenty," said Nolan stiffly. I couldn't blame him for that. He wasn't accustomed to being interrogated by the literal sea witch.

He was a striking man, despite his somewhat old-fashioned clothing and his plummy, outdated accent. He looked and sounded like something from an Underhill production of *The Great Gatsby*, and while I wasn't sure having him along with us was necessarily a good idea, it was nice to see him outside the knowe. He'd spent the better part of the twentieth century in an elf-shot coma, and he was still adjusting to the way the world had changed while he was asleep. This was, so far as I was aware, the first time Arden had allowed him out of her sight for longer than a quick trip to the store. Which meant . . .

"Nolan, have you been to the Duchy of Ships before?"

He turned to me, eyebrows lifted. Then he relaxed, and smiled his prince's smile, and said, "The informality of this era is a delight. Yes, Sir Daye, once. Long ago. It was a short trip, taken in company of my nursemaid, Marianne. I travel in my sister's name, but I am, I admit, hopeful that perhaps someone there might remember her, and be able to tell me where she's gone. We would welcome her home, if she were willing to return. If nothing else, I would like to find her, and see for myself that she's all right."

"And as Arden's seneschal, I'm here to make sure he doesn't get kidnapped by pirates or something," said Cassandra. "It's sort of like going on vacation, except for the part where it's not going to be restful and we're all going to die."

"Cheerful," I said.

She shrugged. "I learned from the best."

A car door slammed in the distance. I turned to see Gillian walking toward us, towing a small suitcase in her wake. She was alone. Danny must have stayed with the cab, and I was grateful for that; I didn't want to explain, again, what was going on, and we'd come too far to turn back now.

She stopped a few feet away, eyes going terribly wide at the sight of Poppy, with her gauzy, undisguised wings, and Nolan, with his sharply pointed ears and inhumanly handsome features. "I thought we were supposed to use illusions when we were out in public," she said, voice wavering. She raised a hand to indicate her own seemingly human face. "Did I do this wrong?"

"There's an illusion on this whole pier right now, courtesy of the Duchy of Ships," said the Luidaeg. "It was necessary."

Gillian frowned. "Why?"

"Because our ride is almost here," said the Luidaeg.

As if on cue, the fog in front of the pier parted and a ship sailed majestically toward us. It was an old-fashioned thing, like it had been stolen from the set of the latest *Pirates of the Caribbean* movie, with tall sails and a stylized mermaid on the prow. Only she wasn't quite a mermaid: her body ended not in the long, scaled sweep of a fish's tail, but in a tangled knot of tentacles, each one carved into an elegant spiral and colored the same coral red as her hair. There was an air of antiquity to the vessel, accentuated by the barnacles on its sides and the tattered edges of its sails.

The flag flying above the crow's nest was unfamiliar to me, showing three black feathers above a background of blue, each tipped in palest gray. The Luidaeg looked at it and smiled before turning to the rest of us.

"I want to make this perfectly, exquisitely clear, and I want to do so right now, while there's still time for you to go home and forget you were ever here," she said. "October is necessary for this to work. Gillian is bound to attend this Convocation. The rest of you are convenient at best and inconsequential at worst, and if you offend or bother me in any way between here and the Duchy, if you try my patience while we're in open waters, I'll throw you over the side without thinking twice."

Dean paled. Quentin patted his arm, clearly trying to be soothing.

He was just as clearly failing. Quentin didn't think of the Luidaeg as a threat, but Dean had grown up in the Undersea, and he understood how dangerous she could be.

"That's a ship," said Gillian.

"Sure is!" chirped Marcia.

"It's . . . it's huge, and no one's coming over here to take pictures or point at it," said Gillian.

"Nope," agreed Marcia. "They can't see it. Or if they *can* see it, they know it's not here for them, and they don't want to mess with anybody powerful enough to summon an Undersea vessel to a mortal pier." She moved closer to Gillian, patting the other woman on the arm. They looked like they were roughly the same age. When had my daughter become a woman? When had the world changed?

Oblivious to my staring, Marcia continued, "I'm Marcia. You must be Gillian. You have your mother's chin. Anyway, I'm Dean Lorden's seneschal, and I'm happy to answer any questions you have. You'll probably come up with a million, and I think I'm the least intimidating person here."

"The man who picked me up was seven feet tall and gray like a boulder," confessed Gillian.

"That would be Danny McReady," said Marcia. "He's a friend of your mother's. He's a Bridge Troll, and a very nice guy. Did he give you his business card? It can be really useful to have someone you can—"

"Please stop calling her that," interrupted Gillian.

Marcia stopped, blinking wide, confused eyes at her. "Calling who what?"

"Calling October my mother," said Gillian. "She is, I know, but . . . it's complicated."

Marcia looked from Gillian to me and back again before she said, "Got it. Anyway. He's a friend of October's. Good number to have." She turned away, shoulders stiff, and moved to retrieve the suitcase she'd abandoned next to Dean, fussily checking the latches.

Gillian grimaced. "I didn't mean it like that," she said.

The Luidaeg clapped her on the shoulder with one hand, snapping the fingers of the other. Gillian's human disguise dissolved in a whiff of fennel, the underlying seawater drowned out by the proximity to the ocean.

"I am the *last* person who should lecture you about family, except for maybe my sister, may piranhas strip the flesh from her poisonously pretty bones," she said. Her teeth seemed sharper than they'd been a few seconds ago: she looked like she could chew through diamond. "But technically, you're part of my family as long as you wear that skin, and once you can't take it off anymore, you're going to be part of my family forever, so I'm going to give you this advice for free: hate your mother as much as you want to. Loathe her. Raise up armies to destroy her and everything she cares about. But for the love of my father, don't go *saying* it. She's a fucking hero of the realm, and you're a brand new Selkie who most of these people will be looking at as a possible tool to use against her. The more dissent they see, the more they're going to aim their designs on you. Be dull. Be unwanted. Be the daughter who broke the chain of Amandine's line, and make yourself seem as placid and pointless as possible. Do you understand me?"

Gillian glared at her, jaw set in a stubborn line. Finally, sullenly, she said, "Yes."

"Good. Because your first test is almost here."

The great ship had sailed closer as we talked among ourselves; now it was almost to the pier. It shouldn't have been able to fit there. It should have run up against hidden obstacles, ancient, rotting support beams and fresh-poured concrete pylons. It did no such thing. It sailed, straight and true, until it pulled up along the pier and a voice called from above, "'Ware below!"

"That means step back," said the Luidaeg.

We stepped back, watching as a gangplank dropped from the side of the ship and landed, neat as anything, against the pier. It was perfectly dry, with ropes along the sides to keep passengers from falling off the ship and into the water as they boarded.

A Satyr appeared at the top of the gangplank, dressed in a long black coat that wouldn't have looked out of place on a pirate ship, with a tricornered hat perched jauntily on his head. His hooves seemed to have been treated with something that helped them grip the deck, because his steps were steady and sure, even as he bowed deeply to the lot of us.

"All who come in peace are welcome aboard," he called, as he straightened. "How many are you?"

"Ten," called the Luidaeg. "Do you know where we're going?"

"I was dispatched to take a gathering to the Duchy of Ships," the Satyr replied, seemingly unoffended by her question. "If I'm not your ship, I'm not your ship, but I'll not be taking passengers anywhere else."

"We're going to the same place," said the Luidaeg. "Poppy?"

"Here, here," said Poppy, hurrying to stand beside her.

The two of them walked up the gangplank. At the top, the Luidaeg offered the Satyr a shallow nod, which he returned. Poppy bounced onto her toes, then hugged him, leaving him looking nonplussed as she followed the Luidaeg onto the ship.

I exchanged a glance with Tybalt, shrugged, and started up the gangplank myself. He hurried to match his steps to mine, and Quentin followed behind us. Dean and Marcia seemed to take that as their cue; they joined us on the gangplank, with Nolan and Cassandra behind them, and Gillian bringing up the rear.

At the top, the Satyr offered me a thin-lipped smile. "Whom do I have the honor of meeting?" he asked.

"Sir October Daye of Shadowed Hills, Knight of Lost Words, hero of the realm," I said, as blandly as I could manage. "I'm accompanied by Tybalt, King of Dreaming Cats, and my squire, Quentin."

"Charmed, I'm sure," said Tybalt, with a thin-lipped smile of his own.

Quentin waved.

The Satyr blinked—once—and looked me up and down. "*You're* Sir Daye?" he asked.

"Last time I checked," I said. "Why?"

"No offense, I beg, but I thought you'd be . . . well, taller. And larger. And terrifying. I expected substantially more in the way of teeth."

"Sorry. No extra teeth here." I shrugged. "Do we need to pay you or anything?"

"No!" Now he looked horrified. "My name's Rodrick; I sail at the pleasure of Captain Pete; your fare has already been paid by the Duchy of Ships. It would be rude, if not immoral, for us to take anything more from you. We'd be naught but common pirates if we did that."

"Got it. Come on, Quentin. Mind your step. The deck might be slippery." I stepped off the gangplank, onto the ship proper, and barely managed to catch myself on Tybalt's arm before I toppled over in disorientation and shock.

The world spun around me, a sudden carousel of light, color, and sickeningly irregular motion. Then it passed, and I was standing on the deck of the ship—but the sky above us was shot through with veins of glittering purple and spectacularly bright gold, and I could count at least eight moons without really trying. We were in the Summerlands. I looked frantically around, settling my gaze on the Luidaeg, who shrugged almost sympathetically.

"The Duchy of Ships is a unique case," she said. "The ships that go back and forth between the coastal kingdoms and the ducal waters are functionally floating knowes. You crossed over when you willingly stepped onboard."

"You could have warned me," I snapped.

She smirked. "Where would have been the fun in that?"

"Right." I forced myself to loosen my grasp on Tybalt's arm, shooting him a wan smile to balance the alarm in his expression. "I'm fine. You know transitions can be hard on me."

"I haven't seen one hit you that hard in a very long time," he said solemnly.

"It's always harder when there haven't been other people with human blood making the transition," I said. My eyes widened as a sudden, horrifying realization hit me. "Marcia!"

"What?"

I whirled. She was right behind me, a politely quizzical expression on her face. The moonlight glinted off the faerie ointment around her eyes, making them seem huge and guileless. She wasn't breathing hard. She wasn't even paler than usual.

Gillian was behind her, making her introductions to Rodrick. I gestured toward the two of them, keeping most of my attention on Marcia. "The crossing," I said. "Didn't it knock the wind out of you?"

"Um, no?" Marcia glanced up, eyes widening. "Oh, wow, look at all those moons. Are we in the Summerlands? I guess we must be. Earth doesn't go around adding moons for fun."

"Yeah," I said faintly.

She flashed a quick smile before trailing after Dean and Quentin, who had gone to find a seat atop some nearby barrels. I looked back to the gangplank. Gillian was now safely on the ship, and two more sailors—a Merrow and a Candela—had appeared to get us ready to cast off. Everyone looked perfectly content with the situation, and with their role in the journey ahead.

Tybalt touched my elbow. "What is it?" he asked.

"That's the problem. I don't know," I replied. "But something's wrong."

He nodded and stepped closer as we pushed away from the pier—still visible through a wavering, crystalline curtain, like it was on the other side of a heat haze rising from a highway in the summer sun. As soon as we were no longer in contact with it, it winked out, and we were sailing on an endless, wine-dark sea, bound for an unknown destination, and everything was water all around us, and there was no turning back.

FIVE

IT TURNS OUT SAILING is intensely dull when you're just riding the boat, not actually doing anything to *drive* it. There were cabins belowdecks, but as we were supposed to arrive at the Duchy of Ships before sunrise, they hadn't been prepared for our use, and the crew didn't like us hanging out down there. Worse, there were no beds—not even cots. The rocking that suffused the whole ship was worse on the deck, and there was nowhere else to be. I heal quickly enough for injuries that would be game over for most people to be only minor inconveniences for me. Somehow seasickness, like migraines from excessive magic use, didn't care. Once my stomach went into rebellion, that was all she wrote.

I hoped the barnacles lining the ship's hull and sides didn't mind being vomited on, because it was happening. It was happening a *lot*. I gripped the rail, trying to keep my eyes closed so the roiling water below wouldn't set me off again. Footsteps warned me of someone's approach. I wondered, half-eagerly, whether this was a surprise assassination attempt. Drowning couldn't have been worse than the nausea.

Actually, I *had* drowned before, at least once, and it *hadn't* been worse than the nausea. I hate puking. Almost as much as I hate being shot, stabbed, covered in my own blood, and everything else that happens to me on a horrifyingly regular basis.

"Did you not bring any Dramamine?" Marcia sounded concerned, but not like she was about to lose everything she'd ever eaten over the side of the ship.

I decided to hate her a little. "Didn't think of it," I wheezed, allowing my head to loll forward, so if I did vomit again—I couldn't possibly vomit again, there was nothing left inside me—it would follow the path of the existing mess. "Never been seasick before."

"Have you ever gone sailing before?"

I shook my head. The motion was enough to set my temples throbbing and make my stomach do another slow tuck and roll. I groaned.

"Poor Toby." Marcia put her hand against my back, rubbing in small, concentric circles. It helped. Not enough to make me feel like I could let go of the rail, but it helped. "We'll be there soon. Miss the Luidaeg says the Duchy of Ships doesn't sway nearly this much. It's too big for that. Well, except when there's a major storm, but the Merrow have agreed to sing the storms away for as long as this meeting is going on. Which could be days. I hope you remembered to clean your fridge before we left."

"May and Jazz are home, and the wards are keyed to Raj," I said. "Food doesn't have time to spoil in my house."

"Oh, that's good," said Marcia cheerfully, still rubbing my back. "Tybalt is having a serious conversation with one of the ship's cats, or at least that's what it looks like. I don't know whether the cat is Cait Sidhe or not. I guess it doesn't matter much. And the prince is up in the rigging. He climbs *really* well, for a prince. If I were a prince, I think I'd spend all my time sitting around waiting for people to bring me things. Bonbons and stuff like that."

I finally took my eyes off the water, peering at her through the disheveled curtain of my hair. "Are you just babbling at me until I start feeling better?"

"Yup!" Marcia beamed. "Is it working?"

My stomach was no longer roiling. I didn't trust myself to stand up on my own, but I also didn't feel like I was about to introduce the barnacles to my breakfast. Again. I blinked. "Actually, yes."

"Sometimes you need to take peoples' minds off their problems if you want those problems to resolve themselves," said Marcia. "Focusing on things can make them worse."

"Not all problems go away if you ignore them. Most don't."

"No, but not all problems can be fixed. Sometimes you have to wait until the situation changes." She smiled sympathetically. "Like if you're on a boat and you get seasick."

"I don't like water." I closed my eyes, trying not to think about the fact that I was completely surrounded by my least favorite element.

"Which explains why you're marrying a cat," chirped Marcia. When I opened one eye to look balefully at her, she grinned. "I know you don't like water. It's a real good thing you're doing here."

I opened my other eye. "Did Dean explain why we're doing this?"

"He did. He's good about making sure his people are kept in the loop. He's trying, you know? They do things differently in the Undersea, and it's not like he can ask any of the local nobility for help without weakening his position, but he's trying." She turned so she could rest her elbows on the rail, facing the ship while I faced the sea.

When she spoke again, her voice was softer. "I meant what I said. It's a real good thing you're doing. There are so many broken parts to Faerie, and sometimes I don't know if they can ever be fixed. What happened to the Roane wasn't just a tragedy, it was . . . it was unforgivable. I know the Firstborn are supposed to be judged by a different standard, but I can't think of any standard that makes killing an entire people because you don't like your sister the right thing to do. This doesn't bring back the ones who were lost. This doesn't make things *right*. But it makes things better than they've been, and maybe that can be enough to let us move forward, you know? Maybe this is where some of the broken bits get fixed."

"Maybe," I agreed. More delicately, I said, "The Undersea doesn't have many changelings. Humans tend to drown before they can get too involved. Aren't you worried?"

She shrugged. "Aren't you?"

I was still mulling over my answer when Rodrick shouted, from the helm, "Harbor ahoy!"

Marcia turned. So did I. So did all the others, and together we beheld the Duchy of Ships breaking through the mist ahead of us.

At first it looked like an island, like some natural combination of rock and sand and location had formed the perfect spot for the Undersea to claim. As we sailed closer, I realized that what I'd taken for trees was a forest of masts, their sails furled and tamped down to keep them from catching the wind; what I'd mistaken for the shore was a conglomeration of docks and hulls and wooden bridges, all of them built over, around, through the bodies of the ships that had come to anchor here and would never sail away again.

"All hands to stations," called Rodrick, and sailors swarmed for the sides, grabbing ropes, hauling on lines, doing a hundred incomprehensible things to get us ready for docking. The cat Tybalt had been speaking with stood on two legs, shaking off her fur in favor of a bipedal form, and ran to join one of the rope crews.

"Huh," said Marcia. "Cait Sidhe after all. Cool."

The other members of our little party—parties, really, since Gillian was here to stand with the Selkies, and Nolan and Cassandra were here to witness this whole thing on behalf of the Kingdom in the Mists—drifted toward us, until we were grouped together once again. The Luidaeg flashed me a smile filled with concern, mostly concealed under a thin overlay of malice.

"Done feeding the fishes?" she asked.

"For now." I kept my eyes on the Duchy of Ships. There was a lighthouse among the masts, an actual lighthouse. I pointed to it. "What is that standing on? Did someone build it on their deck?"

"'There's an island," she said. "A very small one. Big enough for a single lighthouse and a single dock, where a single ship could be moored. The rest of the Duchy grew up around it. Piece by piece, they found ways to anchor the structures they'd need. Merrow placed the stones for their foundations, and Cephali tied the pylons into place, and the Duchy took shape, like a pearl being formed a single layer at a time."

"But why?"

"Because some things are better when discussed in the open air, and not every resident of the Undersea can breathe beneath the waves." The Luidaeg indicated the Duchy with a sweep of her hands. "We claim sailors and their lovers, merchants and those who find no peace on land, and we keep them as safe as storm and sky allow. Here, they can be home. And here, we can discuss things on somewhat neutral ground. We're technically in Leucothea, since the closest mortal cognate is the Pacific Ocean, which means we're in Dianda's waters, if you squint. Queen Palatyne has, quite wisely, ceded rulership of the Duchy of Ships *to* the Duchy of Ships. The people who live here make their own law, maintain their own order, and don't cause problems for the Crown, which means Queen Palatyne can mostly pretend they don't exist, sparing her from needing to justify all these air-breathers to her more traditionalist subjects."

"Ugh." I pinched the bridge of my nose. "I hate politics."

"If you didn't, it wouldn't be nearly as much fun to make you deal with them."

I glared at her. She smirked, and looked like she was about to say something when the ship gave a mighty lurch and a pair of vast, red-shaded tentacles reached out of the water, wrapping around the ropes that had been prepared for docking.

Screaming would have been the sensible thing to do. Gillian, Poppy, and Quentin certainly thought so, although their screams had widely different qualities. Gillian sounded terrified. Poppy sounded delighted, like a kid on her first roller coaster. Quentin was somewhere in the middle, although his scream faded into puzzled silence as he realized none of the sailors looked concerned. They were tossing *more* ropes to the tentacles, which seemed to be guiding us ever closer to the ramshackle conglomeration of ships, docks, and gangplanks.

I shot the Luidaeg a sharp look. "Not funny."

"Pretty funny," she said. She blinked, and her eyes were no longer blue. They were green, like shards of broken bottle rolling across the bottom of the sea, like light reflecting through kelp. I've always wondered if that was the true color of her eyes, assuming anything can be said to be "true" when it's referring to a shapeshifter's appearance.

"Not hiding anymore?" I asked quietly.

"No." She shook her head, eyes on the rapidly approaching Duchy. "If the Selkies die here, Cousin Annie dies with them. She was never anything but a useful reflection, a face in the water. I loved being her. I loved the freedom of knowing people weren't listening to every word I said, waiting for the moment when malice turned into murder. I loved just . . . being. When you're as old as I am, when you have as few friends left as I do, there's something beautiful about just *being*. I was playing pretend but I was never lying to them. It was a loophole, you know? A way for me to breathe. And now it's over."

The Luidaeg chuckled, and the sound was dry and mirthless, bones rattling in a forgotten cave. "I can never have my children back. I'll never be a mother again. I'll be a grandmother, and a great-grandmother, and so on, for a dozen generations, but I'll never look someone in the eyes and know that the ocean they carry inside of them remembers the ocean I carry inside of me. My sister stole that. And I've been stealing it from the Selkies since the day I made them. I trapped them between worlds. They don't get to see their grandchildren born to the waters; they pass their skins, they die, they end. For the sake of my children and for the sake of the Selkies themselves, we're going to make that stop. No more Selkies. Not even Cousin Annie."

I wanted to say something. My throat was dry and my lips wouldn't move, and so I put my hand on her shoulder, pretending not to see the surprise and relief in her eyes when she glanced at me, and we sailed the rest of the way into the artificial harbor of the Duchy of Ships, pulled along by the vast tentacles of the great beast that had us in its embrace.

As soon as the hull came to rest against the dock, the tentacles withdrew, vanishing into the water without a sound. Rodrick barked orders that his sailors rushed to obey. I paused.

"Luidaeg," I said. "That man, Rodrick. He said he wasn't the captain, that he sailed at the captain's grace. Did this ship not *have* a captain?"

"There's only one captain in the Duchy," said the Luidaeg. Seeing my confusion, she shrugged. "The Duchy of Ships is a Duchy because it needs to be *something*, but there's no Duke or Duchess of Ships. It's the captain who keeps things running. Hands on the helm, sails to the wind, all that fun stuff. The other ships have first mates, to keep them under a clear chain of command, but they don't have captains."

"That feels unnecessarily confusing," objected Quentin, who had inched up on us while she was speaking.

The Luidaeg granted him a warm, if brief, smile. "Says the boy who grew up in a system of kings ruling kings. The high kingship is no more confusing than a single captain with a whole passel of first mates. It's all in what you think is normal. Here, this is normal. Now shut up. It's time for us to be announced."

Rodrick, who had apparently been waiting for us to be quiet, bowed extravagantly as he lowered the gangplank. He stepped up onto it, hooves clopping against the wood, and called, in a loud, carrying voice, "The *Jackdaw* is returned safely to port, carrying our contracted cargo!"

A cheer went up from the people on the dock and hanging out

of the portholes of nearby ships. I turned, taking them all in. Where had they come from? It felt like there were dozens of them present, all watching us like we were the most interesting animals at the zoo. I hadn't seen any of them during our approach. Either they'd gathered in a serious hurry, or the Duchy of Ships had some unpleasant tricks up its sleeve.

"Name your cargo, First Mate," shouted a voice, female, even louder than Rodrick's.

There was no cheer this time. Only silence. Rodrick paled, and for a moment, I thought he was going to turn and run to the safety of his cabin. Then he cleared his throat and stood up even straighter, squaring his shoulders like he thought posture was the answer to all his troubles.

"From the Court of Dreaming Cats, King Tybalt of the Cait Sidhe," he announced. Tybalt shot me an irritated glance, apparently not pleased to have been called first, and stepped onto the gangplank, looking along his nose at the assembled crowd. Then he proceeded down to the dock, as was only correct when he had been announced so formally.

"From the County of Goldengreen in the Mists, Count Dean Lorden, and his seneschal, Marcia." Dean stepped onto the gangplank, Marcia behind him, dragging her suitcase. He looked utterly at ease, which made sense; apart from Nolan and the Luidaeg, he was the only one of us who might actually have been here before. Marcia was so busy rubbernecking that I couldn't tell what she thought about the situation. At least she didn't slip and fall into the water.

"From the Duchy of Shadowed Hills in the Mists, Sir October Daye, named Knight of Lost Words, and her squire, Quentin."

I took a deep breath. "Chin up, kiddo, it's time to get judged."

"I've been judged before," said Quentin dismissively.

"Then this should be easy." I stepped onto the gangplank. The wood was slipperier than it looked, and my feet nearly shot out from underneath me. I saved myself from a nasty fall by putting a hand on Quentin's shoulder and bearing down hard, trying to make the gesture look as natural as possible. It wasn't easy, because the smell . . .

The Duchy of Ships was located entirely in the Summerlands, with no mortal population to hide from. There was no reason for any of these people to keep their magic under wraps or to pretend to be anything other than what they were. The air crackled with dozens, maybe *hundreds* of magical signatures, and while "oceanic" scents were dominant—wind and waves and sea grasses, kelp and sand and ambergris—there were plenty of conflicting scents that would have been much easier to interpret if we'd been inland. Or near land at all.

"Toby?" whispered Quentin. "You okay?"

"Lot of magic here," I said, holding onto his shoulder. "Get me to solid ground."

We descended slowly, people watching and assessing us every step of the way. Tybalt was there as soon as we reached the bottom of the gangplank, taking my other arm with the sort of ostentatious flourish that I knew meant he was flexing his possession of me for everyone to see. I would have been annoyed, except that I understood his reasons all too well. They were very similar to the reasons I wasn't letting go of Quentin, and the reason my heart sank as Rodrick continued his introductions.

"From the Court in the Mists, standing in lieu of Her Majesty, Queen Arden Windermere, Prince Nolan Windermere and Her Majesty's seneschal, Cassandra Brown."

Nolan and Cassandra walked decorously down the gangplank. Nolan was still in his rumpled turn-of-the-century finery, but Cassandra had exchanged her jeans and sweatshirt for a dress of blue linen a few shades lighter than the lamplit sky above us. She walked three steps behind Nolan, as was technically appropriate for a changeling in service to a pureblood court, her head bowed and her hands folded in front of her. My breath caught in my throat. I've known Cassandra since she was born, and while there's a fourteen-year chunk missing in the middle, courtesy of my time in the pond, I'd never truly seen her in the context of Faerie before.

She was glorious. She was where she'd always been intended to be. Only our prior ruler's prejudices against changelings had kept Cassandra from this side of her heritage for so long, and I was suddenly, fiercely grateful to see her this way.

"From the Ryan clan among the Selkies, Gillian Marks."

There she was, my baby girl, alone and anxious at the top of the gangplank, hugging her arms around herself and looking around like she wanted nothing more than to leap into the waiting sea and swim away as fast as she could. She didn't have anyone to lean on, and so when she took her first step down, her foot shot out from under her and she went sprawling, landing hard on her behind.

"Gillian!" I was halfway up the gangplank before I realized I was going to move. I didn't stop. I didn't stop until I was beside her, dropping to my knees on the wood, offering my arm so she could pull herself to her feet.

She glared at me and slapped my arm away. "I'm not a part of your fiefdom, remember?" she snapped, and there was a depth of hurt in her voice that wounded me as surely as any arrow. She pushed herself to her feet, wobbling as she turned and stomped down the gangplank, her anger somehow lending her the stability she needed to remain upright. I stayed where I was, baffled and aching from the urge to run after her.

What had just happened? Maybe more importantly, how could I *fix* it?

The people who'd gathered to watch us arrive whispered behind their hands, enthralled by the drama we were enacting for their amusement. I stood, bracing myself as carefully as I could, intending to stalk back to where Tybalt and Quentin were waiting for me.

Naturally, I immediately fell on my ass. Like mother, like daughter, I suppose.

I heal at a rate that's frankly offensive to anyone who believes actions should have consequences, but that doesn't mean I don't feel pain. The impact of my behind on the wood was hard enough to send a shock along my spine, and I sat there for a moment, blinking in shock and surprise. Unfortunately for me, I was *still* sitting there when Rodrick decided he couldn't keep the rest of his passengers waiting any longer.

"From the Kingdom in the Mists, apprentice Poppy," he announced, and Poppy launched herself into the air, stained glass wings beating harder than any pixie's would have needed to, fighting to keep her increased weight aloft. It had taken her a while to learn how to fly again after giving up her pixiehood for Simon Torquill's sake. Still, she made a striking sight as she cut through the air toward the dock, a moving painting in all the colors of the living autumn.

Some of the people surrounding us gasped. A few clapped hands over their mouths, staring . . . and then a man who could have been her brother, only rendered in shades of red and pink instead of orange, pushed his way through the crowd, pulling Poppy into a fierce embrace even as they both burst into tears.

"What the . . . ?"

"When you want to keep something secret, you send it out to sea," said a familiar voice. I tilted my head back. The Luidaeg stood over me, offering her hand. "There are a lot of secrets buried far from familiar shores."

"You said the Aes Sidhe died out," I said, letting her pull me to my feet. Her skin was cooler than normal, like she'd risen from the depths and hadn't had enough time to return to room temperature. "You can't lie."

"I can't, and they did," she said. "A few scattered survivors does not a people make. It's just a funeral in slow-motion." She turned and looked over her shoulder at Rodrick, lifting one eyebrow. "Well? This is where you're supposed to introduce me."

"I . . . I sail at the pleasure of Captain Pete, and that means I truthfully name all who enter these waters, as pleasure can easily become pain," he said. "Annie. We've met before. I *know* you. Why would you write such a thing on my passenger manifest? Are you trying to get me in trouble?"

The Luidaeg lowered her eyes to the deck, holding that position for several long seconds. When she glanced up again, looking at him through sooty lashes, her irises and sclera had blended into a single fathomless darkness, not black, not exactly, but layer upon layer of translucence leading to the same inevitable conclusion. I like to think of myself as relatively fearless where the Luidaeg is concerned. I couldn't look at those eyes for more than a second before I turned away, searching for something—anything—less terrifying.

There was a clatter of hooves as Rodrick stumbled back, away from the Luidaeg, away from her graveyard gaze.

"Does anyone ever really *know* anyone else, or do we act like cartographers, drawing maps of unfamiliar shores, pretending it teaches us their secrets? You've *met* me, Mate Rodrick of the Duchy of Ships, master of the *Jackdaw*, wind-chaser and wave-chaser and son of the sea. You've seen my shores from a distance, through a fog. But to claim to *know* me? That's the purview of greater hearts than yours, and it's not a burden you've ever been called upon to bear. Now announce me, so we can end this little passion play and move on to the business at hand. The fog is clearing. My capital city can finally be named."

Rodrick cleared his throat, still staring at her with a mixture of fascination and horror, like a hiker seeing their first venomous snake. "Y-yes, my lady," he said. His voice was a shipwrecked whisper, the ghost of his former sonorous tones. He cleared his throat a second time, and in that same hollow voice, announced, "From the Kingdom of Albany, in the High Demesne of Albion, most recently in the Mists, Firstborn to Maeve by Oberon, the fair and hallowed lady known as the Luidaeg, called sea witch by all who would avoid her wrath."

Somehow, despite its broken hollowness, his voice carried, silencing the crowds around us. I glanced to the Luidaeg. Her eyes were green again, and she inclined her chin ever so slightly, confirming that the spell which carried Rodrick's voice throughout the Duchy had been hers. I knew, in that moment, that it had penetrated even the smallest and most private of rooms, reaching the ears of every citizen and every visitor. She was coming before them in her truest guise, and that was a sacred, terrifying thing. They deserved to be warned.

Some of the people on the docks began weeping. Others put their hands over their mouths or turned their eyes away, unable or unwilling to look at her, to face the judgment they had to be certain was upon them. The Luidaeg offered Rodrick a smile. He trembled and bowed.

He didn't know her well enough to see the softness in her expression, but I did. She was being gentle. It didn't look like it—it looked like some dire portent suddenly suspended over an entire people, like the sword of Damocles, only waiting for the final thread to break—and yet I knew she didn't need any of this pomp or circumstance. She could have risen out of the sea like the avenging hand of Oberon himself. She could have swept this entire Duchy away, leaving only wreckage and legends behind. She was, in her terrifying way, trying to be kind.

She didn't let go of my hand as she turned and descended the gangplank. The crowds pulled back as we passed, too frightened to stay close, too aware of what offending the sea witch could cost them to flee. When we reached the bottom, Quentin rolled his eyes at us.

"Are all Firstborn overly dramatic, or is that a special gift you have?"

Dean looked horrified. The Luidaeg laughed. I eyed Quentin.

"You won't call Arden by her name, because her title is more important, but you'll back-talk the Luidaeg? I just want to be clear on where your sense of self-preservation fails you."

He shrugged. "The Luidaeg isn't a reigning monarch. She won't get mad at me for being disrespectful. Not in that way, at least. She might get mad at me for being disrespectful in other ways, but I'm pretty good about knowing where my boundaries are."

Dean's horror deepened, until he looked like he might be sick over the idea of what the Luidaeg was going to do to his boyfriend. I offered him a sympathetic smile.

"You get used to it, honest," I said.

A murmur ran through the crowd, sounding relieved and worried at the same time. They began to pull away, and this time, they didn't let fear of offending the Luidaeg stop them. In a matter of moments, they had opened a clear path along the dock, leading deeper into the ramshackle conglomeration of ships and shanties and more permanent structures.

There, at the exact center of the newly-opened path, was a woman. She was about the same height as the Luidaeg, and like the Luidaeg, she looked innocent and ancient at the same time, like a girl barely out of her teens who had nonetheless somehow seen more than any single person should have to see. She was dressed like a pirate from a summer blockbuster, down to the ludicrously large white feather in her battered hat and the cutlass belted at her nipped-in hourglass of a waist. Her shoulders were narrow and her hips were wide and she walked toward us like the rolling ocean, like she had nothing to worry about in the world, like the sea witch came to visit every day.

She was a stunning beauty, in every sense of the word "stunning": she was gorgeous and terrifying at the same time, with skin the color of a shark's belly, streaked here and there with lines of tiny scales that glittered with mother-of-pearl rainbows, shimmering and strange. Her hair was long and black and filled with oil-slick echoes, almost matching her scales. It covered her ears and the lines of her neck, making it impossible for me to tell whether she had gills. I couldn't name her type of fae on sight, and with so many other fae still clustered around us, I couldn't try to breathe in her heritage; I would have knocked myself on my ass again if I'd even considered it.

She smirked as she drew closer, like she knew what I'd been

considering. Then she focused on the Luidaeg. "Gentle winds and kind tides to all who come to my realm with peaceful hearts and honest hands."

The Luidaeg raised an eyebrow, looking briefly amused. "We're doing this the formal way, are we?"

The nameless woman looked placidly back at her.

The Luidaeg snorted. "All right, Petey. Clear skies and trackless shores to all who keep their signal fires burning, guiding home sailors from the sea."

The woman—Captain Pete, I presumed—suddenly grinned and, to my utter shock, swept the Luidaeg into an embrace. Even more shockingly, the Luidaeg returned it.

"It's been too long," said Pete.

"I've had my reasons," said the Luidaeg, and pulled back, shooting a smile at the rest of us. I braced myself. She never smiled like that unless she was about to say something upsetting.

"Pete, this is my retinue for the duration of our stay, along with a few assorted nobles and hangers-on. Retinue and otherwise, this is Captain Pete, keeper of the Duchy of Ships, protector of these waters, and my sister. Count Lorden, you may know her better by her given name: Amphitrite, Firstborn daughter of Titania and Oberon, Mother of the Merrow."

I stared, open-mouthed. Quentin did the same. Tybalt kept his composure better than either of us, offering the Luidaeg's newly-revealed sister a deep, formal bow.

Marcia squeaked in dismay. I turned to see that Dean had hit the dock in a dead faint.

"Okay," I said. "Business as usual, then. Good to know."

SIX

PETE DIDN'T SHARE THE Luidaeg's feelings about interior decorating, thank Oberon. I wasn't up for sitting in waist-deep garbage, pretending not to see the roaches. Her quarters were spacious, airy, and meticulously decorated in a mixture of "pirate queen" and "fae noble" that May would probably have admired and taken notes on, before running the hell away, because my Fetch has more sense than to sit down with an unfamiliar Firstborn for tea and cookies.

The Duchy of Ships wasn't designed to provide its citizens with huge homes, and Pete seemed content to live by the rules she set for everyone else, leaving her with one room that was large enough to serve as social area, kitchen, and bedroom, all at the same time. A decadently soft-looking bed was centered on one wall, and Dean was sprawled in the middle of it, still dead to the world. Somewhat worryingly so, given that he hadn't woken up when Tybalt and Quentin had picked him up from the dock, or during the walk back to Pete's quarters. Marcia and Poppy were off to find the canteen and get him some restorative soup. Also, I privately thought, to reduce the number of bodies in the room.

Gillian was gone as well, swept away by the rapidly-growing Selkie contingent, who had surrounded her while I'd still been trying to get Quentin to calm down about his unconscious boyfriend. When I'd looked up, she'd been walking away, and she hadn't looked back.

Still, Pete was a decent hostess, and she hadn't shown any signs of transforming us into anything unpleasant, which was about all I asked for in one of the Firstborn. My standards may be low, but hey. They've earned it.

"Sorry about that," said Pete, waving her mug of ale toward the unconscious Dean. At least it wasn't rum. That would have been too on the nose, and it was *way* too soon for us to start seriously drinking. She pursed her lips in a small frown. "I sort of overload my descendants until they get used to me. The Merrow are usually so busy running things *under* the waves that they never come up to visit the Duchy, and so I don't have to remember to hide from them."

"Is that why you go by 'Pete'?" I asked.

"That, and 'Amphitrite' isn't exactly what I'd call a modern name," she said. "It doesn't roll trippingly off the tongue the way it did five thousand years ago. I like to move with the times. Keeps me from seeming like a stagnant old fuddy-duddy who needs to be undermined and overthrown."

"Is there anyone around here who *could* undermine and over-throw you?" asked Quentin.

She fixed him with an amused stare. He met it, looking genuinely curious. To my surprise, she was the first to look away, swinging her attention to the Luidaeg as she asked, "How much time have you spent desensitizing this kid to the idea that gods walk among us?"

"I don't know," said the Luidaeg. "A lot. He follows Toby around, and she's not great for nurturing a sense of self-preservation."

"Ah, yes. The famous October." Pete turned to me, and for the first time, I felt the full weight of her regard. Her eyes were startlingly like the Luidaeg's, deep and drowning and comprised of what felt like countless layers of clear water combining into darkness. "Amandine's youngest. Is Amy the only sibling we have standing who's still having kids?"

"She hasn't had one since October, but so far as I know, yes," said the Luidaeg.

"We're all supposed to be gone now, you see, lies and legends and bones at the bottom of the sea," said Pete, still looking at me. "We agreed, when our parents disappeared. We're too big. We're like hurricanes surrounded in skin, storms that walk the world and do more damage than we intend to. Our wars shook Faerie when Dad and the Moms were here to rein us in, and without them, we could have ruined everything. So we withdrew. We stopped telling people who we were. We're oddities and demons now, sea witches and dark lords of the fen, but we're not *Firstborn*. The word carries too much weight. And that means we couldn't exactly go around having kids, since they'd give the game away."

"Our sister had one, shortly after Amy had August," said the Luidaeg.

"Wait, what?" I asked.

"Dawn," said the Luidaeg shortly, her attention still mostly on Pete. "I think she wanted to prove she was still stronger than the baby of the family."

"Eira." Pete's lip curled in disgust. "If there's one thing I truly regret, it's that I share a mother with *her*, and not with you. Not that I don't love my mother, may she remain missing until the stars fall from the sky, but who wants to sit at the family table and admit they're the full sibling of the biggest bitch to ever walk the world?"

"About that," I said. The Luidaeg turned to look at me. Having the full attention of two Firstborn was a bit much, even for me, but I refused to back down. "I thought, well. I thought Titania's children and Maeve's children didn't, you know. Get along."

"We don't, usually," said Pete. "Mom encouraged her kids to be conquerors and kings. She wanted us to carve out empires in her name, and if we could do our carving through the bodies of our half-siblings, all the better, because it meant there'd be less competition. She wasn't exactly what I'd call 'nurturing.' More 'bloody-minded and dedicated to the idea that one day she'd be seen as the one true Queen of Faerie.'"

"She sounds like a nice lady," I said, as carefully as I could.

The Luidaeg snorted. "She sounds like nothing of the sort."

"Anyway, the ocean is mostly Maeve's domain, what with her being the source of water magic and all, and I was Titania's first child who actually took to the depths. Like a fish, some might say." Pete took another sip of ale. "Mom saw me as a chance to start undermining Maeve's interests, and hey, it might have worked, if not for the part where my full siblings treated me like some sort of unwanted spindrift washed up on their shores. I was wet, which meant I was less than they were, so they felt free to act like it. Whereas Maeve's children . . ." She faltered, looking to the Luidaeg.

"We didn't know at first," said the Luidaeg. "My mother wasn't a megalomaniacal bitch who thinks of her kids as useful pieces in a century-spanning game of chess, but that didn't make her a great communicator, and sometimes she'd make children out of random stuff when Dad was away. When Pete showed up, she was just this skinny kid with kelp in her hair and fish guts in her teeth, and we all assumed Mom had fallen in love with the story of a shipwreck or something. It wouldn't have been the first time. When we realized she was one of Titania's get, it was too late; we were already fond of her."

"Good thing, too," said Pete, a look of deep melancholy settling over her face. "Maeve's children were my brothers and sisters, too—most of them, anyway, the ones who didn't have shipwrecks or stories for fathers—and they were kind to me, and they were dying. If I hadn't been their little curiosity, I think they might have killed me, just to even the scales a bit."

"Which would have been a pity, since I like most of the Merrow I've met," I said. "Although speaking of Merrow, you want to explain why Dean's still asleep?" I was starting to get nervous about that. He'd never been prone to fainting, and from the pinched, worried look on Quentin's face, he was going to say something stupid if his boyfriend didn't wake up soon.

"Sorry," said Pete unrepentantly. "The Merrow think I'm dead. Most of them, anyway. The few who realize I'm still up here do their best to pretend I'm not, because if they admitted I was alive, they'd have to listen to me, and I'd tell them to stop tormenting the rest of the ocean to make my mother happy. Titania can go hang as far as I'm concerned."

"That doesn't explain why he won't wake *up*," said Quentin.

Pete gave him a thoughtful look. "You're a prickly little spirit," she said. "No merry wanderer of the night. What family line are you from?"

Quentin's worry melted into an even deeper discomfort. "I'm not supposed to say," he said. "I'm on blind fosterage."

"Right now the only family line that matters is mine," I said, before he could dig his way any deeper into the hole. "He's my squire, I'm responsible for him, please don't turn him into a school of sardines or anything else that makes it difficult for me to finish his training."

"Presumptuous thing, aren't you?" asked Pete. At least she

sounded amused. "Your half-breed is unconscious because he wasn't prepared to look upon my glory. Merrow tend to respond like that when they see me without warning. Or they get really, really pissed and try to kill me. It's almost always one of the two. Does Eira know about him? Is it just *killing* her to know that one of her precious Daoine Sidhe went and lowered themselves to sport with a fish? Please tell me she knows. I'll forgive you for being annoying if you do."

"She knows," I said. "Dean has a little brother, too. Their parents are very happy together."

Now Pete looked surprised. "Wait, they did it more than once? Okay, my blessings on their household, solely because it cheeses Eira off."

"You don't know that," said the Luidaeg mildly.

"I've met our sister," said Pete. "I *do* know that." She looked around our group. "So this is your glorious crew, sailing for the unknown horizon, out to destroy the Selkies. They claim the protection of the waves, you know. I have Selkie families living here."

"There are families everywhere," said the Luidaeg.

"Not like this," snapped Pete, and for a moment, her scales were darker, like stormlight on the water, and I didn't want to look at her too closely, for fear I'd somehow drown in her mere presence. "When I say families, I mean *families*. Human families. Selkies who come here draped in sealskin and then set it aside, and stay, because they're mortal but they're not completely human. They've been touched by Faerie, and they can't go back to being what they were before they held their breath and dove. So tell me, sister dearest, sister mine, why I should side with you instead of with them?"

"Because you love me and want me to be happy?" suggested the Luidaeg.

"If love alone dictated the actions of the Firstborn, our world would be a very different one," said Pete.

"I'll drink to that." The Luidaeg picked up her mug and drained it in a single long pull, slamming it back down on the table and glaring at her sister. "Why should you side with me? Because you know what their ancestors did. What our sister used them to do. This is healing a wound in the world almost as old as Faerie itself."

"That isn't their fault," said Pete. She sounded sympathetic. She didn't sound like she was going to yield. Suddenly, it was very difficult to ignore the fact that we were sharing this pleasant, somewhat archaic room with two of the Firstborn, or to pretend their goals were exactly aligned with my own.

I glanced at Tybalt. He met my eyes, nodded, and shifted position slightly, so he was prepared to grab Quentin by the shoulders and haul him away if it proved necessary. Our places around the table meant he couldn't get to us both, but he was smart—and more importantly, tactical—enough to know that of the three of us, I was the most likely to survive anything Pete and the Luidaeg wanted to sling at each other.

Did I particularly *want* to be the only hero standing when two of Faerie's greatest monsters decided to go toe-to-toe? No. But I wanted the boys out of the line of fire even more. I only wished there were a way to safely extract Dean before things went sideways.

"They agreed to this consequence," said the Luidaeg.

"No, their *ancestors* agreed. We're not humans, Annie. We don't live and die by the sins of the father, nor should we, given the amount of mischief our forebears got up to when allowed. You told a bunch of shivering children who'd just killed their own parents to allay your wrath that they weren't done paying, and they agreed, because they were terrified. You're terrifying, you know. Sometimes you even frighten me."

"Then why are you arguing with me?" The Luidaeg wasn't smiling anymore, and when she spoke, the teeth I glimpsed beyond her lips were too sharp and too plentiful to be ignored.

"Because the Selkies who live here are under my protection, and many of the Selkies who are swimming this way to answer your summons are members of the same clans; they could claim that protection for themselves, if they wanted to. If they thought to do it." Pete leaned forward. "Tell me why letting you do what you came here to do doesn't betray that protection. Please."

"Because no one's going to die," I blurted.

They slowly turned to look at me. I forced myself not to flinch under the weight of their gaze. I was accustomed to being the full focus of a single Firstborn's attention. Two was . . . well, it was a bit much. I could feel their anger crawling across my skin like the static charge before a storm, and I wanted nothing more than to apologize, to throw up my hands and tell them I was sorry, anything to turn that befuddled disapproval aside.

I didn't. Instead, I squared my shoulders, raised my chin, and refused to look away.

"We're not here to *kill* the Selkies, or their families," I said. "I mean, we're here to make it so there won't be any more Selkies in the future, and I can see where that probably sucks if you're someone who's been waiting to receive a skin from a parent or grandparent or whatever, but those skins never really belonged to the Selkies. They belonged to the Roane. When the Selkies agreed to carry them, they did it knowing this was the way things were going to end."

"And they don't get to pretend they forgot," said the Luidaeg, seamlessly picking up the explanation. "I've been there, Pete. Every time a Selkie parent passes a skin, at least on the West Coast, they've done it with me watching over them. This entire generation saw me on the shore, judging them for what they'd chosen. They know about the promise their ancestors made, about the blood on their hands. They know how my babies died. They take their skins with full understanding of the blessing and the bargain, and they don't get to say they didn't know, because they knew. They did this knowing that one day, there'd be a price to pay. I can't lie, because of *your* mother, and I told them this was coming. I'm not going to say I'm sorry that price fell to this generation. It always sucks to be the one who catches the bill."

"Yes, it does," said Pete. She was talking to the Luidaeg, but her eyes were on me, deep and cold and surprisingly sympathetic. "It's terrible to be the one who has to set things right when you didn't play any part in breaking them."

She sighed then, and it was like some terrible tension snapped, leaving the room smaller and less dangerous. Tybalt relaxed. Quentin frowned, looking between Pete and me, trying to understand what had just happened.

"You can do what you came here for, so long as there's no fae blood shed in my waters," said Pete. "I maintain a safe harbor for the people with nowhere else to go. And I'll be wanting some faerie ointment from you, and the promise of more. Some among those families may want to stay here. Why shouldn't they? They've never known anything else."

"I'm a better brewer than you anyway," said the Luidaeg.

Pete punched her in the shoulder, and she laughed, and for a moment, they were just a pair of siblings seeing each other again after a long and not entirely voluntary separation. It was odd seeing the Luidaeg with a family member she didn't hate. There was no love lost between her and Eira—probably even less now that Eira had successfully killed her once, not counting on my occasional, unpredictable ability to exhaust myself by raising the dead—and while I hadn't actually *seen* her with my mother, from the way she talked about Mom, I didn't expect them to be braiding each other's hair.

The door banged open. Every head in the room, except for Dean's, swung around. Marcia, standing in the doorway, flushed a bright, embarrassed red. She was holding a tray in her hands, which explained the force with which the door had hit the wall; she must have bumped it open with her hip.

"Sorry," she said. "I had to find the canteen, and then I had to explain what I wanted, and then I had to go through this long, irritating process of barter, and—"

Pete groaned. "They didn't just give you the stuff when you said it was for my account?"

Marcia blinked, eyes wide and worried. "You didn't tell me it was on your account."

"I'm the reason the lad won't wake up. It seems only fair I should pay to bring him back to the world of the living."

"I'm sorry. I didn't know. Anyway, it didn't cost me much once I'd made people understand what I wanted, just some pennies and a ribbon from my hair—none of my actual hair, I cleaned that off before I handed it over." Marcia looked briefly smug about that. "I know better than to give people bits of me that they could use against me later. I'm no fool."

"Yet here you are, on a floating structure in the middle of the ocean, surrounded by beings who could send you to the depths in an instant," said Pete, rising from her chair. "That seems a little foolish to me."

"Foolishness and bravery look a lot alike if you're not paying close enough attention," said Marcia. She watched nervously as Pete approached, but stood her ground; only her white-knuckled grasp on the tray betrayed how difficult that was.

I wanted to applaud for her. Marcia's always been reasonably unflappable, especially for someone who knows, all the way down to her bones, that she's a small, breakable creature moving through a society filled with much larger predators.

"Is that so?" Pete stopped, cocking her head and looking thoughtfully at Marcia before she said, "You have the protection of my principality until such time as you choose to leave our borders. The next time someone tries to take advantage of you during simple barter, tell them as much. They may sing a different chantey after that."

Marcia bobbed her head in grateful acknowledgment, holding up her tray as she asked, "May I take this to the Count? He's my liege, and I'd really rather not give him a reason to think I'm not doing my job."

"As you were," said Pete, with a casual wave of her hand.

Marcia curtsied quick and shallow, and continued across the room to Dean, settling on the edge of the bed. Quentin moved to join her—not, I noted with amusement, asking anyone's permission—and together they shifted Dean into a sitting position and pressed the brim of a rough ceramic mug to his lips. Quentin pinched Dean's nose closed and tilted his head as Marcia raised the mug. A moment later, Dean sputtered and reared back, opening his eyes.

"Oh, good," said Marcia. "You're not dead. Drink this."

"What is it?" asked Dean, so fixated on the contents of the mug that he didn't seem to realize the rest of us were in the room. That was probably for the best, since Pete was watching the whole scene with faintly malicious amusement.

"No idea." Marcia sounded entirely too happy about that. "I know there's honey in there, and saltwater, but the rest? Who knows. I bought it from a man who said it would wake you up, and—hey presto—it worked. He also said you needed to drink the whole thing if you wanted to be 'inured to the majesty,' which sounds like a good plan to me."

"It is," said the Luidaeg. "Trust me, and drink the damn tincture."

Dean briefly looked like he wanted to argue—but Dean was a son of the Undersea, and the understanding that arguing with the Luidaeg was a swift, not necessarily painless form of suicide had been all but baked into his bones. He grasped the mug with both hands and drained its contents in a long, pained-looking gulp, dropping it back onto the tray with a gasp.

Marcia picked up the bowl that had also been on the tray and thrust it at him. "Here."

"What's *this*?" he asked. He still took the bowl. He had long since learned that doing what his seneschal said was easier than the alternative. Clever boy.

"Kelp and salmon stew," she said. "There's potatoes in there, too. How does a floating duchy in the middle of the Pacific get potatoes?"

"We grow them," said Pete. "We have special bubbles anchored to the bottom of the sea, keeping the water out, and we grow all sorts of things that air-breathers like to eat, because we take care of our own. Hello, little half-Merrow. Ready to look at me now?"

Dean paled as he raised his head and met her eyes. Then he blinked, looking baffled. "I'm still awake."

"You've been inured to the majesty," she said, with amusement. "I'll be honest, you surprised me when you went down like that. Most Merrow attack me on sight. The fainters have almost been bred out of the line. By which I mean, the fainters never get the opportunity to breed, because the other Merrow kill them for being weaklings."

"You're going to like my Mom," said Dean, in a dazed voice. He paused before asking, "Are you really my . . . ?"

"One of them," said Pete.

"I met the other one, too," said Dean. "The Daoine Sidhe First-born. I didn't like her."

"Congratulations: you are now a member of a large and not at all exclusive club," said Pete. "Eat your soup and I'll show you all to your quarters. Welcome to the Duchy of Ships. Don't make trouble, don't pick fights with people who don't deserve it, and for the love of Oberon, don't make me regret letting you in."

"Would we do that?" I asked.

She raised an eyebrow, looking at me flatly. "You, Amandine's daughter, hero, king-breaker? In a damn heartbeat. So let's at least pretend you respect my authority, shall we?"

"Yes, ma'am," I said.

The Luidaeg laughed, and Dean drank his soup, and the world had never been stranger, or safer, than it was in that moment. I was surrounded by water on all sides, but I had people I loved and trusted with me; I would do my job, go home, and everything would be fine.

Really.

SEVEN

ALL THE MEMBERS of our party—save Gillian, who was still off with the Selkies—had been assigned quarters carved from the belly of the same cargo ship, with individual apartments made from sections of hull. They radiated out from the tiny courtyard that had once been the ship's upper deck, making it impossible for any of us to sneak away without the others knowing. I found that oddly comforting. This was a big, unfamiliar place, and while I was statistically the most likely to wind up covered in blood, I liked to have a sense of where they were.

Tybalt and I had taken the apartment closest to the gate on the left-hand side of the entrance, with the Luidaeg taking the apartment on the right-hand side. Quentin was next to me and Tybalt; Dean and Marcia were next to the Luidaeg; Poppy and Cassandra were on the other side of them, and Nolan had an apartment entirely to himself. Small tables made from a ship too damaged to be repurposed as housing dotted the courtyard, accompanied by mismatched chairs and lovingly crafted planters. Each played host to an assortment of plants, ranging from kitchen herbs to lush tomatoes to patches of strawberries the color of candied violets that glowed with their own strange inner light.

The Luidaeg saw me eyeing the strawberries and said, "Those found their roots first in Emain Ablach, which was my sister's country before our father decided we had to be exiled to the Summerlands. They're not like goblin fruit. They won't hurt you. But they do make excellent jam. Breakfast here is going to be a treat."

"See, you say 'my sister,' and I can't help thinking of Evening," I said.

The Luidaeg shook her head. "Here, I'll mostly be referring to Amphitrite. You can trust her, for the most part."

"For the most part?"

"There's no one in this world you can trust all the time. Not even the people you love, not even the people who love you." The Luidaeg looked briefly, terribly tired. This had to be so hard on her. She had moved among the Selkies for centuries, pretending to be their loving, uncomplicated Cousin Annie, a woman whose ancestry contained some life-extending fae heritage but whose shoulders would never be draped in a Selkie's skin. They had loved her and pitied her and let her into their homes, and now she was betraying them. She had never been the woman they believed her to be.

What we were going to do would bring the Roane back to Faerie's oceans, and it was difficult not to see that as a good thing. Evening had wanted them destroyed, and Evening played a long, brutal game. Maybe she'd been trying to hurt her sister; maybe she'd been doing something more complicated. The Roane could see the future, after all. By arranging their destruction, she had closed the eyes of prophecy, and those eyes had been open for a reason.

I don't like prophecy. I don't like anything that smacks too much of destiny, of needing to follow someone else's template for what's to come. But it turns out I like Evening even less.

And despite all that . . . bringing back the Roane wasn't going to bring back the Luidaeg's children. These new Roane would still be the people they had been when Faerie was something they could set aside and walk away from. They would have their own families and their own histories, and they wouldn't be hers, not really. Maybe in a generation or two, she could have a relationship with them. But it wasn't going to happen right away, and it wasn't going to happen on this floating duchy.

Her elbow caught me in the ribs, knocking me out of my wool-gathering. I turned to blink at her. She looked impassively back. Her eyes were green again, the color of sunlight in the shallows.

"You were getting ready to feel sorry for me," she said. "I could see it. Don't. I made this bed for myself, a long damn time ago. If there's anyone you should feel sorry for, it's the second sons and the dutiful daughters who always thought their day would come, and are about to find out they'll never have the waters after all. They're who I'm worried about."

"Worried how?" I asked carefully.

"I bet we find some bodies floating under the dock before sunrise, no matter what promises I make to my sister." Her reply was calm, matter-of-fact: she'd had plenty of time to think about it. "The Law has always been a little shaky when it comes to the Selkies because a Selkie without a skin is just a human. The only way to know *when* one of them was killed, and whether they were wearing their skin when it happened, is to ask the night-haunts. Most reasonable people don't consider that an option."

My ears and cheeks grew hot. "I don't talk to the night-haunts that often."

"You talk to them often enough that one of them chose to give up her wings and move in with you; I'd call that pretty strong evidence that you have no sense of self-preservation."

I wrinkled my nose but said nothing.

Faerie has wondered for millennia where Fetches come from, how they're called, and why they're so rare. They supposedly appear for heroes and great rulers, but I've been through the records at the Library of Stars, and it seems like Fetches just sort of *happen*, usually around people who bleed a lot—which, yes, is a group that's going to include heroes and people who ride the assassination attempt express. Turns out, Fetches are what happens when a night-haunt ingests the blood of the living. Just a little gift from Oberon, who wanted them to stick to devouring the dead. When they feed from the living, they become perfect mirrors of those people, with their faces and their memories and a direct tie to their lives. The sort of person whose blood is likely to wind up in front of the night-haunts is also the sort of person who's likely to die in the near future, and thus the connection between Fetches and death is reinforced, until seeing someone with your own face is almost as good as an executioner's ax.

May has been living with me for several years now. It turns out that while I may be pretty good at dying, I'm equally lousy at staying dead.

"People will die tonight because of what we've come here to do," said the Luidaeg implacably. "More people will die tomorrow, when the sun is in the sky and there aren't any witnesses around. I wish I could say I had a plan in place to stop it, but honestly, I don't think there is one. I think this is the sort of thing that has to play out in its own way, in its own time, because I waited too long for the bargain to come due."

"Why—" I began, and stopped when she fixed me with a cold eye.

"A hope chest couldn't do what I need you to do, and your mother *wouldn't* do what I need you to do, and she made sure your sister wouldn't do it either, because she didn't like the idea of destiny," she said. "She thought if she made the future unknowable, she could keep it from happening. She didn't understand."

"I don't understand," I said.

"I know, and this isn't when I'm going to tell you, so I guess we're both going to be unhappy for a while yet."

I opened my mouth to argue. A door slammed, and I turned instead, watching Marcia emerge into the courtyard. She grinned when she saw me, walking over with only a quick nod for the Luidaeg.

"So how much are we going to pretend my liege isn't sleeping in your squire's room, and how much are we going to ask them to stay focused?" she asked.

"Okay, first, I don't need to know that, and second, they're adults. They can do whatever they like, as long as it doesn't interfere with the reason that we're here." I glanced at the Luidaeg. "It's not going to interfere, is it?"

"Sex complicates things, but no, it's not going to interfere," she said dryly. "The only people who *need* to be here are you, me, and the Selkies. Everyone else is a politically necessary extra, or an annoying additional complication."

I raised an eyebrow. "And where are you filing Tybalt?"

"I think you know the answer to that." She shook her head. "Amy's on the loose, and Dad only knows what she thinks she's doing when she messes with you. I know she was trying to protect you once, but these days it feels like she's trying to punish you for refusing to be protected. I wouldn't leave my lover behind where she could get to him if I were you. But that doesn't make him necessary to what we're going to do, or even relevant. When the time comes, you and I will stand alone."

I didn't like the sound of that. Neither, from the expression on her face, did Marcia. "Count Lorden and I are here to act as go-betweens for the Kingdom of Leucothea and the Kingdom in the

Mists, to be represented by Duchess Dianda Lorden and Prince Nolan Windermere. We're not *useless*."

"Yes, you are," said the Luidaeg, almost kindly. "This is between a Firstborn, me, and her descendant race, the Selkies. The laws of land and sea have no sway here. If I wanted to slaughter them all, you'd stand back and let me do it, because you're smart enough to know not to get between me and something I intend to do. It wouldn't end well for you."

Marcia's cheeks burned red. "I don't think we'd just stand by and watch you commit *murder*," she said.

"You would," said the Luidaeg. She shrugged. "I don't judge you for it. I'd think twice before I tangled with one of my siblings, and I'm strong enough to survive it. Which is, by the way, why we're *here*, and not on neutral ground. By calling the Selkies to a place under Pete's protection, I told them I wasn't planning to slaughter them wholesale." She turned to me. "And with that in mind, it's time for us to go."

I blinked. "Go? We're in the middle of the ocean." I knew what she meant. I knew I was stalling. I just couldn't seem to help myself.

"I know. Isn't it splendid? But yes, go. We need to speak to the Selkies, and let them know the Convocation is officially begun."

I blinked again, harder this time, like I could somehow force the situation to change. Into what, I wasn't sure. Everything about this moment had been inevitable since before I'd even been born. If I was going to choose Faerie over the mortal world, then I was going to be the one standing here, waiting to bring the hammer down on an entire breed of fae.

"Tybalt—" I began.

The Luidaeg cut me off. "He's a big boy, and he knew the deal when he decided to accompany you here. He can take care of himself for a little while. Now come on. The hour is late, and I'd like to have this part of things done before dawn. Marcia, if you'd excuse us?"

Her tone was primly, perfectly polite. Marcia nodded, still looking unsure.

"I'll let Tybalt know where you've gone," she said. "In case he wants to follow."

"Tell him it wouldn't be a good idea," said the Luidaeg, before taking me by the shoulders and bodily turning me so she could look me frankly up and down. "Hmm. I know you hate it when other people change your clothing, but you have to realize that you can't wear *that*."

I frowned, glancing downward at my jeans, sneakers, and as-yet-unstained gray tank top. I didn't look like I was going to visit kings or queens, but I didn't look like a slob, either. I was suddenly, fiercely glad I'd left my leather jacket in my temporary quarters, where I wouldn't need to worry about getting it covered in saltwater. "Why not? This is the sort of thing I wore last time we went to see Liz."

"Yes, but that was just this side of a social visit, not a formal Convocation. Tonight, we observe the forms and formalities. Tonight, we make sure no one can say we cut corners or bent rules. Understand?"

I didn't. As the Luidaeg had so carefully pointed out, there was no one left, except for maybe Amphitrite, who could say a single word about what we were going to do. We were sailing into uncharted waters, far from the safe harbor of Faerie's traditions and laws. Still, I nodded and said, "If you need me to be wearing something different, do it."

Her smile was a flash of sharp, gleaming teeth. "Remember," she said, "you gave me permission."

She snapped her fingers, and my clothes writhed like a veil of live eels, active and intrusive and horrifyingly vital. I stood frozen, resisting the urge to start shoving the clothes away from my body. For one thing, it probably wouldn't work. For another, I was reasonably sure that interfering with the Luidaeg's spell would result in my getting bitten by what had previously been one of my favorite pairs of jeans.

The eels stopped their writhing, settling back into frozen fabric. Like everything else about the Duchy of Ships, my new gown was archaic and piratical at the same time. The skirt was more properly plural, and had been slashed into strips starting at mid-thigh, both to offer me freedom of movement and to show the layer beneath it, which had been similarly slashed to show the layer beneath *it*, and so on. The top layer was a deep reddish-brown, like dried blood, and each successive layer grew brighter, from arterial red to rosy red to pink to a final layer as white as newly-fallen snow. My bodice was black, constricting enough to feel like corsetry, and based on the way it felt when I breathed, properly boned. There were no sleeves. Instead, a cascade of elbow-length ribbons in colors that matched my skirts tangled around my arms, creating an effect that was probably striking from the outside, but was annoying as hell against my skin. My sneakers were gone, replaced by snug calf-length boots with low heels.

The Luidaeg looked critically at my hair. "It'll do," she said. "And before you freak out, your knife is still at your side. Just reach through the slit where you think a pocket ought to be."

Her clothing had changed along with mine, although her new dress was nowhere near so busy, or so modern. She wore a white samite shift in a distinctly medieval style, the fabric glimmering with hints of blue and green and pearl. Her arms were bare, her neck was exposed, and her hair was loose, cascading down her back in heavy curls. It looked like it had gotten longer when the tape disappeared. The Luidaeg is a protean creature. Just because she usually keeps her physical form within a certain set of constraints, that doesn't make her any less of a shapeshifter.

I'm not sure I've ever seen what the Luidaeg really looks like. I'm not sure I want to.

"Come on," she said, beckoning for me to follow as she started toward the mouth of the courtyard. "We need to get this part over with, so the true troubles can begin."

When one of the Firstborn tells you to follow, you follow. I pulled up even with her, matching my steps to hers, and managed not to look back as we stepped out of the hollowed-out ship that was our temporary home, into the greater body of the Duchy.

It was strange to be walking away from my boys. Quentin and Tybalt should have been by my side, letting me lead them into the dangers of the moment, and the fact that they weren't was unsettling. They were probably going to be pretty pissed when they realized I was gone. At least they both understood that when the Luidaeg spoke, it wasn't a good idea to argue.

The Duchy of Ships seemed to have been modeled off a dockside town from the turn of the twentieth century, just one that happened to be floating on the open ocean and constructed so that "vertical" was as much of a civic planning option as "horizontal." Our little slice of space was clearly located in a residential area; we walked past more courtyards like ours, and larger, more defined private homes, some of which had been built from repurposed vessels, while others wouldn't have looked out of place on a San Francisco street.

Gradually, the bigger residences gave way to stacked shacks connected by rope ladders, with clever pulley systems clearly designed to help the people who lived there transport goods. I blinked at the rope, finally realizing what had been bothering me.

"There aren't any pixies," I said.

"Too many things out here think of them as snack foods," said the Luidaeg. "Dangerous as it is for them on the land, it's twice as bad out at sea."

"Huh." It was strange, walking through a fae holding and not seeing any sign of Faerie's smallest residents. The varieties of fae around me were even stranger, largely due to unfamiliarity. I knew some of them—Cephali, Sirens, even the occasional Asrai—but others were new. I wanted to breathe in their heritage, to get a sense of the shape of their blood, but I didn't dare. I had no idea how many spells were woven into the body of this impossible duchy, and the last thing I needed was to be knocked on my ass by too many unexpected magics.

Everyone we passed shied away from us, refusing to meet the Luidaeg's eyes. They seemed to know who she was, better than people normally did when we were at home. In San Francisco, she was the sea witch, but almost no one understood what that *meant*. Here, out at sea, there was no question. She was their mother in mourning and their unforgiving monster, and while she might not have seen the longing in their eyes, I did.

They missed her. They'd been missing her for centuries; they might miss her forever, depending on how things went with the resurrection of the Roane. My heart went out to them, and to her. Why does Faerie have to make everything so *hard*?

We had entered a small market area, packed with stalls selling fruit, vegetables, bread, and less edible goods, when Tybalt stepped out of the narrow space between a spice vendor and a slightly more permanent-looking tailor's shop. He was carrying my leather jacket over one arm, and had an expression on his face that couldn't seem to decide between amusement and irritation.

"Imagine my surprise when I emerged from unpacking to find Marcia saying you'd gone on without me." He fell into step beside us, offering the Luidaeg a nod. "Lady Sea Witch."

"Sir Cat," she replied, without breaking stride. "Don't be too annoyed at October. I told her she didn't have time to go get you. I also told Marcia to tell you not to follow us."

"She did," he said, offering me my jacket. "I elected to ignore her, as is my right as both a cat and a king."

"How did the Cait Sidhe survive past infancy?" asked the Luidaeg.

Tybalt raised an eyebrow. "If any of us would know the answer to that, milady, I would expect it to be you. You were, after all, there when it happened."

The Luidaeg laughed and kept walking.

I shrugged my leather jacket on, taking a moment to fuss with the ribbons that served as my sleeves, trying in vain to make them lie flat, or at least not get all twisted and tangled around my elbows. Tybalt watched this with some amusement, waiting until I was done before he reached over and took my hand.

"You look quite elegant, if a bit anachronistic," he said. "The Luidaeg's work, I assume?"

"I can dress myself."

"Yes, but you generally choose not to unless under serious duress, and I have never once seen you voluntarily trend toward corsetry." Tybalt shook his head. "I fear I'll need to take all responsibility for your wedding gown, lest you show up in one of those abominable knee-length creations."

"They're called skater dresses, and they're very comfortable," I protested.

The Luidaeg looked over her shoulder at us. "Now is when you want to do your wedding planning? *Now*? Do you have no sense of timing, or are you just oblivious?"

"We are surrounded by water on all sides," said Tybalt. "Forgive me if I wish to take my betrothed's mind off the situation."

I flashed him a smile and kept walking. The Luidaeg rolled her eyes and did the same.

The shopping district—if it could really be called a district, under the circumstances—gave way to another residential neighborhood, this one consisting entirely of tiny shacks. It was shabbier here. The air smelled more strongly of saltwater and decaying wood, and the walkways were slipperier, damp with condensation and streaks of drying seaweed. I cast the Luidaeg a curious look, allowing my question to go unasked.

She answered it anyway. "The Duchy of Ships is home to a great many Selkies and their families, but that doesn't make them wealthy, or even particularly well-regarded," she said. "Their inability to breathe water means they can never fully belong to the Undersea. Still, they work as couriers and messengers, and they hold on."

"Can Roane breathe water?" I asked, unable to stop myself.

"Yes and no," said the Luidaeg. "They don't have gills, but their control over the currents is such that they can call air bubbles to themselves, and keep breathing without coming to the surface. It's a relatively common trick in the Undersea. There are several descendant races who are technically air-breathers, but manage to do it subtly enough that they never get called on it. An open secret, if you will. Now can you stop asking me questions about my kids? You know I have to answer, and you know that makes me uncomfortable."

"Sorry."

She shook her head. "It's not your fault. It's just that these are things that should be common knowledge—the Roane should never have been lost—and now I have to explain them like they're trivia. Like they're *trivial*. I hate everything about this. I even hate doing this to the Selkies, although that's not going to stop me. Faerie needs the Roane."

"Why?" asked Tybalt. The Luidaeg whipped around to stare at him, and he put his hands up. "Peace, lady, please. I only ask because . . . because this doesn't return your children to you. This doesn't put their hands in yours, or their eyes upon your face. Why do this, when the ones who broke faith with you are so long gone?"

"I made a promise, and thanks to my stepmother, I can't break them," she said. "I could try. Some people might even argue that I *have* tried, with as long as I've put off calling in this debt that is due. I could have grabbed October here when she was a child, raised her as my own, raised her to think doing this was the most important thing in the world." She glanced at me before resuming her forward progress. "And don't think I didn't consider it. Amy had no right to do what she did to you. *No* right. But I wasn't ready to be a mother again, and Sylvester was glad to step in when I told him he was needed, and I gave the Selkies another fifty years. I've put this off as long as I can. Anything more would be cruel."

"Ah," said Tybalt, with what sounded like genuine sorrow. "My apologies for your unfair predicament."

The Luidaeg sighed and kept walking.

The shacks grew denser around us, until there was no space between them. Sand began appearing on the deck, adding a level of grit and grip to the waterlogged wood. And then, without warning, the lane opened up, becoming a wide, artificial cove, like something out of a Coney Island fever dream.

We were still in the Duchy of Ships: that much was clear from the way everything continued to shift and creak around us, ancient wood settling deeper and deeper into its questionable moorings. But the decks and walkways were gone, obscured by a layer of fine white sand that would have looked exactly like an ordinary beach, if not for the five-foot drop between it and the waterline. The shacks were replaced by tidy little houses built in an almost Cape Cod style and painted in ice cream pastels, their windows thrown wide and their shutters painted in contrasting colors.

There were children everywhere. Small children, two and three years old, rolling in the sand and building complicated castles that collapsed at the slightest touch. Awkward prepubescent children goading each other into diving off the beach's edge, pulling themselves back up to the sand by way of rope ladders, or scaling the pylons that held the whole construct in place. Teenagers, who looked at us, took note of our clothing, and looked away, although I couldn't say whether it was out of dislike of strangers or judgment of our fashion choices.

There were adults as well, moving more sedately, and every other one I saw had a seal's pelt tied around their waist or shoulders. They were the ones who went pale at the sight of us—or, in some cases, froze in place, seemingly unable to even breathe.

"Annie!"

The cry came from our left. I turned to see a freckled teenager with brown-and-silver hair and green, green eyes running across the sand, arms already open for the hug she knew she was certain to receive. The Luidaeg didn't move as Diva barreled into her. She didn't return the hug, either. She just stood there, implacable as the tides, while the girl clung to her.

"I *knew* you'd come, I just knew you would, I told Mom you had to, we were all summoned and that means you, too, and you wouldn't *dare* go against the sea witch—have you seen her? She's supposed to come here, she's supposed to come tell us what happens next, and I'm excited but I'm scared, too, because what if she's not nice? What if she called us here to hurt us? I'm not even in line for a skin, I don't need one, not with the magic I got from Dad, but I had to come anyway, and—Annie?" Diva caught herself mid-sentence and pulled back, squinting at the Luidaeg. "Annie, what's wrong? What's wrong with your *eyes*?"

"I love you," said the Luidaeg softly. My breath caught. The Luidaeg can't lie. "I've loved you since the moment I met you. You were this little wrinkled screaming thing, you were Liz trying to apologize for what she'd done to me, and you were everything. Blood of my blood, bone of my bone. I've never met your father, but I don't need to meet him to know who he's descended from. Your great-great-grandfather's name was Aulay, and he died along with the rest of the Roane, and one of these people is wearing his skin tied around their bodies like a belt, and he deserved better, and so do you. I love you, Diva Ryan, but if you don't take your hands off me right now, I will have to remove them from your body as a warning to everyone watching us. Please. Let go."

Diva stumbled backward, staring at the Luidaeg. Her face had gone pale, freckles standing out like brands. "Annie?" she whispered.

"My name is Antigone of Albany, daughter of Maeve, daughter of Oberon," said the Luidaeg. Her voice was soft, but it carried, oh, how it carried. All around us Selkies turned, faces wan and shoulders shaking as they beheld the instrument of their creation and destruction. "I am here to call the Convocation of Consequences."

"Annie?" Diva whispered again, her voice breaking.

The Luidaeg looked at her with sorrowful eyes, and said, "Get your mother, Diva. It's time."

Diva turned and ran away across the strand, leaving the three of us standing there, surrounded by staring, shivering Selkies. I moved a little closer to Tybalt, who put his arm around my shoulders and didn't say anything. There wasn't anything to say.

EIGHT

THE FIRST PERSON TO approach us wasn't Elizabeth Ryan, but a tall, distinguished man with dark skin and black hair shading to silver at the temples. Like Diva, he had freckles across his cheeks and the bridge of his nose, mimicking a seal's spots. Somehow, they failed to detract from his overall air of solemn dignity. He wore a brown linen suit, which seemed timeless to my modern eye, and was probably shockingly gauche to everyone older than me.

"Mathias Lefebvre," he said to the Luidaeg, bowing deeply. "I represent the Lefebvre clan, from the waters off the Kingdom of Beacon's Home. I am at your service, and your disposal."

I glanced at Tybalt, mouthing "Beacon's Home?"

"Halifax," he mouthed back.

Ah. One of the Canadian Kingdoms. One of the *East Coast* Canadian Kingdoms, even. With my reputation for causing political chaos every time I leave the house, it was a pretty good bet that I was never going to be invited over for a casual visit. Although given that Quentin's parents were offering to host my wedding, who knew? Maybe I'd have the chance to annoy a few more kings before I got myself confined permanently to the Mists.

The Luidaeg raised an eyebrow. "Bold," she said, in a perfectly neutral tone. "What makes you think you have the right to approach me as you do, wearer of a stolen skin? Why should I hear whatever it is you have to say?"

Mathias was unflustered. "The Convocation has yet to begin,

Lady; we stand in a liminal space," he said. "I am here to speak with you before the formal commencement of our funeral, to beg a boon."

"I hardly think you have any stones beneath your feet, but continue," said the Luidaeg. "Only be aware that I reserve the right to slit your throat if you cease to amuse me."

"I suspected your nature long before I became head of my clan and learned your name," said Mathias, and tensed, apparently aware that what he was saying was pretty much guaranteed to annoy the Luidaeg. Her inability to lie to anyone except the Selkies was a sore spot, and she had always treasured her identity as "Cousin Annie," the person no one was afraid of.

Her eyes narrowed, traceries of darkness moving through the green of her irises. She said nothing.

To his credit, Mathias stood his ground, although I could see him fighting the urge to take a step backward. I liked him a little for that. He'd decided to walk right into the arms of the sea witch, and now that he was here, he wasn't going to pretend he hadn't been aware of the risks.

"Why are you telling me this?" asked the Luidaeg.

"Because we are all criminals in your eyes, heir to the crimes of our ancestors, and we are yours to keep and command. You have a Firstborn's duty toward us, for so long as we swim these seas." His voice became more formal as he spoke, taking on a tight, clipped cadence that fit surprisingly well with his maritime accent.

"And?"

"And you favor the Ryan clan over the rest of us, because their waters are so close to your own." He met her eyes and somehow didn't flinch. "Elizabeth Ryan has come into possession of eighteen of the Lost Skins. She increases the size of her clan, and guarantees Faerie to eighteen of her family, while the rest of us receive no such bounty. So I approach you, Lady, to ask you do the same for the other clans, who have always done our best to keep our side of the ancient bargain, who have lived and died knowing we did so solely at your discretion. The bargain comes due. Let us save our children, as we were unable to save yours."

"Elizabeth Ryan received those skins for doing me a favor outside the scope of the bargain between the Selkies and the sea witch," said the Luidaeg. "How many children do you think I had,

Mathias? How many grandchildren? How many Roane would you hope were slaughtered, if it means you can drape their physical remains around the shoulders of your own descendants and mark them for immortality? You're lucky I don't rip the skin from your shoulders merely for suggesting it."

Mathias said nothing. Instead, he dropped to his knees in the sand, reaching up and tugging the knot resting at the hollow of his throat, where I would normally have expected a tie to be. It came easily undone, and he pulled the sealskin from beneath his jacket, holding it out to the Luidaeg with shaking hands.

This time, she raised both eyebrows. "You think this impresses me?" she asked. "You think I can be impressed by an offer to return something that has always been mine? Your gesture isn't 'grand' so much as it's misguided. Be grateful I don't find it insulting."

"Lady, please," he said, in a low voice. "I've spent my entire adult life trying to make amends for a loss you suffered centuries before my birth, knowing it was futile. I have asked you for *nothing*. I have sought to be beneath your notice. I have devoted myself to you. Please, please, I beg. If there is anything to be done, if there are any more skins held in secret, please. Give me only the gift you have given to Elizabeth Ryan. Let me save my clan."

"Get up," she said, and her voice was low and tight and unreadable, even to me.

Mathias scrambled to his feet, the sealskin still resting on his hands. The Luidaeg looked at him flatly, more of those dark threads curling through her irises, chasing away the green.

"Leave," she snapped.

For a moment, I thought he was going to argue with her. For a moment, I thought I was going to find out whether she'd been right when she said that any of us would stand calmly by and watch her commit a murder. Then he backed away, taking three long, quick steps, before turning and running toward the row of neat little Cape Cod-style houses. He didn't look back.

We had gathered a small crowd while he was speaking, Selkies and Selkie-kin pausing in whatever they'd been doing before we came in order to drift closer and listen in as hard as they could. The Luidaeg turned to look at them, and they paled and fled, some following Mathias, others simply retreating along the artificial beach. All but one.

That one—a child, maybe six years old, dressed in a shapeless tunic, with pale blonde hair cut in a pageboy bob—approached the three of us, head cocked curiously to the side.

"Are you really the Lady?" they asked.

The Luidaeg nodded. "I am."

"My mother says the Lady bound Merlin in a tree for a thousand years because he was mean to her."

The corner of the Luidaeg's mouth twitched. "That's not *quite* how it happened, but you should listen to your mother. Mothers have many clever things to say, if you listen closely."

"She says we came here because the Lady is tired of there being Selkies, and she wants the Selkies to stop." The child looked at us solemnly. "Is that so?"

"Almost." The Luidaeg crouched, putting herself on a level with the child. The dark lines vanished from her eyes between one blink and the next, leaving them a clear, untroubled green. She looked heartbreakingly at ease. She must have been one hell of a mother. "I'm here because a very long time ago, the first Selkies made me a promise, and it's time for that promise to be kept. Do you ever make promises?"

The child nodded.

"Is it always easy to keep them?"

The child shook their head.

"Well, then. So I have to talk to all the grown-ups, your mother and the man who was just talking to me and *all* the grown-ups, and they have to talk to me, and together we're going to figure out what happens next. These are my friends, October," she gestured to me, "and Tybalt. They don't get to decide what happens because they're not Selkies, but they get to help make sure everything is as fair as it can be."

The child studied her face carefully before asking, "Does that mean you don't hate us?"

The Luidaeg sighed. I tensed.

The Selkies—and, I suppose, the Roane—are the only people the Luidaeg *can* lie to. They're her descendant race, and powerful as Titania is, or was, she's not powerful enough to get between a Firstborn and their children. But she couldn't lie to Tybalt, or to me, and we were standing right there. Whatever she said, we'd hear her. Would that be enough to bring Titania's geas into play?

Would that even make a difference?

"Sweetheart, I don't know you," she said. "You haven't been alive long enough to make any choices you might regret. No matter how long you live, things are never going to be as simple as they are right now ever again. So run. Run and play and try to forget that I'm here. Everything will be complicated soon enough."

The child wrinkled their nose. "You didn't answer my question."

"I'm the motherfucking sea witch. I don't have to answer your question."

The child's eyes widened. "You said a swear."

"Again, sea witch. I'm allowed."

The child nodded, apparently satisfied, before turning and wandering off down the beach. The Luidaeg straightened, giving me a challenging look.

"What?" she demanded.

"Nothing," I said. "You're good with kids."

"I can't stand them." She smoothed her dress with the heels of her hands, not looking up as she continued, "I haven't been able to since my own went and died on me. So many children in the world, and not one of them is mine. It's not fair."

I bit my lip, and said nothing.

It's not entirely clear how the Firstborn create their descendant races, not even to me. Supposedly, every time they take a lover, they have the potential to create a new facet of Faerie, but it can't be that straightforward. August and I have different fathers and the same Firstborn mother, and we're both Dóchas Sidhe. The Luidaeg has never identified all her children by name, but there must have been at least a dozen of them, if not more. There's no other way for the Roane to have been as well-established as they were by the time Evening decided to arrange for their destruction. It seemed a little unreasonable to assume they had all had the same father.

Maybe if the Luidaeg had gone out and gotten pregnant again as soon as Evening instigated the slaughter of her children, the Roane would have been with us all along. Or maybe she would have created something entirely new. I didn't *know*, and something about that lack of knowledge worried me. There was a piece I didn't have yet. I've learned, to my regret, that missing pieces now almost always mean pain later.

This wasn't the time to dwell on it. The doors on several of the

Cape Cod houses opened and a line of Selkies appeared, walking across the sand toward us. The scattered people who'd still been wandering the sands vanished into other houses, pausing only long enough to snatch up any children who happened to be out in the open. I took a deep breath and braced myself.

That was a wise decision. The Luidaeg raised her head as the Selkies approached, and her eyes were dark as the depths of the ocean, and her skin was underscored with a faint bluish tint, like she'd somehow managed to drown on dry land while I'd been standing right next to her. Even her bones had shifted, rising too close to the surface of the skin. She was unspeakable, a deepwater dream of drowning and despair, and her skin radiated cold.

I didn't know her with this face. But I recognized my friend in the downturned corners of her mouth and the tension of her shoulders, and I didn't pull away.

Three women and two men walked at the head of the group of approaching Selkies. I recognized Elizabeth Ryan and Mathias Lefebvre. The other three were strangers. All five stopped some distance away, forming a loosely curved half-circle, like they feared to come any closer, but feared stopping out of hearing range even more.

"I am Antigone of Albany, mother of the Roane, creator and keeper of the Selkie clans," said the Luidaeg. She sounded almost bored. Only the pulsing cold rolling off her skin betrayed how tense she was. "These are my companions, Sir October Daye, Knight of Lost Words and daughter of Amandine, and King Tybalt of the Court of Dreaming Cats. They stand here under my protection, and are not to be challenged. Who comes to represent the Selkies?"

"Elizabeth Ryan, of Roan Rathad," said Liz.

"Mathias Lefebvre, of Beacon's Home," said Mathias.

"Isla Chase, of Belle Fleuve," said a striking woman with long brown hair and piercing gray eyes that had somehow managed to dodge the usual Selkie deepness. She had a faint French accent, and a strand of glass beads braided behind her left ear.

"Joan O'Connell, of Tremont," said a redheaded woman in a brown broomstick dress that looked like it had come directly out of the nineteen seventies.

"Claude Anthony, of Sweet Water," said a black-haired, brown-skinned man in jeans and a simple button-down polo shirt. He looked even more anachronistic than the others, like he'd just wandered out of some hot new show about attractive people and their sexy problems.

All five of them fell silent after their introductions, looking to the Luidaeg, waiting to see what she was going to say. She took a step forward. Mathias and Joan flinched, but didn't move. None of them moved.

"The Convocation of Consequences is begun," said the Luidaeg, voice clear and calm and carrying. "You represent the five dominant clans of North America. Through you, the word has been passed to all who know these waters. Through you, the Selkies of the world have been called. Are they called?"

I blinked at the phrase "North America," exchanging a quick, anxious glance with Tybalt. Were we going to have to travel outside the continent? Because I didn't exactly have a passport, and if I was worried about my reputation for treason when on lands controlled by Quentin's father, I couldn't imagine what would happen if I went to, say, Europe. They probably didn't like treason very much there. Although, to be fair, no one liked treason very much anywhere.

"They have been," said Liz. Her voice was soft, and more resigned than I had ever heard her sound. "Word has been passed already. The Selkies and their chosen and potential heirs come to the Duchy of Ships from all over the human world, to receive your judgment. The gates will be running all through the night and day, bringing them to port."

Oh, good. We weren't going to need to travel internationally after all.

"We beg your indulgence, Lady," said Isla. "We can send word, but we have no control over the Selkies who swim in other waters, the ones who make their homes on other shores. Some may refuse to come at this summons."

The Luidaeg smiled at that. It wasn't a pleasant expression. "They're coming," she said. "They're all coming."

"Lady?" Isla's voice quavered, like she was afraid of the consequences of contradicting the Luidaeg. Which was pretty smart of her, under the circumstances.

"Each of you wears a skin cut from the body of one of my descendants, powered across the centuries by my own magic, imbued into skin and fur and sacrifice," said the Luidaeg calmly. "Did you really think you had the power to refuse me? That you could run, that you could *hide* when I came to call you home? They come because I called them. As soon as they hear that the summons has been sent, they'll leave their lives and come to us. Some will bring their families and have the opportunity to pass their skins along, if that's what they choose; others will come alone, and have no choices left. Once you sent the word to your people, you sent it to the world."

All five of the clan leaders looked suddenly, profoundly uncomfortable. I couldn't blame them. I wouldn't have looked too thrilled, either, if I'd suddenly been informed that my role in the destruction of an entire fae culture had been larger than I'd originally believed it was going to be.

The Luidaeg took another step forward.

"All of you were content to lead when you thought there'd be no costs, as there had been no costs for hundreds of years. You took up the mantle of your families knowing this day might fall within your lifetimes, and when it did, you regretted it. Your regret measures not even a fragment of my own. Mourn your lost peace of mind as I mourn my lost children, and know that we are not even. We will never be even."

"Yes, Lady," murmured the five, in ragged unison.

"One among your number came to me with a complaint. An accusation, even, of favoritism to one clan above the others."

Mathias stiffened. So did Liz.

"I will not claim to be fair. Fairness is neither my blessing nor my burden. But I do listen. Do any others among you feel I showed favoritism to the Ryan clan when I granted them the Lost Skins in exchange for doing me a direly needed service?"

Silence fell, and lasted long enough that I started to hope this was over. Then Joan cleared her throat, and said, "Any of us would have been glad to do whatever you asked. You didn't ask. You approached the Ryans and granted them a gift the rest of us could never hope to achieve. Yes, it was unfair."

"I needed the girl to be taught, and the girl needed to remain near her mortal family. None of you are near her mortal family," said the Luidaeg implacably. "How is this unfair?"

"None of us had any say in where you settled, Lady," said Mathias. "We would all have been honored to have you near us, ready to ask us for favors as you do the Ryans."

"You didn't say that at the last gathering," said Elizabeth

peevishly. "None of you had a kind word to say about the idea of sharing waters with the sea witch when we weren't getting anything out of it. This is shameful. You shame yourselves."

"Be quiet," snapped Isla. "We all know what *you* did to earn the Lady's favor."

She seemed to realize what she'd said a beat too late to stop herself from saying it. Her mouth snapped shut, her eyes growing wide in her suddenly pale face. Elizabeth looked away, staring fixedly at the waves while the tips of her ears burned red.

And the Luidaeg smiled.

"I always wondered when my past would come back to haunt us," she said, in a conversational tone. "Yes, Elizabeth Ryan was my lover, and yes, I would have kept her with me for as long as her mortal bones could have borne it. I would have lain her to rest in Summerlands soil, in a place where no one would ever disturb her remains, and I would have gone to visit her every sennight until the moons fell from the sky and the sea forgot what it was to sing. But she chose a Selkie's life, and with it, became one of my children in image if not actuality. And if she keeps that skin tied around her shoulders now, if she doesn't set it aside, she'll be mine forever. So no, the Ryan clan has not had my favor for these past thirty years, because the Ryan clan stole my heart when they draped my lover in a stolen skin and called it the sea witch's blessing. She had my blessing and my bed, and she gave them both away to be exactly like the rest of you."

She paused, long enough for her words to fully sink in, before she continued, "But you're right: here, at the ending of all things, it seems only fair that all clans should be treated equally."

Elizabeth went pale. I knew the bargain the Luidaeg had made with her: in exchange for teaching Gillian, who wasn't technically a member of any Selkie clan, and whose continued association with Cliff and Janet made her a threat to Faerie, the Luidaeg had given the Ryans eighteen of what they called the "Lost Skins," Selkie skins that had, through one mechanism or another, found their way back into the Luidaeg's hands and had not been redistributed. It was a gift beyond price, and I could understand why the other Selkies were jealous, even as I could understand why Liz looked so alarmed. If the Luidaeg wanted to take those skins back . . .

"In two days, the ritual will be performed to strip the Selkies from the sea," said the Luidaeg. "At that time, anyone who has a skin will be bound to it, and no longer be able to pass it to their descendants. That was the Selkie way, and the Selkie way is ending. But to be bound to a skin, they have to hold it."

Of the five clan leaders, only Liz seemed to realize what the Luidaeg was saying. She gasped, a small, sharp sound, and looked to me, like I could somehow stop this. I couldn't. All I could do was stand with the rest of them and listen in numb, mounting horror.

"From now until I stand with you once again, I swear that I will neither intervene nor demand satisfaction over any accusation of theft between Selkies. Knock each other down and steal the futures from one another's shoulders. It does no harm to me. The only limit is this: you will not touch the children, and you will not involve any other Selkie's human kin. They aren't yours to endanger. Run and hide and rob each other down to the bones. You have two days. Pass your skins willingly or pass them because you can't protect them. I no longer care. The Convocation is called. When I return, I will have my satisfaction."

The Luidaeg turned on her heel and began marching away down the beach, leaving the rest of us standing stricken and silent.

Liz broke free of the spell first. She ran forward, seizing my hands in hers like she thought she could make me see things her way if she just held on tightly enough.

"Gillian," she hissed. Before I could ask her to clarify, she continued, "Gillian is a damn Selkie now, and she's the least of us, you understand? She is the *least* of us. She doesn't understand her powers, she doesn't swim fast enough to get away, she doesn't know the rules. She has no family among the clans. If this goes forward, she's a target for anyone hoping to settle a skin upon a second child, and if she loses her skin, she dies. You have to make Annie realize what she's doing to us. You have to make her understand what she's doing to your *daughter*."

I was still gaping in open-mouthed horror when Joan and Mathias stepped up and pulled Liz away, yanking her backward until she lost her grasp on my hands. Still she reached for me, straining against the empty air.

"Please," she said. "Please, you have to make her understand, please."

"This is no concern of yours," said Mathias, eyes settling on my face. "The Lady is leaving. Her protection goes with her."

"A *true* Firstborn would find a way to protect her people, no matter what," muttered Isla. Liz was still staring at me, silently imploring me to take her warning seriously.

And I did. I just wasn't sure what I could do about it without offending the Luidaeg. Not that offending the Luidaeg had ever stopped me before.

"Oh, to hell with it," I muttered, and took a step forward, back into the reach of Liz's hands. Mathias was taller than me, but I still did my best attempt at looming over him, drawing myself up straight and arrogant, just like my mother taught me. "Gillian Marks-Daye, of the Ryan clan, is my daughter. She's a Selkie, and I swear to you, if anyone touches her, I will rain down fire upon whichever clan has done it. I'll make you regret ever choosing the sea, because I will drown you in blood. By the root and the branch, the fruit and the thorn, you will regret having ever been born if you so much as look at her too long. Have a nice day."

I smiled, broad and bright and borderline feral, before I spun on my heel and stalked off after the Luidaeg. Tybalt followed me, leaving the Selkies alone with their own problems, standing in the shadow of their own future.

NINE

WE WALKED AWAY FROM the artificial beach in silence. Only once the surface beneath our feet had shifted back to bare dock did Tybalt say, "That was impressively vicious of you. Had I not fallen in love with your ladylike charms long since, I think I might fall in love now, out of sheerest self-defense."

"You're cute when you're trying to placate me." The Luidaeg was up ahead, in sight if not yet in hearing range. "Why the hell did she need to change my clothes if *that's* all we were going to do? I could have stood there and listened to her make threats in a T-shirt and jeans. I'm good at standing around in a T-shirt and jeans. I've had practice."

"Yes, but a T-shirt wouldn't have been nearly as flattering to your figure."

I stopped walking in order to fix him with a baleful eye. He didn't even flinch. "Are you seriously going to stand there and talk about my tits when things are this messed up?"

"Be reasonable, October; I could have been talking about your ass." Tybalt looked at me haughtily. "My interests are far more versatile than you give me credit for."

I blinked at him slowly. Then, almost against my will, I started laughing, great, gasping gales of laughter that evolved, a bit at a time, into sobs, until he stopped smiling smugly and gathered me close, surrounding me in the comforting musk and pennyroyal scent of his magic, which always clung to his skin like mist.

"Ah, little fish, I would take this from you if I could, you know

I would," he murmured, holding me so that his mouth was close to my ear, and his words were mine alone. "You never deserved any of this, and neither did she. It seems the sins of our parents are forever destined to be laid upon the shoulders of our children, generation on generation, until we grow weary of the whole affair. But you will do your best to do right by her, no matter how fiercely she rejects you, and I will be here throughout the whole sordid affair, by your side, to cheer you on."

I sighed, pressing my face into his shoulder and letting the warm fabric of his shirt absorb my tears. Then I pulled away and offered him a wavering smile. "We should catch up with the Luidaeg before she decides we've been kidnapped and comes looking for us."

"As if anyone here would dare?" Tybalt waved a hand airily. "More likely she'll decide we've gone off to have sex somewhere, and come looking for us solely so she can interrupt at the worst possible moment."

That startled another laugh out of me. I wiped my eyes with the back of my hand. "Well, then, we *definitely* want to catch up with her. The last thing I need today is for one of the Firstborn to see me naked."

"Indeed." Tybalt offered his arm, and I took it, letting him guide me down the rickety wooden walkway. I knew the path as well as he did—we'd each walked it exactly once before, in each other's company—but it made him feel better to take the lead sometimes, and I was willing to let him, for my peace of mind as well as for his. If Tybalt was relaxed, I wasn't worrying about him. If I wasn't worrying about him, we could both get more done.

Like worrying about Gillian. When this was over, and she was safe and home and Roane, part of Faerie forevermore, the Luidaeg and I were going to have words about how casually she'd endangered my daughter. I refused to consider any future in which Gillian *wasn't* going to wind up safely in her own bed, with Janet trying her best to keep her away from me. Our family was already fractured. This wasn't the way it would break.

Trailing this far behind the Luidaeg was an interesting experience. It hadn't been obvious before just how much her presence had shut down the normal activity of the stalls around us. Now that Tybalt and I were on our own, people were appearing from all directions, swarming up and down ladders to get to specific shops, leaning out of windows, bartering for wares. A woman who looked like a more delicate version of a Merrow, all the way down to the long, furling flukes of her silver-scaled tail, rode a wicker basket between levels, clinging to the ropes and laughing to the Tylwyth Teg sailor who worked the pulley. Children scampered past, playing some complicated, old-fashioned game with a hoop and a weighted net.

These people were living entirely outside of the mortal world, in the closest thing I'd ever seen to a full reflection of Faerie. Maybe the deeper realms had been like this, dotted with maritime homesteads and private communities that set their own rules and kept their own tempos. Or maybe this was the social equivalent of a changeling, something created from the necessary meshing of two worlds.

The Luidaeg was waiting for us at the end of the marketplace. Her eyes flicked coolly from Tybalt's face to mine before she raised a brow and asked, "Trouble in paradise?"

"Is this paradise?" I asked. "I hadn't noticed."

"It's as close as you're going to get any time soon," she said. "Where were you?"

"Can we not do this now?"

She tilted her head, studying me with more care. "You're unhappy with me," she said finally.

"I know you can't read minds, thank Titania, and I know you can't lie," I said.

"Again, that's on Titania," she said dryly.

I ignored her comment. "What would happen if I wasn't upset? Maybe my face just looks like this."

"Which is why I couldn't say that sort of thing about anyone I didn't know well," said the Luidaeg. "You, however, I know *very* well. I've had years of you darkening my doorstep whether I want you to or not. I can tell when you're unhappy."

"You put my daughter at risk," I said.

The Luidaeg nodded solemnly. "That's true. I did."

"Why?" I demanded.

"Because she was going to be put at risk no matter what. What we're doing here is risky. The destruction of one descendant race to make way for another is something that's only happened once before, all the way back to the dawn of Faerie. It doesn't matter that we're only putting right something that should never have gone wrong. This is going to change the balance of the power in the Undersea. It's going to change everything. Gillian was going to be at risk, because every Selkie is at risk until this is finished."

"You could have told them she was off-limits," I said stubbornly.

The Luidaeg sighed. "I could have, yes," she agreed. "I could have told them she was your beloved baby girl and wearing the skin of my own daughter, and ordered them to leave her alone. And maybe she would have thanked me and maybe she would have spit at me, but she'd have been safe, for now. Only 'now' is a moving target. Tomorrow is coming, and another tomorrow after that, and another after that, until we're standing a century away, and none of the other Roane will even speak to her out of fear that they'll hurt her feelings and the sea witch will sweep in to steal their livers."

I blinked. "You wouldn't do that."

"They think of me as a monster, remember? As far as they're concerned, I'll do virtually anything. Maybe I'm wrong—I'm not lying when I speculate about what the future *might* be, as long as I base it off what I know to be true. But honestly, I don't think I am. These people are going to be her peers for a long, long time, and she's going to be on even footing with them, because none of them know how to be Roane yet. I needed to not start her off in a position of social isolation."

"That's . . ." I paused, shaking my head. "That's way more carefully thought-out than I expected."

The Luidaeg shrugged. "I've had a long time to learn how to read people."

The entry to our courtyard was visible up ahead, and I sped up, anticipating the comfort of being back among people I already knew and trusted. Tybalt and the Luidaeg matched my pace. I barely noticed. Quentin was probably going to be pissed that we'd gone off without him. It was for the best—having him there wouldn't have made things go any more smoothly—but I could still appreciate his reasons for annoyance. Best to get this over with. Maybe he'd been able to spend a little quality time with Dean, and would go easy on me. Maybe—

We came around the edge of the courtyard and stopped, staring at the scene that was unfolding inside. The people we'd left behind were grouped at the center of the space. They had been joined by two newcomers. One, a tall man with burnished bronze hair covered in a thin patina of verdigris, was standing, holding hands with

Poppy and staring at her, mouth slightly ajar, like he'd never seen anything more beautiful in his life. The other, a tawny-skinned woman with straight black hair, was aiming a punch directly at Dean's throat.

Dean dodged the blow with surprising speed, laughing, and swung back, aiming his own fist for the side of the woman's face. She grabbed his arm and twisted, performing a complicated pivot with her lower body that somehow resulted in Dean being flung over her shoulder. He slammed into the deck, landing on his back. He laughed harder. So did she, turning to offer a hand up.

I smiled. It was difficult not to. Both of the newcomers were dressed in the vaguely ahistorical, vaguely maritime style that dominated the Duchy of Ships; whether or not they'd ever been here before, they fit right in. They were clearly at ease in a way they'd never been when they'd come to visit us on the land. This was their home. This was where they belonged.

Quentin looked over and saw us, waving somewhat laconically. So he *was* annoyed, but willing to swallow it for the sake of his boyfriend's parents. Good to know. "The delegation from Saltmist has arrived," he called. "In case you missed it while you were running off and leaving me behind."

Okay, maybe not so much with the swallowing it. "I see that," I said. "Is Dianda actually trying to kill her eldest son, or is this how Merrow say hello?"

"Mostly the latter," said the Luidaeg. "I once attended a Merrow wedding that was three days of the wedding party punching each other. It might have gone on longer, but the guests felt left out and staged a siege."

"Who won?" I asked.

She grinned toothily. "They were all so busy punching each other that they forgot to guard the cake. So, really, I did."

I shook my head. "Right."

Dean embraced his mother, still laughing. I took that as a sign that it was safe to approach: Dianda probably wouldn't have let him get that close if she'd been considering the virtues of a second assault.

Patrick didn't seem to notice our arrival. He kept staring at Poppy, and as I got closer, I saw the tears running down his cheeks—and hers. Poppy's tears glowed with a pale orange light, much like her body used to, back when she'd been a true pixie and not one of the Aes Sidhe. Patrick's tears were just tears, saltwater shed and returning to the ocean, where all such things belong.

Dianda released Dean and whirled on me, reaching out to initiate another hug. Then she froze, eyes going to a point behind me, and I swallowed a sigh. She'd seen the Luidaeg. Of course she had.

"We're here because the Luidaeg called a Convocation," I said patiently. "I think it makes sense that she'd be here."

"Right," said Dianda. The playful violence she'd been displaying when we arrived was gone. Her voice was faint; she looked like she was considering the virtues of passing out.

Under any other circumstances, it might have been amusing to see the normally brash Merrow rendered silent and on the edge of shaking. Maybe. I don't necessarily enjoy seeing my friends and allies suffer. Sure, they don't always extend the same courtesy to me, but part of being a hero is learning how to rise above.

"What's with Patrick?" If I could distract her, she might stop staring past me with that mixture of longing and dismay in her eyes, like she wanted nothing more than to reach for the Luidaeg, knowing with absolute certainty that if she did, she'd pay for her impertinence.

Dianda glanced at her husband and some of the dismay left her face, replaced by fondness. She really did love him. They'd been married for more than a hundred years, and she still looked at him like he was the greatest treasure in all of Faerie. I hoped I'd still look at Tybalt like that after we'd been together for a century.

"The tall orange woman, whose name is 'Poppy,' apparently used to be a pixie," she said. "Did you know pixies could turn into full-sized people? Because I didn't."

"I didn't either, until Poppy did it," I said, all too aware of Tybalt and the Luidaeg at my back. Neither of them had said anything. I was surprisingly grateful for that. "She's Aes Sidhe now. She gave up whatever it is that makes a pixie a pixie willingly, to save Simon Torquill."

Patrick jerked a little, his hands tightening on Poppy's until she grimaced. He loosened his grip. "I'm sorry," he said. "I'm so sorry."

"Don't be sorry," she said, and smiled radiantly through her tears. "You're here and alive and looking at me and I can talk to you, and that's about the better part of everything. I can go back to the swarm and tell Lilac I saw you."

His eyes widened, and the rest of us were forgotten again. "Lilac? She's alive?"

"Alive and thriving and still flying sure and strong."

Patrick's laugh was small and choked. He turned to Dianda. "Lilac is the pixie whose wing I repaired, back when we were first courting. The little girl, the one who'd been injured by someone looking to collect lights for a garden party."

"I remember." She turned to Poppy, bowing her head in respectful acknowledgment. "It's very nice to finally meet you. I'm sorry to have stolen Patrick away."

"We didn't forgive for long and long, but I suppose forgiveness is the thief in the afternoon sometimes, stealing your anger away when you're not paying attention," said Poppy. "He looks healthy and seems happy, so all has been forgiven as far as I'm concerned."

"Did you really give up your home to save *Simon*?" asked Patrick.

I grimaced and stepped forward, placing a hand on his arm. "That's a long story, and maybe this isn't the best time for it," I said. "I promise, though, I'll explain everything. I should probably have explained everything a while ago."

"First, though, the Selkies," said the Luidaeg, finally inserting herself into the conversation. She focused her attention on Dianda. "Are we going to have a problem?"

"Are you going to turn me into a shadow on the surface of the sea?" asked Dianda.

"I could," said the Luidaeg. "Was that a request? Or are you asking me not to?"

"I have a husband, two sons, and a Duchy to take care of, so I'd prefer to remain a Merrow, if that's all right by you," said Dianda. She took a breath, visibly composing herself. "It is . . . difficult, looking at you, knowing the sea did so poorly by one of its Firstborn that you left us for the land. We don't have many left to us."

"Um, Mom?" said Dean.

"In a second, honey," said Dianda. She kept her eyes on the Luidaeg, wary as a predator whose territory has been invaded. Which, in a way, was exactly the case. "I was raised to worship you, Lady. I was raised to offer you the best part of a kill and the sweetest fruit of the harvest, to do whatever was required to keep your wrath from the tides that rock my people. So please forgive me if I don't know how to talk to you. You're . . . daunting."

"See, this is why I left the sea," said the Luidaeg, turning to me. "They're nice people and all, but they can't forget what I am. They can't just let me be a monster."

"I thought you didn't want to be a monster," I said.

"*Mom*," said Dean.

"It's not that I want to be a monster, it's that being a monster means I don't have to deal with people acting like I hung the moons," said the Luidaeg. "Who has time for that shit? My parents wanted to be gods. I just wanted not to get slaughtered by my siblings."

"Mom, *please*," said Dean.

Dianda turned to him, scowling. "What is so important that it can't wait for me to be done talking to the sea witch?"

Dean glanced around, clearly looking for someone to support him. Quentin grimaced and held up his hands: there was no help coming from that quarter. My squire has many excellent qualities, and one of them is knowing when not to get between the temperamental mermaid and her son, even if that son is his current boyfriend. Marcia just looked baffled. The politics of Firstborn and the Undersea were not a part of her daily routine.

"Mom . . ." Dean paused, taking a deep breath, and said, "Amphitrite is here."

Dianda went still.

"What?" asked Patrick.

"The Merrow Firstborn. Amphitrite. She's here. On the Duchy of Ships. I think she sort of technically *is* the Duchy of Ships. She's the captain. All the ships that sail here sail for her. It's hers."

"That's not possible," said Dianda. "Duchess . . . I can't remember her name, but a duchess holds the Duchy of Ships, in the name of Queen Palatyne. Captain Pete sails under her colors, and he's not the Merrow Firstborn. He can't be."

"Have you ever met Captain Pete?" asked the Luidaeg. Her voice was surprisingly kind.

"Once," said Dianda. She frowned, looking suddenly lost. "There was a storm. Not long after the big earthquake. The Duchy of Ships is anchored in a slice of sea that's almost a skerry, so it's in everyone's waters and no one's waters at the same time. They managed to dodge the worst of the aftershocks, and they couriered medical supplies and food to the coastal domains. I was still new at being Duchess, but I remember . . . I met him. I know I did. I just can't remember his face." She paused, frown becoming a sharp-edged smile. "I remember his nose, though. It crunched so nicely when I punched it."

"Yeah, so apparently that's one of the two common reactions Merrow have upon meeting their Firstborn. Either they pass out, which Dean did, or they attack," I said. "Sounds like you attacked."

Dianda shook her head. "No. I'd remember punching my own Firstborn. Or, more likely, I *wouldn't*, since I'd be dead."

"Pete doesn't mind when her descendants assault her, as long as they calm down after the shock passes," said the Luidaeg. "She says it's something in the blood, and she can't hold it against you, when she's the one who went and made you this way. She doesn't leave the Duchy often. You should feel honored, even if she did feel the need to fog your memory after the fact, to keep her secrets safe. You may not even remember she's here after you go home, although I suppose that's up to her. She might decide you're trustworthy."

I wouldn't, said her tone.

Dianda shook her head again, harder this time. "No. I'd remember."

"Sorry, Mom, but yeah," said Dean.

She looked at him, stricken, and said nothing. Patrick gave Poppy's hands one final squeeze and let them go before moving to stand next to his wife.

"Well, this is fun." The Luidaeg clapped her hands. "Can we possibly make this any more awkward, do you think, or should we all stand around staring at each other for a while? Really, the possibilities for discomfort are endless, if we all work together."

"It's nice that you can still be sarcastic," I said. "I think if you couldn't lie *or* be sarcastic, you might literally explode."

"Titania's cruel, but my father wouldn't let her go that far," said the Luidaeg.

Privately, I thought Oberon had allowed his wife to go more than far enough. I wasn't going to say so. There were some family affairs that were well past my pay grade, and this was one of them.

"Where are Nolan and Cassandra?" I asked.

"Shopping," said Quentin. "He wanted to see if some pie dealer he likes still had a stall here, and Cassie's trying to keep him from getting kidnapped or thrown overboard or something stupid like that. Which means he's looking for information about his old nursemaid, and she's trying to stay out of the way. Her job is mostly babysitting."

"Then you should have plenty to talk about, since you seem to think your job is similar," I said.

He wrinkled his nose.

Dianda had taken the pause as an opportunity to recover her composure. She gestured toward a nearby seat. "Do you mind?" she asked. "Keeping myself on two legs for long periods of time is wearying, and I'd like to be able to walk when I need to."

"Of course," said the Luidaeg. "I'm not here to torment my sister's children. Just my own."

Dianda nodded as she sank gratefully into the seat, stretching her legs out in front of her and pressing her ankles together. The scent of water lilies and amber rose around her, and scales rippled across her skin, replacing her legs with a muscular tail that ended in jewel-toned flukes, which she splayed contentedly across the ground. She was lovely. It was easy to see why Patrick was so besotted with her, even after all this time.

"Oh, that's better," she said, bending forward and resting her forehead against the spot where her knees had been. After a moment, she raised her head, still bent double, and looked at me. "How did it go with the Selkies?"

"Shouldn't you be asking the Luidaeg that?" I asked.

"Yes, probably, but I'm still a little freaked out by having her just standing around like a regular person, so for my own peace of mind, I'm taking a moment to pretend she isn't here," said Dianda. She glanced to the Luidaeg. "No offense intended, Lady. This is a lot to take in."

"No offense taken," said the Luidaeg, sounding almost amused. "Please, continue pretending I'm not here. I'll make it easier by not *being* here. October, if any Selkies come looking, I'm sort of obligated to speak to them, but for anyone else, I'm in my room and don't want to be disturbed."

"Got it," I said. I hesitated. "Isn't this the sort of thing Poppy's supposed to take care of? She's your apprentice."

"Yeah, but she's also a bigger flake than you are, and she's understandably distracted. Just do as I say, all right?"

"All right," I said, and was rewarded with a quick smile before she stomped across the courtyard and into her apartment. She slammed the door so hard the whole frame shook, and I laughed. "Drama queen."

"Should you be speaking of one of the Firstborn like that?" asked Patrick.

"Believe me, that's kinder than most of what I have to say about the Firstborn," I said.

"Truth," said Tybalt. "My lady possesses a filthy mouth and a creative mind when it comes to describing our forebears."

"Too much information," muttered Quentin.

I laughed again, turning back to Patrick and Dianda. "I didn't know you were coming."

"What, and miss the opportunity to see our son when he's back at sea, like a sensible Merrow, and not hiding in his inland halls?" Dianda finally sat up. "I wouldn't dream of it."

"Goldengreen is coastal," Dean protested.

"Coastal, but still on dry land," said Dianda.

I looked around. There were no other Lordens. "Where's Peter?" I asked. "I don't think I've ever seen both of you without him." One or the other, sure, but not both at once.

"Peter is safe in Saltmist with Helmi," said Patrick. "We wanted to bring him, but it seemed . . . inadvisable."

"Meaning you thought there might be a slaughter here," I concluded.

Dianda shrugged. "Can you blame us? This is a whole new thing. Anyway, Peter's getting older. He's ready to stretch his fins a little, and if anybody tries to hurt him or take him hostage, Helmi can explain why it's a bad idea."

"Meaning she'll assault them until they go away," I said.

"You get used to it after you live in the Undersea long enough," said Patrick. "Things are simpler there."

"That's one way of putting it." I took a step back and Tybalt was there, putting an arm around my waist and pulling me, ever so gently, against him. If I didn't focus on the fact that we were on a floating demesne in the middle of the ocean, the scene was almost pleasant. Everyone in this courtyard was a friend or an ally, or at minimum, someone I trusted to have my back in a fight. It was a level of security I didn't have very often outside of my home.

Of course it couldn't last.

The sound of marching feet broke our momentary peace. I

pulled away from Tybalt and spun around to see what looked like a full detachment of armored guards enter our courtyard, arraying themselves to either side of the entryway. I didn't recognize their livery, which featured a red-and-yellow chevron with a hippocampus rampant above three radiant sea stars.

Dianda did. She was on her feet in an instant, transforming back into her bipedal form with a smooth, somehow frenetic speed as she moved to place herself in front of Dean and Patrick. That, more than the ceremonial tridents in the hands of the guards, told me something was wrong.

The Undersea is a dangerous place. They still settle disputes the old-fashioned way: by beating on each other until only the victor is left standing. Dianda blustered. Dianda threatened. Dianda had never, in my experience, looked genuinely alarmed. She was protecting the people she cared about. She didn't look openly scared, but there was a tension to her shoulders I'd never seen there before. Not good.

Poppy fell back a step. Marcia didn't. She was pinned between two planters, her hands full of strawberries, and there was nowhere for her to go.

Quentin took a step toward me. I offered him a quick, encouraging nod, and he crossed the rest of the short distance between us, falling into place at my side. The guards were still coming, making a clear display of force. I touched the knife at my belt, and wondered whether calling for the Luidaeg would do any good at all. One of the many geasa she lives under forbids her to injure any descendants of Titania. I couldn't say for sure—I don't have enough practice identifying Undersea fae—but I thought at least some of the guards were Merrow, which would render the Luidaeg powerless to move against them.

Maybe it was better to let her stay inside, where she could watch and take notes, but couldn't wind up stuck in an untenable position. No matter how much better I would have felt with a *really* big stick by my side.

"Toby," said Quentin in a low voice.

"Stand your ground," I said. "We'll figure this out."

The guards stopped coming, and a final man stepped into the courtyard.

Unlike the guards, he wore no armor. His clothing was far more reminiscent of that worn by the denizens of the Duchy of Ships, almost but not quite historical, like something from a maritime fantasy novel. His doublet was the same red as the chevrons on the guards, and he had the hippocampus and sea stars stitched above his right breast, the lines of the insignia picked out in small glass beads that shimmered blue and green and crystal clear. His hose were pale gold, and he carried no visible weapons. He didn't need to. Everything about him radiated quiet power. His arms were thick with muscle, and would have looked entirely out of proportion if not for the breadth of his chest and the thickness of neck. This was not a man who'd spent a single day of his life sitting idly, not when there was something else to be done with his time.

His hair was dark and his skin was golden brown, and I didn't have to ask to know he and Dianda were related. Technically, all Merrow are related, but he looked enough like her that it was jarring.

The man smiled without warmth. It was the cold smile of a predator, something rising out of the deeps to snatch its prey. "Open waters and kind tides to you, Dianda Lorden, Duchess of Saltmist."

"Torin." The name fell from her lips like a stone. "I'm afraid I don't know your current title, little brother, and so can't offer it to you as a peaceful hello. You're looking . . . well."

I swallowed my shock at the word "brother," although I couldn't stop my eyes from widening. This complicated things. As my own experiences with August proved, siblings complicate *everything*.

"I stand heir to the Duchy of Bluefish, as you well know," snapped the other Merrow. His eyes skated across the rest of us, smile twisting into a scowl. "This is the company you keep? Landers and animals and creatures of the air? You shame yourself and your father's name with your behavior."

"It's my name to use as I like, since I'm the one he kept," said Dianda. "Get your own name, if you're so worried about the dishonor done to mine. It's not my fault our mother carries no family name to give you."

Torin's lip curled. He said nothing.

So there'd been a separation. That at least made his existence—and the lack of mention—make sense. When married fae have children, divorce is impossible until those children are old enough to choose which parent's family line they want to claim as their own. Maybe that's part of why fae children tend to come reasonably close together. A couple can be married for hundreds of years with no luck at conceiving an heir *or* a spare, only to get both in less than a decade.

It's hard to say, in Faerie, whether our social customs stem from our biology, or whether our biology has been shaped by our social customs. Honestly, it could go either way.

Some fae, especially among the noble houses, have been known to marry solely for the sake of conceiving that all-precious heir. Once the first child comes along, there's a decent chance of having a second in an irrelevant number of years, and then it's only a few decades before they can separate and get on with their lives. This doesn't mean divorces can't be messy—and while supposedly, parents aren't allowed to pressure their children to choose one over another, that's not how it works in reality. That's never been how it worked.

It looked like Torin, who had chosen to be his mother's son sometime in the deep past, was having second thoughts now.

Dianda yawned luxuriously, stretching her arms above her head, before planting her hands on her hips and looking, narrow-eyed, at her brother. "Well?" she asked. "You brought a lot of guards for a friendly visit. You here to start something with me? Because if you are, you're a coward who knows he can't take me in a fair fight. You couldn't do it when we were children, you couldn't do it when I was sent to school to become a better warrior than you, and you can't do it here."

"Technically, dear, he's not *allowed* to do it here," said Patrick, in the mild voice that meant he was genuinely annoyed. "The Duchy of Ships has strict rules about such things, and attracting the wrath of Captain Pete is less than desirable."

A briefly stricken look crossed Dianda's face at the thought of even being in the vicinity of her Firstborn's wrath, mirrored by a look of abject horror on Dean's. Torin, on the other hand, continued to sneer. Either he didn't realize who Pete was, or he somehow didn't care. Looking at the number of heavily armed guards he'd brought with him, I thought it could go either way. This was a man who didn't believe he needed to play by the rules.

"You think a *Duchy's* rules supersede the rules of Leucothea?" Torin asked, lip curling like he smelled something unpleasant. "That would explain a great deal, given the way you flaunt your perversions and disregard for our traditions. You think yourself an empire, inviolate, unapproachable. You're wrong. You've always been wrong. Every action you've ever taken has led us here, to this inevitable moment, this inevitable conclusion."

I frowned deeply, shifting closer to Tybalt, my hand once again going to my hip, where the hilt of my knife waited under the careful layers of my skirt. For the first time, I really appreciated the artistry of the Luidaeg's design. No one could even tell that I was armed, but I could be ready to defend myself in an instant if I needed to.

Patrick glanced at Dianda, clearly ready to take his cues from her. As for Dianda herself . . .

It was like a light I'd never realized was burning in her eyes had suddenly been extinguished, leaving her a little smaller, a little more breakable. She'd always been a warrior queen, ready to fight the world if that was what she needed to do. Now, she looked almost frightened. She looked almost vulnerable.

Until this moment, I'd never seen her stand like she wasn't sure whether she'd be able to win.

"I think no such thing," she said. Her voice didn't shake: it was still clear and strong and unyielding, and I was proud of her for that. "Saltmist answers to the Queen, as it has always done, as it will always do. I have never set myself above Queen Palatyne's laws, nor would I think to do so. She is chosen of the sea. She will keep us safe through all the storms to come."

"And yet you didn't trust her, or the sea, well enough to marry a Merrow man when he came to you with an offer of alliance."

Dianda visibly bristled. "That was over a hundred years ago. We were ill-suited, to put it lightly. His life would have been a misery with me, and I would have been cruel to him, even without meaning to."

"You rejected a good man of Merrow blood because you wanted to dally with lander filth," spat Torin. He pointed to Patrick, who raised one eyebrow in silent judgment, but otherwise didn't respond. "He has no right to stand on these grounds."

"Patrick's not the only air-breathing scum here, in case you were wondering," I said mildly. His head snapped around, staring at me like he was just registering my presence. It was a nice touch, even though I knew it was a lie. He'd already admitted he knew we were there, and if he'd ignored us that completely, I would have taken him for a fool as well as a bully. I raised my free hand, leaving the other resting against my knife, and offered a tiny wave. "Hi. Not nice to meet you. Sort of lousy to meet you, actually. Anyone ever tell you that you're kind of a jerk?"

Quentin shifted positions until he was more beside me than behind me. Tybalt didn't move at all, but somehow loomed a little taller, the bones of his face subtly shifting to a more predatory mien. Out of the corner of my eye I saw Marcia inching into the shadow of a tomato plant, and that was good; that was exactly right. She wasn't a combatant. If this got ugly, I wanted to know that she was safe. I only wished I could do the same for Poppy, who was continuing to stand and stare with open-mouthed fascination at the scene unfolding around her.

"I should have the tongue from your head for daring to speak to me so disrespectfully," snapped Torin. "Who claims you, *changeling*?" He spat the word like it was the direst of insults. "You're not of noble blood. Not even the land would elevate vermin."

"Weirdly enough, the land *has* elevated this vermin, at least twice," I said. "I was a Countess for a while. It didn't stick. Good thing, too, since I was pretty bad at it. I'm still a knight. Sir October Daye, hero of the realm, at basically anyone's service but yours."

Torin's eyes widened in shock and what looked, momentarily, like delight. "October *Daye*?" he echoed. "The changeling knight? The *king-breaker*? Oh, sister." He shook his head as he turned back to Dianda. "I knew this would be easy. I never expected it to be such a joy."

Dianda glared at him, jaw set, and said nothing.

"By the authority of Queen Palatyne of Leucothea, I place you, Dianda Lorden, under immediate arrest." Torin sounded way too pleased about that. "If you come quietly, you will be treated as any other prisoner. Or you can contest the charges as a Merrow, and face the justice of the sea."

Dean and Patrick both went pale. There was something I was missing. Dianda's hands twitched, like she was longing to throw a punch. She glanced at her husband and son, and her shoulders sagged, leaving her looking smaller than I had ever seen her.

"What are the charges, please?" she asked, voice barely above a whisper.

Torin scowled. "You truly intend to face justice like a weakling? Like a common—"

"What are the *charges*?" This time, her voice cracked like a whip, filled with all the fury and embarrassment her body could hold.

For the first time, Torin looked nervous. "Refusal to do your duty and provide the Duchy of Saltmist with a suitable heir. Sedition. Consorting with the enemy. And now, it seems, treason, for you've brought a king-breaker into our waters. For shame, Dianda. I regret I must call you 'sister,' and hope the tides will never bring us together again once this filthy work is done."

"I am innocent of all charges; even of bringing Toby here," said Dianda. "That was the sea witch. If you want to take it up with her, be my guest. I'd love to watch."

Torin glared. Then he spun on his guards. "Take her," he commanded.

The guards began to advance. Dianda turned, putting her hands on Dean's shoulders.

"Do *not* fight them, any of you," she hissed, but her eyes were fixed on her son, pleading with him to hear her, to understand. "This will all be fine. It's a mistake, we'll fix it, but if you fight, you acknowledge that you would rather be tried as Merrow, and he *will* kill you. So do not fight them. I'll be all right. I promise."

"Mom?" Dean suddenly sounded very young, and very lost.

Dianda pulled him into a quick hug. "Oh, my brave boy."

Patrick touched her shoulder. She tensed, looking like she was fighting the urge to swing. Then she let Dean go and wrapped herself around Patrick, holding him so tightly that there was no space left between them, no room for a shiver or a sigh.

She whispered something in his ear as she released him and stepped away. He closed his eyes, and didn't see the guards grab her wrists and wrap them in chains of rowan braided with silver. He didn't see them pull her toward the exit. He didn't even see Torin plant a hand between her shoulders and shove, laughing as she stumbled. He just stood there, voluntarily sightless, and let the moment pass him by.

I couldn't blame him. There was nothing he could do. There was nothing any of us could do, except stand there and watch Dianda's brother lead her away. She kept her shoulders high and her head up, and he scowled, and then they were gone, and we were alone.

TEN

PATRICK PUT HIS HANDS over his face, standing stone-still in the middle of the courtyard. Poppy flicked her wings, slowly at first, then more and more rapidly, until her feet left the ground and she was hovering a foot or so in the air, looking genuinely distraught. Dean pressed his face into Quentin's shoulder. I was fairly sure he was crying.

I looked around the group. No one, not even Tybalt, would meet my eyes.

"What happens now?" I asked.

"Sometimes I forget," said Tybalt. His voice was soft; almost hollow. "I know your political education has been piecemeal at best, but your mother was Firstborn, and Sylvester only ever wanted to do well by you, and sometimes I forget how much you don't know."

"I'd know if you'd *tell* me," I snapped. "Torin's going to take Dianda to Pete, right? Or the Duchess of Ships. Who oversees Dianda's trial? Where do we need to go?"

"Nowhere," said a voice.

I turned.

The Luidaeg was standing just outside her apartment, back in what I thought of as her "normal" guise: overalls and tank top and pigtails and pain. Her hands were by her sides, and the sorrow in her driftglass eyes was almost painful to behold.

"The Convocation means people can *enter* the Duchy, but they can't leave without Pete's explicit permission," said the Luidaeg. "The docks are closed. No ships sail. I'm sure a few people will sneak away in small boats, but something like this? A fully armed guard trying to take a Merrow Duchess away to stand trial? That's a production. Pete will never approve it. She won't forbid it, because she doesn't interfere in the Undersea like that—she hasn't done so for centuries—but she won't let them leave until she absolutely has to."

"So you can stop this." Patrick uncovered his face and took an unsteady step toward her. "You can make him let her go."

"I didn't say that, Baron Twycross," said the Luidaeg. Patrick visibly flinched as she rested the full weight of her attention on him, even though she looked sympathetic; even though, for her, this was being kind. "You had a hundred years. That's more than most people can ever hope for. I'm sorry."

"She's my *mother*," said Dean. He glared at the Luidaeg. Her majesty seemed to have faded where he was concerned. Good kid. "A hundred years isn't enough."

"It never is," said the Luidaeg.

Patrick took another step. "I'll—I'll make a bargain with you. I'll give you whatever you want if you'll just save her. If you'll bring her home. I'll—"

"No." He turned to stare at me, seeming surprised by my presence, like he'd forgotten I was even there. I shook my head and said it again: "No." That didn't seem like enough. "You can't do that to her."

"Dianda is your friend," he said.

"So's the Luidaeg," I said. "And she's here to finish burying her children. I won't let you force her into a bargain right now. Before you say you wouldn't be forcing anything, remember, if you ask, she has to answer. She doesn't have a choice."

"Impressive," said the Luidaeg wearily. I turned to face her. She shook her head and said, without a trace of sarcasm, "With as much time as we've spent together, you still can't get over thinking of me as a person, and not a salvation dispenser. Most people, when the chips are down, jump straight to telling me what they need and what I should do. It's a nice change."

"I'm a hero," I said. "I can deal with this myself."

"October." She folded her arms across her chest in an almost defensive gesture. "Dianda Lorden is a *Merrow*. She belongs to the Undersea. You can't just go yell at Queen Palatyne the way you would at Arden. You'd drown before all her guards decided to stab you."

"I'll figure something out," I said. "There has to be a way. I'll find someone with a SCUBA kit, or . . . or something."

"The sea witch is *right there,*" said Patrick desperately. "Please. She has to help us. You have to make her help us."

"I know you're new around here, but unless you enter into a bargain with me, I don't have to do anything, and October's not going to let you enter into a bargain," said the Luidaeg. "I can close this door and ignore you all until it's time to bind the Selkies into their skins and bring back the Roane."

Patrick clenched his hands into fists by his sides. "He *took* her."

"I'm sure he did." She looked at him levelly. Her eyes had bled back to driftglass green, clear and pale and exhausted. "I'm sure he put her in chains of rowan and silver, and called her all sorts of names, and led her away. But the Merrow are the descendants of Amphitrite, and Amphitrite is the daughter of Titania, and I am bound not to harm or raise my hand against the children of Titania."

"Wait," I said. "You were able to send Quentin into Blind Michael's lands to find his girlfriend, and the Daoine Sidhe are children of Titania, too."

"Quentin came to me of his own free will. I did him no harm, only offered him the knife and told him how to cut himself. It's not the same thing. It might look like the same thing from the outside, but it's not." She shook her head. "I have no power here, October. The Merrow keep the Law in their own way, and I am not invited to intervene."

"Okay, fine. You said Pete wouldn't let Torin leave with his sister. I'll just go to her and tell her what happened, and—"

"You won't find her."

I stopped, blinking. "What?"

"I said, you won't find her."

"But you just said—"

"I know what I said. She leaves instructions when she sails, and they usually include keeping people where she wants them. There's no way Torin leaves before she gets back." Somehow, the Luidaeg seemed to be growing wearier by the moment. "Dianda's brother came here to arrest her, which means he came with guards, which means Pete sailed on the next tide. She's neutral ground. That's how she keeps herself from needing to face off against Palatyne."

Palatyne. I seized on the name, demanding, "Why *doesn't* she face off against Palatyne?"

"Because we agreed, all of us, to fade back. To let Faerie govern itself in the absence of our parents. We're not gods. We're not perfect. Even the sister I can't name has held by the agreement. She tries to take power whenever she can, but she does it as a *part* of Faerie, not as something held above it. Pete isn't going to save you."

"Then I'll go to Palatyne," I said. "If she's allowing Dianda to be arrested for treason just because I've overthrown a couple of monarchs, she's not a good queen."

For the first time since this conversation started, the Luidaeg looked almost amused. "Are you really going to stand there and tell me Dianda doesn't deserve to be punished for spending time in a king-breaker's company—*your* company—and say in the same breath that Palatyne isn't a good queen? Because that sounds like sedition to me."

I scowled. "That isn't what I meant."

"What you mean and what you say should be similar, or you risk people not understanding you." The Luidaeg sighed. "Look. I know you aren't trying to be insulting when you challenge me on the things I say, I know you're just . . . really fucking young by the standards of anyone as old as I am, and you're trying to make sense of things. I get that, I truly do. But I said I couldn't help you—any of you—and I can't lie to anyone except for the Selkies. I. Can't. Help. You. Whatever happens next is on your shoulders. Figure it out. But know that I won't allow you to get yourself killed in a stupid way. We have a Convocation to complete."

She turned and stalked back into her apartment, slamming the door behind her. Silence fell. I knew what I would see when I turned around, and so I didn't turn around, instead taking a moment to catch my breath.

The silence was broken by the sound of a fist slamming into something solid. There was a horrible cracking sound, like bone giving way. I spun around before I had time to think better of it, and clapped my hands over my mouth when I saw Patrick clutching his right hand against his chest, eyes closed and cheeks red. The table that had been in front of him was on its side. No one else had moved. No one else even seemed to be entirely breathing. Poppy's wings were moving so fast they were a blur, leaving her hanging a foot off the ground, watching him with bleak dismay.

I lowered my hands. "Did the furniture say something mean about your mother?" I asked.

"My mother is safe at home in Boston, and hasn't spoken to me in over a century," said Patrick. His voice was calm and measured, as it almost always was. There was blood coming from between the fingers of his left hand. He'd probably split the skin on several of his knuckles, assuming he hadn't managed to do something even worse. He chuckled darkly, not opening his eyes. "She didn't like me marrying a mermaid. Said it was 'beneath me.' I suppose that's something she and Dianda's family can agree on."

"Dad," said Dean desperately. "Please, let me see your hand." .

"Why? It's only blood. As pure as hers, but that doesn't matter, because I can't breathe water, and she can't be happy on the land."

"It's only blood, but if I have to stand here smelling it, I'm not going to be able to get anything done." I started back toward the group. "Marcia? Did you pack a first aid kit?"

"The Count's as clumsy as a newborn lamb, so yes, I packed a first aid kit. I don't go anywhere without one." Marcia stepped out from behind the tomatoes, looking relieved to have something to do. "I'll be right back."

"Great." I walked toward Patrick, moving slow and careful. He couldn't see me, but he could hear me, and I didn't want to startle him. Under the circumstances, it seemed like a very, very bad idea. "Patrick, Marcia's going to take a look at your hand. You want to sit down while she does it?"

"This was a trap." He finally opened his eyes, turning to face me. "He would never have come here without first securing Salt-mist. Do you understand?"

"Helmi—"

"Is one Cephali. One guard we know is completely loyal. I . . . I know our staff, I know most of them wouldn't turn against us for no good reason, but this is the *Undersea*. You yield to the strongest hand in the room." Patrick's despair was written clear for anyone to see. "Torin must have had someone there, waiting for the day when we left without Peter. Someone signaled him. And then, once his forces took the knowe, all the people who were loyal to us would have changed allegiance to him and not thought for a second that they were doing anything wrong. This is how things are done in the depths. The peace is maintained because once it's broken, everyone shifts sides."

"Helmi wouldn't," I said firmly.

"No," said Patrick. "She's been with Dianda too long. She's sworn to her in a dozen different ways, and she would never betray our family. Which is why I fully expect to hear that only two people from our household died in the fighting."

I began to open my mouth to ask who he thought the second casualty would be. I caught myself, barely, before I could speak.

Peter. He was talking about Peter.

Quentin looked from Patrick to Dean, who was shivering, barely seeming to hold himself together. "I don't understand," he said, and finally looked to me, like he thought I'd have all the answers. And maybe he did. I'd been his knight for years, and he'd learned he could depend on me to know what to do, even if I thought "bleed" was the correct solution.

When none of us said anything, he repeated, louder, "I don't *understand*. How can Torin just walk in here and arrest Duchess Lorden for treason? She didn't do anything wrong. And you can't really be saying he would . . . he wouldn't break the Law to take Saltmist. No war has been declared. He doesn't have the authority to break the Law." Quentin sounded almost desperate.

I understood why. The Law is supposed to be absolute: that's why we call it *the* Law, even though everyone knows it's not the only thing a person can be punished for. Kidnapping, theft, treason—even if Faerie doesn't have hard and fast laws forbidding them, doing those things is likely to make a lot of people angry. Nobles have the power to punish their own subjects for breaking the social code, and even outside of noble households, people police themselves fairly tightly. The one Law, the one inarguable rule of Faerie, is that purebloods don't kill each other.

The Law doesn't cover changelings; it's always been perfectly acceptable for someone to kill me and then claim they did it because I'd looked at them funny, or because I'd been in their way, or whatever. Because Sylvester became my liege when I was remarkably young, as such things go, anyone who'd tried that would have found themselves facing a pissed-off Daoine Sidhe Duke demanding satisfaction . . . but they technically wouldn't have broken the Law.

Peter's parents were both fae. He might be a blend of Merrow and Daoine Sidhe, but that wasn't enough to set him outside the Law. I looked to Patrick, hoping for an explanation.

I got one.

"The Undersea chooses to abide by the land's ideas of what is and is not a war, when they have to interact; it's easier, given how often they can avoid air-breathers, not to force a discussion of what exactly it means to go to war. But the Merrow, much like the Cait Sidhe, have been allowed to develop their own definitions of certain things. During a fight for succession, it's totally acceptable to . . . to . . ." He stopped then, putting a hand over his eyes. Not fast enough to stop a tear from running down his cheek, visible and utterly damning.

"Oh," I whispered. I bit my lip, watching Patrick. He wasn't supposed to cry. It wasn't right. "Okay. We have to . . . don't jump straight to assuming the worst, okay? Helmi's smart, she knows Saltmist, and she's loyal. If she had *any* warning, she'll have gotten Peter out of there."

And if she hadn't received warning, if Torin's people had been quick and careful enough, she and Peter were both lost forever. I couldn't dwell on that. If I did, I'd be useless to everyone, Peter included. He was just a kid. He didn't deserve to be swept up in all this.

"Where will the trial be?" A dire thought occurred to me. "There *is* a trial, right? Torin isn't going to haul her off and have her executed as part of this succession thing? Because if that's the plan, we need to organize a jailbreak right now." The Lordens could be exiles in the Mists, if it came to that. King Gilad had been a friend of theirs. His daughter would never refuse to offer them sanctuary.

Dianda would be miserable on land, but she'd be alive. We could get her a saltwater swimming pool or something. She could be safe. All the Lordens could be safe. Assuming it wasn't already too late for the youngest of them.

No. Screw that. I wasn't going to think that way. I turned and walked to the Luidaeg's apartment, rapping lightly. There was no response. I knocked harder. There was still no response. I started knocking even harder, hammering on the door until the side of my hand ached. The others watched silently, clearly not understanding what I was trying to do—or if they did understand, not seeing a way to help.

That was fine. As usual, I was making this up as I went along.

"Yo, Luidaeg!" I yelled, over the sound of my own hammering. "I heal like it's a contest, remember? I can break my hand on this damn door and keep right on going. So open up, before you get a headache to go with the rest of your problems."

There was a long pause. I kept knocking. Maybe my first appeal hadn't worked, but my second would, or my third, or my fifth—however many it took. We didn't have a lot of time, but this was still where things needed to begin.

The door swung open without warning. I was already in the middle of my next knock, and for one horrible moment, I thought I was going to punch the Luidaeg square in the face. She was capable of forgiving me for a great many things, but even so, that would be pushing it.

She caught my hand. Effortlessly, stopping me in mid-motion, sending a bone-jarring shock up my arm and into my shoulder.

"What," she said flatly. It wasn't a question. I would have liked it better if it had been a question. Irritable, artificially annoyed Luidaeg was something I knew how to deal with. This . . .

She looked exhausted. She looked resigned. Worst of all, she looked sad, like she'd already considered all the ways this might play out, and had found absolutely no happy endings.

Screw that. She was bound not to act against the children of Titania. I had no such restrictions. The Lordens weren't mine the way Tybalt and Quentin and even Marcia were, but they were my friends. They had put themselves at risk for me before, and I'd be damned before I failed to do the same for them.

"You said we had two days before the Convocation would conclude and the Selkies would be bound to their skins," I said. "Is there anything else you're going to need me to do between now and then, or am I free to wander around as I like?"

She blinked once before saying warily, "You're free to wander, although with Pete gone, there's not a ferry back to the Mists. And that's not an invitation to steal a ship and go by yourself. I don't want to answer to Pete when she demands to know why you're commandeering her ships."

"No, that's going to be you."

"What?"

I took a deep breath. "We pass debts back and forth between us like some kind of toy. Now I owe you, now you owe me. This, helping you bring back the Roane, it clears the debts I incurred from you when you helped me to save Tybalt's life. We're square. Right?"

"Right," she said, sounding even warier.

She was probably right to be suspicious. What I was about to ask for existed somewhere in the strange hinterland between ridiculous and suicidal, and honestly, it wouldn't even have been that reasonable if I hadn't been so difficult to kill.

"Luidaeg, I need your help."

"What happened to leaving me alone because I was here to bury my children?" she asked.

"If I leave you alone, he buries his son." I gestured behind me, toward Patrick. "That changes things. Please, Luidaeg. We're both parents. We can't let someone else lose a child."

She started to answer me. Then she stopped, sighed, and asked, "What are you planning to do?"

"Do you remember the time you turned me into a Merrow so I could go to Saltmist? I need you to do it again, so I can go save Peter Lorden. And while *I'm* doing *that*, I need you to commandeer a ship and go find your sister."

The Luidaeg cocked her head hard to one side, a genuinely baffled expression on her face. "Why the *fuck* would you want me to do that? Self-sacrificing behavior from you, sure, I expect that, and we'll loop back in a second, but why are you sending me after Pete? So we can drink mimosas and talk about how annoying our father's other kids are? And his *grandkids*? Because believe me, you're annoying on a level I doubt Oberon ever conceived."

"Patrick says the Merrow have their own interpretations of the Law," I said. "He says they don't require a formally declared war to kill each other."

She nodded. "That's right. They worked that out with Dad and Pete a long time ago, back when everybody was still in play. The Merrow are . . . volatile. I think it's because Titania's brand of magic doesn't like to be submerged, and they're inherently damp people. So they got the rules changed for them. Why?"

"Peter Lorden," I said again, with as much patience as I could muster. We were wasting time. I needed to be gone. But I needed the Luidaeg to help me—willingly—and that meant making sure she understood what I was asking her to do. "He's just a kid, but he's Merrow."

"Ah." She looked at me gravely. "He's worse than Merrow in their eyes. He's a Merrow who can't completely transform. He always has scales, like a common Suire—you've never met one," she added, seeing my confusion. "They're not shapeshifters. They don't come to the surface much anymore. Peter is weak as far as the Merrow are concerned. He shows them in a poor light. Normally, I'd expect a conqueror to keep him alive to show they aren't monsters, just people who have a better claim to ruling the local demesne than the old rulers did. Given Peter's limitations, however . . ." She hesitated, eyes flicking past me.

She was looking at Patrick. I knew she was. And that was part of how I knew that the Luidaeg was not and could never be the monster some people believed her to be. She was a parent. She cared enough not to say certain things where another parent could hear them.

"Right now, Torin's forces have Saltmist, but they haven't had it long; there's still a chance," I said, dragging the Luidaeg's attention back to me. "I'm a hero of the realm, Dianda and Patrick Lorden are friends of mine, and the charges Torin is levying against his sister are trumped-up at best, completely false at worst."

"If he wins, you're committing an act of war against the Undersea," said the Luidaeg.

"If he wins, I'm pretty sure *he's* committing an act of war against the Mists, since Patrick and Dean are considered nobles on the land." Patrick had given up his title when he married Dianda, but that didn't matter. If Torin messed with his family, Arden would find a way to justify striking back.

That would be bad. That would be really, really bad. I needed to fix this as soon as possible, and not just for Peter's sake. For everyone's.

The Luidaeg pinched the bridge of her nose. "And so you want me to turn you into a mermaid, while I leave the Duchy of Ships to convince my sister to do what none of us has done in centuries, and actually command a member of her descendant race to do something. Specifically, 'stop bullying your sister.'"

"Right."

"Even for you, this is ridiculous."

"Again, right."

"You know I can't . . . I can't do this for free. This is too much. I might be able to drape you in scales a second time without charging, because I know how much you hate the water, and that makes it a punishment as much as it is a gift. But you want me to do you a favor that involves risking myself, that I can't spin in any way that turns it into a cruelty." The Luidaeg glanced away, adding, in a softer voice, "Some days I wish I knew where she was, because then I could die trying to kill her for what she's done to me."

"I'm not a big fan of Titania's, either," I said. "Will you do it?"

"I'll need three things from you, if I do, and if you refuse me any of them, I give you nothing." She looked back to me. Her expression was agony. "I'm sorry. I'm fighting it as hard as I can, but I'm sorry."

"I thought you could charge whatever you wanted," I said, hating how afraid I was of whatever she might say next; hating the whine in my own voice. Not much scares me anymore. The things the Luidaeg could potentially ask for . . .

I remembered the look on Simon Torquill's face in the moment before she ripped his sense of home from his chest, and I was afraid.

"I can charge more than a thing costs, as long as the price is in harmony with the request," she said. "I could ask you to bring me the moon and the stars and not violate this geas, but I can't give you things for free that I can't spin around to being selfish. I've tried. It never works. Will you hear the fee?"

I could almost feel Tybalt staring at me. I squared my shoulders and said, "I will."

"All right." She sighed, a sound so deep that it seemed to rise up from the soles of her feet and shudder its way through her body. "First: when next I call on you to aid me, you can't refuse. No matter what I ask of you, no matter how little you want to do what I demand, you can't refuse. Your own magic won't allow it."

"Done," I said.

"Second: I want blood. When this is done, you will come to my home, and I will bleed you until a full day has passed or I feel satisfied with what I've taken, whichever comes first. You will not ask me why I want the blood, or what I intend to do with it. Good or ill or in-between, it's none of your concern."

I hesitated. Magic lives in blood. In Faerie, having access to someone's blood is almost as good as having access to the person themselves. By giving the Luidaeg my blood, I was giving her the ability to mimic or recreate almost anything I could do, including my ability to heal myself. I've been dead at least once, and probably more often than that, and the magic in my blood has refused to let me stay that way. What could the Luidaeg do with as much blood as she could strip from my body in a full day's time?

It didn't matter. Peter mattered, and Patrick and Dianda mattered, and ending this before it interfered with the salvation of the Selkies mattered. "Done," I repeated, with somewhat less force this time.

At least the Luidaeg didn't look surprised. She simply looked at me and said softly, "Third: I want you to bring Simon Torquill home. He's suffered long enough."

I jerked away from her like I'd been shocked. "Luidaeg . . . do you know what you're asking me to do?"

She smiled. There was no joy there. "I'm the one who helped him get lost. So yes, I do. I know exactly what I'm asking you to do."

Damn. I closed my eyes long enough to take a deep breath. Then I opened them and nodded. "Yes. I'll bring him home."

"I knew you would." She leaned to the side, looking past me. "Squire, kitty-cat, come. You'll both want to be here for this. Count Lorden, Duke Lorden, Marcia, Poppy, you all stay out here. If anyone from the Duchy comes to see how we are, make something up."

"Lie?" asked Dean blankly.

The Luidaeg nodded. "Yes, lie. Fiction is a great gift I no longer share, but which you may indulge in to your heart's content. Invent things. Spin wild stories and back each other up. No one's going to come to *me* for clarification; they're all too afraid I'm going to eat them." She turned her attention back to me. "Well? Why are you still standing there? *Move.*"

I moved. Tybalt and Quentin were close behind me, the three of us crowding into her apartment, which was the same small, cozy, maritime design as the ones we were sleeping in. The Luidaeg slammed the door once we were all inside, resting her head momentarily against the wood before she wrenched it open again, revealing her kitchen at home in San Francisco.

"Luidaeg," I said, carefully. "That's your kitchen."

"Yes," she said, stepping over the threshold and heading for the fridge. "Your point?"

Quentin and I exchanged a glance. "If you can summon your kitchen, why did we have to take a boat to get here?" I asked.

"Because I can't just snap my fingers and take away distance for no good reason; the magic doesn't work like that, and let's all be grateful," said the Luidaeg. "There have to be limits, even on the Firstborn. We can't be gods. The world would shatter and turn to dust beneath our feet."

"Some of you would be gods if they were allowed," said Tybalt.

"And all the ones who *would* be gods are the ones who *shouldn't* be gods. My kitchen is here because I need it to do my job, and that gives me the leverage to bridge the distance." The Luidaeg opened the refrigerator door and started rummaging around inside. "Last time I used one of Ketea's scales to manage the transformation, but that's not a good idea when I need your blood to remember that the form isn't yours."

"If it's not a good idea now, why was it a good idea last time?" I crossed my arms, fighting the urge to scowl. It was born of nervousness; I don't like it when people transform me into things. It didn't seem to matter that this time, I'd *asked* to be turned into something I wasn't supposed to be. It was still a transformation, and I still wasn't comfortable with it.

"You were more human last time." She pulled several bottles of fluid off the shelves and set them on the counter. One was white and sparkled like liquid starlight, one was so black it seemed to steal all light from the room, and the last was a swirling, pearlescent red, somewhere between blood and strawberries. "Humans don't understand what it means to lose themselves in a new shape. They're born in one body, they die in the same body, and all the changes they make to it are cosmetic. The bones remain the same."

"And?"

"And you're Dóchas Sidhe, children of the last Ride—and you have no idea what a relief it is to be able to *say* that, to not be waiting for you to figure out the right question to unlock your own family tree—and your blood knows how to become something it's not. Tam Lin isn't your grandfather, thank Dad, or you wouldn't be standing here now, but the magic my mother threw at him splashed onto your grandmother, and it changed her, too, somewhere deep beneath the skin, where the world couldn't see it. It's easy to convince you to be something other than you are. Simon Torquill would never have been able to turn kitty-boy there," she hooked a finger toward Tybalt, "into a fish for more than seven years, and Cait Sidhe are natural shapeshifters. With the brat, he'd have been lucky to get seven months."

"My grandfather turned a man into a linden tree for a hundred years," said Quentin.

"Trees are different." The Luidaeg produced a large glass bowl and began dumping her various liquids into it, doing the measurements by eye. "Trees are slow. A hundred years as a tree is less than a decade as something that has a heartbeat. There's a reason most punishment-through-transformation involves trees. Everyone gets to look impressive, and no one has to live with the long-term consequences of having a pissed-off enemy popping out of the decorative water feature. Toby, you got your knife?"

"Do you even have to ask?" I wearily produced the knife from beneath my skirt, holding it out to her hilt-first.

The Luidaeg raised an eyebrow. "I don't want it. You're all going to be bleeding for me in a moment. I needed to know we had a way to make that happen."

"All?" asked Quentin nervously.

"Well, kiddo, since your lady knight wants to go hang out in the Undersea like a big asshole, you're going to go with her." The Luidaeg flashed a toothy smile. "Call it a learning experience. You're going to learn why you need to get yourself a better knight if you want to live long enough to be High King."

I gaped at her. "I'm not taking *Quentin*."

"She's not *only* taking Quentin," added Tybalt. I turned my gape on him. He raised an eyebrow. "Don't look so offended, little fish. If you must go submerge yourself in a watery nightmare, it's my duty to be by your side."

"Hilarious as the idea of transforming you into a giant catfish is—and believe me, it's funny as fuck—no," said the Luidaeg. "You're here to provide the shapeshifter's spark to my spell and nothing more. I'm too protean to power this. You have two forms, and that's the number we need."

Tybalt narrowed his eyes. "I'm going with her," he said.

"No, you're not," said the Luidaeg. "If you try to negotiate for passage, I'll set the price so high that your own betrothed will stab you in the kidney before she lets you pay it."

"That sounds like me," I said. "But why? Why do I have to take Quentin, who doesn't want to go, and not Tybalt, who does?"

"She's right: I don't want to go," said Quentin.

"Because, currently, this is a two-way war," said the Luidaeg. She plucked a hair from the crown of her head and dropped it into the swirling liquid in the bowl. It dissolved with a faint hissing sound, and the smell of quinces spread through the room. "Land and sea, Divided Court against Divided Court. We're used to this. It hasn't happened often in the last hundred years, but oh, the war of wall and wave used to be practically a sporting event. Taking your squire with you means you'll have backup, and means he'll have a little more understanding of what he's going to be in charge of one day. Add a King of Cats, even one who isn't sitting on his throne, and you complicate things. You make them messy. You make this look calculated, like you were gathering allies before you even set foot in the Duchy of Ships. Trust me, all right? I know what I'm doing."

The liquid, for all her mixing, was still swirled in three colors, like the scales of a calico koi. I suppressed a shudder. "And you'll go find your sister?"

"Yes. I'll go find my sister, and do what I can to convince her to come back and rein in her descendants. I can't promise she'll listen, but I'll try." The Luidaeg sighed. "Now's when you bleed for me. All of you. Toby, I'm going to need a lot of blood from you; Tybalt, Quentin, I need seven drops. Each. Once that's done, the compact is sealed, and everything proceeds."

"What if I refuse?" asked Tybalt stiffly. "If you won't send me with my lady, perhaps I think she shouldn't go at all."

I swung around to stare at him. "You don't get to make that call."

"October—"

"No. *No.* You don't get to make that call. Not now, not once we're married, never. We can discuss things, absolutely. I can make an effort to tell you before I go throwing myself into mortal danger, sure. But you don't make that call, because that call is not yours to make. Peter Lorden is . . . best case, Peter Lorden is in a lot of trouble. He's a kid, and he's alone and he's scared and his parents can't help him, and maybe I can. So you don't get to decide for me. I'm a hero, remember? I didn't want to be, but I am, and that means when a kid is alone and scared and in danger, it's my job to try and make things better. If you think you get to make that call, we're going to have to have a conversation. And I don't think either of us is going to be happy with the results."

My heart was beating too fast and my skin felt too tight and everything was wrong, wrong, *wrong*. After everything Tybalt and I had been through together, the idea that he could try to stop me from saving someone, from saving a *child*, was—

It was—

I couldn't do this. If he really wanted me to walk away when Peter was in danger, I couldn't do this. And I couldn't do it if he only changed his mind out of the fear of losing me. We had to be in this together, even when it was hard, or we weren't really together at all.

Tybalt sucked in a sharp breath, pupils narrowing to slits. Then, slowly, he nodded.

"I've long since resigned myself to the idea that immortality will never be your saving grace," he said, voice even more formal and stilted than usual. "Not because of the human blood in your veins, but because you insist—you *demand*—the world be less unkind. One day, you're going to go up against something you can't conquer, and the only way I make my peace with this is by telling myself, over and over again, that when that day comes, I'll be there to fight by your side, to do whatever can be done to save you. It's not that I . . . I fell in love with a hero, October. I fell in love with you. I would never dream of asking you to change that essential part of who you are. I don't want you to stop fighting. I just want to be fighting with you."

"Right now, you fight by staying in the Duchy of Ships and protecting Patrick and Dean," I said softly, reaching up to touch his cheek. "They're going to need allies. Clever allies. Allies who can pull them into the shadows if Torin's guards come back. Can you do that for me?"

"Can you come back to me?" he asked.

"I can try," I said.

Tybalt nodded, glancing to the Luidaeg. "Lady sea witch, if you would grant me a moment's time?"

"Clock's ticking, kitty-cat, but you do you," she said.

He nodded, and turned back to me, and leaned in, and kissed me.

It wasn't a kind or gentle kiss. It was the kiss of a man afraid of drowning, already trapped by some relentless riptide and being dragged farther and farther from the shore. He kissed me hard and fierce and unrelenting, and I kissed him back the same way, both of us fully aware that this could be the last kiss we ever had the chance to share.

But then, we always knew that. Our lives weren't exactly safe, and one day, one of us wasn't going to come home. We were both panting when we broke apart. His pupils weren't slits anymore; they had widened until they almost consumed his irises, drinking in all the available light. I offered him a wan smile. He returned it, and together we turned to face the Luidaeg.

The blade of my knife was cool against the skin of my palm. I slashed downward, opening my flesh like a flower, and stepped into the Luidaeg's kitchen, positioning my bleeding hand above her bowl. She watched impassively until she could be sure I wasn't making a mess; then she plucked the knife from my hand and beckoned the boys forward.

"Kitty-cat first, then Quentin," she said. "Tick-tock, kids, times a'wasting. You've spent too much of it on your petty little feelings, and now you need to hurry."

Tybalt narrowed his eyes but stepped forward, watching impassively as she ran the already-bloodied blade of my knife across the tip of his index finger. He hissed a little at the pain, and she moved his hand over the bowl, squeezing out the required seven drops.

"Shapeshifter's blood, to make the changes voluntary; they'll need to move between sea and air until this is finished," she said, and released his hand. "Quentin?"

My squire swallowed hard as he stepped forward and held out his hand. The Luidaeg took it gently, and rather than slicing his finger, merely pricked it, holding it above mine.

"Don't worry, kiddo, I'm not keeping any," she said, in a tone that was probably meant to be reassuring.

The liquid in the bowl sparkled and fizzed as our blood mingled with what was already there. When she judged that it had had enough, she handed me my knife and pushed us both backward, turning to rummage in the nearest drawer until she produced two small bottles. They were the sort of thing a sailor stranded on a desert island might use to throw messages out into the shoreless sea, hoping that someday they would go where they were meant to be.

"Once you drink this, you'll have twelve hours," she said, dipping first one bottle and then the other in the bowl. The first bottle came up filled with liquid so dark a blue that it was almost black, shot through with veins of bright, burning gold. The second bottle . . .

The second bottle was for me. The liquid it contained was layered like calico scales, white and red and black, and I knew the shape and texture my fins would take when I drank it. My body remembered what Simon had done to me, would always remember, and whenever I went back to the water, I would go in tricolor autumn, painted like the koi I'd been.

The Luidaeg handed us our bottles, expression grave. "Twelve hours," she repeated. "You'll go to the water, you'll belong to the water, and you'll be cast from the water all within that span. If you're not on dry land when your time runs out, you'll get to experience the wonder and joy of drowning. Toby will probably survive, she'll just wish she hadn't. Quentin . . ."

"I'm not as sturdy; I get it," he said.

"Heroes raising heroes to do heroic bullshit since the dawn of time," said the Luidaeg, almost fondly. She poured the rest of her liquid down the sink. "All of you, get out of my apartment. I'll go seek my sister as soon as I'm sure you're gone. I don't want to see your faces again until you've had your dance with drowning."

I frowned. "Luidaeg—"

"Go!"

We went, out of the kitchen and back into her apartment in the Duchy of Ships, and then out of that to the courtyard where our friends and allies waited, impatient and afraid, to see how much we'd paid for a slim shot at salvation.

ELEVEN

"I COULD GO WITH YOU," said Patrick for the third time, his eyes on the bottle in Quentin's hand. His hands twitched, like he was considering the virtues of snatching the thing from my squire. "I know the way."

"It wouldn't work for you," I said. I wasn't sure of that—the Luidaeg's magic is strong enough to be surprisingly flexible—but I was sure her deal with me had been for myself and Quentin, not myself and Patrick. If he drank the potion, it might work, or it might do nothing, or it might somehow mystically cause my dose of the stuff to curdle and turn useless. If this was going to happen, it would happen according to the Luidaeg's rules. "Now come on. Tell me what else we need to know. What's going to be waiting for us when we get there?"

Patrick sighed heavily. "When you exit the Duchy and swim downward, you'll find the channels connecting the various Undersea domains to this neutral ground. It's how the Selkies were able to get here so quickly. The gate to Saltmist is marked with pearls and ancient teak carved in sea otters and kelp. Passing through it will deposit you at our borders. I don't know what Torin will have done with the guards. Normally, you'd be able to pass through the fields to the palace, and enter through the lowest doors. Right now . . . I don't *know*." He looked at me, briefly, openly hopeless. "They may have destroyed everything. They may have taken it all intact. I don't *know*."

"Then we'll find out." I gripped his shoulder, squeezing hard.

"Tybalt will take you back to the others. Trust him. Until we get back with Peter, it's his job to keep you alive."

"I take my job very seriously," said Tybalt. "You will be safe in my company."

"I don't care about my own safety," said Patrick. "Save my *son*."

"We'll do whatever we can," I said, and glanced to Tybalt. He offered me a small, tight nod, but didn't speak, only touched the leather jacket that hung, folded, over one arm. There was nothing left for us to say to each other, not until I had gone and come back. I returned his nod and turned away, offering Quentin my free hand.

"Now?" he asked.

"No time like the present," I said, popping the cork out of my bottle with my thumb. He did the same, even as he took my hand and laced his fingers through mine, holding on as tightly as he could.

Together, we stepped off the edge of the dock, plummeting toward the surface of the sea. The wind was cold and stung my eyes, sending my hair whipping around my face. I raised my bottle, exactly as we had planned, and gulped down its contents in the instant before my feet hit the water. The liquid was sweet and bitter at the same time, like cherries mixed with battery acid, or honey mixed with snake venom. My body revolted, trying to gag, to spit it out, but it was too late; I had already swallowed, and warmth was radiating out from my belly, filling me.

The speed of my descent was enough that when I finally hit the water, I just kept going, cutting a trail of bubbles down into the depths, until ten feet, fifteen feet, twenty feet of ocean stretched out above my head. Quentin was gone, his hand ripped out of mine by the impact. So was the bottle, returning to the bottom of the sea, which was probably where the Luidaeg had found them in the first place. They could wait there until she needed them again.

My lungs were starting to burn. I closed my eyes, fighting against the panic that was threatening to claw its way out of my gut and overwhelm me, and took a breath.

Water filled my mouth and lungs. I felt like I was choking, the familiar instincts of my body warring with the reality of what I was feeling: water flowing into the places where air had always been before, sustaining and preserving me. I took another breath. The panic began to recede. I opened my eyes, and the water was clear around me, as transparent as the world above. Fae have excellent night vision, and for the Undersea races, that extends to the ability to see a much greater distance underwater. Which makes sense, really. They need to be able to navigate in their watery home.

Something was thrashing six or so feet below, spinning in the water like it couldn't tell up from down. I shifted the angle of my torso, trying to remember the swimming lessons I'd received from Dianda the last time I'd done this. My body knew what to do, courtesy of the Luidaeg's enchantment. All I needed to do was get out of its way.

My flukes beat against the current, driving me downward as I kicked. I pressed my arms against my sides to cut down on the drag, noticing as I did that my clothes had changed along with the rest of me: my rag-cut dress was gone, replaced by a much simpler short-sleeved shirt, tied at the waist with a woven rope belt that also served as a scabbard for my knife. The Luidaeg really did think of everything, when the world gave her the time to think. Too bad it didn't do that more often.

As I grew closer to the thrashing in the water, my suspicions were confirmed: it was Quentin, transformed and panicking, twisting himself into a knot as his body told him he was drowning and he tried to claw his way back to the surface that refused to be in any single, predictable direction. As a Daoine Sidhe, he'd had the same basic density as a human; if he stopped swimming, he would float upward, aided by the air in his lungs. As a Merrow, or a magically-made bootleg of a Merrow, he didn't have that same buoyancy. If anything, he was designed to *sink*, to drop lower when he was in the kind of danger that left him unable to swim.

Real Merrow glow faintly when submerged, their scales generating a soft, luminous light. My scales didn't glow. That was fine. I already knew what they looked like. Quentin's didn't either . . . mostly. There were specks of gold buried in the midnight blue of his tail and streaking his flukes and the fins at his sides, like he'd been briefly dipped in molten metal. *Those* were glowing, more brightly than a real Merrow's would have, intermittently lighting up in dazzling streaks.

It was a pretty effect. I had no idea what it meant. I just knew I needed him to stop panicking. I swam closer, reaching out and grabbing his hands by the wrists. He stopped thrashing almost instantly, staring at me with wide, terrified eyes. There were streaks of gold in his normally blue irises. It was striking and strange. I smiled encouragingly, and he managed to summon a wavering smile of his own, although his eyes were still too wide. I guess "knowing I'm giving the sea witch consent to transform me" and actually experiencing it are very different things.

But then, I already knew that from experience.

I hooked a thumb upward, indicating the surface. We couldn't talk while submerged. Real Merrow have a separate language designed for use beneath the waves. It sounds like whale song, like a heartbreaking melody from another world. It's beautiful and elegant and complex and it spreads along the currents like ink through paper, and I had no idea how to even start. English doesn't have the right shape for use underwater.

To my surprise, Quentin shook his head and pointed outward instead, away from the dark shadows of the Duchy's support pillars, toward the gates that would take us out to sea, toward Saltmist. He wanted to get this over with.

So did I. I nodded my understanding, let go of his hands, and began swimming away, trying to let my body do what it already knew how to do. Quentin followed, surprisingly clumsy in his new shape. I rolled onto my back and half sat up in the water, watching him. He seemed to have the basics of kicking and fluke placement down, but the rest—where to put his arms, how to keep his hair out of his eyes—was escaping him.

I'd been clumsy the first time this had happened, but not *that* clumsy. Was that another side effect of being Dóchas Sidhe? I was easy to transform, but I also adapted more quickly to the changes? I couldn't decide whether that was a good thing or not. I could vanish into another species in an instant, undetectable, concealed.

Like I had when Simon had turned me into a fish and left me in the pond. Panic threatened to overwhelm me again. I was surrounded by *water*. I had scales and fins and there was water in all directions, pressing down on me, smothering me. This was a trick, this was all a trick, I was never going to go home, I was never going to stand on dry land again, this had all been a trick, I—

Quentin grabbed my shoulder, shocking me out of my spiral. I glanced at him. Concern was written clearly across his face, shining in his blue-and-gold eyes. I offered a wan smile in reply, and flashed a thumbs-up.

He didn't look like he believed it. Still, he let go of my shoulder—and my panic had had at least one helpful side effect: he was swimming more naturally now, allowing his body's new instincts to take over and move things where they needed to go.

I wished I had a camera. His parents were never going to believe this one.

The water lightened as we passed out of the shadow of the Duchy's foundations. We shifted to swim directly downward, descending with a speed that would have been unbelievable if we'd still been in our natural forms, even if we'd been using SCUBA gear to speed the process along. The pressure around us mounted without becoming unpleasant; it was like the entire ocean was taking us in a loving hand, holding us close and keeping us safe.

Fish flashed by, silver and blue and a thousand other colors, a fearless living rainbow that moved with casual nonconcern. I didn't see anything that looked dangerous. That was probably part of the ducal wards, keeping sharks and other predators at a distance. Did it apply to the more predatory Undersea fae? Merrow could be plenty dangerous when they wanted to be, and clearly the wards let *them* through. Maybe the wards were keyed to the absence of sentience, which implied some fairly complicated spellwork.

I was concentrating on something irrelevant to keep myself from dwelling on the fact that we were diving deeper and deeper into the literal ocean, moving away from light and air, and doing it while we had a ticking clock counting down the amount of time we had to do this safely. We couldn't move any faster, but I couldn't afford to freak out again.

Water and I are not friends. I was respectful of the stuff before I spent fourteen years as a fish, but that turns out to be the sort of thing that leaves a girl with a complex that verges on becoming a phobia. It wasn't that bad, thank Maeve. It was still bad enough to make me distinctly uncomfortable, and now that I didn't have Quentin's struggles to focus on, I needed to keep myself from getting wrapped up in the existential horror of it all.

The seafloor came into view, studded with homes shaped from water-treated wood and living coral. Fae moved in and around them, or tended the farmlands that dotted the open space between the structures. Some crops grew in open water. Others were enclosed in artificial atmospheres—the covered gardens Pete had mentioned before. They were growing everything from apples to potatoes, and they were doing it at the bottom of the sea.

Luna would probably have been fascinated. Then again, that would have required Luna to be speaking to me long enough for me to explain what I wanted her to see, and she hasn't been speaking to me for a while now. Not since I chose my daughter over hers; not since her daughter chose Daoine Sidhe over Blodynbryd; and certainly not since I'd asked that Sylvester allow me to wake his brother, only to lose him in the process of finding my sister.

Families are complicated. Other people's families are even more so.

We swam over the farmlands, and the gates Patrick had described began to appear, like giant funhouse mirrors tethered to the bottom of the sea by ropes carved from literal wood; oak and ash and rosewood and elm. Each was carved with its own pattern of oceanic images, fish I didn't recognize, sharks, sea dragons, even hippocampi. We swam on until we found the gate Patrick had told us to look for, carved with sea otters and kelp, ringed with irregularly shaped natural pearls. From one angle, it was just a ring in the water, simple, easy to swim through. From another, it was filled with a glistening mother-of-pearl film, betraying the presence of some lasting transportation gate.

I'd never seen anything like it. There are fae who can teleport, the Tuatha and the Candela. There are fae who can access otherwise impossible roads, like the Cait Sidhe and the Shadow Roads. But permanent gates? Maybe those had been possible once, when there'd been fewer humans and we'd had the space for larger workings, designed to span longer periods of time. Not anymore. Even in the Summerlands, things were too crowded, and the taint of iron was too omnipresent, clinging to everything humanity touched.

Down here, there were no humans. Pollution spread more slowly, and the dawn never reached the delicate foundations of the sealing spells. There was more time, for everything.

Quentin and I hung in the water in front of the gate for a long, solemn moment. Then we joined hands and swam through, together.

The transition was about as jarring as that of moving from the mortal world into a knowe that had been closed for years. Everything twisted around us, until it felt like we were on a roller coaster bent on separating us from our lunches and our sense of equilibrium. Even Quentin felt it; his hand tightened on mine, and when I glanced at him, he looked like he was considering the virtues of being sick. What would happen if he threw up in the middle of a bespelled gate?

I so did not want to know.

As quickly as it had started, the feeling of disorientation passed, and we emerged into warmer, brighter waters. We were closer to the coast. I didn't know how I knew that, but I did, just like I knew that the light slanting down on us from above had nothing to do with the sun, but was somehow a reflection of the health of the duchy as a whole. The king is the land in Faerie, and the Lordens had always done their best to do right by the land—or the waters— in their keeping.

Farms still spread out around us, but there were none of the airy domes, and the crops seemed to be, on the whole, both wilder and denser, forming veritable forests of sea pears and undulating kelp.

They were also utterly abandoned. No farmers tilled the soil; no farmhands gathered the ripe fruits; no children played hide-and-seek through the greenery. The fields we'd passed beneath the Duchy of Ships had been alive with the denizens of the Undersea. These were lush and healthy and ready for the harvest, and there was no one there.

Resisting the urge to draw my knife—for comfort, if nothing else—I descended through the water, gesturing for Quentin to follow. The palace stood in the distance, an elegant construct of stone and coral rising from the sea floor in gravity-defying spires and towers that would never have been possible on land. Smaller buildings clustered around the foundations, tucked safely behind lacy walls of living coral. We dipped lower and lower as we approached, until we were swimming along causeways that I suppose technically could be considered streets, although they weren't paved; the ground was sometimes decorated, sometimes cultivated in flowering plants or elaborate playgrounds, but it wasn't meant for walking on.

And still there were no people. I thought I saw motion in some of the windows we passed, but no one came out to either greet or attack us.

Patrick had said the people of Saltmist would have changed sides as soon as the palace was seized. I was starting to wonder how true that was. It was like we were swimming through a ghost town.

I had no idea how much time had passed since we'd gone into the water. I assumed it was about an hour, but I needed to err on the side of caution, given the circumstances. I picked up the pace, urging Quentin to do the same.

There were openings around the base of the palace, tight little tunnels designed for use by servants and household staff. Torin would never have demeaned himself to use them, or even to send his forces through them; according to Patrick, if we were going to find Helmi holed up with Peter somewhere in the palace, it would be in the storerooms of the lower levels. If they weren't there . . .

Saltmist was a Duchy. It spanned *miles*, and all that territory was unfamiliar. I'd been here once before, and most of my time had been spent in the palace. Quentin didn't even have that much to go on. If Helmi and Peter had been moved, or had fled, we were going to be hard-pressed to find them before our time ran out.

We were almost to one of those entrances when something moved, warning us we were not alone. I drew myself back in a hard stop, putting out an arm to force Quentin to do the same, and watched as what I had taken for a piece of masonry uncurled itself, becoming a Cephali man.

He looked like a Merrow from the waist up, and like an octopus from the waist down. The skin of both halves was lemon yellow, although large blue rings marked his octopus half. His hair was an even brighter blue, verging on neon. He looked at us warily, hands moving in a quick, interrogative gesture.

Shit. It made sense that there'd be some sort of sign language in the Undersea, for use when having every word broadcast for miles wasn't a good idea. But if I couldn't speak their verbal language, there was no way I could fake their silent one.

Cephali. Dianda had several Cephali in her employ, including the missing Helmi. *Here goes everything,* I thought, and mouthed, with exquisite care, 'Duchess Lorden sent us.'

It felt silly, like trying to perform a mime show where the price of failure was death. But slowly, the Cephali man nodded. He indicated Quentin with one tentacle.

I nodded back, with substantially more enthusiasm. 'Yes,' I

mouthed. 'Both of us. Looking for Peter.' Grammar seemed less important than getting my point across.

The Cephali man nodded again before withdrawing up the wall, into the shadows. The yellow and blue faded until he looked like part of the wall once again, just another piece of decorative molding.

We didn't have time to wait and see if this was a trick. I dove for the hole, Quentin close behind me, and tried to ignore the way the walls pressed in against us. There was always the chance that we were swimming into a dead end, catching ourselves like crabs in a pot.

I didn't think so. From everything I'd heard, Saltmist was considered a thriving Undersea domain, and part of that could be credited to Patrick's presence. Yes, being married to a Daoine Sidhe meant Dianda wasn't as socially high-ranking as she could have been, if she'd married another Merrow and kept to the standards of her own kind. But it also meant Saltmist was less cruel than it might have been. Her people *liked* her. They liked her family. They might not be willing to fight against Torin, but did that mean they were going to turn on the people who had taken care of them for so many years?

I didn't think so. And so I kept swimming, until I had to stop kicking my tail and start pulling myself along with both hands. Quentin was so close behind me that the top of his head kept brushing the sensitive edge of my flukes. I was almost grateful for that, since I couldn't turn around and check on him anymore, not with the walls pressing in around us. As long as I could feel him, we were okay.

Unless that wasn't him, and he'd been grabbed by one of Torin's people while I'd been swimming. I started pulling myself along faster, gripped by the need to see my squire. When we reached the top, we'd be all right. I'd be able to confirm that it was him, and we'd be all right.

There was no way to know how long we spent forcing our way through that tight, unforgiving space before my questing hand broke through the surface of a still pool and into the air. I grasped the pool's edge and pulled myself up, gasping as water ran from the gills on my neck and my lungs suddenly ached for air. That transition might have felt natural to a true Merrow, but to me, it was disconcerting in the extreme.

All things considered, the heavy object slamming into the back of my skull was even more disconcerting. Something cracked, bone giving way under the brutal force of the assault, and I dropped back into the water, which was suddenly veiled red with my own blood. Quentin thrashed below me, trying to pull me down. I pulled my flukes out of his grasp, keeping him from doing more than tugging.

The attack had come from behind. My skull was already healing, flesh and bone knitting back together with horrifying speed, and the blood in the water was focusing me, filling my nose and mouth as I breathed it in, creating an invigorating feedback loop. My strength is in the blood, even when it's my own.

Whatever hit me, it had been too wide and blunt to be anything other than an improvised weapon. Someone was trying to keep us out of this room. That was a good thing. Torin's guards had been carrying tridents, brutally pointed, with barbed, cutting edges. If I'd taken a trident to the head, I would be in a lot more pain. Logically, whoever had just attacked me wasn't one of Torin's men.

My head didn't hurt anymore. Here went everything. I turned around in the tight tunnel, so I'd be facing the direction the last attack had come from, and pulled myself up for a second time, spitting out water as fast as I could.

"Dianda sent me!" I said, once I could form words again. They still came out a little garbled by the water in my throat and lungs. "Dianda sent me to find Peter!"

The room was small, and dark, and lined with shelves, each of them filled to bursting with supplies that did better when kept dry, flour and sugar and beans and rice. There was even a shelf of what looked like office supplies, which made a certain amount of sense. The Undersea Kingdoms didn't exist in total isolation. They needed a way to communicate with the land, and paper messages sent by courier was probably easiest, as well as being fairly traditional.

A surprising number of fae nobles have email these days, mostly due to the efforts of Countess January O'Leary and her daughter, April. But there's always going to be a place for the traditional ways.

The room was also apparently unoccupied. I couldn't see any sign of the person who'd assaulted me before, although I was pretty sure I could see the weapon: a large box of pancake mix was near the edge of the hole, dangerously close to the water. I thought of the Cephali guard I'd seen before, the one who'd been able to blend into the wall until he decided he didn't want to. We weren't alone. We just *seemed* to be.

I closed my eyes, spat out the last of the water, and breathed in, tasting the air for traces of fae blood. Someone doesn't have to be actually *bleeding* for me to read their heritage; they just need to be close enough for me to pick up on their presence.

My first breath was all saltwater and the lingering scent of my own blood. My second blossomed bright with Cephali. Not Helmi—it wasn't a familiar flavor, for all that I recognized its source—but Cephali all the same.

"I know you're here," I said, opening my eyes and squirming farther out of the hole, until I was sitting on the edge. My scales glittered in the gloom. I tried to remember what Dianda had taught me about transformation, about knowing who I was and who I wanted to be and letting that be enough. The scent of cut grass and copper rose around me, faint but clear, and my scales melted away, replaced by my more familiar legs. My rag-cut skirt also returned, shorter now, stopping just above my knees. Well, that was efficient.

Carefully, I pulled my legs out of the water and stood, barefoot and unsteady on the storeroom floor. Quentin's head broke the surface a second later, hair slicked down and dark with water. I bent to offer him my hands.

"Come on," I said. "We're being watched, but it's cool. I think they're a friend."

"They tried to smash your head," he objected, coughing up water. Somehow, he managed to look dignified and elegant even with water running down his chin. Sometimes I hate purebloods.

"Sure, but whoever it is, they're protecting something really important, and they didn't realize it was me. There's no harm done."

Quentin looked dubious. "I don't like you acting like major head trauma is 'no harm done.' It would have been a lot of harm done if they'd hit me."

"And that's why I go first."

Quentin snorted, taking my hands and pulling himself up onto the edge of the pool. His scales gleamed in the open air, even more beautiful now that they were out of the water and thus not part of their environment. He eyed my legs with open avarice. "How are you standing?"

"Think about how it feels to stand, how it feels to have the body you know you're supposed to have, and then just . . . get up." I shrugged. "Sorry if that's not as helpful as it could be. I had Dianda to walk me through the process, and she was a little more accustomed to the idea than I am."

Quentin gave me a baleful look before closing his eyes and taking a deep, slow breath. Then, planting his hands on either side of the hole in the floor, he stood.

His legs had brought his pants with them when they came back. It was nice of the Luidaeg to consider our desire not to be running around an unfamiliar knowe filled with potentially hostile forces without any clothes on. He didn't get shoes either. I suppose the Luidaeg hadn't thought they were important enough to include them in her spell.

Quentin wiped the water out of his eyes as he transferred his baleful look to the rest of the room. "I wish whoever it is would just come out. I don't like sharing space with invisible people who've already attacked my knight."

"I don't think the Cephali have turned on the Lordens," I said. "Not yet, anyway. I guess they'd have to if Torin kept the knowe, but since we know that's not going to happen, they may be waiting to see. And keeping Peter safe, of course. Dianda entrusted Helmi with her younger son, and the Cephali have a strong sense of honor. They're going to protect the boy until they can't do it anymore."

I was making wild guesses, based on what I knew of Dianda's relationship to Helmi and what I knew about the Cephali as a whole. They're loyal, like the Hobs in the land Courts, but they're more militant than any of the household spirits I'd grown up with. They make their decisions based on the needs of their households and their lieges, and they're devoted to the people they choose to serve. Helmi was sworn to Dianda, not Saltmist, and that meant the rest of the Cephali might have chosen the same carefully-worded loophole.

Merrow, like the Daoine Sidhe, seemed to assume everyone wanted what the Merrow wanted, and thought like the Merrow thought. If I was right . . .

A tentacle uncoiled from the ceiling, already changing colors from chalky shadow-gray to a vibrant shade of green. A moment later, a Cephali girl dropped down to the floor, flipping over in midair, so she landed on her tentacles and not on her head. The octopus half of her body was bright green at the tentacle-tips, shading to a deeper shade of pine near the waist; the skin of her human half was a very pale green, like newly sprouted leaves. She was far too young to be Helmi, but she was armed, holding a wickedly jagged knife in either hand.

"You say you come in the name of the Lorden family," she said. "Prove it."

"A reasonable request, but I can't," I said. "Dianda has been arrested for treason, so it's not like she could give me a token to show you. Patrick and Dean are safe with allies. We're here for Peter. My name is October Daye. I'm the one who found Peter and Dean when they were kidnapped. I'm the former Countess of Goldengreen. I gave up my title so Dean could be Count, and we could solidify the alliance between our domains. I can bleed for you, if you can read the truth in my blood."

"Blood magic isn't a strength of the Cephali," she said. "All our bleeding is spent on growing back our limbs."

"Right," I said. Cephali regenerate. That's a good thing, since their usual response to disappointing the people they care about involves chopping off their own tentacles. "In that case, all I can give you is my word. By the root and the branch, I swear, we're not here to harm Peter. We're here to get him back to his family before someone else can hurt him."

"Who's the boy?" demanded the Cephali, nodding toward Quentin.

"My squire, Quentin," I said.

"He armed?" asked the Cephali.

"We're both armed," I said. "Come on. If you want to fight us, fight us. But if you want to see Peter Lorden safe and out of here until his parents can take their Duchy back, you need to take us to him."

The Cephali hesitated. I held my breath until finally, she lowered her weapons.

"Follow me," she said. "If we're caught, I'll slit your throats myself to show my loyalty to the invaders."

"Must loyalty always mean blood on the floor?" I asked, already stepping toward her. "All right. Let's go."

She eyed me warily as she moved toward the door, not walking so much as undulating, her tentacles gripping and releasing so she flowed across the damp marble like something out of a dream. Quentin and I followed silently, letting her lead the way. It would have been a stretch to say we trusted her, but we didn't have much of a choice. Time was short, for everyone.

I'm not sure how much of the average Undersea knowe is pressurized and filled with air. Because the Selkies are air-breathers, and several Undersea races are equally comfortable in both, I've always assumed air chambers were a standard feature: it's easier to sip wine and preserve royal decrees when you're not trying to do it underwater. The hall the Cephali led us along would have looked perfectly reasonable in Goldengreen or Shadowed Hills. It was laid out in a vaguely medieval style, its organic nature betrayed only by the places where the walls met the ceiling, which were gentle slopes of polished, bonelike coral rather than hard edges. The floor was pink; the walls were white; the décor was elegant, and almost managed to obscure the fact that the place had been grown rather than built.

"Is the knowe alive?" I asked, voice pitched low to keep us from being overheard.

The Cephali nodded but didn't slow. "Grown from a seed by the Duchess Lorden's grandmother," she said. "My parents helped protect it when it was young and small and could have been easily uprooted. Now, it will outlive us all and remember our bones when they fade into its roots."

Quentin and I exchanged a glance. It's one thing to know that attitudes about life and death are very different between the land and sea. It's another to hear a pureblood talking frankly about bones and mortality. Fae are supposed to live forever. That's how they're made. I'm a changeling, and I'll still live for centuries if no one figures out a way to kill me.

Things in the Undersea followed their own patterns. Sometimes that was more jarring than I would have thought possible.

Voices echoed up ahead. The Cephali jerked back, and looked over her shoulder to us. "*Hide,*" she hissed. Then she was swarming up the wall, changing colors as she went, until she was the same white as the coral around her, wrapping her body around a decorative light fixture and fading utterly from view.

I turned to Quentin. "Hide or fight?" I asked.

He bit his lip. "What happens if we hide and they find us?"

"We fight anyway."

"Can we try?"

I nodded. "We can always try," I said. I started to grab for the air, then paused. "You're the Daoine Sidhe. You should do this."

Quentin nodded tightly before snatching the air and pulling it toward himself, whispering rapid-fire, "Hickory dickory dock, the mouse ran up the clock. The clock struck ten, the mouse didn't care because rodents have no sense of time, hickory dickory dock."

The smell of heather and steel rose around us, so strong that I cringed. Surely anyone who came down the hall would be able to smell it and guess where we were standing. Quentin didn't look concerned. I tried to hold onto that. Daoine Sidhe are blood-workers and can detect the scent of a person's magic when it hangs in the air, but they're not as sensitive as the Dóchas Sidhe. If Quentin wasn't worried, we'd be fine. We were going to be fine.

We had to be fine.

The spell settled around us like a fine mist and Quentin disappeared, becoming a part of the wall, much as the Cephali had. If I squinted, I could almost make out the shadow of his outline, but it was difficult, and I was only getting that much because I knew where he was. If he moved while I wasn't looking, I'd lose track of him completely.

Good. A strong don't-look-here should protect everyone involved, even from each other. I pressed myself hard against the wall, getting as far from the center of the hall as possible, and drew my knife, holding it low and close against my hip. If we had to fight, I'd fight. I just hoped it wouldn't be necessary.

I'd barely gotten settled when three guards in Torin's livery came around the corner. Two of them were holding those nasty tridents from before; the third was peering at an oiled parchment map. I couldn't see the whole thing, but what I could see made me fairly sure that it was a map of the knowe. It had the right twisting, curving lines, and it looked like it had been treated to stand up to being submerged.

"There are eight storage rooms on this level," said the one with the map. "If we search them all, we can go back to someplace decent."

"Can you imagine having a palace this defensible and sacrificing half of it for *air-breathers*?" The second guard sounded utterly dismissive. "The county where I did my training had a single chamber set aside for the Selkies, and even that, they knew we could flood in an instant. Kept them in their places."

"Do you really think the Lady is in Ships?" asked the third, nervously. "Rumor says she's come to slaughter the Selkies for what they did. The water will run red, and we'll have to find new couriers."

"Or we could cut off communication with those lander fools entirely, and watch them tear themselves to pieces worrying about war," said the second. He chuckled. "Frightened fish, every one of them. They'll leave the coasts in droves once they realize they can't keep tabs on us any longer—and good riddance. The farther we are from those air-breathing weaklings, the better."

"I heard she was intending to resurrect the Roane," said the guard with the map. The other two turned to look at him. He raised his head and looked impassively back. "Didn't you wonder why the Selkies would be gathering in Ships, and not running for the deepest waters they could find to shelter them? She's not slaughtering them, she's empowering them. Uplifting them. The Lady is bringing back the Roane, and then they'll be bought by the strongest nobles, and we'll finally have the future in our hands again."

Right. That was quite enough of that. We didn't know where Peter was; we couldn't allow these arrogant, careless people with their sharp, sharp tridents and their nasty ideas to get to him before we did. I stepped away from the wall, aware that Quentin wouldn't be able to see me moving until he spotted the consequences of that motion. That was fine. He could catch up.

One nice side effect of healing the way I do: I've basically gone through a massive crash course in humanoid anatomy over the past few years, as people have stabbed, skewered, and otherwise damaged literally every internal organ I have, and a few I'm not sure actually exist. If there's a way to hurt a body, odds are good that I've experienced it, and that makes me uniquely well-suited to challenges like incapacitating three guards without bringing the rest of the invading forces down on my head. Being invisible didn't hurt either, in the moment.

Sliding my knife back into its sheath, I crept up on the two guards with the tridents. Neither of them was wearing a helmet. That would help. Knocking a person unconscious is a lot more difficult than most people assume it is, especially if you're set on doing the job without opening any skull fractures. I found that I was less concerned about skull fractures than I maybe should have been. Dianda had healers on staff, which meant right now, Torin had healers on staff; any damage I did, short of killing somebody, could be undone in short order.

After the things they'd been saying about selling the Roane to the highest bidder, they might be happier with a little head trauma than with me telling the Luidaeg what they'd said.

Silently, I reached up, taking advantage of my invisibility to align my hands at the perfect angles before I slammed the two guards' heads together. They shouted, startled and hurt by the blow, although neither of them went down. That was all right. I hadn't been expecting to take them out with a single hit, although it would have been nice. I slammed their heads together again before they could react, and this time the guard on the left reeled back, clearly injured.

The guard on the right spun around and stabbed her trident at the space where she assumed I was standing. She wasn't *wrong*. The don't-look-here, already strained by my interaction with the world around me, broke in a haze of cut grass and copper as the tines pierced my stomach.

The pain was incredible. I swallowed it as best I could, grabbing the trident and yanking it toward myself. That drove the tines deeper in, which was bad. It also caused the startled guard to lose her grip on the shaft, unable to handle what she was seeing. That was good.

"Someone call for a hero?" I asked, and punched her in the face.

Merrow are militant and violent and always ready for a fight. Dianda is considered a relatively peaceable example of her breed, and I'm pretty sure she'd challenge the wind to a brawl if she had the opportunity. But here's the thing about having a reputation as the biggest badass in existence: people mostly stop hitting you. I had never seen anyone with any sense try to start a fight with Dianda in what I would consider the smart way, by sucker-punching her before she had a chance to respond.

The guard reeled backward, blood gushing from her nose and

split lip. I grabbed the shaft of the trident and yanked it out of my body before the skin could start healing around it. Then I swung it as hard as I could, slamming the end of the shaft into the side of her face, just below her eye. There was a sickening cracking sound. Her eyes went wide before she collapsed, bleeding and motionless, on the hallway floor.

The other armed guard seemed to shake off his disorientation— or maybe he was just too angry to notice how dizzy he was. He bellowed and charged at me, trident lowered, like he thought he might have better luck skewering me than his partner had.

He never reached me. The Cephali dropped from the ceiling, landing on his head and wrapping her tentacles around his face, cutting off all air supply. He grunted angrily and clawed at her, only for her to wrap two more tentacles around his wrists. His struggles slowed and finally stopped, and he fell, not visibly bleeding, next to the first guard.

All this had taken less than a minute. Maybe that was why the guard with the map hadn't moved. He turned slowly, eyes gone wide and face gone pale, and I realized how young he looked. He didn't even look as old as the still-invisible Quentin . . . and he didn't have a weapon.

"Hi," I said. "We're from the other team. I have a proposal for you."

He swallowed hard. "I will not swear fealty to a woman I've just met," he said. His voice shook. I realized he thought I was Merrow, and that, as a Merrow, I was allowed to kill him if I wanted to, thanks to his own liege's declaration of war.

"Not what I'm looking for, so don't worry about it," I said, trying to make my voice as soothing as I could. "My squire—who's still invisible, and could be behind you right now, so don't even think about running—my squire is pretty good with knots. You give me the map, not because we need it, but because I don't want you to have it anymore. He ties you up and shoves you into a storeroom. When someone finds you, you get to tell them you fought just as hard as your friends here." I prodded one of the fallen guards with my toe. It would have been nice if the Luidaeg's spell had left me with my shoes.

"I refuse to sit by while my comrades in arms are killed," he said stiffly, and closed his eyes. "Do me this mercy, and kill me quickly, so I may be ready for the night-haunts to arrive."

I glanced at the place where I assumed Quentin was standing, wishing that he were visible, so I could see him roll his eyes. Then I looked back to the guard. "We're not killing anyone. We're here for Peter Lorden. Once we have him, we'll leave, and you can tell whatever story makes you happy. Be the hero who fought off twenty invisible attackers, or just say you kicked your friends' asses. I don't *care*. Give me the map, let us tie you up, and this ends."

He opened his eyes, looking uncertainly from me to the Cephali still sitting serenely on the other guard's face, and back again. Then he held out the map.

"Good choice," I said, and grabbed him.

It only took us a few minutes to get all three of the guards securely bound and chucked into the nearest small storage room, which was mostly filled with dried beans and packages of instant ramen. Quentin appeared in a wafting cloud of my magic as the last of the don't-look-here gave way. He picked up one of the ramen packages, wrinkling his nose.

"Really?" he asked. "There's so much *salt* in these things."

"I bet when you live at the bottom of a literal ocean, you don't care as much," I said, taking the ramen away from him and tossing it at one of the unconscious guards before closing the door. "We should have a while before the next patrol comes looking for this one. Let's move before we have to do this whole routine over again."

"How are you not dead?" demanded the Cephali, finally breaking her silence. "I saw them stab you. You're covered in blood."

"That's pretty normal for her," said Quentin. "Her fiancé is going to be pissed."

"Not if it all washes off in the water," I said. "There's no need to tell Tybalt I got impaled."

"Again," said Quentin.

"Again," I agreed.

The Cephali's eyes widened. "No wonder the Duchess Lorden chose you as allies," she said. "Not even she would want to face you in open waters."

"Oh, you'd be surprised," I said, and started walking.

Quentin paused long enough to pick up one of the discard tridents before he followed me.

The palace was designed in a series of gentle, organic spirals, which made sense, since it had apparently been grown from a seed coral, not built like the knowes I was used to back on land. I still got the feeling of patient presence from it that I got from the more familiar knowes; it was alive, if not exactly in the way quick-moving, hot-blooded creatures understood living.

If I'd thought it spoke the same language as the land knowes, I would have tried to plead with it for Peter's life. It's a weird trick, but one that's served me well in the past. Instead, I put a hand on Quentin's shoulder, saying, "Don't let me walk into any walls," and closed my eyes.

Blood magic can take many forms, and most of those are shared between the Daoine Sidhe and the Dóchas Sidhe. The Dóchas Sidhe just got them in a stronger form, because our blood magic isn't diluted with flowers. I opened my mouth as I walked, tasting and testing the air, trying to focus on the unique blend of Daoine Sidhe and Merrow that the Lorden boys represented. As far as I'm aware, that's a blending that has never happened before, in all of Faerie, and may never happen again, given how reclusive the Merrow tend to be.

I breathed in and tasted the steel and heather traceries of Quentin's heritage, which made so much more sense to me now that I knew his mother had been born a changeling and given up her human heritage in order to marry her true love. Steel had never seemed like a logical element of a pureblood's magic, but we carry our parents in our veins—sometimes even the pieces they, themselves, have chosen to give away. I tasted the Merrow guards behind us, and the Cephali, a delicate blend of sweet seagrass and something tart and salty that I automatically identified as plankton and filed away for future reference. My internal catalog of magical signatures defies proper description, and is filled with things I've never actually experienced.

I breathed in again, letting Quentin guide me down the hall . . . and there, under the heavier, more present scents, I found a thin thread of Merrow mixed with Daoine Sidhe. It tasted like stone-crop blossoms and young kelp, and I could almost follow those traces back to Patrick and Dianda, and farther, all along their family lines. I'd never gone looking for someone by dowsing through their parents before, and the possibilities were both endless and intoxicating. I shook myself loose, opening my eyes, and pointed down the hall.

"This way," I said.

Together, we hurried toward our destination, and I didn't say anything about the fact that, for me to pick up the scent that strongly, Peter must have been bleeding at some point. I just walked as fast as I could and hoped that I wasn't already too late.

TWELVE

THE HALL CURVED and the smell of Peter's magic grew stronger, until I could pick it up without even really trying. Then it began growing fainter again. I paused.

"Quentin, give me the map."

He held it out silently. I grabbed it, running my finger along the curves of the carefully drawn hallway walls until I was sure what I was seeing—or wasn't seeing.

"Look: there's a door every ten feet or so on this level. They're evenly spaced, probably because the coil of the architecture here supports it. This whole hall matches the map."

"So?" said our resident Cephali. "Maps should be accurate, or they're useless."

"So there should have been a door a few feet ago, and there wasn't." I walked back the way we'd come, studying the walls as I went, until I reached a patch that was a little too smooth, a little too regular, compared to everything around it. "It doesn't make sense for the architecture to start getting weird on us now, not when it's been this regular. Which means someone is trying to hide something."

"You think it's Peter?" asked Quentin.

"Can you think of a better explanation?" I touched the wall. It felt ever-so-subtly wrong, slick and almost icy under my fingers. I smiled. "Aw, good boy, Peter. Look, Quentin, put your hand here. Feel it?"

Quentin pressed his palm to the wall, face scrunching up in

concentration. Then he relaxed, slanting a smile in my direction. "It feels like flower petals."

It didn't feel like flower petals to me. It felt like a glacier, like something that was doing its level best to reject my presence. I wasn't going to argue. Quentin had flower magic in his veins, the same as Dean, and I had only blood. Of course things would feel different to me.

"Now, the sensible thing to do here would be to knock," I said, running my fingertips across the holes in my shirt. The bleeding had long since stopped and the flesh had long since healed, but there was still blood there, thick and ropey and coagulated. I slathered it on my fingers, then pressed my palm against the wall.

The shape of the illusion came into view, looking like a sheet of glittering threads woven into a fishnet formation. It was good, solid work. His father would have been very proud.

"Toby? What are you doing?"

"Untying a knot."

Seeing spells is another Dóchas Sidhe trait, although not the most useful of them, since I can't do it fast and I can't do it without bleeding and there's a lot of "can't" to balance out a relatively narrow amount of "can." But I *can* find the edges of an illusion, and when I find them, I *can* grab hold of them, hooking my fingers into the fabric of the spell itself. I can pull. I can pull until they come apart.

I tugged and the spell unraveled, illusion falling into the distinct, ashen smell of magic that had been dismantled by someone it didn't belong to. A door appeared in the wall in front of us, exactly like every other door in the hallway, except that this door had been magically concealed, and this door was between me and the faint, frustratingly appealing scent of Peter Lorden's blood.

Leaning closer, I knocked on the door and called, "It's October. I have Quentin and a Cephali whose name I don't know with me. We're coming in. Please don't stab us."

"If that works, that's how I want you entering every room from now on," grumbled Quentin.

"Ha, ha," I said, and opened the door.

It was another storeroom, this one filled with apples and potatoes and onions, piled in bushels that threatened to overwhelm the shelves they rested on. There were no visible people. I sighed.

"I know you're scared, and I know you've only met me once, so you probably don't trust me very much, but I promise, I'm here to help," I said. "Your parents are safe in the Duchy of Ships, Peter. I need to take you back to them. The sea witch gave me and my squire the ability to move through these waters without drowning, but the spell only lasts for so long, and we need to move. Whatever it is you need to hear from me, can you please pretend you've heard it already and come out, so we can get the hell out of here?"

There was a rustling noise from one corner before a tentacle uncurled, slowly shifting from nondescript gray patterned with blotches like a bushel of potatoes to the bright, sugary red of cherry cough syrup. The rest of Helmi uncurled a moment later, sliding to the floor and revealing a skinny boy with green-blond hair, enormous gray eyes, and a tail that shaded from slate gray at the hips to silvery-white at the flukes.

Peter Lorden stared at us, hiccupped, and began crying. He seemed angry with himself for not being able to keep the tears in, but that didn't stop them from coming. Helmi put her arms around him and glared, not at me or Quentin, but at the other Cephali.

"Your loyalties have shifted," she accused.

"The knowe has been taken," the Cephali replied. "We cannot raise forces against the Merrow; we would surely die. But we have not served them. They can't command what they cannot see."

"Okay, this is a great little window on Undersea politics and all, but can we maybe hurry up and skip to the part where you let us take Peter, please?" I spread my hands. "Dianda's been arrested, Patrick's panicking—and rightly so, since this all sucks—and I don't trust Torin not to order Peter's execution to solidify his own claim. So, please, if you could just come *on*, we'll get out of here."

"We?" Helmi looked surprised.

"Of course 'we,'" I said. "I'm not leaving you here for Torin's guards to capture. You serve your liege best by *going* to your liege. That goes for you, too," I added, to the Cephali at my side. "Hell, that goes for all the Cephali in Saltmist. If your people would rather hide than be forced to serve Torin, they can come with us to the Duchy of Ships." Hopefully, Pete wouldn't mind that I was offering the hospitality of her home to someone else's vassals. At the end of the day, I didn't actually care. Let her be pissed at me. I'd tangled with the Firstborn before. I could take it.

The unnamed Cephali stared at me for a moment before executing an elaborate bow that mostly involved her tentacles going in what seemed like an impossible number of directions at the same time. "My name is Kirsi," she said. "I am honored to meet you."

"Nice to meet you, too, and if that's not the right form, I'm sorry; we don't have time for a lot of etiquette," I said. Shifting my focus to Peter, I asked as gently as I could, "Do you feel up to changing forms? I know you've been dry for a while now, but this will be easier if we don't have to carry you."

"My . . ." He sniffled, wiping his nose with his forearm, exactly like teenagers the world over, before trying again: "My mom and dad are really okay? They're not . . . they haven't stopped their dancing?"

"Your father is fine, if worried about you; your mother has been arrested for treason, which isn't the same as 'okay,' but means she's probably causing a lot more problems for the people holding her than they expected. She'll come back with bruised knuckles and cracked ribs and a smile on her face." I forced a smile to my own face, trying to look as encouraging as possible. "Right now, you're the one we need to worry about. Your uncle Torin has Saltmist, and that means we have to get you out of here. Can you walk?"

Peter nodded, sniffling again, and pulled away from Helmi, standing at the same time. Most of his scales shimmered and fell away, or maybe shrank back into his body—it was impossible to tell, it all happened so fast. In less than a second, a skinny boy in rough homespun trousers was standing, still shirtless, where the Merrow teen had been. A few scattered scales shimmered on his wrists and ankles. Peter looked at me shyly, chin tilted downward, so he was staring up through the long fringe of his lashes. It was a soft, vulnerable expression.

He was still Dianda's son. I raised an eyebrow. "Are you planning to stab me, or just punch me in the throat?"

Peter allowed his chin to raise, softness becoming stubbornness in an instant. "My mother says never to trust anyone who's offering you something for nothing."

"Your mother is pretty smart that way, but trust me, this isn't something for nothing," I said. "I'm a hero of the realm in the Mists. That means anything that might disturb the Kingdom's peace is my problem. We *like* having your parents in charge of Saltmist. They're allies, and they don't attack us for no reason. I don't trust your uncle to show the same restraint. I also don't trust your mother not to start breaking spines if she finds out you've been hurt. Saving you is the best way for me to keep my kingdom calm."

Quentin shot me a sharp look, seeming offended by my pragmatic approach to rescue. Peter, on the other hand, looked relieved.

"All right," he said. "I'll come with you."

I smiled. "Great," I said. "Let's go."

Helmi had been forced to grab Peter and run when Torin's forces came spilling into the knowe: there hadn't been time to collect any of his belongings. That would make things harder eventually, but for right now, it made things somewhat easier: we didn't have to collect or carry anything. We just had to run.

So we ran.

Five of us, fleeing down a hall that technically belonged to the enemy, past closed storeroom doors, past the scuffs and blood on the floor that marked our battle with Torin's guards. Helmi stayed with Peter, but Kirsi took to the ceiling, somehow keeping up with the rest of us as her tentacles roiled, one over the other, propelling herself along at a seemingly impossible rate.

We were almost to the storeroom we had entered through when another Cephali dropped from the ceiling and the five of us stopped dead in our tracks.

He was larger than Helmi or Kirsi, larger than any two of us put together: if the Undersea had a wrestling foundation, he was probably their star attraction. He had a neck as thick as my thigh, and heavily muscled arms that promised a world of pain to anyone who got within reach. That didn't touch on his tentacles, which were even thicker than his neck at their bases, or the trident in his hands. His smile was thin and cruel, the expression of a man who had been held in check for too long.

Helmi hissed—actually hissed, like water flicked onto a smoking hot pan—and pushed Peter behind herself, falling into a defensive position. Kirsi dropped down from the ceiling, joining the blockade.

The Cephali man laughed. It was a deep, rolling sound, and it set my teeth on edge.

"I had wondered where my kin were swimming when none of you came to our new Lord's command," he said, in a voice even lower than his laughter. His skin was a deceptively cheery shade of baby blue, darkening along the length of his limbs, so that his fingers and the tips of his tentacles were cobalt-dark, like they'd been dipped in someone's inkwell. "Have you lived in peaceful waters for so long that you've forgotten what it means to follow a proper warlord? Duke Torin will lead us to greatness, if we allow him to do so."

"Usurper Torin will lead us to blood and the battlefield," spat Helmi. "He'll leave us in pieces for the sharks to swallow, and cry that we died for the greatness of the Merrow. Who cares for the greatness of the Merrow? Titania is *gone*. There's no reward to gain for following them into dark places. There's only death, and we were made to be immortal. Maeve won't praise us for laying our lives down in service to her sister's descendants."

"Titania isn't the only one missing," said the man. "Maeve hasn't been seen in centuries. If there's no reward for what we do, then what we do must be its own reward. I would prefer to be rewarded with battle."

"Peter, stay behind me," hissed Helmi.

I stepped forward. "Yeah, no," I said. "This is stupid, and I'm not playing."

Silence fell. The man slowly turned to frown at me, squinting as he realized he didn't recognize me and couldn't tell precisely what I was. I might be able to fool a casual onlooker with my vague air of Merrow-ness, but this Cephali had presumably been serving the Lordens long enough to look at me and know I wasn't what I seemed to be. Without the gills, I could have passed for a particularly drab Daoine Sidhe. As it was . . .

"Who *are* you?" he demanded.

"Sir October Christine Daye, Knight of Lost Words, sworn in service to Duke Sylvester Torquill of Shadowed Hills, named hero of the realm by Queen Arden Windermere in the Mists, here in the name of Duchess Dianda Lorden, rightful ruler of Saltmist, to recover her youngest son, who has been detained against his will by her brother, who has no claim to her demesne." I somehow managed to make the recitation of my titles sound almost bored. Gold star me.

Jutting one hip out to the side in a nonchalant posture that anyone who knew me well would have recognized as a sign of trouble to come, I folded my arms and looked the Cephali languidly up and down before lifting an eyebrow. "What are you supposed to be?" I asked. "The wall we have to scale to get to freedom? Because trust me, I'm not in the mood for rock climbing right now. How about you go do something else, and let us walk away nice and easy?"

He sneered. Actually sneered. It was a pretty good display of arrogance and misreading the situation, if I did say so myself. "Out of my way, vermin," he snapped. "This is between me and the traitors."

"Wow, 'traitor' is a moving target around here, isn't it? See, where I come from, the people who are defending the son of the rightful regent aren't the traitors, they're the heroes of the hour. Quentin?"

"Um, yes?" My squire sounded uncertain. I couldn't blame him for that. I was so far off-script at this point that I might as well have been part of an entirely different production.

That was the plan. If even my allies were off balance, the people who were supposed to be fighting me would have absolutely no idea how to handle themselves. "Can I have that big fork you took from the patrol we beat the snot out of?"

The Cephali man glowered, his tentacles curling closer to his body in a move I could only interpret as enraged. They lightened at the same time, that inky shade of cobalt retreating to their very tips.

"I bet they didn't get the Smurfs down here under the Pacific, but trust me, you look like a giant angry Smurf right now, and it's not helping you look impressive." I stuck my hand out. To my immense relief, Quentin slapped the shaft of his borrowed trident into it. "How about we dance, big guy? Just you and me."

"I don't honor vermin with my strength," he rumbled.

"I'm not vermin," I replied. "I am a knight of the Divided Courts—which means, right, the Court that includes the Undersea. You've listed no titles, bucko, which probably means you don't have any. I *outrank* you. If I *am* vermin, that means you're below vermin. You're less than the thing you sneer at. If I'm not vermin, maybe your honor survives the day. Either way, you and me, we're going to do this."

He looked, briefly, confused. "You lack the authority—"

"What I lack in authority, I make up for in big pointy things." I leveled the trident on him. "Come on. Let's go."

I could hear the others shifting behind me, uncertain about exactly what was happening. Quentin would catch on soon, if he hadn't already. He's been with me for long enough to understand that my seemingly suicidal actions almost never are—and that even if they were, it wouldn't stick. I may not be unkillable, but I'm hard to put down for more than a few minutes.

The Cephali continued to look unsure. So I stabbed him in the nearest tentacle.

He bellowed, raising his own trident and jabbing it toward me with a speed and force born entirely of fury. Reasonable fury, even, since he hadn't come here expecting a strange woman from the land Court to stab him. I dodged his blow, wrenching my own trident free, and stabbed him again.

"You can do better than that!" I shouted. "What are you, a guppy?"

He didn't look like he understood the insult. Oh, well. Guppies are freshwater fish, but I'd still considered it to be pretty good. He stabbed for me again, and I danced backward, keeping his attention on me.

"Do they not teach you to fight here in the Undersea?" I jeered. "Have we been worried about invasion all this time for *nothing*? Gosh, wait until I go home and tell the Queen. She'll be so relieved."

He howled and stabbed for me again. This time, I didn't dodge fast enough; one of the tines scratched my upper arm before I could get out of the way, opening a line of pain along the slope of my bicep. I didn't yell. I refused to give him the satisfaction. Instead, I danced away again, glancing to the side as Helmi swarmed up the wall, Peter clutched firmly in her arms.

Cephali don't think about gravity the way most people do. They don't consider it optional, like the air fae, but they do consider it negotiable, and are equally happy sticking to the floor or the ceiling. If my unwitting opponent wanted a chance of beating me, he needed to stay on the floor—an attempt to go up the wall would end with him getting my trident in the side. But that meant the ceiling was clear.

Helmi and Peter dropped down behind him as Kirsi and Quentin started up the wall. They had less of a size difference between them. Quentin clung to her neck, and she kept one arm around his waist, keeping him from throwing her too severely off balance as they climbed. I swallowed my smile and stabbed at my opponent again.

"Hey! Asshole! That the best you got?"

He roared, fury and embarrassment and confusion all warring for ownership of his tone, and stabbed at me again.

Maybe it was carelessness or maybe it was exhaustion, but either way, this time, I didn't get out of the way. The trident caught me right below the rib cage, slamming into the soft tissue of my body with sufficient force to pierce multiple internal organs. The pain was immense and dizzying, making the entire world flash momentarily white. I made a startled, agonized sound, unable to stop myself.

Above me, Quentin tensed. The Cephali man gloated, openly gloated, and began to twist his trident hard to the right.

"Not so cocky now, are you, *vermin*?" he asked, grinning widely enough to show me every single one of his teeth. "You should have known better than to challenge a Cephali warrior. You should have known better than to think that you were *worthy*."

Things inside me were ripping and tearing. Behind the man, Peter stood, drawing himself to his full, if still-diminutive height. His eyes sparked, the air around him growing heavy with undefined magic, and for the first time, I could see the echoes of his mother in the lines of his face. If Dean was Patrick's son, Peter was Dianda's, perfectly matched to her quiet fury and unrelenting willingness to break the world to get her own way.

"Remember, Sir Daye," he said, and every word was quiet, and every word carried down the hall like a proclamation of the end of days. "We're at war right now."

The Cephali man twisted his trident harder, so that I felt things rip and come loose inside of me. I ground my teeth, tasting blood, and did the only thing I had left to do.

I'm sorry, I thought, and shoved my trident into the Cephali's throat.

He stopped moving, eyes going wide with a combination of shock and pain. Blood gushed from the wound, spilling everything he was and could ever have been onto the hallway floor. He made a strained gurgling sound before twisting his trident again, with less force this time, like he was determined to take me with him. Like he knew there was no winning, not anymore. There was only the chance, however slim, that he wasn't going to lose alone.

Pain flared from the wound in my stomach, and before I could fully consider what I was doing, I twisted my own trident, opening the wound in his throat even further. He gasped, unable to get sufficient air to scream.

Then he collapsed, hands sliding off the shaft of the trident, leaving it embedded in my gut.

I dropped my weapon and fumbled to get a grip on the blood-drenched wood of his, grasping it tight and yanking it out of me, along with a great gout of blood and some shreds of flesh I didn't want to think about too hard. The pain of removal was almost worse than the pain of insertion; I dropped to my knees in the gore, bracing myself on my hands as I waited for the world to stop spinning. The characteristic itch of mending flesh came from the wound. I knew if I looked, I would see my own body industriously knitting itself back together, ready to take more abuse.

Sometimes I wonder whether my general lack of self-preservation is a side effect of knowing that nothing can keep me down for very long, or whether it's part and parcel of being Dóchas Sidhe. Even before I knew how powerful my body's ability to heal itself was, I'd had a tendency to throw myself over the nearest cliff and try to pick a fight with gravity.

Chicken and egg questions give me a headache.

"Toby?" Quentin sounded awfully far away, but that was probably a consequence of all the blood loss. "Are you okay?"

"I will be in a second," I said, trying to sound encouraging. I have fortunately had a great deal of practice sounding encouraging while covered in my own blood. "Is anyone else hurt?"

"You fought like a fool who thought themselves a sacrifice," said Helmi. Somehow, coming from her, it wasn't an insult. She sounded genuinely awed. "No warrior of the land has ever been willing to risk themselves so for one of the water."

"I want to be there when you tell Patrick that." I pushed myself back to my feet, using the wall for balance when the world spun.

Helmi scoffed. "The ducal consort is a good man and a better father, but he's no fighter. He never has been."

"Semantics." I took my hand off the wall. The world spun again, but this time Quentin was there to keep me from toppling over. Why did I ever resist having a squire? They're so *useful*. "We need to get out of here."

"We're at war," repeated Peter, entirely too calm for a teenager who'd just seen a man stabbed in the throat until he died. Like mother, like son. "You haven't broken the Law, Sir Daye. My parents will reward you for this."

"Okay, see, that's a weird thing to say and I don't like it, but that's not why we need to get out of here." I started moving, keeping my grip on Quentin's shoulder. The wound in my stomach was almost healed, but the itching hadn't stopped, for all that it was mostly beneath the surface now. That made it almost worse. When my skin itches, I *can* scratch it, even if I'm sensible enough to choose not to. When it's my liver that itches . . .

Complaining that my ability to heal from injuries that should be fatal isn't comfy enough feels sort of like a jerk move. That's never stopped me before.

Together, we made our way down the hall to the storeroom where we had entered. It was thankfully still unoccupied; if any more of Torin's forces had come down here looking for us, they hadn't seen the signs of our arrival, and hadn't decided to stop and lie in wait for our return. The surface of the pool that led to the outside was untroubled, inviting us back into the depths.

I hate swimming. I eyed the water mistrustfully as I said, "Okay. Quentin and I don't speak whatever language it is you use to communicate underwater; once we dive, we're basically going to be incommunicado. You need to follow us to the gateway to the Duchy of Ships. The Luidaeg isn't there right now, but she'll be back soon, and she'll be pissed if I come back without you after putting her to all this trouble. If you have any questions, ask them now."

Peter, Helmi, and Kirsi all stared at me, united in their stunned silence. Bands of color washed across the two Cephali, briefly tinting their skins in sickly pallor.

Peter was the first to find his voice—there was his mother's influence again, teaching him that rushing in was always better than the alternative. Eyes wide and round, he whispered, "You're taking us to see the *sea witch*?"

This thing where the Undersea was still radically impressed by her would have been charming, if I hadn't been trying to get them into the water and out of the knowe before someone noticed the mess out in the hall. I'd just killed a man. Yes, he'd been trying to kill me at the time, and no, I wasn't sorry I'd done it, but wow did I want to get out of here before the night-haunts came.

"I'm not taking you to *see* the sea witch," I said, with as much patience as I possessed. Which was, admittedly, not as much as I might have liked it to be. "I'm taking you to the place where the sea witch is currently planning to be. She doesn't have a lot of patience under the best of circumstances, and trust me when I say that these are not the best of circumstances. Are there any other questions?"

There weren't. Peter gave me a small nod, his jaw still clenched and his eyes still wide, and I stepped into the open circle of water in the floor, and let the ocean take me.

THIRTEEN

THE TRANSFORMATION WAS NO less nerve-racking the second time. It was still someone else's magic dictating the shape of my body, pulling me into a new form and fixing me there, like a butterfly trapped under glass; it was still dropping me into the crystalline depths of my worst fears and leaving me there. I grasped the walls of the narrow tunnel, pulling myself toward the distant promise of freedom. Which, weirdly, helped a lot.

When Simon transformed me into a fish, he'd gone all the way, leaving me without hands or arms or any way to communicate. Even here, silenced by the sea, I could gesture to get my point across. Quentin, at least, would recognize what it meant if I showed him my middle fingers. And that meant I wasn't as cut off from the world as my increasingly panicked thoughts were trying to make me out to be.

The journey through the supply tunnel seemed to take longer this time than it had before, maybe because the urgency was even greater. Time was short—the Luidaeg's spell would have to wear off eventually, and I doubted we had more than a few hours left—and more, there was a mess in the hall that would tell Torin's guards something was wrong. We had to hurry. I hadn't come this far to fetch Peter only to lose him before I got him back to his father.

I was the first to emerge from the hole in the side of the knowe. My flukes were still inside when someone grabbed me by my hair and whipped me around, slamming me into the coral wall. I began to push myself back into open water, ready to fight, only for my attacker to press the tip of a jagged blade against my throat. I froze.

Blood in the water means sharks, means setting off alarms, and even if it won't kill me, having my throat slit isn't my idea of a good time. I stared, wide-eyed and furious, at the Cephali hovering over me. It was the man from before, pale yellow with blue rings, and his expression was unreadable, impassive and calm. Had he been waiting for us to return all this time? I suspected he had.

Quentin came out after me, and froze when he saw the situation. I had no way to signal him, but he seemed to realize what he had to do, and whirled, clearly intending to block the others from coming out.

He was too slow. Helmi pushed through, followed by Peter and Kirsi. All three of them stopped for a moment, staring at the Cephali man whose blade was still pressed—uncomfortably tightly—against the skin of my throat. Then, with a wordless sound that carried through the water, formless and echoing, Helmi threw herself into his arms.

My attacker was good; he didn't drop the knife. Instead, he transferred it to one of his tentacles while he caught Helmi, plucking her out of the current like she was a leaf blowing along on a stiff breeze. He gathered her into a complicated hug that involved at least six limbs on both their parts.

Then she slapped him.

He recoiled, looking startled and confused. She pulled back, pointing to me with one hand while three of her tentacles twined together in a complicated motion that couldn't have been anything other than purposeful, an impression that was only reinforced when the man's tentacles did something similar, if not precisely the same. Kirsi stayed where she was, holding Peter back while the two other Cephali argued.

The man pulled the knife from my throat. I reacted immediately, bringing my tail up and whacking him in the stomach as hard as I could. The reason Dianda depended on that move so much was immediately apparent, as the blow shoved him away with surprising force. He tumbled, not losing his grip on Helmi. I pulled my knife, ready to fight—

—and stopped as I realized he was laughing soundlessly. They both were, like this was the funniest thing they'd ever seen. I narrowed my eyes, glaring. They kept laughing.

Whatever. I've been mocked by better than a few octopus-people, and the longer I hung here having my feelings hurt, the less time we had to get back to the Duchy of Ships. I flicked my fins at him and spun in the water, taking advantage of the lack of gravity to return to Quentin and the others.

Kirsi shot me an amused look. I ignored her, motioning for Quentin and Peter to follow me. They did. Kirsi fell in behind them. Helmi and the stranger fell in behind *her*, and we swam as fast as we could back toward the gate that would see us safely out of these waters.

In Faerie, the king is the land. That's not just a pretty phrase: it's a reality of the way the magic that anchors us to the Summerlands works. A noble can control the weather, the season, even the overall feeling of their demesne. A forest that seems creepy and unwelcoming in the hands of one noble may be airy and open in the hands of another; a place where it never stops snowing may blossom into eternal summer when the head that wears the crown is changed. How extreme the effect is depends on how tightly the landholder is tied to the land. It would take time for Saltmist to adapt completely to being held by Dianda's brother.

But it was already underway. It felt like the water was getting colder, like it was rejecting our presence. The fields still grew green, but there were strands of what looked like an underwater species of briar growing around their edges, reaching upward with thorny, gravity-defying tendrils to catch and claim anything that came too close. We swam by one of the thicker brambles and I saw fish trapped inside, impaled and motionless, their bloodless bodies left by circumstance to rot.

Peter shivered, swimming faster, until he was pacing me through the water. I expected him to pull ahead, but he didn't. Instead, he matched the motion of his tail to mine, pacing me, so I'd be able to protect him if something attacked us. I blinked, surprised, and barely resisted the urge to glance back and see how his Cephali guard had taken this change. There wasn't time. Anything that could slow us down was something to be avoided.

Then the gate was there, appearing out of the gloom like the welcome anchor that it was. I grabbed Peter's hand, ignoring his startled look, and swam even faster, pulling him with me into the glimmering disk.

The world dipped, whirled, and spun, remaking itself as something new. Nausea threatened to overwhelm me. Before it could, the water warmed around us, suddenly pierced with brighter shafts of shimmering sunlight that couldn't possibly have been visible this deep, not according to the rules of the mortal world. Faerie works differently, thank Oberon.

I let go of Peter, who looked frantically around before kicking as hard as he could, arrowing toward the surface like a shot. I took off after him, unwilling to lose sight of him when we were this close to our goal. "I had your son, but I don't know where he went" wasn't the sort of thing that was going to play very well with the Lordens. I didn't know what Patrick's breaking point actually was. This wasn't how I wanted to find out.

Peter swam, and I followed, and Quentin followed me, and the Cephali followed *him*, until together we sketched an arrow across the slope of the sea, six people fleeing from an uncertain future, heading for the questionable safety of a duchy that could still decide that Torin had been in the right to do what he'd done. A duchy filled with anxious Selkies and inscrutable Firstborn and seriously, there are days when I feel like I need a vacation from my life. Is it too much to ask for things to stop being hard for just a few hours? Please?

The shadow of the Duchy of Ships cut through the water, seeming to loom out of nothingness with a speed that shouldn't have been possible. Then the long chains of the anchors and the thick sweeps of the pylons were all around us, turning the formerly open waters into an obstacle course. There were no guards. Pete apparently trusted her people to take care of themselves, and didn't see any point to holding off an invasion that was never going to happen. I couldn't decide whether that was arrogance or confidence. For the Firstborn, I guess the difference doesn't matter as much as it does for the rest of us.

Peter broke the surface first, propelled by his own anxieties. I was close behind. I took a gulping, almost involuntary breath when I broke back into the air. Quentin did the same. The Cephali were more decorous, rising silently, their tentacles curling around them. Then we were looking up at the smooth wooden side of the Duchy, and Poppy was looking back at us, one orange-skinned arm raised in a vigorous, amiable wave.

"There you are!" she chirped. "I was getting worried you wouldn't come back before everything ran out and you drowned yourselves dead, bones at the bottom of the sea and everything!"

Peter looked nonplussed. I nudged him with my shoulder.

"That's Poppy. She works for the Luidaeg, and she's as close as you can get to harmless without becoming a parody of yourself." Cupping my hands around my mouth, I called up, "We need something to help us get out of the water! I don't think I can focus enough to go back to having legs while I'm still wet!"

"We will help," said Helmi gravely, and proceeded to begin climbing the side of the ship, her tentacles pulling her easily along while her upper body remained as graceful and seemingly motionless as a noblewoman making her grand entrance during a summer ball. The male Cephali followed her, and the two of them ascended with apparent effortlessness. Kirsi remained behind, hanging protectively in the water next to Peter.

"I wish *I* could do that," said Peter. "Cephali get to have all the fun."

"Can't argue, kid, although I, personally, will be happier when I have knees again," I said.

Quentin didn't say anything. He'd shifted in the water, until he was so close to me that our shoulders were almost touching. I glanced at him, frowning at the hint of dark confusion in his eyes. Something was really bothering him.

Well, there'd be time to figure out what it was later, when asking didn't mean involving his boyfriend's little brother in whatever he was feeling. Quentin would tell me if he felt like whatever he was dealing with would interfere with him performing his duties as my squire. As long as he didn't say anything along those lines, I could give him space until we could sit down and talk about it privately.

Helmi reached the top and vanished over the rail, followed a moment later by the man—I was really going to need to learn his name before too much longer. Poppy stepped back, out of sight. Peter made a small, unhappy noise. I flashed him a quick smile.

"It's okay, bud," I said. "Your dad's going to be thrilled when he sees you're safe. He wanted to come with us, but we convinced him not to."

"Why?" he asked, a whine in his voice that betrayed his still-heightened anxiety. I couldn't blame him. Being held hostage twice before you turn sixteen has got to be hell on the nerves.

I shrugged. "I'm scared of your mom," I said.

Peter cracked a smile.

"What? It's true! I like her a lot, she's great and everything, but she's also terrifying, and I'm not doing *anything* that might upset her. Taking your father on the kind of adventure that might get him killed would definitely upset her."

"You took him," said Peter, pointing at Quentin.

This seemed like a strange place for this conversation, but whatever; it wasn't like we could go anywhere before Poppy and the others tossed us a rope. "Quentin is my squire," I said. "That means it's my job to take him places that might kill him, at least until he's learned everything I have to teach and can go off to be a hero in his own right."

"Not a hero," said Quentin hastily. "I never want to be a hero."

"I didn't exactly sign up for this," I said.

He rolled his eyes but didn't say anything.

Peter, on the other hand, looked almost excited. "So Quentin won't be your squire forever?" he asked. "You're going to need a new squire one day?"

A horrifying possible future unfolded in front of me like the petals of a large, potentially carnivorous flower: one where, as soon as I was no longer responsible for the care and well-being of the next High King of the Westlands, I had to start taking care of the younger son of the Duchess of Saltmist.

"No," I said firmly. "Quentin was a special case, and I only agreed to take him on because my liege was the one who asked. Once he graduates, I'm done with squires. I'm bad for their health."

"Oh," said Peter. Any potential protest he might have made was cut off a beat later, when a rope ladder dropped from the side of the ship and splashed down right in front of us.

"Come on up if you're coming!" shouted Poppy, leaning over the side and waving enthusiastically. "You've missed buckets and buckets of nonsense!"

Of that I had absolutely no doubt. "You go first," I said, to Peter. "Kirsi, go up with him, make sure he doesn't lose his grip or something."

"Of course," she said. The Cephali guided Peter to the ladder, wrapping the tip of one tentacle delicately around his wrist and guiding it to the lowest rung. He gave her an amused look and began pulling himself up, at first by upper body strength alone, and then, as his magic shimmered around him, putting his legs into it.

I waited until he was about halfway up, Kirsi pacing him on the hull, before I nudged Quentin. "Go on," I said. "Get moving."

"What about you?" he asked.

"I'm pretty sure that, as your knight, I'm literally obligated to stay down here until I'm sure you're not going to fall," I said. "Call it acclimation therapy. Maybe if I float in the middle of the ocean for long enough, I'll be able to enjoy hot tubs again."

Quentin snorted and began climbing. I watched carefully. To be honest, my reluctance to go before him had also been born partially from the desire to see how he managed the transition between shapes. The Luidaeg's spell gave us some of the instincts and abilities of the Merrow, but it hadn't come with an instruction manual: while I knew how to change my fins into feet when I was sitting with my butt solidly on dry land, I had no idea how I was supposed to accomplish the same feat while totally surrounded by water.

The last time this happened, I'd been able to get Danny to pull me onto the dock before I tried to change. That wasn't going to work now. No docks, and no convenient, long-armed Bridge Trolls to haul me out of harm's way. I was going to have to manage this one for myself.

Quentin struggled for the first few rungs, his fishy lower body dangling as he hauled himself laboriously hand over hand. Then there was a shimmer, and he was placing one foot after the other, scrambling nimbly after the rest of our party.

"Everyone is good at this but me," I grumbled, and started for the ladder. Then I stopped.

Something white was floating in the water near the hull, almost hidden by the shadow of one of the many pylons holding the Duchy in place.

It would have been easy to dismiss whatever it was as a trick of the light, or—if it *was* something real—as some piece of meaningless flotsam, a dead fish maybe, or a piece of torn-off fishing net. I wanted it to be one of those things. I wanted it to be something I could ignore.

Instead, I ducked my head under the water, so I wouldn't be able to hear my friends calling me back, and swam toward the thing that shouldn't have been there. I was hoping, still, that it would be nothing; it would be a bit of trash, a bit of foam, anything but what my long years of experience were starting to whisper to me.

Underwater, the scene shifted. Light moves differently in a Summerlands sea than it does in a mortal one, and even the shadows cast by the Duchy couldn't turn the waves darker than a bright gloaming, like a summer twilight. I swam forward, and what I'd taken for a barnacle-encrusted piece of the foundation eddied in the water, becoming clearer. The white thing I'd seen floating was a starfish shape attached to an elegant stem, pale in the shadows, raised in an arch above a moon-shaped circle, crowned with waterweeds that had no discernable color.

Then I blinked, and the scarecrow construct of slices of the sea became a woman, wilted, wound about with the shroud of her own sundress, eyes closed and skin softened by the water that had invaded every inch of her. She was barefoot, wearing nothing but several yards of patterned cotton that tangled around her motionless legs.

Isla Chase. Leader of the Selkies of Belle Fleuve.

Drowned.

She was dead: there could be no question of that. Living women don't hang like statues in freezing water, their chests motionless, their arms moved by the tides around them. But she was a Selkie, and Selkies don't drown. They need to breathe, sure, but the water cares for them, in a way the Luidaeg can't, and it tries its best to be kind. I remembered Connor talking about the sea back when we'd been lovers, when he'd stretched the length of himself out next to me in my bed, his webbed fingers playing in my hair, his toes running up and down my calves.

"Selkies know everything there is to know about drowning," he'd said. "Back in the days when sailors still thought it was a clever idea to steal our skins, we got really good at making sure they understood that they weren't supposed to *do* that. One dead sailor could teach a whole fishing community to leave the seals alone. But we don't drown. When one of us falls into the water, we wash up on the shore. Maybe we'll be bruised, maybe we'll be battered, but we'll be breathing. Every time. Always."

I couldn't remember why we'd been having that conversation—probably because I'd had another nightmare about my days in the pond, when the water had been above, below, and everywhere, when drowning would have been a mercy—but I could remember the wistful look in his eyes when he'd talked about his own inability to drown. Like he couldn't have imagined any better end for himself.

He'd died on dry land. Isla Chase hadn't.

Her body was secured to the pylon with a length of fishing net, so tangled that I couldn't tell whether she'd been tied there or simply drifted into position after someone had tossed her body overboard. I swam as close as I dared, circling her with deft flicks of my tail, and couldn't see any knots. I didn't know whether that was a good thing or a bad one. Whether her body had been disposed of here on purpose or whether she'd been thrown overboard somewhere else, the message she was sending was the same:

Isla had been murdered.

I turned and swam back to where I'd been a few seconds before. When I broke the surface, Quentin, Peter, and Poppy were all staring at me over the edge, while Helmi and the other Cephali stuck to the side of the ship, watching me warily.

"Where did you go?" called Quentin. "Is something wrong?"

I opened my mouth. Then I froze.

Captain Pete had sailed away rather than allow her presence to complicate the process of returning the Roane to these waters. Dianda was under arrest, and for the moment at least, her usurping brother was the ranking Undersea noble onboard. Dean's title wasn't in question, but his authority in these waters, this far away from land, certainly was. Involving Nolan would mean saying I thought the Mists had some sort of claim over this floating domain, so far from the shore. So who did I call? Isla Chase was dead. There was no question about that. But as for the question of who had killed her, well . . .

The Luidaeg had given the Selkies permission to assault and rob each other. Isla could have committed suicide after having her skin stolen. This didn't have to be murder. Would the Luidaeg even *want* me to investigate? Or would she want me to leave it alone, and let the Selkies handle their own problems, at least until the moment when they ceased to exist in their current form and became Roane, forever?

"I can't believe I'm saying this, but I don't think it matters what she wants," I muttered. Hearing my own voice made me feel a little better about what I was about to do. Not much. Not enough. Going against the assumed wishes of one of the Firstborn was the sort of thing only a fool would do.

A fool, or a hero. The two are so often indistinguishable, after all.

Raising my voice to be heard above the waves, I called, "I have a dead body down here. I need you to lower some kind of net, and I need you to do it quickly because this water's getting cold."

Quentin's eyes widened without actually telegraphing any sense of shock. If anything, he looked resigned. "Right," he said. "Just . . . wait there, okay?"

I hung suspended in the sea, my temporary fins holding me upright, and watched as my squire stepped away from the rail. My only company was a dead woman—and Oberon forgive me for my heroism, but I was going to find out how she'd died.

FOURTEEN

ISLA'S BODY SPRAWLED LIFELESS on the deck, somehow looking smaller than she had either in life or in the water. Without the waves to lift her limbs and support her head, she was limp, motionless. Without the waves to keep her up, she couldn't help falling.

The strand of glass beads braided in her hair was broken; half of them were missing. There was something unutterably sad about that. Someone had put them there, whether Isla herself or a loved one. Someone had thought she mattered enough to adorn her before she came here, to the middle of the ocean, to die. She was wearing a sundress and she had glass beads tied in her hair, and that was all she had: her sealskin was gone.

I crouched down, feeling my knees protest the gesture. The old damage that used to make certain things difficult for me had long since healed; this was a new protest, born from the still too-limber joints of my artificially Merrow form. The spell would wear off soon. Until it did, I'd have to live with gills in my throat and the occasional twinge from a skeleton that was no longer sure it loved the land the way it always had before.

Gently, I lifted one of Isla's hands and uncurled her clenched fingers. Her skin was soft and spongy from the water it had absorbed. It would trickle from her for hours, maybe even days, if the night-haunts didn't come to carry her away. Which, I noted with regret, they didn't even have to do. There were no webs between her fingers. They would come anyway. Her blood still held memories for them to carry.

No webs between her fingers, but there were bruises on her wrists. This hadn't been a suicide.

"She died human," I said, making no effort to keep the sadness from my voice. If I couldn't be sad over a needless death, a fae death, I was one step closer to becoming the monster I had never wanted to be. "Someone stole her skin and then they threw her overboard."

There were no obvious signs of injury. If she'd been human when she went into the water, she had drowned, the same way any human could have drowned if thrown into a sea that was unwelcoming to mortal kind.

The night-haunts would have come for her as soon as she'd washed up on shore. With their filmy wings and delicate bodies, they couldn't have come for her in the water; they would have been bogged down and drowned. That was something, at least. We were still dealing with the original Isla, and would be until we left her body alone for the night-haunts to collect. She could still tell us her secrets.

I drew my knife, ignoring Peter's voice asking shrilly what I was intending to do, and sliced the flesh of her right wrist. It was a shallow wound, and I was lucky, according to some definitions of the term: she hadn't been dead long enough for her blood to fully settle.

"I hate this part," I said, and bowed my head, and drank.

I came to, flat on my back, with the others standing around me in a circle. Peter looked terrified. The Cephali looked bemused. Quentin looked like he couldn't decide between the two states, and so had settled on furious as the best way to split the difference.

"You just *drowned*," he informed me, voice a little too shrill. "On the deck. With no water. You *drowned*."

"That explains why my throat hurts," I muttered, sitting up and coughing. A little more water was dislodged by the movement, and ran down my chin to soak into my shirt. I grimaced. "Okay, one, that's disgusting, and two, I don't think I can ride Isla Chase's blood."

"What was your first clue?" asked Quentin, voice still too shrill.

"The drowning was too traumatic for her, and for me. It's blocking out everything else." I looked at the body. "I could wait and try to talk to the night-haunts, but they've asked me to stop doing that, and I don't have what I'd need to make a safe summoning ritual. The risk is too great. I'm sorry. I should be braver."

"I think I'm glad you're not," said Quentin. He took a short, sharp breath through his nose. "What do we do now?"

Go the hell home and let the Luidaeg deal with this, I thought, and stood. Aloud, I said, "We find out who did this. Whoever it was has to pay."

"Pay *how*?" asked Peter. He was showing far too much interest in the body, watching it with an avid fascination that was barely balanced by Quentin's restraint. It was true that he'd grown up in a more militant part of Faerie, but still. Childhoods in the Undersea were clearly very different. "It's only against the Law to kill purebloods, and sometimes not even that."

I opened my mouth, prepared to answer. Then I froze, really thinking about his question.

The Law, Oberon's Law, is very simple: no one kills purebloods. Not changelings, not other purebloods, and certainly not humans, not unless they feel like finding out how cruel Faerie can be when it comes to devising punishments for people with no one to speak for them. There are exceptions, like wartime, or like the deal the Cait Sidhe made with Oberon when it came to their fights for succession. The Cait Sidhe are allowed to kill each other, providing they can come up with an explanation that satisfies their Kings and Queens. The denizens of the Undersea are allowed to kill each other, as long as they declare a state of war before they draw their weapons. Anyone's allowed to kill a changeling, any time they want to, without necessarily facing any consequences.

And anyone can kill a human. Humans have even less protection under the Law than changelings do. At least we're a part of Faerie. Humans are . . . in the eyes of many purebloods, humans are livestock. They're animals, here to die, and so helping them along the way to their inevitable destination is not a big deal.

Isla was human when someone pushed her over the rail. Isla was human when she hit the water. In the eyes of Faerie, the only thing her killer had done wrong was an act of theft.

I stood where I was, looking at her body and swallowing the bile that threatened to rise up in the back of my throat. I hadn't lost my lunch at a crime scene since the supposed death of Evening Winterrose. I certainly wasn't going to do it now.

The scent of pennyroyal and musk reached me a heartbeat before Tybalt did, giving me sufficient warning that I didn't tense or pull away when an arm slid around my waist, pulling me close. I might normally have objected to that sort of distraction while I was looking at a body, but under the circumstances, I welcomed it, letting my head sag to the side until it rested against Tybalt's shoulder. I allowed my knees to buckle a bit at the same time, not enough so as to drop me on my ass, but enough to take some of the tension off. I knew he wouldn't let me fall.

"She was a fair lady," he said, eyes on Isla. "We met her on the beach, did we not?"

"We did," I confirmed. "Isla Chase. She was the head of one of the Selkie clans. She was sort of snippy, but I guess I can understand, under the circumstances." I paused as a thought struck me, and pulled away, twisting until I was looking at Tybalt.

He met my gaze without flinching. Then he blinked, looking briefly bewildered. "Your eyes," he said.

"What about them?" I somehow managed not to reach up and touch my face.

"They're not meant to be so colorful." He shook his head, a wry smile tugging at the corner of his mouth. "I suppose if the sea witch can dress you in scales, she can tint your eyes to match. Still, it will be a pleasure when the fog rolls in, and you look at me like yourself again. What question can I answer for you?" I must have looked confused, because his smile lost its edge of wryness, turning genuinely amused. "You only look at me so when you have a question gnawing at your tongue. Out with it, then, before it chews its way free."

"Yeah, well, you only talk this much like a period drama when you're worried," I said, and took a deep breath. "The Cait Sidhe have the authority to rule themselves, correct?"

"Granted by Oberon himself," he said, smile fading into wariness. "Why do you ask?"

"What would happen if one of your subjects killed someone, another Cait Sidhe, for no good reason? I don't mean if they challenged you for rank and one of you didn't walk away, or anything like that. I mean a murder. Oberon's Law wouldn't necessarily apply if it happened in the Court of Cats."

"No," said Tybalt slowly, choosing his words with evident care. "Were I to slit another King's throat in a knowe of the Divided

Courts, an argument might be made that I had, through murder, disturbed the peace, but it would be a difficult needle to thread. When a cat kills a cat, there are no consequences."

"No consequences *under the Law*," I said, stressing my words. "I know you don't let your subjects go around killing each other willy-nilly. I've been to your Court. Things are too steady for that."

Quentin had realized where I was going with this. He was leaning forward, watching Tybalt with a silent intensity that I realized, with a start, he'd learned from watching me. I was shaping the next High King of the Westlands in ways that might or might not be good for him.

Oh, well. Too late now.

"There would be . . . consequences, yes," said Tybalt. "There aren't so many of us that we can afford to waste lives on petty arguments. The killer would be brought before me, or before their liege if they were not of my Court, and a punishment would be devised."

"Gotcha." I whirled, facing Peter. "Who's in charge of the Selkie clans?"

He blinked. "What?"

"They skirt the line between land and sea, between human and fae. They're purebloods under the Law when they wear a sealskin, but they care for and protect their human kin, and they're allowed to tell those kin about the existence of Faerie. So who's in charge of them? If a Selkie is murdered, who gets involved?"

"They're our subjects when they're in the water, but they belong to someone else on the land," said Peter. "They mostly govern themselves, I guess. Mom never talks about it. She says the Selkies are someone else's problem."

"Meaning the Luidaeg's, but she's not here right now, and we don't have time to wait for her," I said, and glanced at Quentin. "How about you. You ever hear of someone claiming to be in a position of absolute authority over the Selkies?"

Quentin shook his head. "No. They fall under the jurisdiction of the Divided Courts when they quarrel with others among the fae, but when they keep to themselves, they're allowed to go about their business as they see fit."

Quentin's father was the High King of North America. If anyone on the continent claimed absolute authority over the Selkies, Quentin would have known about it. "Meaning the clans handle their own shit. Excellent." I flashed the group a thin-lipped smile. "Poppy, please lead our Cephali friends to our quarters. Patrick will be relieved to see Peter is alive and well." I should probably have felt a little bad for making him wait to find that out. Feeling bad wouldn't make Isla any less dead. "Helmi, can you take the body with you?"

I hated to tote a corpse around the Duchy like a sack of potatoes, but I hated the idea of leaving her here for someone else to stumble across even more. The fae don't do well with the idea of death. Most purebloods refuse to even acknowledge that it's something that can happen to them. And until Captain Pete got back, I wasn't sure whether there was anyone within the Duchy itself in a position to take responsibility for the body. First Mate Rodrick? Someone else? Better to keep Isla with us, at least for the moment.

Helmi looked at Isla thoughtfully before she nodded and said, "We are strong. We have to be, to serve our purpose in the Courts. We can take her." The other two Cephali nodded as well, echoing her sentiment if not her statement.

I spared a brief thought for how Cassandra and Nolan were going to react when a bunch of half-octopus guards came strolling into the courtyard with a dead woman in their tentacles, then waved it aside. There wasn't time to worry about the details right now.

"Quentin, Tybalt, you're with me," I said.

Tybalt turned his eyes heavenward. "Thank Oberon," he said. "The lady sees sense."

"Quiet, you, or I'll come up with a good reason for you not to come," I said, earning myself a disdainful look. I swallowed the urge to laugh. A little levity was fine—the urge to whistle past the graveyard is a very normal one, and one that's served me well in the past—but Isla deserved better. I'd barely met the woman. She could have been a terrible person, cruel to children and animals, and that didn't matter. Someone had murdered her. She was going to receive whatever justice I could provide.

The three Cephali wound their tentacles carefully around Isla, lifting her off the wood of the dock, building a bier from their own bodies until she was perfectly supported, hanging between them like a jewel on a string.

"I suppose that's mine to lead them, then," said Poppy, voice shaking with nerves. She offered Peter her hand. "Come, young lord, and I'll take you to your father and brother, and to tea and cakes and whatever else we can shake out of the larders. Young lords like that sort of thing."

"We do," Peter agreed, and slipped his hand willingly into hers. I let out a slow breath, my shoulders relaxing. Poppy knew where to go, and Helmi wouldn't let anything happen to Peter. Between the two of them, he was as safe as he could possibly have been.

That didn't make me feel any better about walking away from him. Which meant it was time to go. I turned before I could come up with another excuse to stay, walking away from the little corner where I'd done my examination, heading into the maze of docks.

"We could take the Shadow Roads," said Tybalt, matching his pace to mine. "It would be swifter."

"I want you to conserve your strength, and my hair is wet," I said. "My body heals. My hair doesn't."

"Vanity, little fish?"

"Practicality. I'm practically sure Stacy will *murder* me if I wind up bald this close to the wedding. She's looking forward to braiding things into my hair, and I know better than to disappoint her."

Tybalt blinked, looking startled. "You think . . . you truly believe we're close to our marriage?"

"Well, yeah." I glanced at him. "You said you didn't want to wait forever. I mean, I don't think we're going to elope tomorrow, but I figure I wouldn't have time to grow my hair all the way back."

"You better not be eloping," said Quentin. "The High King has offered to host the ceremony. You don't run off and leave the High King with an outstretched hand and no vassal to hold it. It's not done."

"I am a King of Cats," said Tybalt. "Your High King has no authority over me."

"Maybe not, but he has authority over *me*, and I'd rather not piss him off." Making an enemy of the High King of North America would be impressively stupid, even for me. He could call Quentin back to Toronto any time he wanted. That meant keeping him happy was essential.

"I suppose I accepted certain complications when I elected to tie my future to a daughter of the Divided Courts," said Tybalt without rancor. He sounded oddly pleased, and was smiling as he reached over to twine his fingers with mine.

The Duchy of Ships bustled around us as we walked, and if some people cast curious glances in our direction, they were smart enough, or well-mannered enough, not to say anything. I surreptitiously checked my shirt, and was pleased to see there wasn't any blood from my earlier fight with Torin's guard. The water had washed it all away.

"Don't think you're escaping judgment quite so easily," said Tybalt, in a pleasant tone. "I can still smell it. Not strongly, but enough that I know it's *your* blood, and not the poor drowned woman's."

"Also there's a big hole in your shirt," chirped Quentin.

I shot him a baleful look. "You're not helping."

"Sure I am. I'm making sure there are consequences when you let yourself get stabbed in the stomach. Maybe that way, you'll do it less, and I'll have fewer nightmares. Everyone wins." Quentin shrugged, unrepentant. "You're the one who taught me how to cheat. Just think, if you'd been more scrupulous about following protocol, I might not be betraying you now."

"I can't believe you're using the 'I learned it from watching you,' excuse," I muttered. "I can't decide whether I'm proud or pissed off."

"See, I'm happy either way," said Quentin.

I huffed and kept walking.

The shops we'd seen before were open now, and the marketplace bustled with people—merchants hawking their wares, customers sorting through them, looking for the perfect pearl, or lobster, or pearl-encrusted lobster. Everything I could think of needing was for sale somewhere, with the obvious exception of electronics; this far into the Summerlands, even April's modified cellular service didn't work. That was sort of nice, since it meant she had actual limits. It was also sort of vexing. It would have been nice to be able to call home and summon as much backup as we could cram into a rowboat.

I narrowed my eyes and focused on the people. Most belonged to the Undersea races, Merrow and Sirens and people with pearlized eyes or shimmering scales dusted across their skin, whose heritage teased my tongue with signals I didn't quite know how to puzzle out. I might be a walking encyclopedia of magical signatures, but that doesn't give me the ability to recognize types of fae I've never seen before. They were a mystery to me, their shoulders draped in fishnets and strings of coral beads, their brows covered with bandannas or graced with curving seashell horns that grew directly from the bone.

Every time I breathed in, the part of my magic that was dedicated to tracing the magic of others tucked their individual scents neatly away, earmarking them for later. I'd be able to follow a single spell cast by any of these people halfway around the world. It was a slightly unnerving thought. The more I learn about what it means to be Dóchas Sidhe, the more I wonder how many of my choices—becoming a private investigator, following trails I probably shouldn't have followed—have been guided by my magic trying to find a way to assert itself on the world.

It was an unnerving thought, and so I shunted it aside and focused on what I *wasn't* seeing around the stalls. I wasn't seeing any Selkies. With as many as I knew were in the Duchy, they should have been everywhere. Selkie children should have been getting under the feet of the merchants; Selkie adults should have been poking through the available wares. Keeping the still technically human relations back at the beach would have made sense, but the absolute absence of the Selkies as a people was strange. I didn't like it.

Tybalt and Quentin frowned at my expression, then at each other, and kept walking. They'd done enough of this sort of thing to know that I'd speak up when I felt it was safe to do so, and not before.

"Are you sure we're going the right way?" asked Quentin.

"Even with as overwhelming as the magic in this place is, I can't lose the Luidaeg's trail," I said. "It's like a fishhook in my nostrils. I could follow her anywhere." The scent of her magic wasn't normally this strong. She also wasn't normally this open about her true nature. The more of her masks she set aside, the easier it got for me to track her.

That explained a lot—including why August hadn't been able to find Oberon when she'd run off on her fool's errand and gotten herself lost for more than a century. If the Firstborn can mask themselves to the point that their terrifyingly powerful magic becomes nothing more than a vague parlor trick, how much more than that can the Three do? Can they disappear so that no one can follow them?

Can they ever be found?

The beach opened before us as we came down the final stretch of dock, its sands shimmering in the moonlight. There were no children playing outside now. There was no one. The whole place was empty, and if not for the candles flickering in the windows of the little Cape Cod-style houses, I would have thought there was no one here at all. I stopped, squinting at the houses.

Selkies didn't tend to use much magic beyond that which came to them from their skins. The Roane were prophets and storm-singers, almost as skilled at controlling the waves as the Merrow, but none of that had carried down to the people who'd stolen their place in Faerie. We were probably going to have some nasty weather patterns when the Roane were reborn and had to rush to learn how to keep their natural gifts under control.

That was a problem for another day, and frankly, for someone else. I was just here to bring the Roane back into the world—and now, to get justice for one Selkie woman who hadn't deserved to die the way she did.

I stopped, squinting at the row of small, semi-identical houses. Tybalt and Quentin waited patiently, until I raised my hand and pointed.

"There," I said. "Elizabeth came out of that one." Out of all the Selkie clan leaders, Liz was the one I actually knew and felt like I could talk to. She might listen to what I was going to propose. The fact that the Ryan clan had claimed responsibility for Gillian didn't have anything to do with it, honest.

All right. Maybe it had a little bit to do with it.

We trudged across the sand, the waves crashing against the pillars of the boardwalk and the wind whistling around us, and we could have been anywhere; we could have been in Santa Cruz, or Half Moon Bay, or Ventura Beach, any place where people lived alongside the sea. It was a cunningly constructed little community, allowing the people who lived there to pretend that they weren't on a floating duchy in the middle of the empty ocean. It was probably good for the mental health of the Selkies, who could, as we had seen so brutally demonstrated, drown.

The curtains were drawn at Elizabeth's house. There was no doorbell, which made sense, given the level of technology around us. Raising my hand, I knocked briskly.

There was no answer. I knocked again.

When there was still no answer I sighed, leaned closer, and called, "The Luidaeg isn't with me, Liz. It's just me, Toby, and a few of my friends. Let me in. This is important."

There was a long pause, long enough to make me question

whether she was there at all. Maybe she'd gone somewhere. Maybe all the Selkies had gone somewhere, choosing to flee rather than stay here and face the Luidaeg's justice. Maybe—

The door swung open, just a crack, wide enough for me to see a single blue eye peering out at me. Like all Selkies, Elizabeth Ryan had stopped aging when she'd received her skin. She was a woman in the prime of her life and always would be, unless she elected to pass her own skin along before the deadline passed and it was too late. And for all of that, she had never looked older, or more exhausted.

"I'm sorry, but I'm not really up for visitors right now," she said. "You should go."

"We can't," I said. "Let me in, or we'll do this with me standing on your front porch. I don't think either one of us is going to enjoy that, do you?"

There was another pause, even longer than the last, before she huffed and pulled the door all the way open. "Fine," she said. "Come on in." She turned and stomped away, not waiting for us to enter.

I exchanged a glance with Tybalt. Liz seemed antsy, but that made sense. She didn't seem scared.

She didn't know.

"Nice place," I said, stepping inside and looking around the room. It was larger than it looked from the outside, decorated in a quaint, old-fashioned style that managed to look almost modern when contrasted with the rest of the Duchy. While Pete's quarters, and the quarters we'd been assigned, were like something out of a period drama about piracy, Liz's house was all white wicker and faded damask. It looked like the sort of place that should come with a kindly grandmother pre-installed. The only piece that carried any of the shipwreck aesthetic of the other rooms I'd seen was the table, wide and ragged around the edges and apparently carved from a single piece of some sunken vessel's side. There were even barnacles on the bottom, dried out until they became ashen and cracked.

"It's not mine," said Liz, with a careless flap of her hand. She kept walking until she reached a sideboard and picked up a green glass bottle, its sides too clouded to let me see the liquid inside. She considered it for a moment before setting it aside in favor of another bottle, this one red and equally obscured. "It belongs to whoever leads the Ryan clan. Which, I suppose, means it's about to belong to no one. We won't need clans anymore, not once you're done with us." She laughed unsteadily as she uncorked the bottle and poured a stream of dark purple liquid into a tumbler. "Anybody want a drink?"

"No," I said.

"No," said Quentin at the same time.

"I would be delighted to have some of whatever you're having," said Tybalt. Quentin and I both turned to stare at him. He rolled his shoulders in a shrug. "I'm not 'on duty,' as you might so quaintly put it; I'm not the hero here. I'm merely an onlooker, raised in a time where, if someone offered you a drink, it was considered polite to accept their hospitality."

"I like you slightly more than I like the company you keep, which means I still don't like you at all," Liz informed Tybalt, filling a second tumbler and thrusting it toward him. "Why are you here? Come to laugh at the wake, when there's never going to be a funeral?"

"Where is everyone?" I asked, as Tybalt took the glass and sniffed curiously at its contents. His nose wrinkled. I did my best to ignore him, focusing as much as I could on Liz. "There were children earlier. Playing in the sand. Remember?"

"How could I forget?" She fixed her gaze on me, and it was all I could do not to recoil. We had never been friends, had only met in the company of the Luidaeg, but she had never looked at me like that before. She looked at me like I was her executioner, come to drag her away from everything she'd ever known. "That was when my lovely Annie, my dear, beloved, only true love *Annie*, stood before a council of my fellows and said there'd be no punishment for anyone who wanted to steal a skin. You didn't seem overly concerned about the children then. You just stood there and let her do it."

"She's the sea witch, Liz. It's not like I exactly have a lot of leverage with her."

Her laugh was low and bitter and more than a little inebriated. The drink in her hand was far from her first. "You have more leverage than any of the rest of us do, and substantially more than you think. She *needs* you, liar's daughter, or she'll never be rid of my kind. So yeah, you could have said something."

"She said the children were exempt."

"Because they don't have skins to steal, for the most part," said

Liz. "Doesn't mean it won't hurt them to see their futures stolen, or to see their families attacked. Just because no one attacks them, that doesn't mean they're going to get out of this unscathed. You could have *said* something, and you didn't. You cared more about your own hide than you did about theirs." She laughed again, wildly this time. "Hide. What a good word for this mess. We should all be doing it, in order to save it."

"Okay, so she's discovered the joy of homonyms and it's a little creepy," said Quentin.

Tybalt shot him a fond look. "My lady love has ruined you for courtly matters."

"I wasn't trying to," I said, and focused on Liz. "Liz—Elizabeth— I need you to listen to me, please. It's important that you listen to me. When was the last time you saw Isla?"

"Isla Chase? Oh, that would be shortly after she tried to stab me in the shoulder so she could knock me down and peel the sealskin from my body. Clumsy scag." Elizabeth sipped her drink, trying to look nonchalant. "I kicked her in the groin and ran. Most of us are hiding in our homes, if we made it clear of the fray. Things aren't *really* bad, not yet. The deadline is still far enough away that most are biding their time, waiting for the rest to get here. Newcomers will be easy targets for the rest of us, right? Show up late, don't get all the information, lose. Lose big time. Mostly, right now, it's people looking to settle scores, and people going after the easy targets. The weak. The unaffiliated. No one's taking care of *them*."

There seemed to be a stone stuck in my throat. Something about the way she looked at me when she said the word "weak" was setting off alarm bells in the back of my mind. "And Gillian?"

"See, she's the reason I would have expected you to say more than you did when Annie decided to put a bounty out on my entire clan—and not only because those skins my darling love traded for your daughter's education are what kicked off this whole mess." Liz's lip curled as she lowered her glass. "If I were a more vengeful woman, I would have left that girl standing on the sand when I pulled the rest of my people to safety. You're lucky I take my responsibilities seriously. You're lucky one of us knows what it means to be a mother."

Tybalt took a step forward, toward her. He didn't say anything. He didn't need to. Out of everyone in the world—everyone except for me, and May, who remembered being Gillian's mother even if she never had been—Tybalt understood the best how much it had killed me to let her go, even when she'd been demanding I do exactly that.

I caught his arm, preventing him from going any further. Liz looked at him impassively, either too drunk or too resigned to her fate to be concerned about the fury in his eyes.

"Go ahead," she said. "It's not like you'd be casting my clan into chaos. Hundreds of years of governing ourselves, keeping ourselves safe and tucked away and not violating the laws of either Faerie or humanity, and this is how it ends. No more need for Selkie clans, not when there aren't any Selkies anymore."

I forced myself to take a breath, in through my nose and out through my mouth, focusing on how much we needed Liz to help us voluntarily, and not how much I wanted to punch her in the face. It wasn't easy. Quentin looked as furious as Tybalt, but he was channeling it into a perfect stillness, one that spoke of his early training in his parents' Court, where he'd been expected to be the perfect prince at all times, poised and polished and deadly.

Sometimes I think Faerie is way too hard on our kids.

Finally, I said, "Elizabeth Ryan, I'm here *because* the Selkie clans are permitted to govern themselves, at least so far as their relationship with their mortal kin. But you need to tell me where my daughter is and whether she's all right before I can continue." If she said Gillian had been hurt—if she said Gillian had been *killed*—I was going to—

I didn't know what I was going to do. Except possibly go looking for the Luidaeg and get myself killed trying to challenge the sea witch. The Luidaeg had always said she was going to kill me one day. If Gillian was dead, that day might well be today.

"Your brat is fine," said Liz. She took another drink from her tumbler, deeper this time, almost gulping. "She's with a bunch of the kids, showing them how to make paper cranes. She's still new enough to be good with her hands. The webs'll slow her down soon enough."

Connor's hands had always been a little clumsy, hampered by the webs that connected his fingers to the first knuckle. But he'd done well enough. Gillian would, too. I forced my shoulders to relax as much as possible, letting go of Tybalt's arm.

"What do you do when someone hurts one of your human clan members?"

Liz blinked slowly, finally putting her glass down. "What do you mean?"

"You take care of them, you protect them, you tell them about Faerie—the Law doesn't cover them, because they're not purebloods, but that doesn't matter to the Selkie clans. What do you do when someone hurts one of your human clan members? It's not a difficult question. Or should I go looking for an alchemist who can mix you something to sober you up? Because we don't have a lot of time here." Isla, dead in the water, shorn of her sealskin and left to drown like any other human. That wasn't what the Luidaeg had approved. She'd given the Selkies permission to steal from each other. She'd never given them permission to kill. Sure, once a Selkie lacked a skin, they were exempt from the reach of the Law, but if I was right about Selkie governance . . .

"The Law." Liz laughed again, bitter and unsteady, like she couldn't believe she was having this conversation. "Did you know, I didn't even know there *was* a Law until I received my skin? My parents always told me to stay away from the rest of the fae, said they wouldn't understand how a human girl could consider herself part of Faerie, or worthy of speaking to them. My mother said if I ever wound up in a situation where I couldn't hide what I knew, I should pretend to be the au pair of some noble house. They steal humans for that. Almost always girls. I can't decide if that's tradition or chauvinism."

"A little bit of both," I said.

"There was a time when stolen girls were less likely to be missed," said Tybalt. He had the good grace to sound ashamed, even as he kept talking. "A time when sweeping them away into Faerie might have been considered a blessing for all concerned, as they could be fed and safe and not subject to the affections of the first man to make their fathers an offer he felt he couldn't turn down. In those days, it was tradition. Now, when someone insists they must have a woman to tend their young, because their parents did, and their parents' parents before them, it's pigheadedness and a refusal to understand that times have changed, and keep on changing."

"I love you," I said, before returning my attention to Liz. "Oberon's Law doesn't protect changelings, and it doesn't protect skinless Selkies, but you don't go around murdering your human kids and dumping their bodies in the Summerlands where the mortal authorities would never find them. So what *do* you have?"

"We have our own covenants," said Liz. There was a suspicious glint in her eye. She could tell I was getting at something, even if she hadn't figured out precisely what it was. Boy, was she going to be surprised. "We don't kill our human kin, if that's what you're asking. We sometimes imprison them in our clan homes, for their own good, when they cross certain lines. And when they . . ." She stopped and swallowed. "When they seem like they might become a threat to Faerie, we have ways of stopping their tongues. We don't like to do it. It's small and petty and cruel and unfair, but it's sometimes necessary."

"Magically, you mean," I said.

Liz glowered. "Yes, magically. What do you take us for? The fact that our place in Faerie has to be earned doesn't make us less a part of it than you. If anything, it makes us *more* a part of it. We *chose.*"

So had every changeling, ever, but somehow that never seemed to get us a better place at the table. I looked at her expression and decided it might be better not to point that out. "So is it ever, under any circumstances, acceptable to kill one of your human kinfolk? Just so I know we're on the same page here."

"No," she said, utterly affronted. "A Selkie without a skin is still a Selkie where it counts. We respect the Law among our own kind, even if no one else will."

"Wait," blurted Quentin. We turned to look at him. His cheeks flared red, but he pressed on, saying, "I thought if a prospective Selkie refused to accept the skin, you, um, drowned them. So they couldn't go back to the others and tell them the truth about where you all come from."

I didn't remember the Luidaeg telling him that part, but that didn't mean anything: I wasn't always there, and the two of them had a relationship that existed outside of their mutual relationship with me. I turned back to Liz, waiting for her response.

"We drown our children, yes," she said. "It kills me that we do, but it's the agreement we made with the sea witch when she put the enchanted sealskins into our hands, and we keep our word. If you're asking whether *I've* ever drowned a child, the answer is no. I had to have an heir when I became head of my clan, but I sought out a Roane man, and I lay with him to get my Diva. She'll never need a sealskin to reach the sea, and so there was never any need to offer her the betrayer's bargain. And before you say it, yes, I know I cheated, and yes, I know the sea witch would be within her rights to strike me down for going against the spirit of her deal with us, and no, I don't care. I was never going to sacrifice a child to the water."

"Okay, that's . . . really awful, but given what the Divided Courts do to changelings who choose their human parents, I don't think I get to judge you," I said.

"Nor does the Court of Cats," said Tybalt. "It's rare for our children to choose anything aside from Faerie, and those who are born in feline skins never need to make the choice at all, but when it happens that a human-born child selects the mortal world as their home, their blood is on our hands. You shall find no censure here."

Liz looked briefly startled. "Well, good," she said, voice gruff with unshed tears. "Why are you asking me this?"

"I have one last question, and then I can explain," I said. "What would happen if someone killed one of the skinless Selkies? Not Diva—I'm not sure she's technically a Selkie at all, if she doesn't need a sealskin to be part of Faerie—but one of your mortal kin."

"If the killer was of Faerie but not of the clans, we would approach the local regent," she said. "In Roan Rathad, that would mean approaching Baron Aberforth and hoping he was in the mood to listen to our petition. Not because that person would have done anything wrong in the eyes of the Law, but because sometimes, we can convince those in charge that our human relations are our property, and at least get the perpetrators fined for their crimes. It's not enough—it's barely this side of wergild—but it means they don't do it casually."

"And if they were a Selkie, or a human?" I asked.

"A human, we'd drown." Liz scowled at me before draining the last of the purple liquid from her glass. "Is that what you wanted? To be sure we were killers? I could have told you that in a much less roundabout manner."

I wasn't so sure of that. For all that being a Selkie meant she'd spent at least a portion of her life as a human, Liz had been a part of Faerie for much, much longer than she'd belonged, even in a sideways manner, to the mortal world; she thought more like a pureblood than I did. And purebloods are notorious about refusing to give a straight answer where death is concerned.

"What if it were a Selkie who killed one of your human kin?" I asked.

Liz bared her teeth in what might charitably have been called a smile. I knew better. I'd been sharing my bed with a King of Cats for long enough to know a threat when I saw one.

"One nice thing about being partially outside the law: no one interferes when we choose to take it into our own hands," she said. "I'd skin them myself if that was what it came to."

"Good," I said. "I need to talk to you about Isla Chase."

FIFTEEN

ELIZABETH LISTENED IMPASSIVELY as I explained how I'd stumbled over Isla's body: the way she'd been tangled in a net, fixed to a pylon, in a way that seemed more accident than intent. How her hair had floated in the current, giving the illusion of motion.

How she'd drowned, and what that meant in terms of both the Luidaeg's permission to rob each other and the Law.

When I was done, Liz tilted her head and said, "It's not that I don't believe you—I'm not quite stupid enough for that—but why were you in the water?"

Quentin and I exchanged a glance. Telling Liz exactly what was going on with the Lordens seemed both unwise and unkind. Their problems weren't hers, and she had plenty of things already on her plate. Still . . .

"Duchess Dianda Lorden of Saltmist is currently indisposed, due to a challenge posed by her brother," I said, as diplomatically as possible. "Her husband, the ducal consort, was concerned about their younger son, who had been left home with his caretaker when they came to witness the Convocation. I agreed to go get him. As that meant traveling to an Undersea Duchy, it was necessary to allow the Luidaeg to make a few small changes. They're temporary."

I reached up and swept my hair aside with the back of my hand, showing her the slits of my closed gills. Liz blinked, slowly. Then, to my surprise, she started laughing.

"Of *course* you let Annie transform you into something you're not supposed to be; why in the world would you tell her 'no, that's all right, I'd rather be myself and rent some SCUBA gear,' when she could just," she made a swirling motion with her hands, "whizz-bang and you're a mermaid? Oh, October, I wish I'd known you better when Connor was in love with you, so I'd have a better idea of how far you've fallen."

I bristled. I couldn't help it. It was blazingly obvious that she was trying to push my buttons, but that didn't make it any harder for her to do. "Fallen or not, we brought Peter back to the Duchy of Ships to be with his parents, and I'm missing their reunion because I thought you might want justice for Isla."

"Justice? For Isla Chase? That woman was mean as a moray and half as principled. She'd have slit my throat without a second thought if she believed it would get her another skin for her clan. She tried to do essentially that. Why would I want justice for her?"

"Because she drowned. Because someone stole her skin and threw her into the element that had been hers for her entire life, and they thought they'd get away with it, because she was human when she died. Humans deserve kindness, too. She was ours. She belonged to Faerie. She deserves answers."

Liz still looked like she didn't get it. I silently reminded myself that throttling her, while not a violation of the Law, would probably be considered impolitic at best, and really rude at worst. No matter how nice it would be in the moment, it wasn't worth the long-term ramifications.

"If someone's decided that having permission to steal skins means permission to go around killing your human kin, they need to be stopped," I said, as clearly and patiently as I could. "This is not the sort of person you want to step into immortality with, and Isla deserves better, no matter how awful she was. No one should die cold and frightened and alone. Now will you help me?"

"How?" asked Liz. "And *why*? You're here to put an end to us, and a Selkie without a skin is no concern of Faerie's. Why in the world would you be willing to do this—why do you *want* to? You should be glad to know that there's one more possible security flaw patched over and left to be forgotten."

I took another deep breath. "Were you this terrible when you were living with the Luidaeg?" I asked. "Because if you were, I'm sort of amazed she didn't turn you into something nasty and leave you for the seagulls."

"She turned me into a bitter, broken-hearted drunk when she refused to tell me *why* she wanted me to turn away the birthright I'd been dreaming of for my entire life," said Liz. "Is that crime enough, or should I go looking for something more direct that made me the way I am now? I gave her everything. I wanted to spend my life with her."

"You gave her everything but the courtesy of leaving your back bare of her dead child's skin," said Tybalt mildly. "I have no living children: I've never been so fortunate. But if you appeared before me with my dead daughter's pelt around your shoulders, I'd make you something other than a drunkard. I'd make you a corpse."

"Okay, there's going to be blood on the floor in a minute if we keep going down this road, and while that's sadly tempting right now, it's probably not the best thing for us," I said. "Why do I care, Liz? Because when someone turned me into a fish and took me away from my family for a decade and a half, the Law said no crimes had been committed, and no one came to save me. The places where Faerie rubs up against the mortal world are unpoliced and unprotected, and Isla deserved better. You all deserve better. The fact that the Luidaeg is willing to let the Selkies steal each other's skins for the chance to become Roane doesn't mean she wants anyone slaughtering the defenseless."

At least I hoped it didn't. I didn't think it could. The Luidaeg was one of Faerie's oldest, weariest monsters, but she wasn't cruel, not to children, not to the defenseless. The fact that she'd been able to love Liz before the other woman had draped herself in sealskin proved that. It was only the Selkies themselves who broke her heart, not their human kin.

Liz closed her eyes and took a deep breath. Finally, opening them, she said, "We should speak to Mathias. He isn't my biggest fan—he's always believed I owe my position to having been Annie's lover, and maybe he's right; maybe this was the best punishment she could think of for my many, many sins—but he knows I care for my clan, and he had reason to be well-inclined toward Isla. He'll want to see her, and he'll want to find the person who did this."

"Excellent." I hesitated, looking around the room, before I asked my next question. "Where's Gillian?"

"I told you, she's with the children," said Liz. "They like her. She's charmingly ignorant by their standards, and they get to feel clever when they teach her the things she doesn't already know." She looked at me levelly. "I'd strip that skin from her shoulders in a second to give to one of them, if she didn't have Annie's protection, and if she wouldn't drop dead without it. Your girl doesn't know how lucky she is."

"Given the number of times Faerie has ruined her life, I'd say she knows exactly how lucky she is, and one day we're all going to burn for it," I said. "Take us to Mathias."

Liz cast one last, longing look at her bottle of purple liquid. Then she sighed and started for the door. We followed.

The beach outside was as empty and silent as it had been when we approached. Even our footprints were gone, stolen by the wind blowing off the sea. It wasn't hard to imagine that the place had been deserted for years—as it would be, after the time of the Selkies ended. Their human children would grow old and die even if they stayed here in the Summerlands, unable to ever truly touch the sea, and the strange, liminal culture the Selkies had crafted for themselves in the gap between humanity and the fae would be lost forever.

Had the Luidaeg known this was going to happen when she'd chosen to preserve the last pieces of her lost children by binding them to living bodies? Had she even suspected she was going to create a population in exile, not quite human, not entirely fae? She was a monster, by her own admission and by her sister's design. I'd never really considered her cruel. If she hadn't known, if she hadn't been able to wrap her immortal mind about the fast, impatient way that mortal beings lived their lives, that was one thing. But if she had done this on purpose . . .

If she had done this on purpose, she was more of a monster than I ever could have believed she'd be.

Liz led us down the row of houses to one identical to her own, raised her hand, and knocked. A long moment passed before the door was cracked open, just wide enough for a man to peer suspiciously out at us.

"It's Elizabeth Ryan, René," she said—snapped, really, with a hectic, impatient air that wasn't going to make this any easier. "I need to talk to your husband. Let me in."

"There's a war on, in case you missed the news," said the man—René—in a mild voice. He had a French accent, as maritime as the winter is long, and a wary air about him, like he expected Liz to shove her way inside. Which maybe he did. I had no idea how she ranked among the Selkie clan leaders, whether she was considered one of the stable ones or whether she was the one the rest of them warned their children about. She was the unfriendly drunk who had mourned for Connor, who had loved the Luidaeg, who had gone to sea to get herself a daughter with eyes as green as an untouched forest. Everything else had been someone else's problem.

"It's not a war so much as it's a series of uncoordinated assassinations, and people are mostly being polite about it," said Liz. "This is Sir October Daye from Shadowed Hills. She's a hero of the realm back in the Mists, where my clan is unfortunate enough to rest our rookery, and she has something she wants to say to Mathias. Now are you going to let us in, or are we going to stand out here and make a scene until someone decides they can use the distraction to sneak through your window and steal a few skins?"

Quentin leaned closer to me. "She makes you look like you have manners," he murmured.

"Quiet, you," I said.

The door opened wider, revealing a stocky man with blond hair streaked in Selkie gray, and the deep sea eyes characteristic of his kind. The sealskin around his shoulders was almost an afterthought. He could never have been anything but a Selkie.

"You're Toby Daye?" he asked, focusing on me. His eyes seemed to skip over Quentin, like he didn't dare look directly at my squire. I swore inwardly. Beacon's Home was in Halifax. I didn't know enough about Canadian geography to say for sure how close that was to Toronto, but from the way René was trying not to admit he could see Quentin, I was willing to bet it was close enough that he'd seen the High King and his family at least a time or two. He knew what the Crown Prince looked like.

If this was how Quentin's blind fosterage was finally spoiled, I was going to laugh until I cried.

"I am," I said. "Hi."

"My name is René Lefebvre, but I was born René O'Dell," he said. "Connor was my cousin. Second cousin, on my father's side. I'm terribly sorry for your loss."

He sounded so sincere, and so genuinely sad about the man I'd mourned and moved on from, that I felt unexpected tears spring to the corners of my eyes. I swallowed my grief, taking what comfort I could from Tybalt's proximity. Connor was gone. Connor was never coming back. But that didn't mean I was alone, or that I was ever going to be alone again.

"I appreciate that," I said. My voice hardly shook at all. Something else to be grateful for, under the circumstances. "Is Mathias home?"

"As if I'd allow him to be anywhere else, or he'd allow the same for me, given the circumstances?" His sadness faded, replaced by exhaustion. "Neither of us is leaving this house for any reason short of danger to the clan itself, and even then, we'll go together. Why should we let you inside? Connor was a Ryan, by the end. You could be here because you want them to be the last clan standing, and help their leader strip the skins from our bodies."

"Okay, first, I'm not loyal to any specific Selkie clan; it's not like Connor and I ever reached the stage of visiting his family for the holidays. Which is almost a pity, because Selkies throw *amazing* parties, but that's neither here nor there. Second, I'm engaged, and my fiancé would be cranky if I let the memory of a man he wasn't exactly friends with muddle my actions."

"Hello," said Tybalt.

René blinked. "The rumors are true? You're really marrying a King of Cats?"

"I'm going to ignore the part where they're apparently gossiping about me in Halifax, of all places, and move on to my third point. Namely, it doesn't matter if Liz is trying to trick her way into your house, because I'm not. I'm a knight sworn to the service of Duke Sylvester Torquill and a hero in the service of Queen Arden Windermere in the Mists, and neither one of them would put up with me lying my way into a private home."

Well. Sylvester wouldn't, anyway. Sylvester had always been very clear on the need for his knights to be honest, chivalrous, and true, and maybe if he'd done a little better of a job at living up to those standards himself—at least the "honest" part—we wouldn't be functionally estranged. His lies weren't the only things that complicated our relationship, but wow, had they been enough to do a lot of damage.

Arden had spent over a century hiding in the mortal world, pretending to be a human woman, selling books and sitting for children and generally lying to everyone around her for the sake of staying alive. Her approach to the truth was probably a little more flexible than Sylvester's, and for good reason.

"Let them in, René," called a voice from deeper inside. "It's not as if I wasn't expecting a challenge." Mathias sounded . . . smaller, somehow, almost deflated, like all the fight had gone out of him.

René's fingers tightened on the edge of the door. But he nodded, and said, "Of course, darling," as he pulled it wider open, and let us step inside.

The front of the little Cape Cod was almost identical to the one where we'd spoken to Liz, which made sense: these weren't their personal homes. These were temporary quarters maintained by the Duchy of Ships for the comfort of their Selkie guests and the human family members who traveled with them. Mathias and René probably shared a home that was filled with things only they would have chosen, touches and traces of the men they were, the life they shared with one another. This was . . . a motel, practically, a way station between home and harbor.

Mathias was sitting on the couch, a tumbler of amber liquid in his hand. It could have been part of the same set Liz was using, and her eyes locked on it almost instantly. His chuckle was both dark and bitter, like strong coffee served on a winter morning.

"Don't get too excited, Lizzy," he said, and took a sip. "It's apple cider. I prefer to keep a clear head when people are trying to do me ill. Although if you'd like something stronger, I can have René fetch it for you. A drunk enemy is a sloppy enemy, and I need all the advantages I can get."

"Feeling sorry for yourself, are you?" Liz spat. "This is your fault."

"I'm well aware, and believe me, I wish I felt as comfortable numbing the edges of the world as you do." Mathias took another swig of cider before swinging his attention around to me. "Ah, the sea witch's errand girl is here for a visit, with her entourage. Come to issue more veiled threats against anyone who touches your child? Believe me, we got the message. She's as safe as houses, at

least until the deadline gets closer and people grow more desperate. Come back in a few hours if you feel the need to frighten
someone."

"I'm not here about Gillian," I said, and it was only half a lie.
"I'm here because I need to talk to you about Isla Chase."

"Why not go talk to Isla herself? We're not *friends*, no matter
what you may have heard about our history. We simply do a better
job of tolerating each other than many of our peers."

He sounded honestly confused. I couldn't be sure that he hadn't
been involved with the plot that killed her, but . . . I didn't think so.
He had no reason to be that good of an actor.

"Isla's dead," I said.

There was a gasp behind me. I turned. René was staring at me,
eyes wide, one hand clutching the front of his shirt, like he thought
he could keep his heart from leaping straight out of his chest.

"You were friends?" I asked.

"She's my sister," he said. He moved quickly then, crossing the
room to reach, not me, but the couch where Mathias sat. The other
man opened his arms and René fell into them. He wasn't sobbing;
he was shaking, his entire body rocking with the force of his grief.

Mathias looked at me over René's shoulder. His eyes were cold.
"You had best not be playing some sort of joke on us, or I swear, by
Maeve's grace, I don't care if the sea witch sent you, I'll have your
bones for bangles."

"And since I'm a changeling, you wouldn't be violating the
Law," I said. "I know."

"I would still gut him like the fish his seal-shape so resembles,"
said Tybalt. "I would also prefer you not go around reminding people that your government, such as it is, cares so little for your life."

"You're cute when you're murderous," I said.

"That explains why you think he's cute all the time," muttered
Quentin.

Mathias barked a laugh that sounded halfway to becoming hys-
terical. "The Crown Prince of the Westlands is in my living room.
He's in my living room, having opinions about a changeling
knight's love life. Maybe none of this is happening. Maybe we're
still on our way here from Halifax, and when I wake up, we'll
be able to try all this nonsense again, in a slightly less horrifying
fashion."

"Sorry, but this is real," I said. "And we'd prefer it if you didn't spread that whole 'secretly the Crown Prince' thing around. Quentin's with me on a blind fosterage. No one's supposed to know who he is."

"But you don't deny it," said Mathias.

"No, because I said I wasn't here to lie to you, and this isn't the time to start." René was still clinging to him, shaking. I watched the back of his head for a moment. The Selkie clans were all interrelated; they had to be. How else could their human kinfolk marry and raise families of their own? No one who'd grown up purely in the mortal world would be able to understand them, and even with a geas to stop their tongues and keep them from spilling Faerie's secrets, there would be gaps. Places where the lies were too apparent.

More and more, what we'd come here to do felt *wrong*. The Luidaeg's punishment might have been right and just when it began, but that was generations ago, before any of these people were alive, before the Selkies were a thriving, functional part of Faerie. I couldn't tell her "no." I couldn't stop her. But was I going to be able to live with myself once I'd done what she demanded?

I didn't know.

"I'm sorry to be the one who tells you this. I'm more sorry that it's happened. But . . ." I stopped, caught myself, and began again. "When the Root and Branch were young, when the Rose still grew unplucked upon the tree; when all our lands were new and green and we danced without care, then, we were immortal. Then, we lived forever."

René finally made a sound, sorrow and disbelief and shocked horror bound together in a small, tight gasp. He turned, still clinging to Mathias, to face me.

I continued. It was the only thing left for me to do. "We left those lands for the world where time dwells, dancing, that we might see the passage of the sun and the growing of the world. Here we may die, and here we can fall, and here Isla Chase of Belle Fleuve, leader of the Chase clan of Selkies, has stopped her dancing."

René nodded, closing his eyes and sagging into the couch. Mathias stroked his arm, even as he glared daggers at me. I'd rarely seen a man that openly embracing his hatred while not actively trying to murder me. It was a nice change, even if I didn't like the circumstances.

"Why are you *telling* us this?" he demanded. "The sea witch granted us permission to steal from one another, and to be rendered human against your will is the next best thing to being murdered. My clan's children are hiding in their rooms, crying, because what happens to them if someone comes to hurt their mommies or daddies? One death shouldn't be enough to summon a hero. Not unless you're intending to slay our Firstborn."

"She's a friend of mine, so no," I said. I had spent a lot of time cultivating a good relationship with the Luidaeg. Even if some of that time had been accidental, I didn't want to waste it. There was also the little matter of my having brought her back from the dead once, after her sister Eira had broken into her apartment and attacked her. That sort of thing makes it difficult to commit to slaughter. "I'm here because whoever stole Isla's skin murdered her. She didn't fall. She didn't commit suicide. She was murdered."

René made a small snuffling sound and pressed his face into Mathias' shoulder. Mathias, thank Oberon, sat up a little straighter, some of the malice leaving his face, to be replaced by amazement.

"Meaning you're throwing this upon the judgment of the clans," he said.

"Yes. The Luidaeg gave you permission to steal from each other. She didn't supersede or dismiss clan law, and clan law, according to Elizabeth, forbids the unnecessary killing of your human kin. Isla died human."

"You mean the Lady intended her to live and suffer all the days of her life, knowing what she'd lost," said Mathias witheringly. "Whoever killed her may have been trying to do her mercy."

"We're fae. We don't do mercy." I kept my gaze steady, not allowing myself to waver. "I'm a hero of the realm, Mathias Lefebvre. Will you allow me to fulfill my duty, and find the one who killed your . . ." I faltered. "I don't know the term for 'you're both leaders of Selkie clans,' but that's what I want to do. Liz has already said I can. There are only four of you left. If two of you give me permission, then I can do whatever needs to be done and not worry about someone saying I'm not allowed to be here."

"She was my fellow chief, and my kin through René." Mathias put a comforting arm around his husband's shoulder. "We rarely saw eye to eye, but we were friendly, for his sake. Yes. You have my permission to find the one who killed her."

"I want her skin," said René, with sudden, brutal fierceness.

I turned to him, blinking. "What?"

"My sister's skin. I want it. You say someone stole it from her, rendered her human, and killed her? I don't care what the sea witch gave us permission to do. She was murdered, and I can claim recompense, and I want her skin. It's been in our family since the beginning. It was our mother's. I want it back."

I bit my lip, glancing to Tybalt, who looked hopelessly back at me. Under most circumstances, it would have been nice to see him as baffled as I was. This wasn't most circumstances.

"René . . ." I shifted my focus back to the Selkie man, who was staring at me, impatient and defiant. "You know this Convocation ends with the Luidaeg using me to bind the skins to their wearers and bring back the Roane."

"I know," he said. "Mathias and I don't have any children. We've been trying to decide how we want to do that. Neither does . . . neither *did* Isla. There wasn't time. She thought she had so much longer than this. But our clan has children, and my sister wouldn't begrudge me giving her skin to one of them, any more than I would have begrudged her giving mine to a child of Belle Fleuve. We knew when we went to different clans that this day might come. You always hope it won't. You always understand that it will."

One more complication was exactly what we didn't need, especially with Torin prowling around, Dianda in custody, and the Luidaeg sailing off to find her absent sister. Looking at René's eyes, I realized I couldn't tell him I wouldn't at least try.

"I'll do what I can," I said. "If the skin has already been passed to a new owner . . ."

"I need to meet them," he said. "I need to know whether they're someone my sister would have approved of. If they're not, I'll take it back, and screw the sea witch if she doesn't like it."

Mathias looked horrified. Liz looked like she wanted a drink. Quentin grinned.

"I like this one," he said.

"Lovely: the Crown Prince approves of my husband." Mathias scowled at his cider. "I suddenly find myself wishing I shared my colleague's lack of caution where alcohol is concerned."

"A drink a day keeps the crushing weight of the universe away," said Liz, with something that actually resembled good cheer.

"Right," I said. "Mathias, Liz, you should stay here, and stay together. We can't afford to lose any more clan leaders, not when things are getting ugly. René, will you come with us?"

"What?" said Mathias and Liz, in remarkably close unison.

"Of course," said René, and started to rise.

Mathias caught his arm, dragging him right back down again. "You will *not*," he snapped. He sounded furious. His face told a different story.

He was afraid.

I could understand his reaction. I went through something similar every time I needed to send one of my boys away. Tybalt could take care of himself, and even Quentin wasn't the helpless courtier that part of me would always insist on seeing him as, but that didn't stop me from worrying whenever shit was going down and they weren't close enough for me to watch over. Mathias was a man on the verge of losing everything—his way of life, his people, even the specific nature of his ties to Faerie. Adding René to that list was just one step too far.

"He will," I said gently. "I need someone who can walk me through the community you have here, however temporary it is, and I can't take you or Liz."

"Why not?" he demanded.

"Because maybe Isla was killed because she was convenient, and maybe she was killed because someone held a grudge, but maybe she was killed because someone is targeting Selkie clan leaders, and I'd rather not walk you right into their targeting range." I shrugged. "Call me weird, but I think the Selkies—Roane, whatever the right term is when this is all over—will do better if they don't have to deal with their world changing and their leaders dying at the same time. It's just a thought."

"It's not a bad one," said Mathias. "Don't . . . please, *please.* We're not friends. You have no reason to do anything I ask of you, and every reason to want to see me suffer, but please. Don't let them hurt him."

"My lady is not so cruel as you'd imply, and I would be most pleased if you would choose your words more carefully in the future." Tybalt's voice was mild. His eyes told a different story. His pupils had narrowed to thin threads against the banded green of his irises, and he looked at Mathias the way a predator looks at a small, scurrying thing; like he was considering how good the other man might taste. "Please do not provoke me."

"Did you feel like you weren't getting in your daily quota of being unnecessarily threatening, or are you just showing off for the new people?" I asked.

"Can I vote 'both'?" asked Quentin.

Tybalt snorted. "I'm allowed to defend your honor. You granted me that right when you accepted my suit. Please don't take away what small pleasures I can preserve in the face of far more danger than I care to contemplate."

"Fine, you can threaten people."

"I appreciate it," he said, cracking the narrowest line of a smile.

I turned back to Mathias. "Sorry about that: my fiancé is pretty protective. But that means your husband will be walking with a very impatient, very highly-strung King of Cats, and a hero of the realm, and her personal squire. He'll be as safe as we can make him."

"Your personal squire, the Crown—"

"Okay, I *really* need you to stop saying that," I said. "Please. Quentin is with me on a blind fosterage, and if news of his parentage gets out in the Mists, or news of his location gets out back in Beacon's Home, it could endanger him and force his parents to call him home. I'm not done training him, and even though it would mean a serious reduction in my grocery bills, I've gotten fond of the little jerk. So do me a favor and stop endangering my squire."

"Or the King of Cats will eat me?" asked Mathias.

"No, but you'll piss me off, and I'm pretty sure that's worse."

"She's right," said Quentin. "It's way worse. I would prefer the flesh wounds."

"I can't tell whether I'm being insulted or you're being flattered," said Tybalt.

"Again, go with 'both' and move on," I said, keeping my attention on Mathias. "You need to let René go with us. I will do my utmost to guarantee that he stays safe."

"Let her," said Liz. "She has a remarkably good track record, all things considered. She almost never comes back with unexpected corpses."

"That's not encouraging," said Mathias . . . but he let go of René's arm. The other man rose, turned back, and bent to press a kiss to Mathias' forehead, lingering there for a long moment.

"I'll come back to you," he said softly, voice so low and intimate that I felt almost like I was intruding. Only almost. Their farewell was important; so was the dead woman.

"See to it," said Mathias.

René nodded and walked over to join the rest of us. There was nothing left to say, and so we simply left. We had work to do.

SIXTEEN

THE BEACH WAS STILL deserted. I paused, frowning.

"René, your sister—you lived with her at some point, right? After you'd both received your skins?" Most fae have extremely low birthrates, a consequence of being functionally immortal. If we bred the way humans do, we would have overrun the world centuries ago, leaving no room for anything else. Sometimes I think that might have been better. Most of the time, I think we would have just come up with different ways of ruining absolutely everything.

René nodded. "Her skin was worn by our mother; my skin was worn by our grandfather. There's a tradition in our family of marrying kin who were never offered a skin of their own. That way, we never lose sight of the fact that mortality comes for us all. That's why I had to leave for Beacon's Home when I fell in love with Mathias. He wasn't clan leader yet—he wasn't even sure he was in the running—but he couldn't come to live with me, because by my clan's rules, we couldn't have been married. We were both Selkies, and that simply wasn't done, especially not by the old chief's son."

"Okay, the family history is nice, but irrelevant to my actual question. Can you describe the scent of your sister's magic? In as much detail as possible, please." I'd never had the chance to smell Isla in the act of spellcasting. The scent might linger on her seal-skin, but I wouldn't know that for sure until I found the person who'd stolen it.

"Chicory and phlox," said René. "It's a lot like mine. Here." He held out his hand, brow furrowing as he whistled a few notes of a song that sounded distinctly similar to the sort of weird maritime folk that Quentin sometimes decided to blast in the middle of the day. That's the real connection between folk music and the fae: it's easier to whistle than heavy metal.

The smell of chicory and cypress filled the air as the space above his palm transitioned from perfect clarity to cloudy gray, finally becoming a black-and-white image of a younger Isla, laughing as she spun on the bare toes of one foot, her other foot held out at a stabilizing angle. She wasn't particularly graceful. Selkies never are. But there was a joy to her that had been absent the one time I'd seen her alive, a lightness that spoke to the way she saw her place in the world.

"Everyone thought I was going to take over when Mom passed her skin along," said René, eyes on the spinning specter of his sister. "I'd been a Selkie for almost five years before Isla was chosen. I'd carried myself with dignity and pride. But then Mathias happened, and there was no way for us to be together and me to lead the clan, so I stepped aside, and Isla had to change her plans."

"That sucks," said Quentin softly. His eyes were on the spinning Selkie woman, and I didn't know how to read the expression on his face. We'd been together long enough that I could usually tell what he was thinking, but now . . .

He had a sister in Toronto. Penthea, second in line for the throne. If he chose to step aside for some reason, he'd be doing to her what René had accidentally done to Isla. For the first time, I saw why his parents might be concerned about his attachment to the Mists. After all, we were the ones with the power to turn a prince's head.

"Yeah." René closed his hand. The dancing figure of Isla disappeared as he looked at me. "Did that give you what you needed?"

"I guess we're going to find out," I said, and closed my eyes, taking a deep breath.

What felt like hundreds of magical traces struck me at the same time, and I staggered. Tybalt was there to catch me and hold me up, one hand under my right arm and the other clamped around the curve of my waist, supporting and stabilizing me. I clutched at his arms, eyes still closed, and breathed in again, even deeper this time.

The magical assault on my nose and lungs was actually, physically painful. I swallowed, forcing myself to keep going. *This shouldn't be so hard,* I thought, reeling under the assault. *This is what I was made to do.*

The Dóchas Sidhe. Faerie's bloodhounds—literally. We're more attuned to blood than any other kind of fae I've ever encountered, and that includes both the Daoine Sidhe and the Baobhan Sith. We can bend it to our desires, shifting a person's body along the scale between immortality and the grave, and since magic is a function of the blood, we can track individuals by the scents they leave behind as they walk through the world. But there was so *much*, and it was so *thick*—

Not letting myself think too hard about what I was about to do, I closed my teeth on my tongue, wincing against the bright bolt of pain that followed. The wound was already healing by the time I unclenched my jaw, flesh knitting back together with a distracting, tingling itch. Hot blood filled my mouth. I swallowed as much as I could, hoping it would be enough to prevent me from needing to do that again. I've gotten over a lot of my issues with blood—it helps that I've been covered in the stuff so many times at this point that I'd never get out of bed if I hated it like I used to—but it's always better when I can avoid bleeding more than absolutely necessary.

The world seemed to slow as the blood reached my stomach, amplifying my magic in an almost indescribable way. How it can work when the blood is my own doesn't make sense; I shouldn't be able to use my magic to *fuel* my magic. But it does work, and that's what matters, especially when I need to find the place where an innocent woman died.

I breathed in, and the magic flowed around me, neatly separating into its component parts, saltwater and freshwater and kelp and roses, always, always roses. I kept breathing in, looking for anything that sang to my memory of René's magic. Chicory and phlox, that's what he'd said; chicory and phlox.

There. It wasn't much, barely more than a whisper, but it was enough. I let go of Tybalt's arms and started walking forward, eyes still closed, trusting him and Quentin to stop me before I could walk over the edge of the ship. With my luck, the Luidaeg's spell would wear off between the dock and the water, and I'd get to enjoy drowning. Again.

I *hate* drowning.

Chicory. Not René's chicory, which was sweet, mellow, well-aged, like a spice that had been sitting in a kitchen cupboard for years, waiting for the chance to be used. This was sharper, more bitter on the tongue, fresh-wrung from the root and still grieving for its marshy home. I followed it across the sand, and when the scent told me to turn left, I did, feeling Tybalt's hand briefly clamp down on my shoulder to protect me from some unseen danger. It was good to have people I could trust like this. There was a time when I wouldn't have been able to make this walk, because there would have been no one to stop me from going over the edge of the world.

Had Isla been alone when she'd walked this way? She'd been bleeding magic, but that isn't uncommon for fae in fae spaces. We're as twitchy and unfocused as the humans are, when we're not forced to stay on edge to protect ourselves from discovery. She had probably been making illusory balls to toss from hand to hand, or filling the air with small sparkles. Selkies have limited magic by pureblood standards—most of their strength goes into their skins, into keeping them alive and capable of transforming—but they have enough to fidget with.

Had Isla known she was heading toward her own death? I hoped not. I hoped she'd been calm and casual, maybe a little nervous, since the Luidaeg had essentially declared open season on Selkie skins, but confident in her own ability to keep her skin safe. I couldn't bring her back, and so I had to believe she'd been caught unaware, that it had happened quickly and completely and left her with very little time to realize what was happening.

I knew I was lying to myself. Her actual death told me that much. Unless she'd been unconscious when she hit the water, her death had been neither quick nor peaceful, but had been an agonizing struggle for survival, surrounded by an element that had, until not long before she fell, loved her. Selkies loved the sea; the sea loved Selkies.

The scent of chicory and phlox grew stronger, until I felt like I wouldn't lose it even if my eyes were opened. I couldn't take the chance. I walked and kept walking. The smell grew stronger still. René gasped. It was a small, strangled sound, powered by pain.

I opened my eyes.

We were standing under a boardwalk. There was still sand

beneath our feet, but this was no longer the peaceful artificial beach designed to keep visiting Selkies comfortable: this was a part of the Duchy of Ships, and not the nicest, or best-maintained part. The wood around us was slick with water and ripe with rot, blotching the structure in lurid greens and oranges. As soon as I acknowledged the presence of the decay, I could smell it, mundane odors overpowering the magical. That didn't matter. We were where we needed to be.

The sand in front of us had been disturbed, thrashed up by what looked almost like a localized whirlwind. The wind couldn't reach it here to smooth the damage away. A string of cheap glass beads lay off to one side, a few rolling loose to mingle with the sand. That was where René's attention was fixed, not on the damage, but on the little glass beads.

"I . . . I want those when you're done," he said, in a strangled voice. "Most of them were our mother's. She used to wear them braided in her hair, just like Isla did."

"I appreciate you not grabbing for them," I said, beginning to circle the disturbed area.

He made a small sound that I might have interpreted as a laugh under other circumstances. "I watch a lot of police procedurals with the kids—I'm one of the teachers in Beacon's Home. We need to prep our children for the mortal world, since most of them will wind up living there, and television helps. Gives them a sort of skewed idea of America, but since they'll never move that far from home, that's fine. Let them think it's a dangerous wasteland full of guns and drugs and murder."

"To be fair, that's pretty close to my experience, and I *do* live there," I said, continuing to circle.

There weren't as many distinct strains of magic here: this was a place where most people didn't go. That made sense. It was dark, gloomy, and decayed, which would put off a lot of the locals, and it wasn't dark, gloomy, or decayed *enough* for the rest of them. This was a liminal ground, splitting the difference between so many factions that it wound up equally inimical to all.

Breathing shallowly in through my mouth and out through my nose brought me the mingled scents of our magics, musk and pennyroyal and steel and heather blended with my own copper and freshly cut grass, and the nearly-twinned scents of René and Isla, but nothing else distinct enough for even me to name. Whoever killed Isla, they had done it without using magic.

There was information in the absence. I didn't know how to interpret it yet, but I knew there was an answer there. It might not be a good one, but . . .

"If one of the human kinfolk who came here with the Selkie clans had killed Isla, would they already be wearing her skin?" I asked, looking toward René.

He shook his head slowly. "I don't know. I want to say yes—I've never known one of our kin to be able to resist the singing of the sea, and we can hear it when we're near an unattached skin, like it's trying to lure us into the depths—but I've also never known one of us to *kill* for the sake of a skin. It's not our way."

"Murder is everyone's way, given sufficient incentive," said Tybalt. "I've never in my life known a person who couldn't be moved to the killing floor."

"You know me," protested Quentin.

Tybalt fixed him with a steely eye. "Yes," he said. "I do."

"All right." I can track magic for miles, but Selkie skins don't have the same sort of personalized scent. The Luidaeg's spell is a part of them, buried in every strand of fur, and I can't follow them. Tybalt, on the other hand . . . "We know where Isla's body ended up. What I want to know is what happened to her skin."

"Because whoever has her skin is the killer?" asked Quentin.

"Not necessarily." That would be too easy. "Tybalt?"

He transferred his unflinching gaze to me. "You're about to ask me to transform and try to sniff out the trail of a killer, aren't you? How many times must I tell you that I'm not a bloodhound?"

"Oh, believe me, I know you're not," I said. "I want the killer or the skin, or both. Any of the above will help me start figuring out what happened."

"Scent doesn't cling well to sand," he said.

"It's better than nothing."

Tybalt sighed, sounding exquisitely put-upon—and slightly relieved at the same time. If I was doing this *with* him, I wasn't going to be tempted to run away and do it *without* him. "As you wish," he said, and folded forward and inward at the same time, the scent of musk and pennyroyal filling the air as he landed on all four feet in the sand, a tabby cat instead of a nearly-human man. One of his ears was tattered, the artifact of some fight long before we'd come to know each other. His eyes were the same. I would always, always know him, by those eyes.

Tybalt sauntered over to wind himself around my ankles once, twice, three times before stepping more delicately toward the circle of disturbed sand, his tail low and twitching behind him, his nose pressed close to the ground and his whiskers fanned forward as far as they would go. He sniffed, sneezed, and then began slinking toward the far end of the sand, toward the place where the artificial land dropped away and became all too real ocean.

At the very edge, he stopped, yowled, and looked back over his shoulder at me. I knew a cue when I saw one. I walked over and looked down . . .

. . . and there, floating in the tangled kelp that matted around the pylons, was a gray sealskin without anyone to wear it, cast aside like so much garbage. My stomach churned, threatening to bring up my last several meals for a repeat engagement.

"René, stay back." My voice was remarkably steady. I wanted to be proud of that. I couldn't quite manage it.

Isla's killer hadn't been content with ripping the skin off her shoulders and pushing her into the sea to die. They had thrown her skin in after her. I wanted to believe they'd thrown them both in at the same time, giving her a fighting chance, even if she hadn't been able to stay alive long enough to benefit from it. I couldn't. I knew, without any proof beyond the gnawing in my gut, that her killer had waited until she went under before they threw her skin after her. Selkies learned to swim while they were still human. They had stood here, skin in their hands, watching her drown. Only when there was no chance the sea could still be kind had they thrown her skin in after her, willing to let it be lost forever.

Maybe that had been the plan for Isla and her skin alike. Let the leader of one of the Selkie clans disappear the day before the Luidaeg's long-delayed judgment was finally to be passed, and see what *that* did to the rest of them. Could any of the Selkies resist the urge to run, if they believed Isla had been able to get away clean?

And if they had run, if they *had* believed . . . who would have benefitted from that? Who would have stood to gain from having the Luidaeg's oaths broken?

René moved to stand next to me. I gave him a careful sidelong look. He was staring at the skin with open avarice, and I had to wonder at the coincidence of it all. The murdered clan leader was the sister of another clan leader's husband, one who had been seen publicly questioning the Luidaeg. If he got his hands on his sister's skin, would we ever see it again?

The chain of evidence matters, even in Faerie. I shrugged out of my jacket, offering it to Quentin, who had appeared—as expected—by my shoulder. "Keep René up here," I said. "Whatever you do, don't let him into the water."

"What are you—"

His question cut off mid-sentence as I did the only thing I *could* do and leapt off the edge of the dock, arms pinwheeling wildly as I plummeted toward the waiting sea. Two immersions in one day. Three, if I counted entering and leaving the knowe at Saltmist as separate incidents. Lucky, lucky, *lucky* me.

The wind whipped at my face as I fell. I barely had time to close my eyes and hunch my shoulders before I slammed into the water like a stone flung through a window. The impact knocked the air out of my lungs and shoved me well below the surface. I gasped, unable to help myself. Water filled my mouth and throat, and for a moment, I knew what it had been like for Isla when she drowned, betrayed by a world she had believed would always, always love her.

The Luidaeg's magic flared around me, and my body changed without my urging it to do so, acquiring fins and scales and most importantly, gills. I took a grateful breath, feeling the water fill me as a source of life, not death. It seemed lighter now, more welcoming. I turned over, getting my bearings back, and flicked my tail to drive me toward the surface.

Isla's sealskin was there, tangled in the kelp. I took it in my hands, and nearly let it go again as it began singing through my skin, offering me the waves, the world—an escape.

Put me on, and you won't have to worry about the prophecy made for your mother's sake, it whispered. *Only a child of Amandine's line can be so bound. You could be free. You could be with your daughter forever, for eternity, for always. Put me on, and be remade.*

It was tempting. Of course it was tempting. The skin wanted to be worn. Whether it was a compulsion charm or simple self-preservation, the skin wanted to be worn, and I was the closest available wearer.

No wonder the Selkies had always worked so hard to make sure their skins were passed hand to hand, and not left to sit fallow on a shelf, waiting for a worthy bearer. An unworn skin was a skin seeking a shoulder to wrap itself around.

Well, it wasn't going to be mine. I knew how Selkie skins worked, thanks to the Luidaeg tying one around my daughter. If I draped it over myself, even for a second, everything I was would be re-made, Dóchas Sidhe replaced by Selkie-maid forevermore. It would be a way for the Selkies to save themselves: without me, the Luidaeg wouldn't be able to resurrect the Roane. My place in Amandine's line would end, leaving only Mom, and August, to play whatever role Faerie intended for our messed-up little family.

"They have to be taken voluntarily," I muttered to myself, tightening my grip on the skin, resisting the urge to cast it aside as fiercely as I could. "They aren't leeches, they can't just latch on." For all that the skin felt hot and vital in my hands, it wasn't moving. It couldn't grab me.

Now there was just the question of how I was going to get back up. I twisted in the water, looking toward the edge of the dock high above me. Tybalt and Quentin were both leaning over the edge. Tybalt was back in his human form, making no effort to hide his displeasure as he glowered down at me. I raised one hand in a small, sheepish wave.

"Hi," I called. "Either of you got a rope?"

SEVENTEEN

THEY DID NOT, in fact, have a rope. Or a ladder, or even so much as a pool floaty. What they *did* have was a traumatized Selkie who wanted his sister's skin back, and was perfectly happy to jump into the water after me. Since that wasn't currently an option, a bunch of yelling followed, while Tybalt and Quentin tried to restrain him without looking like they were restraining him. Fun for the whole dysfunctional family.

After consulting with René, it was determined that the fastest way to get me back into the Duchy of Ships without causing a panic among the rest of the Selkies would be to swim around to the merchant docks and hitch a ride in a fishnet. Surrounded by fish. Because that wasn't going to give me nightmares for the remainder of my semi-immortal life.

"I hate water," I muttered, kicking along with my head just above the surface. Several enterprising waves had already slapped me in the face, but it was better to be able to see my people pacing me on the dock above than to potentially get myself lost somewhere under the Duchy and be stuck there when the Luidaeg's spell wore off.

Another wave slapped me, as if in response to my comment. I spat out saltwater and glared at the ocean, which was generally unimpressed.

"I hate water, I hate waves, I hate fish, I hate *everything about this*." I spat again for good measure, trying to get the salt out of my mouth. It didn't work. Everything tasted like brine, and probably would until the next time I ended up with a mouthful of blood.

I would have preferred that at the moment, and that alone was a terrible statement about my situation.

Quentin and Tybalt didn't look any happier than I felt. Tybalt kept casting sharp looks in my direction, and had twice caught Quentin before he could throw himself over the side. I understood why Quentin wanted to—the Luidaeg had enchanted us at the same time; if I was safe in the water, so was he—and was still thankful Tybalt was stopping him. The spell was due to wear off at any time. I could drown and recover from it. Quentin couldn't. For him, dead was dead, and I did *not* want to try explaining that to his parents.

As if in answer to my thoughts, the water grew colder around me, like it wanted me to remember that this was not my natural environment. My gills stung in my throat, feeling less like a part of my anatomy and more like an injury that was somehow refusing to heal. I swam faster, conscious of the need not to outpace my guides, but equally conscious of the fact that if I reverted to my normal shape while I was submerged, I could be in a whole new world of trouble.

Please, Maeve, I don't ask for much, but I've heard your daughter call on you: please, let me reach the nets, I thought.

Ships began appearing in the water up ahead, some large and stately, ready to take on cargos of both material and passengers, others small and swift and low to the water. I could pull myself into one of those smaller ships, if I really needed to. I might, depending on what happened next. I could see the nets René had mentioned now, long systems of ropes and pulleys helping the individual fishermen bring their catches up to the level of the dock itself. Taking a deep breath, I ducked under the water and swam as fast as I could toward my goal.

I was almost there when the spell wore off.

It began with a tingling at the tips of my flukes, spreading through my scales until, with a wrenching, shuddering sensation that was distressingly akin to being sliced in half, my tail split in two, transforming back into legs. I kept kicking, less effectively now. My gills sealed over and my lungs began burning, alerting me in no uncertain terms to the fact that they desperately wanted air. I kept swimming. It was all I could do.

The Selkie skin draped over my arm seemed to sing even louder now, promising hope, promising harbor, promising—most importantly of all—freedom from the threat of drowning. All I had to do was put it on and the burning would stop. All I had to do was put it on and the water would welcome me as a friend and confidant, as a part of its greater self, and all my troubles would go away.

That's not true, I thought fiercely, still swimming. The water was colder now that I had a less maritime metabolism. It was biting into my skin, seeming to burrow all the way down into my bones. It was getting harder to keep thrashing. *My troubles wouldn't go away. I'd just wind up with all new troubles.*

But oh, it was tempting. I wouldn't have to remake the Roane and destroy Selkie culture for the Luidaeg's sake: I wouldn't be able to. She'd have to talk August around, and good luck with that, since Mom was currently protecting her older daughter like she'd never been willing to protect me. I could learn the things that Selkies knew. People would stop asking me to be a hero, because I wouldn't be Oberon's anymore. Gillian and I would be the same. For the first time in her life, she'd have a mother who was actually exactly like she was, a mother who wouldn't keep disappearing.

Of course, I'd need to break that nasty habit I had of getting covered in blood every time I turned around, but I'd gone years with nothing more than a few flesh wounds. It was only since I'd come back from the pond that I'd developed a tendency to ruin my favorite jeans with bloodstains. I could do better. I could *be* better.

The sealskin was getting better at tempting me. I shoved those brutally appealing thoughts away and kept swimming. What's an ocean but a bigger pond? No, thank you. I was *not* choosing to run away from my responsibilities only to return to a larger version of the prison I'd fought so hard to escape.

My lungs were still burning and I knew I was going to take an involuntary breath soon. I started to turn toward the surface, and stopped as my flailing hand struck something rough and fibrous. The net. I'd reached the net.

Slinging the sealskin over my arm, where it continued to murmur wordless enticements to me, I put my fingers through the netting and began pulling myself up, hand over hand. Fish thronged inside the net, packed together until they could barely do more than twitch and flop. The feeling of their cold, scaled sides against my skin almost made me lose my grip in disgust. I pushed the feeling aside and kept climbing.

My head broke the surface and I took a huge, greedy gulp of air, filling my lungs with what felt like equal parts oxygen and sea-foam. I coughed and wheezed, trying to clear the spray out of my throat as I climbed. Somewhere above me, a voice shouted dismay and displeasure at my ascent. I ignored it and kept climbing. What were they going to do, stab me when I reached the dock? Fine. Whatever. I've been stabbed before, by better people than some confused deckhand who doesn't know what to do with a half-drowned hero.

Tybalt, Quentin, and René were waiting at the top of the net. René was engaged in a vigorous argument with several of the people who'd been working the pulley, shouting at them in a dizzying mixture of French and English that I couldn't even dream of following. Not that I would have had the chance. Tybalt grabbed me as soon as my feet were on the dock, pulling me into a tight, un-yielding embrace.

"Never, *never* do that to me again," he hissed, lips up against my ear, creating a shell of semi-privacy for the two of us to occupy. "Bleed if you must. I know you'll recover from that."

"I recover from drowning, too," I protested, but didn't pull away or ask him to let go. He was warm and dry—or had been dry, before he'd put his hands on me—and most of all, solid. Real.

I hadn't realized how long I'd gone without an anchor before I'd found one. Life was so much easier when I wasn't constantly afraid that I was on the verge of drifting away.

"Do you recover from being swept out to sea, gnawn upon by sharks, drowned again, trapped in a discarded fishing net, and pris-oned at the bottom of the ocean for a hundred years? Because even if you do, I fear my heart could not." He thrust me out to arm's length. His pupils had expanded to their widest point, wiping away all but the thinnest sliver of green. "Do *not* do this to me again, Oc-tober. Do *not*. I can lose . . . so many things. I can't lose you. I would, unquestionably, fail to survive it."

Silence fell. I turned to see René and the dockhands staring at us. Quentin, for his part, had rolled his eyes skyward so hard that I suspected there was a good chance they were going to roll clean out of his head.

"Is he *always* like that?" asked René.

I nodded. "Most of the time. Sometimes he gets flowery and

overblown, but I don't mind. It's sort of soothing at this point, you know?"

"*Ostie*," muttered René. "They should offer the man in shops to inspire our husbands to be better."

"Please, no," said Quentin. "I'll jump into the ocean if we start acquiring extra Tybalts."

"You don't appreciate the finer things in life," said Tybalt.

"I appreciate not watching five of you fight over one of Toby," Quentin countered.

That was an image worth revisiting later, and at length. Right now, however . . . "I have Isla's skin," I said. It seemed to shiver in my hands, like it was protesting the lost opportunity to sway me toward the sea. I shuddered, a bigger motion that made its small twitches easier to dismiss as my own bone-deep chill. I can heal from practically anything. I still get cold.

René's face immediately sobered. He took a step toward me, one hand partially outstretched. He hesitated then, looking at my face. "May I?" he asked.

"I'd prefer it if you did, as long as you understand that if you try to run, Tybalt will chase you down and make you stop," I said. "It keeps talking to me. Do Selkie skins always talk?"

Tybalt grinned, putting teeth—literally—behind my threat.

René cast an anxious glance at the dockhands, who were working the pulley, ostentatiously ignoring us. He looked back to me. "Talk, no," he said, gently taking the skin from my hands. "Some can form words, but most can't at this point. They're worn smooth, like driftglass, like stones in the sea. The elders say *their* elders could converse with the spirits of their skins, but if that's true, and not just some foolish fancy, that time passed very long ago. Before my mother's mother's mother swam the seas."

Meaning the Luidaeg had been draping the Selkies in ghosts all this time. Hungry ghosts, no less, who wanted the chance to live again, no matter how limited their form. I shivered, this time not from the cold. What did the night-haunts make of the Selkies? They were wrapped in magically preserved slivers of the Roane, who had faded from the flocks centuries ago—but when they'd been lifted up on autumnal wings, had they done so with fleshless faces, flensed and left to rot?

It was a chilling thought. I didn't like it, and so I shunted it aside.

"René, I know you want to pass Isla's skin, but I need to ask you not to do that," I said. "It has to stay with us until this is settled. I'm sorry."

"I don't want to let my sister's skin out of my hands," he said reluctantly. "I'd trade it for Isla, alive and human and here, but since I can't have that, I don't want to let it go. And yet . . . I think you're right. It wouldn't be safe with me. Too many people are desperate, for their children, their loved ones, all the ones who'd been content to wait when they thought that waiting could be fruitful."

"I understand," I said—and I did, I really did. To be a changeling is to be something like to a Selkie, inside and outside Faerie at the same time. The hope chests offer us a way to cross that line and become fae forever, if that's what we want. That's what they were created to do, and that's the reason they've all been locked away, hidden from the people who need them most. We're not seen as worthy, and part of that supposed unworthiness comes from the fact that we have to fight for everything we get. Faerie has never given us anything freely.

I took a step back, so I could see all three of my traveling companions at the same time. "We'll take you, and the skin, to our quarters. There's always someone there, and we're traveling under the Luidaeg's protection. No one will interfere with us." I pitched my voice a bit louder than necessary, to be sure the dockhands would hear me. From the way their shoulders tightened, they did. Good.

It wasn't that I thought they were necessarily dishonest. I didn't know them well enough for that. It was simply that we were out in the open, and there was no way to be sure we hadn't been listened in on. Once we got the skin home, we could keep it safe until things were settled.

And we could let René see his sister's body.

"Do you know how to get to the visitor's apartments from here?" I asked.

René shook his head. "Selkies have their own space. We don't travel deeper into the duchy when we don't have to."

"I know the way," said Tybalt. I blinked at him. He smirked, although the expression lacked his usual heat. "I had plenty of time to explore while you and your boy wonder were off playing at being merfolk. Follow me."

He turned on his heel and started walking, a little faster than normal, but not so fast that I couldn't keep up. He was annoyed, not actively angry. That was fine. Annoyed, I could work with. Angry meant yelling and apologies and pain, and I was way too tired for that.

We walked through the Duchy of Ships in a ragged line, fixed on our destination, trying to ignore the way people pointed and whispered behind their hands. Whatever temporary "ignore them, they're strangers" field we'd started with, we'd lost it somewhere between rescuing the son of an imprisoned Merrow Duchess and pulling a drowned woman from the sea.

Tybalt glanced my way, annoyance melting into a far more welcome wry amusement. "I see your reputation is spreading. You have fans again."

"I never asked for fans," I said, walking faster, as if that would be enough to shift me out from under the weight of all those staring eyes.

"Yet you charm everyone you meet in the same unfaltering manner," he said. "It seems difficult to believe that it is entirely accidental."

I hit him in the arm. He laughed, and things were, if not okay again, at least a little better.

The door to our courtyard appeared ahead of us like a beacon, offering the promise of safe harbor. We kept going until we could smell the fresh green scents of our private garden, and hear the sound of voices. Patrick, and Peter, both talking loudly enough that I could tell them apart even before we were close enough for me to pick out words.

"—not the land, Father! You can't keep thinking of it like it is!"

"We don't have an army right now, Peter. You have to slow down."

"Mother has been *imprisoned*!"

"Does it help at all if I say the sea witch is working on it, and is just as annoyed as the rest of us?" I stepped around the edge of the courtyard.

Patrick and Peter, who had both frozen in place at the sound of my voice, turned to look at me. They were virtually nose-to-nose, Patrick towering almost a foot over his son, yet still seeming somehow evenly matched. Dean and Marcia were off to one side. Neither of them made any effort to hide their relief at my appearance. Cassandra and Nolan were on the other side, looking utterly, profoundly confused. I guess suddenly being dropped into Undersea politics without a primer would do that.

"And where's Poppy?" I asked.

"She's in her apartment with the—with the thing you found," said Dean, haltingly.

"The body," I said. "You mean she's with the body."

He nodded, looking like he was about to be sick. Getting that boy out of the Undersea was the best thing I ever did. He was a good Count, thoughtful and patient and fair. Staying in Saltmist would have eaten him alive.

I turned to René. "We can take you to your sister momentarily," I said. "Will your traditions allow you to leave the skin with her body until this is resolved? Even if the night-haunts come for her, they won't touch the skin." If they'd been able to find sustenance in Selkie skins, all chance of the resurrection of the Roane would have been eliminated ages ago.

Looking sick, René shook his head. "The skin can't be given to the dead," he said. "The magic won't allow it. Some of the first Selkies tried to have their skins buried with them, thinking that was a way to break the bargain, and their children and siblings found those skins draped over chairs at the kitchen table the next day."

"Delightful." I pinched the bridge of my nose. "René, may I introduce you to Duke Patrick Lorden of Saltmist, his son, Peter Lorden, Count Dean Lorden of Goldengreen, his Seneschal, Marcia, and Crown Prince in the Mists Nolan Windermere, and his 'please don't cause a diplomatic incident because you don't understand what's happening' Cassandra Brown."

"I feel I may have just been insulted," said Nolan, sounding puzzled.

"Aren't you supposed to introduce princes and the like first?" asked Marcia.

"Not when we're in an Undersea fiefdom, surrounded by ocean on all sides," I said. "There's etiquette and then there's common sense, and they don't always agree. Everyone, this is René. He's married to the head of the Beacon's Home Selkies, and Isla was his sister."

"I am terribly sorry for your loss," said Nolan. He managed to make the proclamation sound like it actually meant something, and wasn't just the sort of thing people said when they didn't know what else to do.

"If we can't leave the skin with the body, what are we supposed to do with it?" asked Quentin. "Can you stick a Selkie skin in a closet?"

"The Luidaeg does, but I don't know how you keep them there," I said.

"I may be able to help," said Marcia. We all turned to stare at her. She flushed red, the color traveling all the way up the sides of her ears, and said, "Lily had custody of a Selkie skin for a few years, while she was waiting for its owner's daughter to be old enough to claim it. The, uh, owner had been clanless, so he handled the dispensation of his own skin."

"We allow people to select their heirs," protested René.

"Even when someone dies, and their chosen heir is too young?" asked Marcia. Her voice was cold and gentle at the same time, like the first swirl of snow on a winter morning. She looked unflinchingly at René. "He came to Lily because he was afraid that if something happened to him, his skin would be given to the 'most deserving,' and his daughter would have to wait until someone else died without an heir—assuming that if and when that happened, she'd be found more deserving than everyone else in her position. I don't know why he was so sure he was going to die. Maybe he'd found an actual seer, or maybe he just had a bad feeling. Whatever the reason, Lily agreed to safeguard his skin if anything happened, providing we could get to it before the Selkies did."

"I remember that," I blurted. "She paid me and Julie to break into a man's apartment." It had been small, and dark, and very, very clean, the kind of place I would only later come to appreciate as the loving home it was. There had been a man in the kitchen, bullet wounds in his chest and throat. The night-haunts had already been and gone, replacing the original corpse with a perfect, convincingly human replica.

The sealskin we'd been sent to retrieve had been neatly folded off to one side, presumably by the night-haunts themselves. It had seemed like an odd courtesy, but they loved the Luidaeg in their strange, windborne way. Maybe they'd been trying to honor her long-dead child as they took care of their latest meal.

He hadn't been my first dead body, sadly. I'd been with Devin long enough by that point to have learned the world wasn't all moonlight and roses. The sight of him had still been enough to wrench my dinner back out of me. I'd made it to the bathroom, barely, and promptly wished that I hadn't, when I'd seen the color-ful flotilla of rubber duckies sitting in the bottom of the dry tub, waiting for a bath time that was never going to come.

Whoever had killed him hadn't been doing it for his skin. Julie had been the one to carry it back to Lily's, maybe because she'd heard it calling to her, maybe because she'd known I—back then, before the pond, before the discovery of my actual heritage, when I'd thought of myself as a defective Daoine Sidhe and not a perfectly functional Dóchas Sidhe—would be vulnerable to temptation.

I'd never met the daughter. I wondered, suddenly, whether she was here.

Wrenching myself out of the memory, I focused on Marcia. "What do we do?"

"We'll need a willow basket lined with wax and filled with oil," said Marcia. "I can find the herbs I need here in the garden if some-one can get me the basket."

"I think I saw a booth selling crab baskets in the market," said Quentin.

"Don't go alone," I said.

"I'll go with him," said Cassandra. "The air's a little thick in here."

"Meaning my father and brother have been yelling at each other since we all stopped crying," said Dean, in a dry, weary tone. "I'd go also, if I weren't afraid of being arrested the second I stepped foot outside the courtyard."

"It seems the Lady sea witch's name carries some weight even with those who would trouble us, as none of the ruffians have been willing to cross our threshold," said Nolan. He turned to René. "I can take you to your sister, if you would like."

"I would appreciate that," said René. Nolan beckoned for him to follow, and the two of them walked across the courtyard to the apartment where Poppy was sitting with a dead woman, counting down the minutes of her decay.

"It makes sense that the people who live here wouldn't want to piss off the Luidaeg; she's their own personal nightmare," I said, as Quentin and Cassandra made their necessary, clearly much-desired escape. "Peter, why are you yelling at your father?"

"He just—he just *stood* there and let them take my mother!" he snapped, eyes flashing. "He could have fought for her! If he'd been Merrow, he would have fought for her!"

"If he'd been Merrow, your uncle would have needed to find a different excuse for arresting an innocent woman." I somehow managed to say that with a straight face. The thought of Dianda as "innocent" was barely this side of ridiculous. "Also your father would probably be dead, since your parents didn't bring an army." I paused, frowning, as I looked around the courtyard. "Where are Helmi and the others?"

"We decided it would be better if any further attackers received some bad information about how well-defended we are," said Patrick. As if on cue, what I'd taken for a curling vine lifted away from the wall, its edges tinting orange as it waved languidly in my direction. Then it reattached to its original place, the color draining away.

If I squinted, I could follow that long tentacle to a motionless shape I was pretty sure was Helmi. The other two Cephali were completely camouflaged, blending so flawlessly into their surroundings that I would have needed to cheat and bleed to have a chance of finding them.

"That isn't unnerving *at all*," I said, and returned my attention to Marcia. "Do you need anything else?"

"Basket, oil, herbs," she said. "And a pony, but I never get that, unless you count the Kelpies, which I don't. Kelpies are too naughty to count as ponies."

"They're also horrifying and full of teeth," said Patrick.

"Like I said: naughty." Marcia turned and walked into the herb beds, beginning to pluck sprigs of whatever caught her fancy.

I wanted to go with her, to see what kind of marshwater charm was used to preserve a Selkie's skin away from a living Selkie. I couldn't. Marcia would probably feel like I was checking her work—the last thing I wanted to do right now—and more importantly, Peter was still glaring at his father, a look of heartbreaking betrayal in his eyes. I sighed.

"I mostly know Dianda as my punchy friend who sometimes helps me out of nasty scrapes," I said. "We don't hang out, we don't talk about our feelings, we don't braid each other's hair. But I know her well enough to know her family is the most important thing in the world to her. She wouldn't want you to be fighting right now. Not each other, anyway. This is Dianda we're talking about: she'd absolutely want you to be fighting everyone else."

Patrick actually cracked a smile at that. "My wife has somewhat militant ideas about conflict resolution," he said.

"Yet you married her anyway," said Tybalt. "Fascinating."

"Don't say bad stuff about my mom," snapped Peter.

"Believe me, child, I am not," said Tybalt. "Even if I wished to mock your father's taste in wives, he would need only to point at my own choice of bride as proof that I am a man living in the metaphorical glass house."

"Root and branch preserve me from men who think they're clever," I muttered. Louder, I said, "The Luidaeg has gone to find Captain Pete and see if something can't be done about this whole 'treason' thing. In the meantime, I have at least one dead Selkie, and I no longer have the ability to go diving around under the duchy itself to look for more of them. Any suggestions about how to deal with all this would be greatly appreciated."

"Why do we care about dead Selkies?" demanded Peter.

"*Peter*," said Dean, appalled.

"What?" Peter looked from his brother to me, hands spread, trying to make us understand. "Mom's been arrested. For treason. She could die, Dean. She could be put to death because of lies Uncle Torin is telling about her. Selkies *always* die. They're barely better than humans that way." He suddenly seemed to realize he might have gone too far, because he glanced at me, grimaced, and added, "No offense."

"Oh, offense taken," I said. "You don't get to decide where the offense goes. But, please, continue."

Peter swallowed. "I—I'm sorry. I know you have more humans in the land Courts, and I know I'm supposed to be kind and . . . and forgiving of their faults, but they're so weird. How can they be people *and* mortal at the same time? People aren't supposed to die unless they do something stupid enough to deserve it. But changelings are mortal, and they're people. And Selkies are mortal sometimes, and they're people, too, and it's all weird and confusing and I don't understand it. They have my *Mom*. She's locked up somewhere, alone and scared, and they're going to hurt her, and I can't let them."

"Dianda isn't scared," I said, trying to be reassuring. "She's scary. Scary things don't get scared."

"Sometimes they do," said Patrick. His voice was very soft. "Sometimes they get so scared they can't breathe. Peter's right to be worried about her. We have to get her back."

"And we're working on it," I said.

"How?" Peter asked. "What are you doing, right now, to save my mom?"

I paused, long enough to count to ten and remind myself that Peter was still a teenager, and on the young side of teen at that, with all the impatience and insecurity of his age. Some things will never change.

Once I was sure I could be calm, I said, "Right now? This second? I'm waiting for the Luidaeg to come back with the one person I believe can actually dispute the treason charges with any authority, and I'm not antagonizing your uncle more than I absolutely have to. We brought you here so he couldn't use you as leverage to make your mother plead guilty to the charges he's trying to levy against her. She's brave, and she's fierce, and she's terrifying, but she's still your mom. If it was your life or hers, I'm pretty sure I know which she would choose. I know this goes against everything the Undersea teaches you, but sometimes you have to be patient."

"Not everything," said a voice from behind me. I managed not to scream as what I'd taken for a bush unfurled and straightened, changing colors as it did, becoming Kirsi. She looked at Peter with frustrated sympathy. "Merrow are hot and fast and angry. They lead us in part because letting them lead is easier than fighting with them. But when a Merrow and a Cephali go fishing, the Cephali will come back with the greater catch, because we know how to be still. We know *when* to be still. Have faith and keep your peace, young lord. Sir Daye hunts as a Cephali does. She will have her quarry, or she will make them pay for denying her."

"I think I'm flattered," I said.

"You are," said Tybalt.

I returned my attention to Peter. "The situation sucks, okay? I'm juggling too many things at once, and as soon as we have Isla's skin preserved, I need to go find the first mate and ask him whether there have been any other mysterious deaths. This may have been personal. It may also have been part of some kind of plot to panic the Selkies right before they're supposed to repay their debts to the Luidaeg. I don't *know*. I can't know until I find out whether we have any more missing skins. So right now, I am helping your mother by not making things worse for her. All right? It's the only thing I can do."

"Fine," muttered Peter sullenly.

Patrick put a hand on his shoulder. "We trust you."

That was nice. I wasn't sure *I* trusted me, under the circumstances. I was tired and sore and the memory of almost drowning was far too fresh in my mind. I was going to have nightmares the next time I tried to sleep, and poor Tybalt was going to be lucky if he didn't wind up getting smacked in the face. Repeatedly. Sometimes love leaves bruises, no matter how hard you try to prevent it.

"Good," I said gruffly, turning away. "Marcia? How's it going over there?"

"I have almost everything I need." She straightened to show me the bundles of green in her hands. A few of the stalks were crowned in tiny starbursts of flowers. I didn't recognize most of them. "Once the basket gets here, I can put the skin in stasis indefinitely."

Marshwater charms can be surprisingly effective when woven the right way, and Lily had been an excellent teacher. "All right. Can you keep things under control here?"

"You're leaving before Quentin gets back?"

With the Beacon's Home Selkies running around recognizing him, leaving Quentin in the courtyard seemed like the only way to avoid a truly awkward situation. I nodded. "We'll move faster this way. Once we're back and René's done paying his respects to his sister, we'll walk him back to the beach. Tybalt?"

"As my lady wishes," said Tybalt, sounding quietly relieved. He fell into position next to me, and together, we walked out of the courtyard, away from the people I was still struggling to save, out into the Duchy of Ships.

EIGHTEEN

"**PLEASE DON'T THINK ME** ungrateful, or that I wouldn't follow you to the very ends of the Earth if given the opportunity, but where, precisely, are we going?" asked Tybalt.

There are no true days or nights in the Summerlands, which exist in an eternal, tangled twilight, but time still passes, and we'd been in the Duchy of Ships long enough that most of the people who'd been awake when we arrived were in bed by now, leaving the docks and byways largely deserted. Not entirely: there's always someone awake in Faerie, no matter what the clock tries to say. Humanity has their night owls, and the fae have their morning people.

Some of them looked at us curiously as we passed, but none reacted as if they knew who we were. Either the news of the Luidaeg's presence—and entourage—had failed to spread, or they simply didn't think it mattered. Interesting.

"Pete's quarters," I said. "She's not there, but she didn't give me the impression of being a lady who likes to live alone. She's a pirate queen, right? Well, they have crews. I want to talk to her crew." Specifically, I wanted to talk to Rodrick, her so-called first mate. If anyone would know what was going on, it would be him. With Pete gone, news of any mysterious deaths would land squarely in his lap.

Maybe sending the Luidaeg—our biggest threat, and biggest dissuasion for anyone who wanted to make trouble—to find Pete had been the wrong call. But Pete wasn't Evening. Pete had promised to minimize her impact on Faerie, and that meant leaving when Dianda and the others showed up. And without Pete, we weren't going to get Dianda's name cleared, and if Torin successfully seized Saltmist, it would destabilize the region. The Mists had enjoyed multiple centuries of relative peace. A war would risk everything. Our people, our ability to hide from humanity, *everything.*

The thought hit me with such force that I actually stopped walking, eyes going wide as I stared into the middle distance. I was dimly aware of Tybalt also coming to a halt, turning to look at me with bemusement and no small amount of concern.

"October?" he said. "What is it?"

"I think we've been looking at this the wrong way," I said. "I think it's not about the Selkies at all, except for the part where it's entirely about the Selkies. Who knew—"

That was as far as I got before a fist slammed into my jaw, sending me reeling. My assailant hit me again before I could do anything more than see stars and blotches of vivid blackness dancing across my vision, like my head had suddenly become the site of the most exciting rave in the Westlands.

Tybalt roared, rage and—I suspected—relief: here was something he could deal with. Here was something he could *hit.* I took another step back as I heard the distinctive sound of an enraged Cait Sidhe slamming into whoever'd been foolish enough to attack me. My jaw felt broken. I touched it gingerly, trying to will the bone to knit back together faster, before the situation got worse.

Pain is not my friend. Neither are broken bones, which may bleed, but mostly do so internally, where it doesn't do me any good. My body is full of blood all the time, and it never helps. Only blood in the open air helps me.

Tybalt snarled again. The flashes of light and darkness were clearing, enough that when I raised my head, I saw him duck a blow from Torin. The burly Merrow had a wicked-looking knife in one hand, a jagged thing clearly designed for gutting whatever it hit. His other hand was empty, although I was living proof that he didn't need a weapon to do damage.

He and Tybalt seemed to be evenly matched. Tybalt was faster, and technically better armed, thanks to his claws, but those claws didn't give him the ability to split his opponent open with a single blow. Torin was already bleeding from several minor wounds, none of which seemed to be slowing him down. He looked like he could do this all day. So did Tybalt.

I had my own knife. It wasn't enough, especially not with that fishing knife in play. Being gutted wouldn't kill me. It would definitely slow me down.

Sometimes the right answer is not to play. "Tybalt! Come on!" I shouted, and ran toward the end of the dock.

Did he understand what I was doing? Maybe. Maybe not. It didn't matter, because as soon as he saw me running, he ran after me, moving fast enough that he caught up before I could go over the edge. He grabbed me by the shoulders, spinning me around, away from the water.

"What in the world are you trying to accomplish?" he demanded.

"You can—" I began.

The knife hitting me in the back stopped me.

I saw Tybalt's eyes go wide and his mouth go slack, hands starting to lose their grip on my arms as he realized what had happened. I grabbed his wrists, keeping him connected to me. Blood was filling my mouth, bitter and bright as a new penny. It hurt, oh, how it hurt, but I was grateful for the pain. If Tybalt hadn't moved me to keep me from falling, the knife would have hit him in the chest.

"Run," I whispered, and pitched forward, slamming into him, sending us plummeting over the edge. I was getting really tired of falling.

Come on, Tybalt, I thought, unable to convince my mouth to do any more heavy lifting. *Figure it out.*

His arms closed around me. There was a rustling sound, like a curtain being thrust aside, and instead of falling through the open air, we were suddenly falling through freezing cold and absolute blackness. I smiled despite myself, closing my eyes and relaxing as he slung me up into his arms. We were on the Shadow Roads. We'd be fine.

There was a jolt as his feet found whatever passed for ground here, and I focused on holding my breath, staying still, and bleeding as little as I could. The last of those wasn't exactly within my control, but as I felt my wounds ice over and struggle to heal at the same time, I felt reasonably confident I wasn't going to be leaving a gory trail through the dark for the next Cait Sidhe who came along to follow.

My lungs burned. I was almost used to that, at this point, and this was just suffocation, not drowning. I let the warmth of Tybalt's body soothe me, the smell of his magic hanging in my nose like a promise that this wasn't going to last forever. The darkness could hold sway for a time, but it would have to pass eventually. It always had before.

As if that had been the incantation to bring us back into the light, the atmosphere shifted around us, cold airlessness becoming ordinary heat. I could see flickers of brightness through my eyelids. I couldn't open my eyes, since my lashes had frozen together, but that was fine; the warmth of wherever we were now would melt them soon enough.

"October." Tybalt sounded distressed. Tybalt usually sounds distressed when I'm wearing more than a certain amount of my own blood. If fae could get gray hair from stress, he would have been a silver tabby by now. "The knife is still in your back, and I'm afraid to leave it there; your body is trying too hard to heal, and may refuse to let it go later. I am so sorry, love, but I have to do this."

The ice on my lips cracked as I smiled. "It's all right," I said. "I would have asked you to pull it out if you hadn't volunteered."

"The edge, it's—"

"Yeah." I'd seen the spikes before they'd been sheathed in my body—in my *spine*, which definitely hadn't been intended for this particular purpose. There was a reason I hadn't asked him to pull it out before we ran. If he'd taken the time to work it free of my flesh, we might both be dead by now. And with my luck, being dead would have stuck with him and not with me, leaving me alone again. "It's going to hurt like hell, and you're probably going to see some pieces of me that you never wanted to. It's all right. You're not the one hurting me. Torin is. You're the one helping me get better."

He hesitated before saying, "You're awake and coherent. Could you remove it yourself?"

"I don't have the leverage." The ice on my lashes was melting. I still didn't open my eyes. I didn't want to see the look on Tybalt's face, which was doubtless unhappy enough to make me reconsider my stance on removing the knife from my own back. All I'd be able to do was hurt myself worse. No: this was the only way.

"I'll need to put you down."

"Where are we?"

"I . . . believe . . . this is the local manifestation of the Court of Cats," said Tybalt. "It's small, and there's no scent that would alert me to the presence of a King or Queen, but it's stable all the same, and I believe we should be safe here, for now."

"Great. So get this thing out of me." There was something wrong with the knife. It wasn't just the pain, which was coming in bigger waves now that the ice was melting and leaving my already raw nerves exposed to the air; it was the shape of it, the way it felt tangled with flesh and bone and . . .

Oh. Oh, yes; that would be a problem. I squeezed my eyes a little tighter shut and added, in a small voice, "Please." Silently, I added still further, *Forgive me.*

There was a long pause, as if Tybalt could hear everything I wasn't saying. Then, gently, I was lain on my side, stretched out on what I thought might be a pile of canvas sacks. The things that got lost in a floating Duchy would have to be different than the things that got lost on the land. Although maybe the Court of Cats here also had access to shipwrecks, vessels lost at sea and thus technically within their purview? They could drain the rooms they added to their slowly evolving architecture, and the dampness would fade. Or maybe they focused on air-filled rooms, or chambers that had somehow never been opened to the sea. Maybe—

The feeling of the knife being jerked out of my spine was a pain like nothing I'd ever felt before or wanted to feel again. Pain has flavors, and I've become something of an unwitting connoisseur of the many terrible forms that it can take. The dull, aching throb; the pointed sear; the jabbing agony. This was something greater than any of them. This was something so big and terrible that it somehow managed to cross from pain into numbness and back again. I'd intended to hold my breath when the moment came, to keep back what air I could in case the worst happened. The pain was so big it knocked every bit of air out of me, leaving me wrung-out and gasping.

And then I *couldn't* breathe, because nothing below my neck was responding to my commands. Even the pain was gone, cut off so abruptly that it left a great, aching chasm in my awareness. It was like the sensation of having a rotten tooth pulled, only in this case, the tooth was my entire body.

"Oh sweet Maeve." Tybalt's voice was barely more than a horrified whisper. "October, I think I'm holding a piece of your *spine*."

I closed my eyes. That was what I'd thought I felt, when I was trying to sort out the shape of the knife jammed into my body. Torin might not have had the time to aim as carefully as he wanted to, but luck had been enough to put his blade right next to my spine, and to hook it through one of my vertebrae.

I'd never had a piece of bone entirely removed from my body before. Academically, I wondered whether it was going to grow back, or whether this would be a step too far for even my magic to deal with. I'd risen from the dead, probably multiple times. I'd healed from injuries that should have been, could have been, and *had* been fatal. But could I recover from this?

Tybalt hissed, dropping to his knees next to me. "You insufferable woman," he muttered. I tried to listen through the haze of oxygen deprivation and shock. This was like being back on the Shadow Roads, almost, except that there was light here. There was warmth. There was air, even if I couldn't reach it. All things being equal, this was a much more pleasant place to die.

A hand cupped my chin, turning my face even further toward the light. I still couldn't feel anything below my neck. My lungs weren't even burning, just . . . failing to pull in any additional air. That was going to be a problem very soon. It was probably a problem already.

"You are direly fortunate that I love you," said Tybalt, and pressed his wrist against my lips.

Blood filled my mouth, bright and hot and brimming with memories that weren't mine. I swallowed involuntarily, and swallowed again as the act of swallowing seemed to unlock something in my chest, making air feel, if not fully achievable, at least like something that might return to the world one day.

Then the red veil of Tybalt's memories slammed down over me, and the condition of my own body ceased to be quite as important. It wasn't like I could feel it anymore.

There's too much blood.

The baby is coming early—Anne said this evening that she hadn't felt any kicking in over a day, and she was worried—and now the baby is coming, and there's too much blood. I've never seen a human give birth before, but this can't be normal. Cait Sidhe women bleed in birthing, and when they do it on two legs, they're built in so many respects like their mortal counterparts. Surely I would know if there were meant to be this much blood. Surely someone would have told me.

Anne is bleeding, and I don't know what to do. I've never been a healer. The local King of Cats has one at his disposal, but he'll not give them leave to come to me, may the night-haunts steal the eyes from his skull and leave him lost in his own lands forevermore. The King and Queen of Tremont have already turned me away. None of them will help a human woman deliver herself of a changeling child. The Divided Courts see me as a beast; the Court of Cats sees her as a burden. No one will save her. No one will save either one of them, and there's too much blood, and Anne can't stand much more of this—

I sat up with a gasp, air flooding back into my floundering lungs, tingles spreading through my body as it seemed to wake up all around me. The room I was in was small, with a low ceiling and bare wooden walls. It looked more like the hold of a ship than anything else although it wasn't moving, and there was no smell of saltwater in the air.

What there *was* was the strong smell of blood, my own and someone else's, mingled with the musk and pennyroyal scent of Tybalt's magic. I turned my head. He was sitting on the floor next to my makeshift bed, a strip of canvas wrapped around his wrist, a look of strained terror on his face.

"Pray reassure me that I've remained awake long enough to see your recovery, and not lost consciousness from blood loss, only to dream a better ending to our tale than the one reality offers," he said, in a wan voice.

"You're awake." I slid off the pile of canvas and wrapped my arms around his shoulders, not pausing to think about what I was doing. This was not the time for careful contemplation. This was the time to reassure my fiancé, who looked like he was on the verge of throwing up, blacking out, or possibly both. "I'm awake. *We're* awake. I promise, we're awake."

"Oh, thank Oberon." He buried his face against my shoulder, letting out a shuddering gasp that became, somewhere toward the end, more of a sob. "Thank Oberon, thank Maeve, thank all the lords and ladies of the Courts that came before us. You can't *do* that to me, October. You *cannot*. I forbid it."

I might normally have taken umbrage at the idea that he could forbid me to do anything. Under the circumstances, I kept holding on as tightly as I could, breathing in, letting the scent of his skin and his hair and his magic fill my nose until I could almost ignore the smell of blood that underscored everything around us.

"I'm okay," I whispered. "I'm okay, I'm okay, I'm here and I'm awake and I'm okay. I swear to you, I'm okay."

Tybalt pulled away, far enough to rest his forehead against my own and look into my eyes. His pupils were narrowed to slits, despite the dimness of the room around us, making him look alien and terrified at the same time—both accurate descriptions, in their own way.

"When I pulled the knife from your back, it carried a piece of your spine with it," he said. "Bone never meant to see the light, brought into the open. You stopped moving, stopped *breathing*. I thought . . ." He shuddered, like a horse that had been ridden too hard before being stabled by a careless owner. "I thought you were leaving me. Please, October, I beg. Don't leave me so soon. I know you cling to your mortality out of love for your father and concern for yourself, and I know it means you may leave me, one day, whether you will it or no, but please. Not so soon as this."

"I'm not planning to leave you," I said. "I'm not ever planning to leave you. I'm not going to say I'm sorry for jumping in front of that knife, because if it did that to *me* . . ." I let my voice trail off.

Every kind of fae has their own strengths and weaknesses. Cait Sidhe, like Tybalt, are shapeshifters and fierce fighters and graceful illusionists, able to hide themselves from prying mortal eyes without struggle. But they don't heal the way I do. They don't bounce back from what should be mortal injuries. They heal faster than humans, sure, but that's not enough. Past a certain point, that's nowhere *near* enough.

Tybalt let out a shaky breath that sounded almost like a laugh as he pushed the hair back from my face with blood-tacky fingers. "I cannot fault you for wanting me to stay and order you to stay in the same breath. But please, October, please. My heart can't take much more of this."

"I know." I put my hand over his, holding it there for a moment before looking around. "This is the Court of Cats."

"A sliver thereof, yes," he said. "There are sufficient Cait Sidhe in this place that they've called it into being. I've not seen any sign of a King or Queen to anchor the place to the Shadow Roads;

odds are none of the resident cats have ever been here, nor ever shall be."

That explained the dusty emptiness of the room around us, and the way it seemed to blur around the edges, like it was barely holding itself to this level of reality. I pulled away, turning to peer into the corners, then looked back to him.

"Would this happen to the San Francisco Court if you didn't have Raj to take over?"

Tybalt nodded. "Given enough time, yes. The Shadow Roads are stable there from long use, and as long as my subjects stayed within the Court, it would not collapse upon them. But if they ever left it standing empty, it would seal itself, reducing in size, until it vanished entirely."

Like the knowe in Muir Woods. It had been sealed after Gilad's death, and reopened fully only when Arden asked it nicely. I could have counted its rooms on the fingers of both hands in those first days. Now, I had no idea how big the place was, and it seemed to get larger all the time, expanding according to some private blueprint designed by its original owners and shaped by Arden's specific needs.

The king is the land. In Faerie, everything else may be negotiable, but it remains unchangeable and essential that the king is the land.

I took a deep breath. "Torin attacked us just as I was about to tell you my suspicions about the Selkies. Did you notice?"

Tybalt raised an eyebrow. "I realize you've just lost a great deal of blood *and* a portion of your spine, but do you honestly think I might have overlooked your being attacked? There are things I can't miss, no matter how much it might help my peace of mind to do so."

"I know you noticed the attack." I pushed his shoulder, trying to seem playful. All I actually succeeded in doing was make him look concerned, as my shove barely stirred him, while sending another wave of exhaustion washing through me. I grimaced. "Sorry about that."

"Never apologize for showing weakness to me." He grabbed my hand and brought it to his lips, kissing my fingers lightly. "It is a true honor, that you feel me safe enough to do so."

"Safe. Right." I took a deep breath. "I think Torin had been following us for a while. We know the Undersea has their own alchemists; someone could easily have bottled the Cephali camouflage for him, if he wanted to listen in on us with his own ears."

"It seems risky," said Tybalt. "As we saw, the one who follows is the one who risks being hurt."

"Yes, but Torin's an Undersea noble, not a land noble," I said. "They take a lot more risks on a regular basis. They have to, culturally speaking, if they want to hold onto their fiefdoms. I don't think he *could* ask anyone to risk getting hurt on his behalf, not if he wanted them to respect him enough to keep following where he led. Especially not with Dianda still insisting on her innocence."

"She might not be."

"I'm sorry—have you met Dianda? He might have been able to blackmail her into lying and claiming she'd committed treason if he had the boys, but Dean and Peter are safe with Patrick, and there's no way she'd take his word for it if he said he was going to hurt them. He'd have to show her proof. He doesn't have proof. She's got to be resisting whatever he wants her to do, and that's slowing him down."

"Why do you think he has a time limit on prosecuting treason?" Tybalt asked.

"Pete left as soon as he got here, because she doesn't like to involve herself in Merrow affairs," I said. "Okay, fine. That works. But what if Torin's not actually here to involve *himself* in Merrow affairs?"

Tybalt frowned. "Now you've lost me."

"Torin has never made a claim on Saltmist before. It's pretty clear he and Dianda's parents had a 'just until we get some heirs' marriage. Right?"

"I suppose."

"So he never expected to get Saltmist through legitimate means. He filled the duchy with troops who are loyal to him, and he expected Dianda's people to go along with it because that's how things are done in the Undersea, but honestly, why now? Dianda has left Saltmist before. He could have taken the Duchy during my bachelorette party, or when she was in Goldengreen having dinner with Dean. Honestly, if he wanted her to give up easy, he *should* have taken it one of those times. Peter can breathe water. Peter can take care of himself. Patrick can't. She would have given in and done whatever he wanted, if her husband was in danger."

Tybalt frowned slowly. "Perhaps he didn't desire it before now."

"Please." I waved a hand. "You don't assemble a force like the one we saw in Saltmist overnight, not even in the Undersea. You don't decide to gamble everything on a whim—and he *is* gambling everything. Dianda isn't going to forgive this."

"Merrow fight. Perhaps this is their equivalent of a family squabble."

"Except, again, he involved her children. Can you honestly tell me you'd forgive any Cait Sidhe who endangered our kids in an ordinary dominance challenge?"

Tybalt froze. For a long moment, he stared at me, eyes wide and strangely, painfully hopeful. Finally, he asked, in a small voice, "You would consider having children with me?"

I managed, barely, to suppress my wince. It helped that I still felt shaky from blood loss, which made most of my responses a little sluggish. "I don't think this is the time for that conversation, do you?"

"No. No, of course not. I simply . . ." He kept looking at me, hope still bright and visible in his eyes. "I never thought you would want that with me."

We were in an unstable Court of Cats. An enraged Merrow was stalking the Duchy of Ships, and since we still didn't know his exact motives, we had no way of knowing whether he was going to try taking his fury out on our friends and loved ones. Somewhere on the nearby sea, two Firstborn were deciding whether or not they were going to come back and help us. This wasn't just not the time for a serious talk about our relationship, this was practically the textbook definition of the worst time possible.

But there'd been a time, not that long ago, when I'd been afraid I was losing Tybalt forever, thanks to my mother's unwanted interference in our relationship. Faerie doesn't have anything as sensible as a modern conception of therapy; every inch of ground Tybalt had gained back, he'd gained by leaning on his friends and trusting that we were telling him the truth when we said that we still loved him, treasured him, and wanted him to be a part of our lives. And yeah, a lot of that heavy lifting fell to me, as the woman who was planning to marry him. Whether or not this was a good time didn't matter nearly as much as the fact that he was vulnerable, and had been for quite some time.

What mattered was that he was *mine*.

"Not right this second, no," I said. "But once we're married?

Once Raj is the King of Dreaming Cats, and you're free to be my husband and figure out what you want to do with your days? I think yeah. Yeah, I do. If you do."

This was not the time or the place for this conversation. But Tybalt's face lit up, suddenly relieved, relaxed, rejoicing, and I knew there had never been a better time, or a better place, for any of this.

"They'll be amazing," he said. "You'll see. Any child of ours could be nothing less."

"That's what I'm afraid of," I said. "Now can we focus? Please?"

"My apologies." Tybalt cleared his throat, getting himself back on task. "So you're posing the theory that Torin acted, not because he desired Saltmist, or to undermine his sister, but because he wished to . . . what?"

"Distract us," I said. "Which I guess means keep us from focusing on the Selkies. But why would someone from the Undersea want us not to focus on the Selkies? They're a security risk. They always have been. They have human friends, human family members, their skins can be stolen—and they're not like Swanmays or Raven-maids. If someone puts on a Selkie skin, they *change*. That's a huge gap in our ability to stay secret."

"Rayseline stole a Selkie skin. She didn't change."

"No one ever said she used it. If she had . . . it was a mask for her, but she never asked it for transformation."

"She infiltrated Saltmist."

"There are other ways of breathing water."

Raven-maids and Raven-men transform using feathered cloaks. They're born with them, coming into the world with bands of pinfeathers set into a strip of leather tied somewhere around their bodies. They can be caught like any other skinshifter, and if someone takes their cloak away—in Jazz's case, the cloak is more of a hair ornament, but the concept holds—they're functionally mostly human until they get it back. The keyword there is "mostly." A Raven without a cloak is still immortal. They won't age or die of natural causes. They don't need fairy ointment to see the traceries of Faerie moving around them. They *can* handle iron, and I've always assumed that's both why they exist, and why they're largely confined to the Oversky: when a piece of iron finds its way into the Cloud Kingdoms, they need someone who can get rid of it. Having people who can put their fae natures on and off like a, well, cloak of feathers . . . that's useful.

But if a human or a changeling found a Raven-maid's cloak and tied it in their own hair or slung it around their own shoulders, they wouldn't become fae. They'd just be thieves and earn the undying enmity of the skies. Selkies worked differently, because Selkies hadn't occurred naturally. They'd been created. The rules weren't the same.

They were a security risk. What Rayseline had done to get into Saltmist proved that. I couldn't imagine *any* pureblood in a position of power looking at them and thinking things were fine as they were. Killing them had been out of the question in the beginning, because they belonged to the Luidaeg, and then as that information had been lost or forcibly forgotten, the Selkies had been incorporated, rightly or wrongly, into the Law. But now the Luidaeg was ready to clean up her own mess, and someone was trying to stop us by creating complication after complication to make it impossible to follow through.

"Why would anyone object to bringing back the Roane?" I asked.

Tybalt sat upright, eyes widening. Then, slowly, he said, "I've met Roane before. They're rare, but not extinct, and I had some dealings with the Undersea when I was younger. The first I ever met was a woman named Naia, who came to the Court of Londinium to warn the populace of a terrible fire that was to come. She could see no way for it to be turned aside, and the potential loss of life was great enough that she was willing to leave the Undersea to bring us a warning we couldn't easily ignore."

"Like Mary," I said. "The Roane woman who came to see me when the Lorden boys were missing. The one who worked for Dianda and Patrick." A stab of guilt lanced through me. I hadn't even thought to look for Mary when I'd been in Saltmist. All my attention had been focused on finding Peter.

"It's said the Roane could foresee everything except their own destruction; that death was the one true mystery the world had to offer them," said Tybalt. "We came here so that you and the Luidaeg could return them to the seas in the numbers they once knew."

I stared at him in slow-dawning horror, the pieces of the puzzle slotting neatly into place around me. "Someone wants to make sure the Roane don't come back."

He nodded. "I can see no other answer. Can you?"

"Nope." I stood. "Come on. Let's go ruin someone's day."

"Do you know whose?" he asked.

"I'm pretty sure I'll figure it out when people start trying to kill me. Again."

Tybalt rolled his eyes, but took my hands, and we stepped together into shadows.

NINETEEN

THE COURTYARD WHERE we'd left our friends, allies, and the body of Isla Chase was in chaos. Cephali clung to the walls, waving spears and tridents in a display that was more threat than actual aggression, while Torin's guard threw themselves against the closed gates. The man himself was nowhere to be seen. Tybalt and I stepped out of the shadows between two of the small residence structures and stopped, pausing a moment to take it all in.

"I swear on Oberon's *ass*, I can't leave you people alone for *five minutes*," I said, not making any effort to keep my voice down.

Quentin, who had been shoving a trident between the bars of the gate, turned at the sound of my voice. There was a shallow cut down his left cheek, deep enough to bleed, but probably not deep enough to scar. "Toby! Where the hell have you been?" There was a beat before he added, less confidently, "Why are you covered in blood again?"

"Long story. Get away from that gate before you get hurt." I strode forward. "Seriously, you cut your face? What's Dean going to think of that? Where *is* Dean?" Only one Lorden was in evidence, Patrick, who was throwing small glass bulbs filled with violently yellow liquid over the gate and into the scrum on the other side. He was grinning nastily as he did it, and I was quite sure I didn't want to ask what those bulbs contained. Ever.

"Poppy and Dean hauled Peter into one of the apartments and locked the door," said Quentin. "We were letting him fight at first, only it turns out he's skinny enough to fit between the bars, and

after he nearly got grabbed, twice, we decided it was better if we
kept him out of reach."

"Good thinking." I looked around again. Marcia was filling glass
bulbs—that explained where Patrick was getting his armaments—
and René had a vicious-looking wooden sword with jagged thorns
running along its cutting edge. Nolan had produced a longbow
from somewhere and was standing atop a table taking carefully
nonfatal aim, with the air of someone who had all the time in the
world to shoot the people who had shown the bad sense to disrupt
his evening.

Cassandra, thankfully, was cowering on the other side of
Nolan—at least until she saw me. Then, her eyes widened and she
rushed from her hiding place to grab hold of my arm, jerking hard
enough that it nearly knocked me over.

"Aunt Birdie! You have to stop them! You have to stop them
before they do something that can't be taken back!"

None of the attackers had ranged weapons. The only ones who'd
made it over the gate were the Cephali, and they were less "fighting" and more "going through the paces of a stage combat improv
class." The Cephali in Torin's service were clearly less than thrilled
about their so-called leader. I frowned.

"What are you talking about, Cass? I mean, there's reason to
worry about Nolan putting an arrow in someone's throat, but I'm
pretty sure this is a skirmish of war right now, so he's not going to
get in *too* much trouble if he does." The Undersea made the rules.
We were just cheerfully exploiting them for our own ends.

Cassandra shook her head, so hard her hair whipped around her
cheeks. "No, no, *no*. Not our people—theirs. They're going to do
something they can't undo, and you're going to lose your temper,
and things are going to get bad when that happens. Please, you
have to stop them before it's too late."

I hesitated. This didn't seem like a good time to try consoling
my adopted niece. But the fight was going on with or without me,
and sometimes the best path through a battle is the one that doesn't
seem available. "Honey, what do you know? Did someone tell you
something?"

"I—" Cassandra hesitated. Then, in a rush, she said, "I can read
the future in the movement of air sometimes. I'm an aeromancer. I'm
sorry I didn't tell you, I really am, but Karen said not to, and she's
always been better at seeing the clear paths than I am, I'm sorry."

Suddenly, Arden's interest in Cassandra made a lot more sense, and I was a lot unhappier with it. "Cassie . . . are you saying you're a soothsayer?"

"Yes." She nodded firmly. "I am. Not the best, but I am. That's why I knew I had to convince the Queen to send me on this trip, with or without Nolan. Bringing back the Roane changes things. It makes the future easier to see, but it also makes it more malleable. There are people who don't want that to happen."

"What about you?"

A glass bottle smashed against the dock; Patrick cheered. Cassandra grimaced. "I don't think it's mine to decide, and this has been coming for a long, long time. This is *supposed* to happen. Things have been broken for hundreds of years, Auntie Birdie, and the air moves too fast for me to see how the fixing ends, but I know we're supposed to be fixing things. Nothing can be broken forever and stay stable. We have to move through this. But you, you have to stop them before they go too far."

"Who is 'them,' honey?"

A rousing cheer rose from Torin's guards. A chill swept over me, even before I heard the small, familiar voice whimpering under the shouts and jeers of the attackers.

"Sir Daye, it seems I have something that belongs to you."

Torin's voice was hectoring, smug. As far as he was concerned, he'd already won. The second he'd acquired the target of his little plan, he'd won.

I turned.

Torin was none the worse for wear from his encounter with Tybalt. There were a few scratches on his cheek, but he stood as tall and proud as ever, giving no sign that his injuries were slowing him down. The light from the hanging lamps around the courtyard's walls glittered off the glass beads stitched to the breast of his doublet, a mocking mimicry of the way the light had glittered off Quentin's scales when we'd been in the water.

One of the strands of beads had snapped down the middle. I looked at the broken, glittering line, and I finally understood. I understood everything.

He hadn't returned alone. A hulking Cephali stood beside him, skin flashing warning bands of blue and orange. The Cephali was holding Gillian's arms behind her back with two of his tentacles, twining them around her arms so there was no chance for her to break away. Not that she wasn't trying. My girl was thrashing as hard as she could, a snarl on her face that I recognized all too well from my own mirror. She had never looked so much like my daughter.

She saw me and shouted, "Toby! Get these fuckers *off* me!"

The sound of her voice, of my name, was enough to break the paralysis that had settled over me. I strode toward the gate, aware that I was a blood-drenched nightmare of a woman and fully prepared to use it to my own advantage. I didn't bother stopping outside of spearing range. Anyone who stuck one of their little toys into me was going to live to regret it.

"It's obvious you have her because you think you can use her," I snarled, eyes on Torin. "You're wrong. Let her go."

"I don't know," he said. "It seems to me that she's been plenty useful already. You're not fighting off my people anymore, when they were only here to collect what was mine by right. What will you give me for the girl, Sir Daye? Your own hand? Your own head? Or maybe the proof of my sister's degeneracy? Give me the boys, and I'll return your Selkie brat."

"My sons are not for sale," spat Patrick. He had a glass bulb in each hand, and looked ready to start throwing again.

I had no idea what was actually *in* those breakable projectiles, but given that half of Torin's people were on their hands and knees, vomiting, I was fairly sure it wasn't anything I wanted getting spilled on Gillian.

"*Sale* implies I believe you deserve some compensation," Torin countered sharply. "You have no rights in the Undersea, lander. You're a pet. A filthy, foul pet who dallied with my sister and needs to be put down for your transgressions. The children aren't yours to claim. They'll learn manners when they come to serve me." He didn't sound angry. If anything, he sounded . . . eager, like he was excited to get started.

The thought sent shivers along my spine, and not only because he had Gillian. At least she seemed to be unharmed, if furious. That was good. As long as he wasn't hurting her, I wouldn't have to take him apart.

"This is *not* smart, Torin," I said. "I'm a hero of the realm. I'm sworn in service to Duke Sylvester Torquill. He's not going to like you threatening my daughter."

"You should have considered that before you dressed her in sealskin for the sake of the sea witch," said Torin. He sounded far too pleased with himself. It made sense. He thought he'd won. I didn't have to like it.

Out of the corner of my eye, I could see Tybalt walking toward the shadows at the side of the courtyard. He was making an effort not to draw attention to himself, and thus far, it seemed to be working.

They don't have Cait Sidhe in the Undersea. Unlike Dianda, Torin didn't seem to have spent any measurable amount of time on land. It was possible neither he nor his people knew how dangerous Tybalt was. Even seeing us vanish over the edge of the dock wouldn't necessarily have shown our hand since, apparently, people around here jump into the water all the time.

"I'm not a particularly patient woman, you know," I said. "Gillian doesn't look like she's hurt. That's a point in your favor. Let her go, right now, and we can keep our dislike for each other at its current levels. Still not great for you, since you *did* stick a big-ass knife in my back, but better than it could be."

For the first time, Torin's expression of smug self-satisfaction flickered. "The knife hit you, then."

"Yeah, it did." I put my hands on my hips. "Where did you think all this blood came from? Blood Costco? It came out of me, when we had to pull your knife out of my body. You've already pissed me off today. Don't make it worse."

"You're bluffing." His lip curled. "Or lying."

"Uh-huh. How did you get my daughter? She was supposed to be locked up with the other Ryan kids."

"She wanted to talk to you, didn't you, poppet?" Torin turned to smirk at Gillian, who glared at him. "Thought her hero of a mother could help to calm the other Selkies, make them stop fighting among themselves. Thought she'd be safe as long as she had your name on her lips."

I sighed. I couldn't help myself. "That sounds like Gillian. It doesn't make her yours to use as a bargaining chip."

"Doesn't it?" Torin produced another of those wickedly jagged knives from his belt, holding it up until the light glistened off its edge. "How about I start slicing strips off her and see how quickly you change your song?"

Gillian struggled against the Cephali that held her, terror and bleak rage in her expression. My heart went out to her, even more than I'd expected it to. She was my daughter, yes, but she hadn't been raised to this—hadn't even been raised knowing this could happen. In my own way, I'd done the exact same thing to her that my mother had done to me. I'd let her grow up thinking the rules were one thing, when they had never been anything remotely close.

At least I'd done it accidentally. My mother had done it all on purpose.

Accidents . . . "You didn't mean to kill Isla, did you?" I kept my voice as mild as I could, like I was making an observation about the weather.

Torin froze. Only for an instant, but long enough for me to know my guess had been correct and my barb had struck home.

Gilly, sweetie, please trust me, I thought. *I'm doing this for you.* "What happened? Were the two of you planning to run away together while everyone was distracted by the chaos in Saltmist? She'd already answered the Luidaeg's call. She could have slipped out with the tide. So something must have changed. Did she tell you she was planning to pass her skin along after all? If you didn't plan to keep Saltmist, someone must have paid for those troops—you were supposed to stop the resurrection of the Roane, weren't you? Did she tell you it wasn't going to work? Is that why you lost your temper? Or was betraying her always in the plan? You don't seem too thrilled to have mixed-blood nephews. Maybe she wanted more than you were willing to give her, and you realized she was a liability. Or maybe you're the one who wanted more. Did she realize you weren't happy being her secret? Did she want to change things?"

His eyes narrowed. "Shut up."

"Not denying it. Interesting. I mean, sure, killing a human isn't against the Law, but killing your lover has to sting, no matter what she is when she falls off the edge of the world."

Gillian stared at me, fighting against the Cephali who held her with renewed vigor. "What do you *mean*, killing a human isn't against the law? That's sick! Faerie is sick!"

My stomach sank as Torin's head swung around to her, his attention finding a new target. "Faerie *is* sick, little girl, that much is true, and creatures like you are the sickness." He took a step toward her, expression thoughtful. "I could make it healthier."

I rushed forward, grabbing the bars of the courtyard gate. One of Torin's guards stabbed at me with her spear, but half-heartedly, like she was too confused to really commit. I grabbed the shaft and yanked it toward me, pulling it out of her hands.

"No spears for you," I snapped. "No swords or tridents or anything else, either. You don't know how to use them responsibly."

"Rowan and thorn, you're such a *mom*," said Quentin.

"Quiet," I said, eyes still on Torin. "You get the *fuck* away from her, Torin, or you're going to wish you'd killed me when you had the chance. Do you hear me? I'll declare war on the Undersea all by myself, and I'll win, unless you move away from my little girl."

Gillian looked like she couldn't decide between terror and irritation, and settled for rolling her eyes, moving as far from Torin as her living chains allowed. The Cephali who was holding her pulled her a little tighter, until her back was against his chest. That just made her fight harder. It was a vicious cycle, and one that wasn't going to end well for anyone.

"*Torin!*" I shouted. "Look at me!"

He didn't turn around. Not as I yelled, and not as Tybalt stepped out of the shadows, moved in close behind him, grabbed him by the throat, and *yanked*.

Torin shouted, confusion and fear wrapped into a tidy little package, and his guard swung around, ready to attack the invader. They were too slow. There were a lot of shadows clinging to the dock, and Tybalt was already gone, hauling Torin with him into the darkness.

"Try not to kill him!" I shouted, probably already too late to be heard—but that part didn't really matter, not as much as having at least pretended to try. Privately, I'd be thrilled to know that the man who had menaced my daughter, arrested Dianda, and thrown a knife at my fiancé had met his end in the freezing cold and endless dark of the Shadow Roads.

"Mom!" wailed Gillian.

I whipped around. The Cephali had wrapped one thick tentacle around her neck, squeezing slowly. He glared at me, hatred in his eyes.

"Give him back," he said. "Give him back, or I'll—"

Whatever he was going to say died as he made a thick gurgling sound and slumped forward, revealing the sword protruding from his back. It was long and sharp and far less dangerous than the scowling woman who stood on the deck behind him.

Captain Pete folded her arms and glared at the lot of us. "I'm going to have to apologize to Chryseis, assuming she's still alive, for killing one of her descendants. Someone want to tell me why this was worth it?"

Silence fell.

TWENTY

GILLIAN STRUGGLED OUT FROM under the fallen Cephali, sobbing as she pushed away the heavy tentacles that had bound her. There were sucker marks on her arms and throat. Those were going to bruise, leaving her marked for days, if not weeks. She'd have to wear even more illusions around the house as she concealed the damage from her father. It felt like my heart had become lodged in my throat, making it hard to swallow or breathe.

It was almost anticlimactic when Tybalt tumbled out of a patch of shadow, dragging Torin's limp, motionless form in his wake. Anticlimactic for me, anyway: not for René. The Selkie man snarled and dove for the unmoving Merrow, stopping only when Quentin and Patrick caught his arms and held him back.

"Let me *go*!" he howled, following the demand with a string of curses in French. I didn't understand any of them. Quentin did, and from the look on his face, they weren't pleasant. René thrashed, trying to break loose, coming dangerously close to hitting one of them with his sword. "He killed my sister! You heard him! He as much as admitted to killing my sister!"

"You just *had* to go and summon your Selkies to my fiefdom," said Pete. She stepped over the fallen Cephali, the heel of her left boot coming down on the edge of one of his tentacles with a vicious squelching noise. Gillian was still struggling to stand. Pete offered her a hand and a sympathetic smile. "It's all right, kid. No one's going to hurt you while I'm here."

"I gave the Selkies permission to rob one another, not to attack the rest of your guests," said the Luidaeg. "And self-defense has always been permissible in the Duchy. It's the aggressor, not the victim, who gets punished."

"Uh-huh." Pete frowned as Gillian stared at her outstretched hand like it was some kind of venomous serpent. "Do you *like* being on the deck, kid? Because barnacles like being on the deck. You want to be barnacles?"

Gillian switched her wide-eyed stare from Pete's hand to Pete herself. "You stabbed that man," she accused. "The octopus man."

"The one who was strangling you, yes, I did," Pete agreed. She glanced at me. "She's not super bright, is she? But you love her, and that's what matters."

"Can someone unlock this damn gate?" I shook the bars. "Please?"

"Um, sorry. That's my bad," said Marcia, stepping timidly forward. She glanced at the Luidaeg and then shied away, like a frightened animal trying not to attract the attention of a larger predator. "I locked them. When the—you know. Angry people with spears showed up." She hesitated, looking at Torin's remaining guards. They were standing frozen, clearly unsure of what they were supposed to do now. "Are they going to stab me when I unlock the gates?"

"Only if they really, *really* want to be barnacles," said Pete, with a vicious good cheer that I was all too familiar with, thanks to my long association with the Luidaeg.

One of the Merrow whimpered. It was forgivable; she was being menaced by her own Firstborn, after all.

"Okay," said Marcia. She grabbed a sprig of rosemary from behind her ear and ran it down the seam between the gates, murmuring something under her breath. The gates sprang open, nearly dumping me on my face as I found myself without anything to hang onto.

No matter. Quentin and Patrick had René contained, Tybalt was taking care of Torin, and I needed to get to my daughter. I half-ran, half-staggered the short distance to where she was still sprawled on the dock, dropping to my knees and sweeping her into my arms.

For one short moment, she returned my embrace, burying her face against my shoulder and closing her arms around my chest, holding me as close as I was holding her. It was everything I'd ever wanted in this world, and it was all I could do not to cry when she finished by pushing me away, looking from me to Pete, not even pretending to conceal her fear and fury.

"I wanted to ask you to make the sea witch tell the other Selkies to stop fighting," she said. "I wanted to ask you to *help*. But instead, these people grabbed me, again, and they hurt me, all so they could make you do what they wanted you to do. Is that how this is always going to be? Am I always going to be a target because people want to make you suffer? I can't do this, Mo—Toby. I can't."

She scrambled to her feet, gathering her bruised dignity around herself like another form of sealskin, and looked imperiously down her nose at me and Pete in the same motion. Gillian hadn't been a part of Faerie for long enough to understand what it meant to snub a pureblood ruler in their own domain—and she didn't even realize Pete was Firstborn. She had no idea how brave she was being. My wonderful, foolish daughter.

"I'm done," she said. "I'm part of Faerie now, and I know that means I can't walk away entirely, but I'm still done. I can't take this. I am . . . I'm so sorry I was mad at you for all those years, for leaving. You didn't have a choice. Now I'm mad at you because you won't stay away. So please, stay away. Whatever the hell it is you're a part of, leave me out of it. I don't want it."

She turned and stalked away, deeper into the Duchy of Ships. I gaped at her, barely able to comprehend what had happened. Then I turned to the crowd in the courtyard, fixing my attention on the first person I saw who wasn't in the middle of doing something terribly important.

"Quentin, go after her."

He looked at me like I'd just said something entirely unreasonable. "Sort of busy here," he said, still hanging off René's arm. René, for his part, had yet to stop screaming at the unmoving Torin. I couldn't tell whether Dianda's brother was dead, but even if he was, René seemed perfectly willing to stab him a couple of times on general principle.

"I've got the man," said Tybalt, standing and moving to grab hold of René. "Do as your knight tells you. Aren't squires meant to be obedient?"

Quentin rolled his eyes, let go of René, and trotted after Gillian. I turned back to Pete and the Luidaeg.

"So," I said. "You came back."

"So," said Pete. "You decided that in our absence you could, what, throw a massive rager of a party? Enterprising. I mean, I'm not your mother or anything, but this is pretty classic, I'll admit."

"You're technically my aunt," I said. "If I'm trashing the place, it's probably allowed."

"Only in a John Hughes movie."

I decided not to ask why Pete knew who John Hughes was. The answer would only hurt my head, and Firstborn are allowed to have cable. I didn't know how she got it to work out here. Piracy, probably, which was both fitting and mind-boggling.

"Right." I took a deep breath, trying to recover some sense of my equilibrium. "If you'll excuse me for a moment, I'm going to go find out whether the man who caused all this trouble is dead."

"If he is, see if you can bring him back." The Luidaeg's smile bristled with teeth far too sharp to be friendly. "It'll be good practice for later."

I shivered, doing my best to hide it, and turned away.

René was running out of steam. While he was still jerking against Tybalt and Patrick, he was starting to repeat himself; I recognized most of the words he was using, even if I didn't know what they meant. I ignored him as much as I could as I moved to kneel next to Torin, pressing the first two fingers of my right hand against his throat.

"We have a pulse," I announced. Glancing at Tybalt, I asked, "What did you do?"

He shrugged. "Pulled him into shadow, as I've done many times before with those who needed to be calmed somewhat."

"And?"

"And it's possible I also hit him a few times in the stomach, to remove any oxygen he might have thought to set aside for later use." Tybalt looked down his nose at Torin. "I doubt his gills served him very well in a place with neither air nor water."

"Gills, of course." I rolled Torin's head to the side. His gills were raw and inflamed, standing slightly open despite the fact that he was in the open air. They looked like they'd suffered a bad case of frostbite. "He must have panicked and tried to breathe any way he could. He probably did some damage to his throat."

"Good," snarled René, and spat, before resuming his struggles. This was getting old. I stood, stepping forward until we were nose-to-nose, and said calmly, "The sea witch is *right there*. I'm standing in front of you. I think I speak for both of us when I say you're embarrassing yourself, and I need you to stop, right now. Please. Unless you want her to explain to you why you need to stop."

"Happy to," called the Luidaeg.

René stared at me, mouth working silently. Then he sagged, apparently trusting Tybalt and Patrick to hold him up. All the fight seemed to have gone out of him like a branch being broken, leaving him wrung-out and empty.

"She was my sister," he said. "My *sister*. She knew me better than anyone else in the world. She took my place when I wanted to marry Mathias. She was my *sister*, and she's dead, and nothing is going to bring her back to me, but he's still breathing. He's still here. It's not right, that he's still here and she's gone. I should be allowed to make things right."

"You should, but you're not," said the Luidaeg, walking toward him. She touched Tybalt on the shoulder; he let go of René's arm and stepped aside. She moved smoothly into his place, taking René's hand in hers. My breath caught. I'd never seen her voluntarily touch a Selkie. Not even Liz. She'd played at being their cousin, but she had always held herself apart from them, keeping her distance, in anticipation of this day.

"This isn't your task, and it isn't your duty," she said, voice gentle. "This is something people older and more burdened than you have to take care of. You honor her by holding her memory. You honor her by passing her skin. You honor her with love, and life, and not letting this man drag you down. Let him go. Set him aside. I promise you, justice will be done."

René turned to look at her, eyes brimming over with unshed tears. "Did you . . . did you know she was gone?" he asked.

"Not until I saw you," she said. "But I know every Selkie. I know who carries every skin. I know you, René, and I know Isla, and I know there are only two deaths in the entire world that could push you to this point." Her smile was fleeting. "I also know that if Mathias were dead, we'd have needed an army to keep you from slitting this fool's throat. Not because you loved her any less than you love him. Because you made him promises you never had to make to her. Let *go*, René. Let us avenge her for you."

He broke, sagging against the Luidaeg, burying his face against her shoulder and sobbing so loudly that it hurt my heart. Gillian had rejected me—again—my squire was chasing her through the Duchy of Ships without backup, and somehow none of that was as terrible, in that moment, as René's sorrow.

"I know," said the Luidaeg, stroking his hair with one hand. "I do. I'm sorry." She looked over his head to me, raising an eyebrow. "Well? What are you waiting for? Tie that fucker up before he comes to and I have to slit his throat for looking at me funny."

"On it," I said, and bolted for my apartment, where I knew I'd find rope.

The Luidaeg's voice chased after me, holding a hint of wild laughter in its depths: "And change your damn shirt! You look like a slaughterhouse!"

The more things change, I guess.

The courtyard had calmed into something resembling order when I emerged a few minutes later, wearing a clean shirt and carrying a long twist of rope over one shoulder. Torin's guards were all standing to one side, divested of their weapons, eyes cast toward the dock. Helmi, Kirsi, and the male Cephali whose name I still didn't know were positioned in front of them, holding tridents and scowling in a way that seemed more performative than anything else. They were showing off how good they were at their jobs.

It was easy to guess who they were showing off *for*: Captain Pete was standing near the mouth of the courtyard, speaking with Patrick and his sons. I couldn't hear what she was saying, but her expression was grave, and Patrick was nodding. Dean looked awestruck and confused. Peter just looked angry. I was getting the feeling that was pretty standard, for him.

Cassandra and Nolan were sitting at one of the courtyard tables. Oddly enough, Nolan acknowledged me first.

"Sir Daye!" he called jubilantly. "I hope you're prepared to tell my sister of the glorious battle we fought here!"

"Yeah, because 'hey, I took your brother to an accidental war zone' is going to really endear me to the queen," I said.

"She knew you were a scorpion when she picked you up," said Cassandra, and clutched the side of her head with one hand. "I wish you could offshore some of that ridiculous healing of yours."

"Sorry," I said, turning my attention toward the fallen figure of Torin. The Luidaeg and René were standing nearby. She had a firm grip on the Selkie's elbow, preventing him from doing anything she was going to make me regret later. That was nice. I liked it when my allies didn't wind up inexplicably covered in blood. Tybalt wasn't there.

I blinked, getting ready to start demanding a location for my fiancé, only to relax as the dark circle on Torin's chest raised its head and yawned, showing me a mouthful of extremely sharp white teeth.

"Got tired of having thumbs again, huh?" I asked, as I approached the pair.

Tybalt closed his eyes and purred audibly.

"I think it was more 'he got tired of people trying to ask him why you were covered in blood,'" said Marcia, falling into step beside me. Her hands were filled with green things, mint and rosemary and basil and feverfew. I didn't want to ask, and so I didn't. Sometimes silence is the best weapon of them all. "I tried telling them that it's an occupational hazard with you, but mostly they weren't listening."

"The Luidaeg knows I get covered in blood the way some people get rained on," I said.

"Yes, but it was more fun watching your kitty squirm," said the Luidaeg. She looked approvingly at my rope. "Good. Now hogtie this fucker so we can move on."

"Couldn't you melt his wrists together or something?" I asked.

"Child of Titania, remember?" The Luidaeg glared at Torin, making no effort to soften the venom in her gaze. If looks could kill, her geas would have been broken on the spot. "Nothing that would do him any harm, unless he comes to me and pays for the privilege of his own pain. Nothing that would *inconvenience* him. You, on the other hand, have no such limitations. Feel free to cut off his circulation."

"Or not." Pete strolled over, thumbs hooked into her belt, looking more like a Jack Sparrow impersonator than ever. She had more of an honest nautical air about her than Johnny Depp ever had—an impression that was only amplified as she hooked the toe of one low-heeled boot into Torin's side. "I'm glad he's not dead, cat. I would have hated to need to stand against you for the crime of hurting my descendants."

Tybalt yawned again, showing his teeth in jagged array. Pete chuckled.

"I love Cait Sidhe. If there's one thing I regret about being naturally nautical, it's the paucity of cats. It would be nice to have more people around being shitty to me." She swung her gaze toward Marcia, eyes narrowing. "I don't know you."

"I was introduced when we arrived here," said Marcia nervously.

"No, I remember that," said Pete. "Your name is Marcia, and you travel with the Count of Goldengreen. They *said* all that. But I don't know you. Something about you isn't right. Who are you?"

"I'm nobody," said Marcia, taking a half-step backward, like she was getting ready to run. She seemed to think better of the motion and stopped, trembling, clutching her pilfered greenery to her chest. "I work for . . . I work for Dean Lorden, I'm not . . . I'm sorry . . ."

"She was my seneschal when I was Countess of Goldengreen," I said, pulling Pete's attention to me. I knelt next to Torin, rolling him onto his side and roughly grabbing his wrists. "I was the one who insisted Dean hire her when I stepped down."

Tybalt jumped off of Torin's chest, making a disapproving grumbling noise. I snorted.

"You want to be a cat, you get treated like a cat, and that means sometimes you'll have to move when you don't want to. If you don't like it, get bipedal."

"I'm amazed a King of Cats tolerates being spoken to in that manner," said Pete.

I shrugged. "He's planning to marry me. I think he's figured out that I don't do 'respectful' unless someone's holding a sword to my throat. Please don't hold a sword to my throat. It's hard to tie people up when I'm being threatened."

"You would know," said the Luidaeg.

I wrinkled my nose at her and turned my attention to tying Torin's hands. Not a moment too soon, either. As I was finishing the third knot, he twitched, then bucked against the rope, nearly banging the back of his head into my nose. I recoiled.

Tybalt was there, back on two legs, to hold down Torin's feet. I flashed him a smile and moved to finish tying the man up before he could get to his feet or cause us any further trouble.

"Filth!" Torin shouted, voice rough and ragged from the damage to his throat. "Unhand me this instant! Release me, or I'll—"

"You'll what?" Pete leaned over him, expression curious and predatory at the same time, like some deep sea creature trying to decide whether it wanted to play or plunder. Torin went very, very still. It was possibly the smartest thing I'd seen him do since the moment we'd met.

"Hi," said Pete, in a companionable tone. "My name's Captain Pete. I'm in charge of this place. Everything around you belongs to me. I hear you've been a bad, bad boy. Want to talk about it?"

She smiled.

Torin screamed.

TWENTY-ONE

ISHOULDN'T HAVE BEEN SURPRISED that Pete's receiving room was located in the main room of the lighthouse. It was the core of the fiefdom, the single stable structure around which everything else had been constructed. The anchor, in other words. It only made sense that as the anchor, it should be the focal point of the knowe.

I shouldn't have been surprised, but I was. Having solid ground beneath my feet again was a silent reminder of how very far we were from home, and how much farther I'd have to go in order to return to the comforting and the familiar. I stood at the center of the open space in front of Pete's chair—which was less a "throne" and more "a large, ornate, excessively gilded prop that wouldn't have looked out of place at Disney World"—and tried not to squirm.

It wasn't easy. There were things about the situation that helped, like my being back in my own fully blood-free clothes, including my leather jacket, and my allies being in eyeshot, even if they weren't all standing with me. Tybalt and Quentin flanked me. The Luidaeg and Patrick stood nearby, the one looking faintly bored, the other stone-faced and silent. Everyone else was at the edge of the crowd, watching. Waiting to see what was going to happen next.

And it was quite a crowd. What seemed like everyone in the entire Duchy of Ships had turned up, summoned by some silent signal to gather on all sides. There were people in the rafters and perching on the windowsills. Poppy and her Aes Sidhe friend were sitting together on one of the higher perches, their wings half-open, so that they became almost tangled. It was an interesting form of intimacy, and one I'd have to think about more later.

Pete herself was nowhere to be seen, having peeled off shortly before we took up our places in front of the dais. I shifted from one foot to the other, trying not to look at either Torin or the empty space where Pete should have been.

Torin was looking somewhat the worse for wear. His former guards had been given the task of standing guard over him, and whatever Pete had said when she ordered them to do it, they were taking her seriously. They had untied his feet, but his hands were still firmly bound behind his back. His gills were still red and raw. Even if he transformed back into his fishier form, I somehow doubted he was going to be swimming easy for a while.

Something wet touched my foot. I glanced down. A runnel of water was snaking its way across the perfectly level floor, moving like something with purpose and intent. I danced to the side, almost stepping in another runnel. It was joined by another, and another, until tiny streams were pouring in from all directions, pooling together at the base of the dais.

They flowed into a small pond, shimmering silver as it accumulated. Then, as if gravity held no relevance at all, the pond flowed up the dais steps, joining with still more runnels that had come down the walls and through the open windows. I glanced to the side. The Luidaeg was smirking, seeming tolerant and . . . amused?

If she thought this was funny, it was probably nothing to be too alarmed about. Probably. She found some pretty upsetting things funny, but she liked Quentin, and she was very firm on the idea that she'd eventually be the one to kill me. It was going to be okay. It was.

The water on the dais pulsed once, twice, and finally twisted upward into a column. I realized what was happening just before it started sculpting itself into the vague outline of a woman, naked and statuesque and gorgeous, from her broad hips and swelling bosom to the sturdy pillars of her thighs. The water surged upward and then burst, cascading down over the form of Captain Pete—of Amphitrite—in a final mighty wave.

Because this wasn't the pirate queen, no, not at all; this was no figure from a storybook or play. This was one of the Firstborn, standing revealed with no illusions, no constraints. Her dress, such as it was, was a sheet of dark and living water, wrapped around her like a lover and slithering as sinuously as an eel, giving us glimpses of scaled, shark-belly skin, enough to tempt, enough to terrify. Her hair was braided with black pearls and small white beads that I suspected were bone, and her throat was exposed, revealing the gills I'd suspected she hid behind her hair.

There was a soft thudding sound as two of Torin's former guards lost consciousness and tumbled to the floor. Amphitrite smirked and settled in her chair. At least the way she moved hadn't changed. She still swaggered, still sauntered, still walked through the world like it owed her several favors and she had come to collect. What she wasn't doing anymore was making any effort whatsoever to dull down the sheer volume of her presence. She had weight in the world. The world was damn well going to acknowledge it.

"Each of you is a guest in my home, a passenger on my ship, sailing on a starless sea," she said. Her voice was low, even intimate, but it spread to fill every corner of the room, like ink curling through clear water. Her legs shimmered beneath their watery gown, feet unfurling into fins as her lower body transformed into sinuous twinned tails. "Some of you, however, have been rather impolite. Not behavior befitting a guest."

Her gaze swung to Torin, making it clear to whom she was referring. He cringed but didn't step away. I would have been impressed by that, if he hadn't been standing in the middle of a field of heavily armed guards. Trying to run would have been a good way to wind up with a perforated kidney.

"Care to explain?" she asked, leaning forward, resting her elbows on the gentle curves of sinew and scale that had been her knees. "I like it when my hospitality is respected. It makes *me* feel respected."

"I . . . I . . ." stammered Torin.

"Yes, you," she agreed. She looked toward Patrick, and then back to Torin. "Unless a closer member of your family than myself wishes to speak for you, you'll do all your speaking on your own behalf."

"People think of my wife as the cruel one, because she wears her edges on the outside," said Patrick. "I'm supposed to be the gentling influence on her anger. I'm not feeling very gentle right now. Maybe Dianda would speak for her brother, but I have nothing to say for my brother-in-law. He's the man who tried to break my family. Let him drown."

"Hmm," said Amphitrite, attention not wavering. "You haven't been making many fans here, have you, great-great-grandson? Now's the time when you tell me why you did what you did, and what you were hoping to accomplish. Maybe you'll woo me with your words. Maybe I'll understand why you chose to smash your ship against these shores."

"The sea witch is moving against you," blurted Torin.

Amphitrite's eyebrows rose. "Really?" She turned to the Luidaeg. "Really?"

"If I am, I'm not aware of it," said the Luidaeg. "I got out of the backstabbing and betrayals business when I lost the ability to lie. It's hard to plot against people when they know you'll tell them the truth if they just ask."

"Hmm." Amphitrite settled in her seat, eyes once more fixed on Torin. "How, then, is the sea witch moving against me? Be specific. I don't have all night."

"She's planning to restore the Roane." There was an air of triumph in his voice, like he'd just dropped the mother of all bombshells on us.

"And?" asked Amphitrite. "I knew that. I told her she could use my place as neutral ground. How is she moving against me when she asked me before coming?"

"They died for a *reason*," spat Torin.

The Luidaeg was suddenly very still.

"I'd be careful if I were you," said Amphitrite. "The sea witch doesn't like it when people imply that her children didn't deserve to live. Why would you say such a thing?"

"Because it's true! Lady . . ." Torin dropped abruptly to his knees. It was a bold move for a man whose hands were literally tied. He wouldn't be able to get back up without assistance. "The Roane spread lies across the water and attracted the eyes of the land. Remember how it was in the days when they swam freely. The land Courts felt entitled to the gifts of prophecy. They sailed into your waters, they attacked our fiefdoms, and for what? For a glimpse of a future that could yet be changed? The Roane died to grant peace to the rest of us. Allow them to stay gone. Allow the waters to stay safe."

"Who told you this?" asked Amphitrite.

Torin ducked his head. "She bid me not to say."

The Luidaeg stepped forward, stillness forgotten. "Did she have hair like the deeps during a storm, and skin like sun-bleached bone? Coral lips and seafoam eyes?" When Torin didn't answer, only shivered, she spat and turned her face toward Amphitrite. "I should have killed her when I had the chance. My own death would have been worth it."

"Eira will have her reckoning, one day," said Amphitrite. "Here, today, the reckoning belongs to Dianda Lorden, and to Isla Chase."

"Please, don't say her name," said Torin.

"Why? Because you killed her? Poor boy. There's a great deal more drowning in your future." Amphitrite leaned back in her chair as she slowly, deliberately tilted her head to the side. Her hair was a black waterfall across her silvery shoulders; her eyes were unreadable.

"I remember," she said, voice soft. "I remember the day my sister the sea witch brought her firstborn child to our father, so he could see the boy. I remember the way my father, *Oberon himself*, raised that child up and called him 'grandson.' I remember how he smiled to see the waters so blessed. I remember *many* things, Torin, descendant and disgrace, who would see his own sister bleed for the crime of falling in love with a man who I have never found to be anything other than perfectly appropriate. I remember how the storms raged when the Roane died, until it seemed as if the very oceans wept. I remember blood in the water, blood enough to float an armada, and I remember that the killings didn't happen out of any altruistic urge to make Faerie a safer place. They happened because another of my sisters was cruel as a tsunami and shallow as a cove, and she couldn't bear to see any apart from herself happy."

She crossed her scaled tails at what should have been her ankles, eyes fixed on the now quailing Torin.

"If I were my sister, if I had transformations in my fingers and curses in my palms, I would cast you out," she hissed. Her voice was barely more than a whisper, but still it carried to every corner of the room. "I would say the man you refuse to call brother is more Merrow than you could ever hope to be; that if you yearn to kneel at my eldest sister's feet so badly, you should have that dubious honor. I'd strip my contributions from your blood and bones and give them to him, because I would much rather have *him* for a descendant. Let you go to bleed and break and beg a place upon the land."

Torin paled, until it looked like he might lose consciousness from the lack of blood in his face. For the first time, I thought kneeling might have been the right move. He couldn't fall down if he wasn't on his feet.

"Sadly, and happily, I'm not my sister," said Amphitrite. "I don't have knots in my hands; I can't tangle and tie you into something you're not intended to be. But I can do these two things, Torin of Bluefish, and you had best heed them, or I'll see you gone and gutted. I may not be able to cast you from my bloodline, more's the pity. I can cast you from my sight. You shall find no favor from me. You can keep your demesne, for as long as you're allowed, but I will not find in your favor if anyone does you harm, or if you bring complaints to lay at my feet. You are no descendant of mine."

"Lady," said Torin, in a strangled tone.

"And as to the other . . . you claimed the authority to arrest your sister, Duchess Dianda Lorden of Saltmist, on claims of treason, on the accusation that she had brought a king-breaker into these waters, where never such a thing should stand. But you lack that authority, because the Duchess Lorden committed no treason. The closest she has ever come is in her marriage to a Daoine Sidhe, which she did with the full blessing of Queen Palatyne and King Windermere, unifying land and sea. So here is the second part of your punishment. You have to watch what follows."

Amphitrite turned to face Patrick, smiling like the star that leads lost sailors home from sea. "Come to me, Patrick Lorden, ducal consort of Saltmist, and have no fear."

Patrick stepped forward. Amphitrite snapped her fingers. Another rush of impossible water flowed into the room, forming a column next to her dais before it shattered, revealing Dianda. She wore no chains; her dress was kelp and shining scale, and somehow managed to be beautiful, despite seeming like something that should have washed up with the low tide.

Dianda gasped, running hands over her hips and torso, like she was reassuring herself they were still there. Then she saw Patrick, and without waiting for leave from her Firstborn, she flung herself into her husband's arms. He let out a shuddering breath that bordered on a sob and buried his face against her shoulder, holding her like a drowning man holds a rope.

"I'd cast him out for you, if he weren't off-limits to me," said the Luidaeg genially, seemingly immune to the touching scene unfolding in front of her. "I can tell Toby I'd like to see how he looks with broken kneecaps, if you want. There are ways to get around anything, if you try hard enough."

"A Merrow without the name won't hold their fiefdom long," said Amphitrite, giving the Luidaeg a tolerant smile. "He'll be outcast and alone before the seasons turn, swimming the seas with neither shelter nor respite. The only post open to him will be ambassador to the land, where they neither know nor care about the specifications of our politics. It's not exile. Exile would be too kind. It's a room with only one door, and that door leads to voluntary isolation." She turned the same smile on Torin. It had edges now; it had teeth. "He'll have to be the traitor he accuses his sister of being if he wants to survive. It seems a fitting punishment for someone who'd betray his family."

"Please," gasped Torin. "Lady, please." He swiveled, turning his entire upper body at once. "Dianda, I beg you, tell her this is too much. Please."

"Excuse me?" Dianda let go of Patrick, enough to lean back and look blankly at her brother for a long moment. "You'd ask me for forgiveness? You, who swam away and never once looked back until it seemed convenient to you, who would have happily seen my husband drowned, my sons broken for the crime of being born of love, want me to say the Lady is being too harsh? I'd have your spine for jewelry if it wouldn't make her angry. I'd make flutes from your bones and play them with my boys every time someone thought it would be a good idea to threaten us. She's not condemning you. She's sparing you, from me. You should thank her for her mercy, not look to me to save you from it."

"The Law forbids me from killing you, and far be it from me to threaten a man in front of his own Firstborn, but if my wife wanted to risk Amphitrite's fury for the sake of spilling your blood in the tide, I wouldn't tell her to stop," said Patrick mildly.

Amphitrite smiled again, more broadly this time. "You married well, little mermaid. If I've never told you that before, consider my blessing given now."

Dianda paled and said nothing. I wasn't sure I'd ever seen her speechless before.

Amphitrite glanced to the Luidaeg. "He killed one of yours, sister. Do you demand any recompense?"

"I have her skin," she said. "Without demanding his life, I'm not sure what else I could ask for."

"And I won't kill him for you," said Amphitrite. There was genuine regret in her tone. "I'd cast him out if I could, but I refuse to go against our father's wishes so completely."

"I know," said the Luidaeg. "Antigone of Albany asks nothing more. Justice hasn't been done, but sometimes justice is an impossible ideal. I'm as close to satisfied as is possible for me to be."

"Then the matter is closed," said Amphitrite. She swung her attention back to the guards who stood, silent, behind the kneeling, now-sobbing Torin. "Take him away. Hold him until the Convocation is done and all who might still be . . . annoyed . . . at his recent actions have left these waters. I'd prefer not to taunt the sharks."

The guards hauled Torin back to his feet and dragged him away. Amphitrite turned back to the rest of us, looking thoughtfully across the group before settling on the Luidaeg.

"You are my sister and I love you," she said.

"I sense a 'but' coming," said the Luidaeg.

"This is supposed to be neutral territory," said Amphitrite. "It's meant to be a place where all the children of the sea can come together without fear, belonging to none of the Three before the other two, held by no authority but my own. Do you understand why I might not be overly pleased about you deciding to give your descendants carte blanche to assault each other?"

"It was necessary," said the Luidaeg.

"You and I have very different definitions of 'necessity,'" said Amphitrite. She sighed and was Captain Pete again, glamorous and terrifying and ordinary and small enough to fit in her chair without seeming to fill the entire room. She was built to scale with the rest of us. It was comforting, and oddly unnerving at the same time. The way the Firstborn could diminish themselves on command would never fail to unsettle me.

"You're not welcome here for the next seven years," said Pete. "Once you set sail, that's it: no visits, no Convocations, no nothing. It's the least punishment I can justify for breaking my rules."

"Rules matter," said the Luidaeg. She shrugged. "I can't say I'm thrilled to be exiled, but I also can't say it's not fair of you. Once I go, I won't turn back."

"Excuse me," said Quentin, and only flinched a little as Pete's attention fixed on him. "Are we *all* exiled, or only the Luidaeg?"

"Why?" asked Pete. "Were you thinking you want to become a regular visitor to my sandless shores?"

"No," he said. "I just like to know what's going on. And, you know. Um. Prince Windermere was looking for someone, and I don't think he's found her yet."

"Sorry," I said. "I haven't exactly provided him with a stable knightly environment. It's left him a little anxious about certain things."

Pete, thankfully, looked amused. "I see. No, young squire, the rest of you aren't exiled. Only my sister, who needs to grant me seven years of peace before she comes and disrupts everything again."

Seven years was nothing to the Firstborn. They weren't just immortal, they were centuries old, measuring their lives in the slow rise and fall of nations, religions, *continents*. This was more of a show punishment than anything else. I still thought the Luidaeg looked sad as she turned away from her sister, like she hated to have even this one narrow door on her remaining family closed, for however short a time.

"I appreciate the clarification," said Quentin, and offered a shallow bow.

"Finish your business soon, Annie," said Pete. "The tide's about to turn."

The Luidaeg nodded. I swallowed, hard. What I was going to do next . . .

Well. No one ever said that heroism would be easy. If it were, everyone would have done it.

TWENTY-TWO

THE DOOR TO THE Luidaeg's temporary apartment closed with a soft click, quiet as a sigh. Poppy was sitting on the couch, dreamily twisting a length of ribbon through her fingers. She looked up, blinked, and frowned at the sight of us.

"Is there a wrongness here?" she asked.

"Not sure," said the Luidaeg, cheerfully enough, although I suspected her overly bright tone was partially a reaction to the possibility that wrongness might be coming. She'd looked that way since I'd taken her elbow on the way out of Pete's receiving room and asked if we could speak in private.

I guess when someone's been alive for as long as the Luidaeg, they get a sense for when things aren't entirely going their way. Even when they're powerful enough that things go their way more frequently than not.

Tybalt and Quentin stayed by the door, not saying anything. They'd insisted on coming with us when we went to speak in private, and I'd been happy enough to have the moral support, even if neither of them entirely knew what I was about to do. The fact that they had my back was more than enough to put a little strength into my spine, keeping me upright as I waited for the Luidaeg to turn and focus on me.

When she did, I almost wished she hadn't. Her eyes were a clear driftglass green, and tired. So very, almost infinitely tired.

"Well?" she asked. "Is something wrong?"

"Yes," I said. My tongue felt thick and my throat felt tight. I didn't want to do this to her. I didn't want to stand here and make things harder, for either one of us. I didn't want to look the sea witch in the eye and tell her that I didn't want to serve her.

Sometimes heroism sucks.

"What you want to do to the Selkies, what you want *me* to do to the Selkies . . . it isn't fair."

Slowly, the Luidaeg blinked. Slowly, she stepped toward me, until we were almost nose-to-nose, until I could feel her breath against my skin. I stood my ground. It was the only thing I could think of that might keep this from getting even worse.

"What do you mean, 'fair'?" she asked, voice barely above a whisper. "Is it fair that my children are dead? Is it fair that the night-haunts found them butchered on the shore, their magic and hearts carved away, so there was no sustenance for the flock in the feasting? I called my sister's children to me when my own were lost, hoping to see their beloved faces on the wings of the wind, and all I found was weeping, because they *weren't there*. Was that fair? When did you become so concerned with fairness?"

"When people kept pushing me into situations that demanded I figure out how to be a hero," I said. "It's not *fair*. The Selkies here aren't the ones who killed your children. Most of them wouldn't have any idea how to hold the knives. They're scared and confused and they don't want to give up everything they've ever known for the sake of a single day's repayment, but they're not your enemies. They're your descendants. Sort of. Technically." They belonged to her as much as the Roane had, as much as the scarce surviving Roane still did. They were her creations and her responsibility.

"Whether or not it's fair is beside the point," said the Luidaeg. "I said I'd do this. That means I have to do this. That's the way it *works* for me. I can't lie, and breaking my word on purpose would make me a liar. Do you want to see what happens to me if I try to break my geas? Because I don't. I've . . . I've seen it before, and there was no point in you saving my life if you're going to make me throw it away on some wild fit of idealism. Do you understand? I don't have a choice. There's no reason for us to have this conversation. It can't change anything."

"It doesn't have to change everything, but I think we can change *something*," I said doggedly. "I ran with Devin for years, remember?"

The Luidaeg lifted an eyebrow. "Okay, I'm used to following

your wild and slightly ridiculous leaps of logic—sometimes I even enjoy them—but this one is losing me. Why does your criminal past make a damn bit of difference here?"

"Devin carved out a place for the changelings in the Mists when the Queen was actively anti-changeling, when no one wanted to give us the time of day." When me being knighted had been the scandal of the century, despite the service I'd performed for that same Queen—and despite who my mother was. If I needed any proof that prejudice was unthinking and irrational, it was that. Too many people had known Amandine was Firstborn. I should have been treated like a princess, and instead I'd been a pariah. "He didn't do it by lying, not all the time, not to everyone. Liars get caught. He did it by twisting the truth until it screamed, but never *lying*."

The Luidaeg was ageless, immortal, and had been cursed for centuries with an inability to lie. How did she not already know this? But she was looking at me with a blankly inquisitive expression on her face, like nothing I was saying made any sense to her.

"Look," I said, desperately, "you joke. You say things that aren't flat statements of truth. You must have learned how to do that after you were geased. Right?"

"When Titania laid the binding on my tongue, it took me years to be able to answer anything more complex than a yes-or-no question," she said slowly. "I couldn't even say my name unless I was in the presence of the Roane, because I didn't know what it *was*. I could lie to them. I could tell them my name was 'mother' in whatever language I liked, and my breath didn't stop, and my senses didn't dim. They were the ones who carried my name back to me, until I could say I was the Luidaeg, the sea witch, that I was Antigone of Albany, and that I was not going to forgive Titania for what she'd done. Not then. Not ever."

I started to speak. She wasn't done.

"*She* was the one who told the sister I can't name to put those knives into the hands of my children's killers. *She* was the one who wanted to see the children of Maeve wiped from the world. It's her fault my babies are dead. And I won't forgive her. I can't forgive her. Not while she still binds me, because she forbade me to be a liar, and it was in honesty that I pledged to hate her until the stars went cold, and it's with honesty that I hate her now."

"The Selkies are not Titania," I said. "Are you going to stand there and tell me the sins of our parents are things we can never, ever put down, no matter how hard we try? Because Pete is Titania's daughter, and you seem to love her. I'm Amandine's daughter, which is awful, and Janet's granddaughter, which might be worse. People keep attacking Gillian because she's my child, even though she's never done a thing to any of them. Where does it end, Luidaeg? When do we stop even seeing each other, because we're so busy attacking over the crimes of our ancestors? When do we get to *rest*?"

She stared at me, threads of black drifting through her seaglass eyes, and asked, "Would you be this calm if someone were standing here talking about *your* child's body, *your* child's murder? Would you be willing to listen to mercy masquerading as reason? Or would you want to raise the seas and drown them all?"

"That last one," I admitted. "At least at first. I like to think that after a couple of centuries, I'd be able to see things more clearly—and you've had a lot more than a couple of centuries. But most of all, I believe, I truly do, that I could forgive the children of the children of the children of the people who hurt her. We have to start forgiving somewhere. If we can't even do that, why are we still bothering?"

The Luidaeg took a deep breath, and then another, visibly composing herself. Finally, in a light tone, she said, "I should turn your organs into fish and watch you die as they suffocate inside your skin for speaking to me like that."

"Should, but won't," I said.

She pulled her lips back in a snarl. "How can you be so sure?"

"Because you were lonely. When I showed up on your doorstep chasing a killer, you let me in, even though it was Luna who sent me, even though you didn't have a lot of love lost for her. You let me in, because you were lonely, and you let me keep coming back, because you were lonely, and you let Quentin in, and Raj, and even Poppy. You don't like being by yourself. I don't think many people do. Your family died or left you or turned out to be assholes, and that sucks, I can't even start to say how bad that sucks, but Luidaeg—Annie—there's a lot of different ways to make a family. We're your family, too. All of us." I waved a hand, encompassing Quentin and Tybalt. "We're your weird, dysfunctional, foundling family, and we love you, and I think you love us. So you're not going to turn my intestines into eels or my heart into an octopus.

You've spent too much time grieving to do that to someone you'd have to mourn."

For a moment—just a moment—she looked stricken. Then, in a small voice, she said, "You know I can't lie."

"Yes."

"You know I've said I was going to kill you. Repeatedly."

"Yes." I shrugged. "I try not to think about it most of the time. When I have to think about it, I figure we'll find a way to break Titania's geas before you get too close to the knives. It's going to be okay. I really do believe that. But we need to figure out what to do about the Selkies. We can't punish them for the crimes of their ancestors."

"And I can't let them swim free," said the Luidaeg. "I made a promise. I have to keep it. We're trapped, Toby. This is a closed cove: no one who swims here gets away."

"No." I shook my head. "We're *fae*. We're not trapped. I refuse to be trapped. We're just not sure yet where the exit is."

"May I?" asked Tybalt. His voice was surprisingly timid.

I turned.

He had moved forward a bit, closing half the distance between us and himself, so that we formed a line across the room: the Luidaeg, me, Tybalt, Quentin. His hands were out in front of him, palms turned toward us in a beseeching gesture that was oddly theatrical, like he was getting ready to deliver a grand soliloquy. I guess it was someone else's turn for a change.

"When I watched the players of the Globe, they were forever mending their costumes," he said. "Money was never so plentiful that a thing could be discarded when it still had life left in it. A gown would be cut down to become a cloak when it was too well-worn at the seams, and that cloak might go on to become a doublet, a vest, a jerkin. Nothing was thrown away until its time was over."

"Yes, people know how to sew," said the Luidaeg, with more confusion than impatience. "It's sort of vital if you don't have magic and don't want to be naked all the time."

"But if you asked someone who wore a vest made from a cloak made from a gown if their vest had been used in the production of *Romeo and Juliet*, they would tell you 'yes,' and proudly, because their vest *had* been used in that production, merely in another form."

"I genuinely hope that you're not suggesting what I think you're suggesting; that whole 'intestines into eels' thing is still on the table," said the Luidaeg.

"It wasn't that specific when you said it," I said.

"I like your style."

I kept my eyes on Tybalt, puzzling through what he'd said. Then I turned to the Luidaeg, and asked, "Where did the Swanmays come from?"

She looked suddenly, inexplicably tired. "They're descended from Aiofe of the White Wings. Another of my sisters. As far as I know, no one's seen her in centuries. She doesn't have some mystical stockpile of feather cloaks to hand out; Swanmays are born with their wings wrapped around their shoulders, where they can be easily set aside."

"Were they the first skinshifters?"

Slowly, the Luidaeg nodded. "Yes. They were born first, and then the Artio came after."

"When were the Ravens born?"

"They weren't."

For the first time since we'd entered the room, Quentin spoke. "That doesn't make sense," he objected. "We *live* with a Raven-maid."

"The first of them weren't born." The Luidaeg was speaking more slowly, like each word was an effort. I wondered how many older prohibitions against speech, either magical or personal, Titania's geas was overcoming. "Aoife had a sister, born at the same time. Aine. And Aine didn't like people touching her. Ever. At all. Aine wanted her own descendant line, but the thought of getting pregnant, of being with someone in that way, for long enough to conceive, was repugnant. So she and Aoife pooled their thoughts and their strength, and they wove a cloak of raven's feathers to match the cloaks of swan's feathers that Aoife's children wore. They *made* the Ravens. Their wings are proof of a sister's love and a mother's determination."

"You used that working to breathe life back into the skins of the Roane," I said.

The Luidaeg nodded.

"But you did it alone. Selkies aren't born holding their skins; they have to depend on the skins they're offered. Why?"

"Because my sister—my *sister*, my eldest sister, who I foolishly thought might care about me—had just orchestrated the destruction of my entire world, and I didn't trust *anyone*," snapped the Luidaeg. The blackness was entirely gone from her eyes. Even her pupils were green, the color of kelp in deep water. I couldn't help feeling like this might be the closest I'd ever come to seeing the real Antigone. "I poured everything I had into those skins, so one day I could stand here with the answer to resurrecting my children. So I could bring them home. That's all a mother wants. To bring them home." Her voice broke on the last word, turning hollow.

"My mother hadn't been born yet."

"No."

"You had no way of knowing *I'd* be born."

"No. Only something one of my daughters had said to me. That it was all right to be scared when I was lonely, because the answer would always come, given time."

That felt more like the sort of thing a massage therapist would have cross-stitched and hanging on their wall than a good reason to create and then destroy an entire fae race. I decided not to say so. It wasn't going to make things any better.

"What if you had help?" I asked carefully. "What if another Firstborn was willing to help you do what Aoife and Aine did? To make more cloaks, only out of sealskin, not feathers? They'd still be the skins of your children. There'd just be . . . more of them, like there should have been all along. The Roane haven't been making more Roane, because there are too few of them to successfully regenerate their race, and they haven't been making more Selkies, because there were only so many skins to go around."

"Nice thought, but we don't ha—" The Luidaeg stopped in the middle of the word, looking briefly like she was struggling for air, like she was suffocating. Then she coughed, rubbing her throat with one hand, and looked at me with wide, wondering eyes.

"We have another Firstborn," she rasped. "Pete."

"Pete," I agreed. "If she's willing to help you . . ."

"It won't work." Her face fell. "I swore to destroy the Selkies, and that's what I have to do."

"But did you swear to destroy the Selkies, or to bring back the Roane?" I asked. "Because maybe those don't have to be the same thing."

For a long, seemingly endless moment, the Luidaeg was silent. I held my breath, counting the seconds. If I hit twenty, I thought it might be a good idea to run. The sea witch might extend me more patience than she did most, but it wasn't limitless, and when it evaporated, I was going to be left high and dry and stranded on the cliffs of her regard.

Finally, in a low voice, she asked, "What would you have me do?"

And I told her.

TWENTY-THREE

W E BEGAN WITH ISLA'S skin. She'd died without formally passing it along: currently, technically, it had no owner, not even René, who hadn't been allowed to take it. Marcia carried it into Pete's receiving room, which seemed larger and eerier without its gathered crowds. Every sound we made echoed up into the rafters, bouncing back and forth between walls and windows until it became the insensate roaring of the sea, stripped of meaning and nuance.

Pete was there when the rest of us arrived, standing behind a vast round table that looked like it might have started life as a tall ship's lookout, only to be pulled down from the mast and pressed into a different sort of service. She was back in her pirate's attire, hat perched on her head, weight resting on her fingertips as she leaned against the table's surface. She looked at us gravely, studying each of us in turn, before she settled on the Luidaeg, back in white samite, her hair a tempest of black curls that sometimes seemed to flash silver, like they mirrored the ceaseless swirl of an angry sea.

"Annie," Pete said, voice barely louder than a sigh. "What stars do you steer by?"

The Luidaeg somehow mustered a smile. "They haven't bound me or tricked me or anything of the sort, I swear. They just convinced me to try another way."

"Another way." Pete gave the rest of us a dubious look. "Centuries I spent asking you to find a way to talk yourself out of doing this, and these people, these little, temporary people," her eyes flicked over me and Marcia on the word "temporary," like it was the kindest way she could find to remind the Luidaeg that we were mortal, "managed to do it in less than a week's time? I'm dubious. You'll forgive me for that."

"I've forgiven you for worse," said the Luidaeg. "Please, Amphitrite. Because you're my sister, and my friend, and because I didn't argue when I let you exile me, help me now. Help me find out whether this is the way forward, or only another anchor to weigh me down."

"You know what it'll cost if you fail."

The Luidaeg nodded. "I do. I don't know why, Dad help me, but I've decided it might be worth it. To know. To know whether I'm about to make myself into the monster they've all wanted me to become."

Pete nodded, expression grave. Marcia stepped forward, putting the willow basket on the table. Its contents sloshed faintly, and my stomach lurched. This was a dead creature's hide, a skin passed who knew how many times over, and there was no blood left in it. This kind of death existed away from and outside of my sphere as one of the Dóchas Sidhe—but it was also exactly the sort of thing Faerie had made my mother—and by extension, me—to do. It was a spell, tangled and ancient and intricate as anything. Age couldn't change its essential nature.

Marcia started to step back. The Luidaeg's hand lashed out, quick as a striking snake, and latched around Marcia's wrist. Marcia squeaked, and froze.

"Weren't you tempted?" asked the Luidaeg. "A Selkie's skin, no witnesses, and all the sea standing ready to welcome you home. I've seen the way you stand in the shallows, looking toward the deeps. Weren't you *tempted*?"

"No," said Marcia. She met the Luidaeg's eyes and didn't flinch. "I have other paths to walk, and other roads to run. I can't do them wrapped in a sealskin that isn't mine. I'm sorry. I'm sorry for the woman who died, and for the people who died before her, all the way back to the boy who died to make the skin in the first place. But me being sorry doesn't give me the right to take what isn't mine."

"Ah," breathed the Luidaeg. She let go of Marcia's wrist. Marcia danced back, out of her grasp. The Luidaeg didn't seem to notice.

She was busy opening the basket, sliding her hands into the oil it contained, and pulling out the sealskin I'd found tangled in the kelp beneath the Duchy of Ships.

"His name was Beathan," she said. "He was my grandson. He was strong and clever and bold and not always good about making the right choices. Most of the futures he saw had to do with fishing. He kept his family fed. He was a good provider. He would . . . I'm sure he'd rather be alive right now than be a part of what we're to do here, but he would approve of this, I think, if he were asked. He would understand that he was saving people."

She pulled the skin fully out of the basket and stretched it out across the table, where it clung, gleaming, to the wood. She looked at Pete, and then at me.

"I've never done this before," she said.

"I don't think anyone has," I said. "Can you turn the skin over? I want to see the magic inside it." The top was a shining pelt, sleek and smooth and perfect as if it had just been cut away from the back of the boy who'd grown it. The spell had to be anchored to the leather. It was the only thing that made sense. I'd touched Connor's skin a hundred times while he was wearing it, and never heard the tempting promises Isla's skin had made when it was hanging across my arms.

The Luidaeg and Pete exchanged a look before carefully, oh-so-carefully, grasping the opposite ends of the skin and turning it so that the burnished leather underside was toward the ceiling. It looked perfectly ordinary, the sort of thing that could have come out of any hunter's stockpile.

Wordlessly, I held my hand out toward Tybalt. He sighed, and the next thing I knew, his claws were drawing hot lines of pain across my palm, splitting the skin. The deepest wound was at the heel of my hand. I brought it to my lips as quickly as I could, and was rewarded with a hot gout of blood, filling my mouth, overwhelming my senses with the taste of cut grass and copper. I could taste the ghost of the Luidaeg's magic there as well, and that was fine; under the circumstances, that was almost ideal.

I blinked and the magic appeared on the leather like a map, or a fishing net of delicate lines older than any modern nation, any mortal dynasty. They were clearly of the Luidaeg's making, but they were infused with an ageless anger and a deep, unspeakable grief.

As if in a dream, I leaned forward and rested my fingertips on the air above the skin, the taste of blood still clinging to my lips. The wounds on my hand had already healed. Tybalt would have to hurt me again if I needed more blood.

"There are four places you can cut without breaking the bond between the working and the weave," I said. My voice didn't sound like my own. "No more than that. Divided further, the spell would fail, and it would just be so much dead fur. I can show you where to cut, but I don't have the power to make the cuts myself. They'd seal over." So much of the magic was dedicated to preserving the skins, maintaining the immortality that had been theirs by right when they'd been living, vital parts of Faerie, and not memorials to commemorate the lost. Anything short of massive trauma wouldn't be enough to break the spell or destroy the skin.

In that, we were the same. Both of us had been created by the Firstborn—me in a slightly more standard manner—and both of us were essentially indestructible.

"Four cuts, five skins," sighed the Luidaeg. She touched the skin with the tips of her fingers. "My brave, beautiful boy. Let's see whether we're gambling everything on the right tide or the wrong one. Let's see whether you get to rest."

"Where?" asked Pete.

I touched the skin where the spell was thinnest, in four places. Pete nodded, and I stepped back from the table. Tybalt was there, to put an arm around my waist and draw me close. Quentin and Marcia stood nearby, seeking comfort in proximity. All of us were silent, aware that we were present for something that no one had seen in centuries, that maybe no one had ever seen at all. Two Firstborn, a daughter of Maeve and a daughter of Titania, working together to change the world.

Magic gathered in the corners of the room, gently at first, like a wave lapping at the shore, and then with more and more strength, until it was everywhere, until we were drowning in it. I leaned against Tybalt and struggled to keep breathing as the magic chased the air from the room. The Luidaeg and Pete bent over the skin, their movements silent and precise and nowhere near as fascinating as the magic they were generating. I closed my eyes and inhaled.

The Luidaeg's magic was familiar to me, more familiar than it had any right to be. It smelled of brackish water, of the point where sea meets shore, where freshwater blends with salt. It smelled like peat and moss and loam, like blooming bog myrtle and sweet blue-bell. Its complexity was dizzying, and enough to remind me that Faerie gets simpler with every generation. Most of us only have two elements to our magic. She had an entire world.

Pete's magic was softer, gentler and crueler at the same time, because it wasn't a cudgel, wasn't a hammer: it was a knife slipped between the ribs and into a lung, it was a blade in the dark that cut and cut and never stopped slicing. It smelled like clean sea air immediately before a storm, wind and wave and ozone and impending doom. It smelled like driftwood, bleached bone-dry on the shore, and like sand bathed in moonlight, like ambergris and mist. Half those things shouldn't have been scents, but I knew them all the same, and as I breathed, they blended with the Luidaeg's magic, tying complicated knots all around the room.

The Luidaeg moaned when she made the first cut in her grandson's skin. It was the sound of something dying. Pete hummed in wordless encouragement, and it was the sound of that same thing rising from the depths of the sea, coming back to life, coming home. I opened my eyes again. It was the only way to keep myself from being overwhelmed.

I could have stayed there forever, bathed in the painful radiance of their magic. I could have turned and run and never looked back. In the end, I needed to do neither of those things. In the end, the Luidaeg dropped her knife and put her hands over her face. Pete stepped back.

Five sealskins lay on the table, each shining, perfect, and as large as the original. They weren't quite identical; their spots and striations had apparently spread out from the piece of Beathan's skin that had been used to make them, creating five subtle but genuine variations.

"Come on, Annie," said Pete gently. "Let's go see if these work."

The Luidaeg nodded, and said nothing.

We walked together through the Duchy of Ships. The Luidaeg carried Marcia's basket, now containing all five skins, against her chest, keeping her eyes fixed on the dim, distant line of the horizon. Nolan and Cassandra met us at the start of the shopping district. The Lordens didn't. Their ties to the Undersea were too strong: this wasn't for them to see. This was for the Luidaeg, and the few people she was willing to share it with, and for the Roane, who had been lost for so very long.

It was hard not to wonder whether the Roane had seen this moment. Whether some of them might have wept over the sight of their mother, their grandmother, walking with a basket clutched in her arms, her shoulders bowed by the weight of centuries they hadn't been able to set aside. The future can always be changed. There's never once been a prophecy that couldn't be somehow undermined or averted. Why hadn't the Roane set their own deaths aside?

What about this moment had been worth losing so very much?

The Selkie clan leaders were waiting when we reached the artificial beach. René stood alongside the others, his hand clasped in Mathias'. I was glad to see that. One way or another, they were going to find a way through this. They had to.

The rest of us slowed our steps, even Pete, until the Luidaeg approached the Selkies alone. She stopped a few feet away from them, the wind whipping her hair around her face, even though it barely ruffled the others. Her eyes were still green. Still so green.

"I promised on the day the Selkies were created that I would see the Roane swimming freely in the seas once more, and I keep my word," she said.

Joan closed her eyes. Claude clutched his webbed hands into fists. Mathias and René shifted closer together, until there was barely any room between them. Only Liz remained exactly as she was, watching the Luidaeg with the mixture of longing and loathing that always stretched between them.

"But words are malleable," continued the Luidaeg. "I was reminded of that today. I was reminded that sometimes, justice and mercy can exist in the same breath, in the same shining space."

Joan opened her eyes.

"René Lefebvre, your sister has stopped her dancing. For that, I am truly sorry. I granted permission to the Selkies to steal from one another out of bitterness. I did *not* grant permission for a cruel Merrow to slay your sister. It was wrong and unfair." The Luidaeg held the basket out toward him. "I can't bring her back to you. But I can let you see what we've made of her loss."

René bit his lip before letting go of Mathias' hand and stepping unsteadily forward to remove the basket's lid. He slid his hands into the oil, eyes widening with surprise before he pulled out a sealskin.

"It's hers," he said. "But it's not hers at the same time."

"The rules have changed," said the Luidaeg.

René blanched. He didn't hand the skin back. The Luidaeg didn't reach for it.

"The tide is flowing out on the Selkies," she said. "I made a promise, and I'm bound by Titania's own grace to keep it, whether I want to or not. But I can bend the way it's kept. Each of you will give me your skin. All the gathered Selkies. Every single one. I know you're all here; I know none of you could avoid my summons."

The Selkie clan leaders drew closer together, horrified and afraid. All, again, save for Liz, who didn't move.

"My sister and I will split it along the seams of the spell that has kept it alive," continued the Luidaeg. "It will happen today. We'll make as many new skins as we can. After that, I'm banished for seven years."

Hope was dawning on the faces of the clan leaders.

But the Luidaeg wasn't done. "Your skin will be returned to you, as will the new skins we've made from the substance of it. They'll be passed as you see fit, and all but one will be bound to their holders. The Roane return. Tonight, the Roane return. And the Selkies remain: one for each original skin. You'll have time to settle your affairs. Some of you may still choose to set aside the sea. In seven years, when my exile is ended, we'll come here one more time, and the final binding will be done."

"I'm sorry," said Joan. "I don't understand. Are you saying we don't *have* to be Roane?"

"No. I'm saying I understand it was unfair of me to give you all this time to learn how to be Selkies, and then to be angry when you had forgotten how to be Roane," said the Luidaeg. "The tide is going out. I can't catch it, any more than you can. I can't keep it here. But I can grant you time to make this an easier transition. I can give you gentler waters."

"When do we start?" asked René.

The Luidaeg smiled. "Right now."

TWENTY-FOUR

$\int$ELKIES FILLED THE BEACH. Some were grown, as old as Liz, if visibly no older; like all fae, their clocks stopped upon reaching physical maturity, even if, for them, that stop was artificially induced. Not for very much longer. Soon, most of them would be as bound to the sea as the Luidaeg herself.

Others were children, wide-eyed and wondering and clutching their newly-split sealskins around their shoulders like they were a lifetime of birthday gifts rolled into a single narrow piece of fur. Some of the teenagers were crying, stroking their sealskins with shaking fingers, clinging to their parents. It was the end of an era. It was the beginning of a new one.

Not every skin had been divisible by five. Some could only split into two or three; a few rare ones had been divisible by as many as seven. In the end, only Gillian had a fully intact skin wrapped around her shoulders, because losing contact with it even for the duration of the spell would have killed her. There were still humans in the crowd, family members without a skin to call their own . . . but most of them had refused the offer, had chosen humanity and everything that came with it. They got to choose, and they got to live, and somehow, that seemed like a miracle.

The Luidaeg put a hand on my shoulder. "Well, here we go," she said. "The largest expansion of Faerie since Dad's day. You feel up to this?"

"No," I said flatly. "I do not."

"Too bad," she said.

"I think it's beautiful," said Marcia dreamily. "Faerie should always be like this, fluid and changing and willing to work for a better world, for everyone."

The Luidaeg glanced at her. "It's not too late. We could find you a skin."

"No." Marcia shook her head. "No, it's another ballad for me. I won't sing the song of the sea, not right now, not today."

"Suit yourself." The Luidaeg turned to fully face me, taking a deep breath. "I know you don't have a choice about this. I'm still grateful. I'm glad to know you, October."

I blinked. "I . . . okay."

I glanced over my shoulder toward Tybalt and Quentin. Quentin flashed me a quick, anachronistic thumbs-up, and it was all I could do not to laugh. Then the Luidaeg was leading me to where Gillian was waiting, her sealskin tied over her shoulders, a haunted look in her eyes.

"Gilly," I said. "I—"

"No." She shook her head. "I still don't want to talk to you. But I want to live. So do this. Make it last. Make it forever." Her laugh was small and tight and uneven. "I can't spend the next seven years wondering if I'm going to die for the crime of tying a bad knot—not if I don't have to. Especially not when the end result is going to be the same. I'm Roane either way."

I bit my lip and nodded, reaching out to take her hands.

Gillian was my daughter, blood of my blood, even if her own blood had been sea-changed by the sealskin around her shoulders. I wondered, briefly, how the Luidaeg had been planning to accomplish this change before I had a child among the Selkies, and put the thought firmly aside. I couldn't be distracted. Not right now.

The Luidaeg set her hand on my left shoulder, and the air around us crackled with the smell of cut grass and copper, my magic amplified and thrown into the wind, surrounding the assembled Selkies, seeking out their similarities to Gillian.

Somewhere, Torin was locked away, waiting to be cast out of everything he'd ever known. Isla's blood would still be on his hands, but he wouldn't hurt anyone else in these waters. It was a small condition. It had to be enough.

On the beach behind me, the Lordens stood, all four of them, together for this short stretch of time as they watched me change our world forever. They had arrived as a group, and while I couldn't turn to look at them, I knew Patrick and Dianda would be holding onto each other, as inseparable as salt from the sea.

To the side, a bit apart from Tybalt and Quentin, Nolan and Cassandra watched, waiting to see what this would mean. We were all together, here in this place beyond the end of the world, where the waves clawed at the pillars holding us away from the sea, where one of the last Firstborn held her sway.

I reached for the magic in Gillian's veins, and when I found it, I reached for the magic in the skin around her shoulders. They were tangled but distinct, two parts of a greater whole. I bit my tongue, filling my mouth with blood, filling my mind with the feel of it. Then I swallowed, and said, as softly as I could, "Blow, oh, blow ye winds blow, the world's greatest graveyard's one more soul to keep: I said blow, oh, blow ye winds blow, the star of the west is at rest in the deep."

The magic caught, seeking sympathy, fueled by blood, cast wide by the Luidaeg's net. Gillian made a small sound of dismay. I closed my eyes and kept chanting, kept casting, kept pulling the strands of magic in flesh and in sealskin and tangling them together, until there was nothing but the braided unity, until there was nothing but the single greatest piece of blood magic I had ever performed.

If only my mother could see me now, I thought, and there was an edge of hysteria to the idea, a fraying. I pushed harder. The spell gathered, crested—

—and shattered around us, raining down on the beach full of laughing, weeping, rejoicing, grieving Roane. I opened my eyes. Gillian ripped her hands out of mine, raising them to the level of her face and staring at the delicate changes in the webbing between her fingers as the dried-out husk of her sealskin slipped from her shoulders and fell to the sand, unheeded. Her eyes were so green. No one in our family had ever had that much color to them.

I staggered, a wave of dizziness sweeping over me, and there was Tybalt, catching me and pulling me into the safe harbor of his embrace. I mustered a wan smile. My head was pounding.

"Ow," I announced.

"Ow, indeed, you infuriating woman," he said, and propped me against him so I could watch the waves of joy and grief and confused, giddy relief passing through the figures on the beach. The doors of the little Cape Cod houses were opening, the Selkies who'd been chosen to spend another seven years dancing between land and sea pouring out to exclaim over their changed kin.

The world was different now. We had done this. There was no taking it back.

I let myself relax against Tybalt, closing my eyes again, and wondered how much more the world would change before it was finished. Would I even recognize it when all was said and done? Would I even want to?

The waves were high and the wind was good, and there were still Selkies in the world, for at least a little longer, and there were Roane in the waves again. The Luidaeg was laughing, and finally, the thin, jagged edge of sorrow that had always lingered beneath the sound was gone.

Let that be enough. For here, for now, until tomorrow, let that be enough.

Read on for
a brand-new novella
by Seanan McGuire:

HOPE IS SWIFT

True hope is swift, and flies with swallow's wings:
Kings it makes gods, and meaner creatures kings.
—William Shakespeare, *Richard III*

ONE

May 1, 2014

THE SHADOWS RIPPLED and separated as a skinny Cait Sidhe a few years younger than me stepped out of them. They were wearing human street clothes—blue jeans and a Pokémon T-shirt—and the glitter of a human disguise sparkled around them. The spell wasn't very well-cast, and their hair was still gray streaked with white. Not a common color for a mortal teen.

This is why we have hair dye. Just saying.

"Well, Cal?" My tone was harsher than I meant it to be. I sounded pissed, which wasn't great if I wanted them to tell me what I needed to know. I took a deep breath, forcing myself to calm down, and asked, "Are they gone?"

"They set sail for the Duchy of Ships an hour ago." Cal let their human disguise wisp away, leaving the faint scent of pine hanging in the air.

October would have sniffed once before rattling off a list of scents, like some sort of magic sommelier. Honestly, she'd be super annoying if I didn't like her so much. She's pretty annoying anyway. "Pine" was as much as I could manage, and even that was halfway guessing.

Without their illusions, Cal's hair was still gray streaked with white. Their skin was too pale, like they'd been dusted with chalk, except for the darker bands that slashed across in a pattern that seemed random on a human but would have made perfect sense on a cat. Their eyes were a bright yellow-green, and their ears and teeth were equally pointed. They grinned, clearly pleased and just as clearly waiting.

"You did well, Cal," I said, trying to emulate Uncle Tybalt's imperious tone.

They visibly preened. Cal has been trying to get close to me since we were kits. They decided a long time ago that we were going to be friends, and I was going to take them into my confidences. They've never quite understood that the reason we *can't* be friends is because I'm going to be in charge.

Uncle Tybalt doesn't have friends within the Court. He has subjects, some more useful than others, but not *friends*. Friends make things complicated. Friends put themselves in danger without considering the consequences. I can't have friends any more than he can. Not within the Court. Outside the Court, I have Helen, and Quentin, and Chelsea, and even Dean. Inside the Court, I have . . .

Cal. Who never wanted anything more than they wanted to please me, and who couldn't seem to understand that they were trying too hard.

I sighed. "But if they left an hour ago, why are you telling me this *now*? 'Go, follow them, tell me when they leave' is a pretty easy job. Why did it take you so long?"

Their satisfaction faded. I would have felt bad about that before I'd been required to take up my duties more devoutly, back when I'd been free to run around the city as I pleased, without anyone telling me to stop. Cal should have been able to get what they wanted. We should have been making mischief together, not held apart by the necessary formalities of my rank.

As October is so fond of reminding me, Faerie has never once, in all its long and varied history, been fair.

"You didn't say to come straight back," they said, watching me with suddenly wary eyes. "I watched them go, and then I went down to the Castro to pick some pockets. Then I bought dinner at Orphan Andy's. They're open all night and they make the best strawberry milkshakes. Then I checked the dock to be sure they were still gone, and so I could follow the trails of the people who'd come and left again without getting on the boat."

"Were there many?" I asked, managing to swallow my second question, which would have been less than helpful. "Why didn't you bring me a milkshake?" is not an inquiry befitting a Prince of Cats.

"Lots of humans after the fog they used to hide themselves wafted away; mostly homeless, a few drunk, two who smelled like law enforcement. A few changelings I figure wandered through the fog but didn't know what it was there to hide. The Troll who drives the cab, and the thin-blood who spends time with your October."

A warm feeling suffused my chest when they called her "my October." She'll never be to me what she is to my uncle, and I'm glad: I don't have a thing for self-destructive changeling women four times my age, especially not when they're engaged to someone who could kick my butt around the Kingdom without breaking a sweat. But she'll never be to Uncle Tybalt what she is to me. Mentor, teacher . . . knight. I'm her squire as much as Quentin is, even if we can't make it official. Cait Sidhe aren't knighted by the Divided Courts. It isn't done.

But maybe it could have been, for me. If Uncle Tybalt hadn't fallen quite so in love with her, quite so quickly, we might have been able to make my squiring official before he agreed to give up his throne. She could have been my knight in name as well as deed. I could have been the first of our kind to kneel and pledge myself to the root and the branch, the rose and the thorn. I could have shown those arrogant fools who call the Cait Sidhe honorless beasts that we've always been as good as they are.

Guess somebody else is going to have to be the first. I should be happy with what I have—I have so much more than most of my kind can even dream of—but it's the nature of cats to want more than we can have. If we were content to be content, we'd be little better than dogs, and what's the use in that?

"The thin-blood's name is Stacy," I said, keeping the pleasure from my voice. "Her oldest daughter is chatelaine to the Queen in the Mists, and her middle child is as good as apprenticed to the sea witch. Treat her with respect, or the allies of her children might move against us."

Cal rolled a shoulder, clearly unconcerned by my vague threats. "I've done as you've asked, my Prince. Is there anything else?"

This was where I was supposed to praise them for doing a good job. All I could manage was a vague wave of my hand, dismissing them. Cal gave me an amused look, all too aware of my mood, and vanished into the shadows, leaving me alone. Again.

Alone. It's the lot of Princes to be alone. The lot of Kings is much the same, if not worse, since the whole Court rests on their shoulders. They're going to make me a King sooner than I ever thought they would. I'm going to be fenced in for the rest of my life. I'll never be a wild thing again, if I was ever a wild thing in the first place.

My mother—may she rest peacefully among the night-haunts—named me Rajiv in honor of her father, a man I never knew. My father, may he *never* rest peacefully, recognized the power in me the first time he held me, a mewling infant with my eyes stuck shut and my ears plastered against my head. My mother's magic was never strong enough to let her transform. She lived, loved, and left us, all in her feline form, and so I'd been born the same way, growing through the early stages of infancy as fast as any kitten.

Sometimes I liked to tease Quentin about how, even though we were technically the same age, I was actually older than he is since I was walking and talking by the time I was four months old, and he was still a helpless burden on his family. He usually responded by hitting me. That was how I knew we were friends.

My father saw what I could be, what I *would* be, and set out to benefit from it. He changed my name, shortened it to "Raj," which means "king," and contacted every Court of Cats in North America that didn't already have an heir. I could have gone anywhere—could even have grown up in Quentin's backyard, detesting the secretive Crown Prince of the Westlands—but I ended up here, in San Francisco, in the Court of Dreaming Cats.

Father used to say Uncle Tybalt had offered the best arrangement of any continental monarch, and that he had no interest in traveling abroad. I think, considering my childhood, that it was more a matter of Uncle Tybalt being willing to tolerate my father's presence. Most Kings of Cats wouldn't do it; they'd view the presence of another adult male in their new heir's life as a threat to their sovereignty. After all, had Father killed my uncle after I was named and known as heir, he could have claimed the throne as my regent— the closest he could have come to being a King in his own right.

He tried. After Mother died, when Uncle Tybalt became too openly enamored of October, finally admitting what the rest of us had known for ages, my father attempted to stage a coup. He failed, and I guess I was never as good a son to him as I'd always wanted to be, because I didn't mourn for him. Not when he died, and not now.

I mourn my mother. I will for years yet, if I ever stop. But my father got what he deserved, and when he's forgotten, I won't be sorry.

I slid from my perch—a pile of old orange crates with peeling paint—and stalked deeper into the court. If I had a tail when I walked on two legs, it would have been lashing. Uncle Tybalt says it's improper for a Prince to look more bestial than necessary. Shade—the Queen of Cats in Berkeley—agrees, so I guess he's right. Again. It's annoying how often he's right about things. Just once I'd like to be the one with the correct answer, while he's left standing confused on the sidelines.

Shame followed the thought; I hunched my shoulders and walked faster. He'd be standing on the sidelines of the Court of Cats soon enough, when Ginevra judged me ready and told him to come back so I could challenge him. Or when he came back for his throne, let the Court see that his heart wasn't in it anymore, and I challenged him. Every path ended with claws bared and blood on the floor. Every future led to me sitting on his throne, his crown on my head, his subjects bowing down before me and calling me their King.

I don't know what else they'll call me. Princes and Princesses take new names when they claim their rightful places, to make it perfectly clear that we aren't the children we used to be, that we have to be respected and obeyed even by the people who used to wipe our noses. I don't know what they'll call my uncle, either. "Tybalt" is his King-name, and he'll have to set it aside when he forsakes the crown.

All these changes and choices gave me a headache. I stalked on, down a hallway lined with patches of plywood and through a room filled with bolts of fabric. Some of them looked like they were decades old. I paused to note the room's location. Helen had a fondness for vintage clothing, and her sewing machine saw more use than anything else she owned. She might appreciate a few bolts of fabric, call me her thoughtful boy and reward me with kisses that tasted like mint tea and sugar cookies. I might not be as good at identifying magic by scent as October, but I could recognize the taste of it on my tongue.

Helen's kisses tasted like coming home.

That was a problem. I mean, it wasn't like I was planning to propose or anything—we'd been dating for three years, and we'd only recently reached the stage where she let me touch her breasts sometimes, below the shirt but above the bra. They were very soft. I liked them. I didn't want to give them up, or stop dreaming about the day when she agreed that maybe the bra could go.

And that was the shallowest, most hedonistic way of considering my relationship. I *liked* her. I liked that she had no respect for my position, not because she thought the Court of Cats didn't count— she respected it as much as she respects any other form of nobility— but because she felt it was time for Faerie to set aside kings and queens and move into a more modern, more enlightened era. She would abolish all monarchies if she could, bringing about free elections across the Summerlands.

She was *not* going to like it when I told her we had to break up because I was going to be King. It wouldn't matter that the rules were the same for Princesses as they were for Princes; she'd call it patriarchal bullshit, and probably several worse things, and then she'd cry, or throw things, or tell me never to speak to her again. That last was my deepest fear. She was my friend. I didn't want her to stop being my friend just because we were never going to be lovers.

When I married, if I married, I'd have to marry another Cait Sidhe, to avoid the conflict of interest that was costing my uncle his throne. Kings of Cats rarely breed true; eventually, I'd have to do as my uncle once did, and spread the word that I was ready to adopt an heir. The cycles repeat. The cycles always, endlessly repeat.

The last hall ended in a chasm. I stepped lightly over the edge, landing in a pit filled with carpet remnants. Wading to the edge, I pulled myself free and bowed.

"Lady Ginevra."

"Prince." My uncle's regent smiled at me, tolerant and amused. "You sure know how to make an entrance."

I straightened, looking down the length of my nose at her, and said nothing.

Ginevra's father, Jolgeir, has been King of the Court of Whispering Cats in Silences for more than a hundred years. When *he* fell in love, it was with a human woman. Somehow, that wasn't considered a conflict of interest, maybe because she didn't come home covered in blood as often as October does. Together, they had three daughters. Three *changeling* daughters.

And then October came along and offered Jolgeir's daughters a chance so many changelings never got. She could give them the Choice for real, not just as a formality. She could bring them fully into Faerie, if that was what they wanted, or turn them fully mortal. All three of them had chosen Faerie. The eldest and youngest are Cait Sidhe now, learning their new place in the structure of their father's Court, elevated and empowered. The middle daughter . . .

Ginevra is a Princess of Cats, her father's heir, and one day, she'll be Queen.

Her hair was a delicate shade of cream-white, trending to a richer orange at the tips; her eyes were very blue. She was attractive enough, in an irritating sort of way that had enchanted half the occupants of the Court. I think they're infatuated with novelty. Her powers were still new to her—I was teaching her as much as she was supervising me—and her grasp on her bipedal form was sometimes questionable. As now, when two fully-formed cat's ears poked up through her hair.

None of our shared subjects were in attendance. I allowed myself a smirk.

"Far be it from me to question a lady's choices, especially a lady as refined as your lovely self, but it's the custom to keep our ears to more refined dimensions here in the Mists." I tapped the point of my own ear in illustration. "Does my lady intend to set a new fashion trend? Should I be modifying my own default forms?"

Ginevra reached up with both hands, grimacing as her fingers found the furry slopes of her ears. "Oh, *dammit*," she said. "I thought I got it right this time. Raj, can you . . . ?" She let go of her ears and gestured helplessly.

Sometimes the fact that she was in San Francisco to supervise *me* felt like some vast practical joke on the part of the universe. But unless I wanted to challenge my uncle for his throne immediately, which I didn't, I needed a regent. Ginevra was unquestionably powerful. It radiated off her, crackling in the air like electricity before a thunderstorm. She'd learn to mask it eventually, concealing her potential behind polite illusions, but until then, she was like a signal flare on a dark night. No one was going to challenge her. Not when she could vaporize them for trying.

Sadly, this didn't make her good at the delicate things, and that's where I've always excelled. I stepped forward, offering her my hands. She took them gratefully, the points of her claws pressing against my palms.

"Close your eyes," I instructed, waiting for her to obey before I did the same. I breathed out, and when I breathed in again, I reached for her magic, tangling it with my own.

I couldn't have done it without her consent. She was too strong for that: if she'd decided to fight me, we could have battled each other to a standstill, all without moving or letting go. My magic brushed hers, and hers surged forward, until they were a braided chain suspended between us, her power and mine in perfect balance.

It was foolish of her to trust me this much. It would have been even more foolish of me to abuse that trust. I slid my awareness forward, finding the space where she kept her image of herself. It was still malleable. She'd known how to be a changeling for her entire life, unable to control how much of the cat and how much of the woman she wore. I could see the shadow of her former self in the open spaces around the image she was crafting now: she'd been one of the unfortunate changelings born with a fully proportional tail, as well as the fluffy ears that currently graced her head. No adornments befitting a Queen, those.

But then, why not? Why do we feel the need to style ourselves after the Daoine Sidhe, who will never see us as their equals, no matter how carefully we imitate them? We should be free to choose our own destinies, and the forms we wear as we approach them.

"Relax," I said, and pulled on her magic, guiding it away from who she'd been and into the space opened by who she was trying to become. My magic flared hot in my hands. I let go and stepped back, opening my eyes.

Her ears were shaped more like mine now, pointed and proud, but not animal. Her teeth were smaller. Her eyes were no less luminous, and her coloring was no less outside the human norm. She would have been an ornament in any Court of the world, pretty and perfect, suited to any royal table. A pang of melancholy regret mingled with my regard. She looked lovelier to me now because she looked less like a Cait Sidhe.

How much of our potential is spent on the endless, aching need to *hide*?

"Better," I said. "Queen Windermere would be delighted to receive you."

Ginevra reached up to feel the tip of her left ear, smiling when she found it smooth and furless and immobile. "Oh, that's good," she agreed. "Your uncle taught you well."

"My uncle has been preparing me to be King since I was old enough to understand what the position would entail," I said.

"I can't say the same about my dad." Ginevra's mouth twisted in a wry curl. "He always said he felt like I would have been a Princess if I weren't a changeling, but I *was* a changeling, so it didn't matter because the Shadow Roads would never anchor themselves through me. And then, Toby, you know," she waved a hand, encompassing the whole of her fae self, "and suddenly I had a lifetime of lessons to catch up on in like, five minutes. I wouldn't change it, not for the world, but wow am I going to mess things up."

"Yes, well, you're messing them up while technically standing regent over me, so this will be fun for both of us," I said stiffly.

Ginevra laughed.

It was hard to stay unhappy with her; she had a joyful heart, and it showed. Still, I kept my face schooled to neutrality as I said, "The ship has gone. Uncle Tybalt and October are bound for the Undersea, and won't return until they've fulfilled their duty to the Luidaeg."

Uncle Tybalt, and October, and Quentin, and even *Dean* were bound for the Undersea, Dean, who loved my best friend in a way that could never have been open to me, and would now share an adventure with him that I would never truly understand. It wasn't the betrayal it seemed, but oh, it burned.

So many things burn, these days. I've always known I'd be King, have even reveled in waiting for it. But I never wanted to be King so *soon*.

"All right," said Ginevra. "I'll double the patrols, tell everyone to watch for signs that someone's sniffing around our borders, trying to take a measure of what's happening here."

"There's no need to fear a challenge," I said. "As a regent, you have seven years of peace before anyone would consider that right or proper."

"I don't quite understand that," said Ginevra. "Everyone likes to tell me the Court of Cats is violent and complicated, but as soon as I said I'd hold the throne for you, the Court of Dreaming Cats gets seven years of no one bothering them? How does that work?"

"It's rare for a regent to be called for any reason other than an orphaning," I said. It was a struggle to keep the frustration from my tone. We'd had this conversation several times, and it seemed likely we'd have it several more before Ginevra accepted it as the way things were done. "Cait Sidhe can be brutal, yes, and our methods of succession are more direct than they are in the Divided Courts—in part because our heirs are so rarely a matter of blood. Your father is lucky to have you. You'll be able to take his throne without killing him, when the time comes."

Ginevra blanched. "You say that so casually."

"Because to me, this *is* casual," I said. "This is how the world works. We're animals, but we're not beasts. If Uncle Tybalt had died and you'd been called to stand regent, I'd be half-trained and grieving. There's no honor in taking a throne from a child. So I'm to be allowed my grief, while you protect me and give me time to recover from my loss. In a customary regency, I'd be expected to fight you to show I was ready to claim what had always been mine."

Unlike a normal succession fight, I wouldn't be expected to do more than cursory damage. As long as she was defeated, I could claim my place, and she'd be allowed to return home in honor, having done her duty to a child of her own kind.

Our politics are as complicated and tedious as the politics of the Divided Courts. It's just that they follow other rules, and have no interest in compromising themselves for the expectations of anyone else.

"You should know I hit like a freight train," said Ginevra. "Dad says I don't understand my own strength, so it's sort of like trying to wrestle a bus. Yeah, you may have technique and training on your side, but it's still a *bus*."

"That's why I'm supposed to teach you how to control your power." Being my regent's teacher was weird. It would leave us both better prepared for our futures. She'd be a better Princess when she went back to Silences, and I . . .

I'd be a better Prince. That was the only thing I needed to be. Better Princes make better Kings. That's just logic.

"If milady does not need me, I would like to be excused," I said, with a quick, shallow bow. "I have business to attend to."

"Does the business involve wandering around the city unsupervised? Because I'm not comfortable with the way you keep doing that."

I raised an eyebrow—a gesture I learned from watching my uncle, and refined over the course of many long hours with my mirror—and looked at her silently, waiting for her to explain.

"You're still a teenager, and San Francisco isn't the safest city in the world," said Ginevra. "I'm not sure what the safest city *is*, but I know this isn't it."

"I realize your kittenhood was spent as a changeling, that your experiences will have been accordingly different from my own, but I am a Prince of Cats born and raised, and I've always been aware of my own power," I said. Once again, I regretted my lack of a tail. It would have been nice to have something to lash. "I'm not in the habit of taking anyone with me when I go to visit my friends."

I left unmentioned the fact that once, I would have been. Before Blind Michael—before the terror and the trauma, before the fear that I would be lost forever to the dark, before October, and Quentin, and Helen, had come crashing into my life and forced me to reshape it—I would no more have left the Court of Cats without a full escort than I would have supplicated myself before the Divided Courts and offered my services as a ratcatcher. I was spoiled and small in those days, content to live in a narrow world until the time came for me to take my rightful place upon the throne. It took a kidnapping to show me that a gilded cage was a gilded cage. It took imprisonment to tell me how much I wanted to be free.

Perhaps I would have been a better King if I had never changed. I would certainly have been a more willing one. It's difficult to see one's freedoms as limited when one fails to understand what they are, or what they have the potential to eventually become.

Ginevra looked unsure. I decided it was time to offer her the greatest incentive I had left.

"If you allow this," I said portentously, "I will give you the password for the Wi-Fi."

Ginevra blinked, her pupils expanding to swallow her irises whole. If her ears had still been feline in form, I had no doubt they would have been pressed flat against her skull. "*What* did you just say?"

"I have the password for the Wi-Fi. I'll give it to you."

"We're in the *Court of Cats*," she said. "There's no Internet here!"

That would have been true once, before Quentin befriended April O'Leary, the cyber-Dryad sometime-Countess of Tamed Lightning. April has a certain understanding with electrical systems. She understands that she wants them to do what she tells them, and they understand that it's best not to argue with her.

Since April entered the questionable orbit of my life, many things have gotten better. Mostly our phones, but also the availability and stability of wireless Internet in places like the Court of Cats.

"It's not the best Internet," I said. "I don't recommend trying to stream something while also downloading something. And it's terrible for gaming. I do all my gaming at Quentin's place. But yes, there's Internet, and I control it, and I have the password."

"I'm your regent," she said. "I could order you to tell me."

I nodded. "You could. Shall we find out together how well that works?"

Ginevra glared, and I smiled at her. It's always nice, the moment when I know I've won. It's always something to savor.

TWO

The air outside was all the sweeter for having been so skillfully bargained for. I walked with eyes half-closed, enjoying the scents and sounds of the midnight air.

Helen's family lived near the Castro, in a residential neighborhood that had been new when her fae father decided he was ready to settle down. His neighbors would probably be way more pissed about how little he'd paid for his home than they were by the fact that he wasn't human. If anything, they might take his fae nature as another statement on the gentrification of the city. Can't live here unless you're rich or supernatural.

They're not as wrong as they would have been, once. The Court of Cats has swelled incredibly over the last several years as stairways and rooms and paths once inherently connected to the city's shape have been lost, cast away by the humans dedicated to remaking the place in a shiny new image. It's nice to know such things can be preserved, and yet it stings to know they must be lost in the first place.

A twig snapped behind me. I kept walking, but stopped sniffing the air for the sheer joy of it, and began sniffing for some sign of who was following me. Ginevra wasn't *completely* wrong about the city's dangers, annoying as that was to admit; muggings do happen, and a slim, relatively slightly-built teenage boy walking alone down darkened streets could be said to be inviting trouble.

Any human thief who tangled with me would find themselves facing more trouble than they bargained for. But I might get hurt in the process of teaching them a dearly-needed lesson, and then I'd have to explain myself to Ginevra, who would probably take this as an excuse to confine me to the Court of Cats any time my uncle so much as thought about leaving the Mists for an afternoon. No, thank you. My freedom has an expiration date, and I'm still a cat: I intend to enjoy every scrap of it that I can.

The air smelled of night-blooming flowers, of eucalyptus, of full garbage cans awaiting the morning's collection . . . and ever so faintly, of pine. I sighed and stopped walking.

"You can come out, Cal. I know you're there."

There was a pause long enough that I began to worry that I'd been wrong, and worse, that I'd just invited a mugger to come over and make my acquaintance. Then Cal said, in a wounded tone, "How did you know it was me?"

"You switched forms too close to me," I said. "You were probably following in feline form until I switched over, and then you did the same. Rookie move. If you'd stayed a cat, I wouldn't have heard you, and I certainly wouldn't have been able to smell your magic."

"You could smell my magic?" Now they sounded awed. "I can't smell magic."

"Of course not. You're not a Prince." A keen sense of smell is part and parcel of being Cait Sidhe. Being able to detect signs of spellcraft, however, is more the bailiwick of the nobility.

I sometimes wonder if that wasn't part of what originally attracted Uncle Tybalt to October. What might have seemed like a party trick to most must have looked like a common changeling treading far too close to mysteries that were meant to belong only to those with the strength to deserve them.

I winced a little at the thought. For a moment there, I'd sounded almost like my father.

Cal scoffed. "Good thing, too, or they'd need to come up with a whole new title for me. I'm not a stupid Prince. I'm not a stupid Princess, either. I'm *me*."

"Accurate and yet unnecessary, as you lack the standing to require refusing either title." I turned. "Why are you following me?"

"Regent's orders." Cal looked at me unrepentantly. "She outranks you, so don't think you can tell me to leave. I won't."

"Root and branch preserve me," I muttered. "Has Uncle Tybalt *ever* asked you to follow me when I was going to visit Helen? I'm fully capable of doing this without a babysitter."

"Regent's orders," Cal repeated.

"Meaning you're more afraid of her than you are of me," I concluded grimly. "You do understand that I'll be your King for much, much longer than she's your Regent, yes?"

Cal rolled one shoulder, unconcerned. "Nothing says I can't go back to Silences with her if I decide I don't want a King my own age. So maybe this is me making sure I keep my options open."

"Is it?"

"No." Cal smiled, showing white, slightly crooked teeth. "I just like getting on your nerves."

"Did she order you *specifically*?"

"No. She asked for volunteers."

"And you were the only one to put your name forward?"

Cal shrugged. "It seemed like a fun way to spend an evening, and it's not like you ever want to spend time with me when you don't have to. So here I am, and here you are, and every minute you spend arguing with me is a minute you're not spending with your girlfriend."

I hissed at them. It wasn't a very princely thing to do. In my defense, I wanted to. Doing something simply because I want to do it is an *extremely* princely thing to do.

Cal looked blandly back at me, unruffled.

"Fine." I threw up my hands. "You are not to enter Helen's home. You are not to attempt to cajole her father into giving you something to eat. You may lurk on a neighbor's porch if you like, so you can see the door, but that's as close as you come. In exchange, I promise not to try to sneak away. Are we in agreement?"

"I don't see why I need to bargain with you," said Cal. "Your regent sent me."

"I'm sure that excuse will keep you very good company when you're on my bad side and no one with any sense is willing to be seen with you," I said. "Ginevra is temporary. I'm forever. Are you truly prepared to risk my eternal enmity simply for the sake of one evening's entertainment? Consider your answer carefully."

Cal looked at me sullenly before looking at their feet. "Fine," they said. "I'll stay on the porch."

"Excellent. Now return to feline form, please. You'll attract less attention that way." I turned my back on them and resumed walking. They would follow instructions. Cal enjoyed playing the rebel, but they wouldn't risk my genuine annoyance.

Sure enough, there was a rustling behind me as Cal stepped into the bushes beside the nearest house, followed by another rustle as they leaped out of the brush on four legs. I kept walking, not giving them the satisfaction of looking back. They would only take it as proof that they were getting to me, and keep going.

Cal and I have known each other since we were kittens. We've never been friends; as Prince, I was never encouraged to socialize with the common children of the Court. It was only after my father's death that I began to ask myself how much of that had been his idea. Uncle Tybalt was always happy to leave my rearing to my parents, and Father's will was always stronger than Mother's. He was the one to stress how important I was, how powerful and special, and how much I needed to hold myself apart from the people I'd eventually rule.

I felt a pang of guilt at that. But the past is past—it can't be changed—and while I might regret my paucity of friends among the Court, I'm too aware that Quentin's time in the Mists is short and growing shorter; the only question now is whether he has to leave before I'm forced to become King. Call me a coward or call me cruel, but I have no wish to widen my social circle further, not when I'm about to lose my best friend in all the worlds. I'm a cat. We don't share well.

Seen from the street, Helen's house was as dark as the others around it. I started up the porch steps, smiling as I felt the magic grow thick and taut around me, like a bowstring drawn back and ready to be released. If I'd been human, I would have been repelled long before I reached the top step, shoved gently back by the field which concealed the lights from sundown to sunup every night. Helen's father has tried to explain the parameters of his wards before, and the reason he lowers them during the day—something about postal workers and Girl Scout cookies. To be honest, I've never been able to bring myself to pay attention long enough to understand his apparent cleverness. The house is secure; Helen is safe. That's all I care about.

One more step carried me to the shabby welcome mat just outside the front door, and the spell released me with a soft, nearly audible sigh, allowing me to see the house as it truly was: brightly-lit and fully awake. The windows were open. Pixies swarmed around the hummingbird feeders, sipping sugary red juice and squabbling with each other in high-pitched voices.

I rang the bell. Footsteps thumped down the stairs inside. Then the door opened and Helen tumbled into my arms, her lips seeking mine, safe from prying human eyes within the shell of her father's illusion.

Oh, Helen. My Helen. She wasn't going to pose any competition to Helen of Troy any time soon, and I didn't want her to; the sort of beauty that can launch a thousand ships is the purview of the Daoine Sidhe, may they choke on it, and it doesn't belong in my arms. I have friends among the Daoine Sidhe—Quentin is virtually my brother—and I still don't think I could love one of them. Their power is too much about how perfect they are, and not enough about the things they do.

A human mother and a Hob father had left her on the short side, not quite five and a quarter feet tall. Her hair was brown, curly, and inclined to mischief; I'd found myself with a mouthful of it more than once, when I was trying to play the skilled lover and plant kisses on her throat, jaw, or shoulder. Despite the scent of it, her shampoo didn't taste like mint or melon. It tasted like soap. I didn't like it.

I liked everything else about her. She was curvier than she'd been when we first met; puberty had been kind. There was nothing about her I didn't like, and I'd never been shy about telling her so when she got self-conscious. She'd called me a pig a few times because of that. I would always sniff and reply that I was a cat, and she would always laugh, no matter how many times she heard it. That was how I first realized that she really loved me. She'd never have put up with me if she didn't.

Her face was sweet, pleasant, and kind; her eyes were brown. Her ears were pointed, although not as much as mine or Quentin's, and stuck slightly out from her head, like the handles on a jug. Her hands were a little bit too large for her body, and thick-skinned enough that I'd seen her pick up burning coals without noticing the heat. They were still gentle, and sensitive enough that she could feel my lips against her palm.

I adore her. Call it selfish—I knew that I should peel myself away now, before things went any further down this road, which could never be ours to walk. Call it foolish and irresponsible. I don't care. She's the fire in my hearth and the heat in my home, and if anything is going to make me regret my eventual kingship, it's her.

"You came," she said, finally breaking off our kiss, if not our embrace. Her cheeks were flushed, her eyes glittering, and she'd never been more beautiful. "I was afraid you wouldn't be able to, with your uncle out of town."

"My Regent saw the wisdom of granting me my freedom," I said solemnly, and kissed her nose. "Want to go inside? I'm sure your dad's ready and waiting to remind me that he can break bricks with his bare hands. He really, *really* likes reminding me of that."

"He's just trying to make sure you won't hurt me. I can't blame him for being overprotective." A shadow crossed her face, there and gone quickly enough that I might not have recognized it if I hadn't been so incredibly familiar with it. "He's in the living room. You should say hi before we go to my room."

"Lead on," I said.

I don't have my Uncle Tybalt's skill with flowery, archaic declarations of love, a fact for which I'm genuinely grateful—sometimes listening to him is like listening to the audio version of some dreadful period romance, the sort of thing where the men are constantly losing their shirts and all the women keep swooning at the shameful sight of their exposed pectorals. Besides, I might not be as fancy as he is, but I'm good enough for Helen. She smiled, glancing up at me through her lashes, and grabbed my hand, dragging me with her into the house.

Dean is surprisingly fond of romantic comedies, artifice-filled narratives where boy meets girl—always boy meets girl, which is remarkably limiting and pedestrian for a genre supposedly built on the shoulders of love—through some contrived coincidence, structurally called a "meet cute." Well, Helen and I didn't "meet cute." We met in blood and terror, when Blind Michael's Hunt stole us from our beds and cast us, defenseless and unprepared, into the unending fog of his private domain.

Helen doesn't like my friends. October frightens her, reminds her too much of those terrible days when we both believed our bodies would be forfeit to a Firstborn's whims. Quentin is too imposing—and that's without her knowing that he's going to rule the whole continent when he's older. She's never met Chelsea, or April, or Dean. She prefers the safety of her home, the locked door, the closed window, an Internet connection keeping her tethered to the world. She's a modern anchorite, unwilling to venture farther from safety than her porch.

I understand it, and I don't. Blind Michael was able to take her from her bed, was able to take me from the Court of Cats, where I should have been safe even from Titania herself. A locked door could never have saved us.

Blind Michael is dead. October killed him with iron and with silver and set us free from the monster. She couldn't free us from the memory. That will haunt us for all the long centuries of our lives, and we will never find comfort in a hunting horn or in the flicker of a candle's flame. He stole us, and he stole *from* us, and sometimes when I look at Helen, I wonder whether he stole too much for her to ever recover.

The front door led into a small, brightly-lit living room, decorated in rich, warm colors, like we were stepping into a snapshot of the living autumn. Despite the time of year, a fire burned in the fireplace, crackling and bright, casting flickers that were too bright and too steady to be mistaken for candles across the walls. Hobs aren't technically fire fae—they could no more survive in a volcano's heart than I could—but they find comfort in the presence of a hearth, drawing peace and strength from the flame. This was as traditional as they could get in a mortal neighborhood in the middle of San Francisco.

Helen's father, Willis, was sitting on the couch pretending to read a book. It was the same one he always pretended to read when I came a visit, some dire medical thriller with a picture of an elegantly dead woman on the cover. Why is it always the women who are elegantly dead? I would make a perfectly lovely corpse, if the need arose.

"Good evening, Raj," he said, looking at me over his book. "Slipped the leash again?"

"Leashes are a canine affectation," I said. "But yes, I'm at liberty for the remainder of the night, and thought your lovely daughter might enjoy my questionable company for a few hours before dawn."

Helen giggled. Willis, who had looked as if he might say something, settled deeper into the couch, an eloquent look passing between us. He knew as well as I did that my time with Helen was limited; that one day duty and the division between our Courts would pull me away. He feared that the longer I stayed, the more I'd break her heart when the time for leaving came, and to be fair, I couldn't say he was wrong. But he hadn't been with us in Blind Michael's lands. He didn't understand how much I was already going to break her heart . . . or how much we needed each other if we were ever going to heal.

Quentin is my brother and October is my knight and both of them went into that damned country voluntarily, with their eyes open, with consent lingering on their lips. Helen and I lacked that sweet decision. We were wounded, and we were going to stay that way for a long time yet to come.

"Hi, Dad, bye, Dad, don't wait up, Dad," said Helen, and grabbed my hand, dragging me out of the living room toward the stairs.

I could feel Willis' eyes on my back every step of the way.

Her room was the first in the upstairs hall. She pulled me into it and kicked the door shut behind us, her mouth already finding mine as her hands went to my hair and snarled themselves there, thumbs brushing the curve of my ears in not-so-subtle indication that the time for illusions was over, at least for now. She preferred it when I was myself before her. Ego said that it was because she couldn't live without my handsome face. Logic painted a grimmer picture.

She wanted to be able to see me because if she could see me, she'd know for sure that it *was* me. That I hadn't been replaced by some dire Rider, come to finish what their fallen Firstborn started.

I released my illusions with a wave of my hand, the other hand clamped tight against her side, holding her to me. She made a small sound of delight, mouth still fixed to mine, pushing me backward toward the bed.

It had been a hard day, then. Some nights she wanted to talk, to show me silly videos online and discuss the affairs of the day. Those nights came after days where she slept deeply, where the horrors of our past allowed her some small measure of peace. Other nights, she wanted nothing more than to speed toward some unseen and unseeable cliff, trusting me to pull us back from the edge.

It would have been so easy to be the boy her father fears, the boy who'd take advantage of her needy, gasping fear. I could hurt her badly, and I could do it without meaning to. That's part of why I had to stay with her. It wasn't merely that I adored her, the scent of her hair, the roughness of her hands. I *cared* about her. She was my friend. I'd be a coward if I walked away from her now, when she still needed something to hold onto, something to believe in.

I could be her safe harbor, at least for a time. And if I knew I would have to leave her one day, I could try to make sure that when that inevitable day arrived, she would be prepared to stand on her own.

We reached the bed. She sat, pulling me with her, pulling her mouth from mine and burying her face against my shoulder as she started crying. I put my arms around her and held her close to me.

There was nothing else I could do.

THREE

As was so often my wont, I stayed too late. Helen's tears had been followed by more kisses, and then more tears, need and grief alternating until well past the hour when I'd intended to return to the Court. The sun was teasing the edges of the sky when I stepped onto the porch, the sound of her father's footsteps on the stairs a whisper of sound behind me. He knew what it meant when I stayed that late and came downstairs with wild, haunted eyes. He'd go to her and offer her a father's comfort, feed her breakfast and brush her hair and do everything in his power to help her go to bed feeling safe and loved and unafraid.

Sometimes he could achieve it. Other times she'd call at noon and beg me to come over, to sit with her, to keep the night at bay. October attributed the amount of time I spent asleep at her house to my dual natures as teenager and cat. My uncle, I knew, suspected there was something more.

I dropped to all four feet before darting off the porch and into the nearby bushes. I wanted to run, to clear my head, before I returned to the Court and to Ginevra's judgment. I glanced back. Cal was asleep on the porch where they had gone to wait for me.

Well. I'd promised to come out via the front door, and not to try and sneak away. I'd said nothing about waking my erstwhile chaperone. If they woke on their own, they might be able to track me. If not, well. I couldn't be blamed for acting on my nature, now could I? I'm a cat. Cats are not meant to be confined.

The bushes ended at a fence. I scaled it easily, running along the top of it until I dropped down into a narrow alley. From there, I ran down a set of residential steps, feeling my muscles warm up and relax with every loping stride. The air was sweet and the sun had yet to rise and the city was stirring, neither fully awake nor fully asleep. I might as well have already been King, for I had all the freedom of the world, and all the stars to share it with.

That, perhaps, was my mistake. I was so wrapped up in the joy of running and the pride of my own strength that I darted into the street without looking first. There was a screech of brakes and the honk of a horn. I looked back, intending to gloat at the human motorist who'd stopped for my sake. They'd never stood a chance of hitting me.

The car that had slowed was already roaring away. But Cal, in feline form, was frozen in the middle of the street, ears flat and fur puffed up in all directions, seemingly hypnotized by the headlights of the second car that was bearing down on them.

There wasn't time to think, to consider the possible consequences of my actions. There was only one of my subjects in immediate danger. I wheeled and ran back to the street, slamming my body into Cal's, sending them tumbling out of the way.

The car hit me.

It sounds so simple, put like that. Four little words. The car hit me. The car *struck* me, fender slamming into my body before I had a chance to move out of the way, momentum launching me into the air like I weighed nothing, like I was nothing. There wasn't any pain, or perhaps there was too much pain: I could almost taste it, something huge and implacable and amorphous nibbling at the edges of my awareness, ready to swallow me whole.

I tried to breathe. I couldn't breathe.

The pain descended, and the world went away, taking me with it. In the span of a single failed breath, I no longer existed; I, Raj, was lost, swept away in a tide so much greater than myself that it would have been foolishness to protest. Even Blind Michael couldn't have stood up to this, this *nothingness*, this cessation of being.

I was gone.

I don't know how long the silence lasted. When it began to break, it was in flickers and sparks. Light, too bright to be either pixie or flame, steady and white and burning. Voices raised in agitation. The pain began to return. I tried to pull away from it, and something pricked my leg, distinct from the greater agonies only in its newness. I mewled, once, and then I was mercifully gone again, down into the dark, down where nothing mattered.

I'd always been afraid that if—that when—I died, Blind Michael would be waiting for me, ready to finish what he'd begun. But he was nowhere. There was only the darkness, the blessed darkness, and I allowed myself to fade into it with a sigh and a murmur of thanks. Whatever came next, I'd meet it on a night-haunt's wings, and I would know no more of fear, or pain, or loss.

My last thought was of Helen.

And then even that was gone.

FOUR

The air was bitter with disinfectant and sickness. It stung the back of my throat and the inside of my nose, making breathing difficult.

I sneezed, and the force of the gesture sent waves of pain through my body, awakening injuries that had been content to sleep until that moment.

If there was pain, I wasn't dead. October had taught me that, whether she meant to or not. I've seen her get up from injuries that should have incapacitated her permanently, half her blood outside her body and still fighting. If she could do *that*, surely I could do something as simple as opening my eyes.

Thinking a thing and actually doing it are sometimes sadly different. I struggled to force my body to obey my commands until finally, exhausted, it gave in, and I was able to part my eyelids slightly. Even that small effort left me panting, and filled my mind with more questions than answers.

I was looking at the bars of a cage. Across from me, in what I assumed was a similar cage, a Siamese cat glared from a nest of blankets, a bandage wrapped around one paw and a long plastic tube taped beneath it, running some clear liquid from what looked like an IV bag from one of Chelsea's hospital dramas. A great many of them share cast members with her beloved science fiction shows, and it seems that once a starship captain, always a starship captain, at least in her eyes.

Wait.

Digressions are normal things—May once likened a conversation between Quentin and myself to watching two kits chase a ball of string around the house—but not when things are actually happening. We're capable of focusing. *I'm* capable of focusing. The fact that I was suddenly trying to remember the name of every show I'd seen Chelsea watch meant something was wrong with the way my mind was working. I turned my head, fighting the exhaustion that threatened to pull me back into the dark. There was a similar bandage wrapped around *my* paw, connected to a similar length of tubing.

They were doing something to me. They were putting something inside my body that didn't belong there, and it was making it difficult for me to think the way I needed to. I would never be able to escape with this . . . this *medication* flowing into my body, unasked for and unwanted.

I would bite it. Yes. I would bite it, and then it would stop, and my thoughts would clear, and I could escape through the shadows.

The shadows! I blamed the tube in my arm for not thinking of them before. They would take me away from this dreadful place, get me out of this cage and back to someplace familiar, where I could think. I reached for them, or tried to. Everything was fuzzy. There were shadows pooled in the corners of my cage—I, a Prince of Cats, in a *cage*—but they were ordinary, mortal things, and they seemed entirely unaware of my presence. I reached again, and when they failed to respond, I went limp, panting from the effort.

No. Tube first, *then* shadows. The order mattered. I tried to bite at the tube, but I was too tired, and my body had no desire to obey me. Exhaustion stole over me like a thief, and I fell asleep again, mouth only half-open, tube still securely in my arm.

When I woke for the second time, a woman in pastel scrubs was standing over me, a clipboard in her hands. I opened my eyes. I considered her through the fog of pain and weariness and what I now understood to be some sort of drug, dulling my reflexes and keeping me from doing more than lying motionless, presenting myself like prey.

I am not *prey*. I am a *Prince of Cats*. I fought my way once more through the exhaustion and hissed at her, reminding her that I was a predator to be feared and respected.

It came out as the smallest squeak of a sound, barely even worthy of the name. The woman smiled.

"Well, hello, you handsome little fellow. Good to see you feeling better. And those eyes! Dr. Bailey will be thrilled to know that she's won our bet. See, some of us think you're an actual Abyssinian, with that coat and that bone structure, and we just needed to see your eyes to be sure. You have the right eyes. Someone's got to be missing you, buddy."

Her voice was sweet, even soothing; she spoke to me like she believed the sound would help, even if she clearly assumed I wouldn't understand a word she said. I decided against hissing at her again and simply stared, watching as she made notes on her clipboard.

"You did a very brave, very stupid thing. The nice man who brought you in said that you ran right out into the middle of the street to make a different cat move before it could be hit by a car. Were you friends? Were you fighting? Was it a female in heat? You're not a stray, not with that coat, but whoever owns you did you no favors by keeping you intact."

That's an ominous way of phrasing things. I attempted to hiss again. All I managed to do was pant.

"Aw, poor guy, you're exhausted." She put down her clipboard and produced a syringe from her pocket. It was quite small compared to her hand, but *I* was quite small, compared to a human, and I wanted nothing to do with her needles or her human attempts to cure what ailed me. I needed to get back to the Court of Cats, where someone who was currently stronger than I could go and fetch me a healer. That Ellyllon from Shadowed Hills, perhaps, or an alchemist—Walther. Walther would be an excellent choice. He knew me and wouldn't make any nasty jokes about my attempts to argue with a car. He'd just fix whatever was broken inside of me, and he'd do it without *needles.*

The woman unhooked the front of my cage, swinging it open. I lay where I was and panted, wishing I had the strength to run. Anything would have been better than being vulnerable and exposed, an easy target for whatever she wanted to do.

"It's okay, buddy, it's okay," she said, leaning into the cage. She was large enough to block the rest of the world. Humans had never seemed so big before, and I had never felt so small.

Humans have no magic, not without fae blood in their veins. Humans have dull eyes, unable to pierce the dark, and soft hands, unsuited to battle. But they drove Faerie into the hidden places with their iron and their fire and their sheer numbers. Even the most fertile of fae can't stand up to the least of humans. We were outbred and outbled, and we ran. For the first time, as I watched the human woman lean over me with her needle, I understood how it had happened. I understood how we could lose.

The needle slid into my shoulder with barely a prick. Her hands were nimble, practiced; she had done this before, so often that she had no need to hesitate or assess. In a matter of seconds she was pulling back, the syringe in her hand now bright with stolen blood. My blood.

Chelsea enjoys mortal forensics, likes to make us watch television shows that focus on them, their techniques, the way they can ferret out secrets. Would the blood in that syringe give *my* secrets away? To mortal eyes, did my blood differ in any substantive way from an ordinary cat's? I didn't know. I might have endangered all of Faerie by saving Cal from that speeding car.

The thought was immense enough to be exhausting. I blinked, intending only to grant myself a few seconds of peace. When I opened my eyes again, the cage was closed, the woman was gone, and so was the Siamese across the way. The cage where they had been was sterile and shining, devoid of any sign that it had ever been occupied. My heart sank.

When I was a child, Uncle Tybalt used to take me to the animal shelter, using my small stature and silence around humans as a mask while he claimed to be looking for the perfect pet for a young boy. We would walk along the rows of cages, sniffing out any captives with fae blood, and return for them after night fell, stepping through the shadows and into their places of imprisonment. The air there always smelled very similar to the air here, disinfectant and damp litter and misery. Despair has a scent. It cakes the nostrils and dizzies the senses, and if I never had to smell it again, I wouldn't complain.

Night after night, we'd gone to the shelters, returning home with thin-blooded kittens, with halfbloods whose fae gifts didn't include the ability to change their shapes—once, even, with a pureblood whose wife had died and who had retreated so far into feline form that she no longer remembered what it was to walk on two legs, to reach for things outside a housecat's grasp. We had carried them back to the Court of Cats, and some of them lived there still, content with their second chances.

Once, just once, we had arrived to see a family in the process of finalizing the paperwork to adopt their new companion. He had been a tabby-striped tom, cradled in the arms of a little human girl who gazed at him with all the adoration and wonder in the world, and he had been half-fae at the very least. I had started to move toward them, automatically, thinking the rescue of the kitten to be a vital part of our mission, when Uncle Tybalt's hand had tightened on my shoulder, holding me in place.

That night, rather than returning to the shelter, we had gone to an apartment, stepping out of the shadows behind the television. The kitten had been waiting for us, his tail curled around his haunches, his eyes bright and alert.

"My mother warned me of the cats who move like men," he had said, before either of us could utter a word. "She said that one day you might come for me, as you came for my father. She said if I refused you, you wouldn't take me. I refuse you. Go away. My pets are sleeping, and I'll not have you waking them."

The language of cats isn't that grammatical and doesn't sort itself so neatly into sentences and phrases, but I thought more like a person than a feline, most of the time, and the translation had been automatic. I had frowned, looking to Uncle Tybalt.

And Uncle Tybalt had bowed.

"Take good care of them, brave one, and remember that the Court of Cats is yours," he'd said, and drawn me back into the shadows.

When we had emerged into the Court of Cats, when I'd tried to pull away, he'd placed his hands on my shoulders and said, voice solemn, "The world is hard for our kin. They fight all their lives for a place to belong, a warm spot to sleep, a meal to fill their bellies. All too often, they find hands raised against them and hatred in the hearts of those who should be kindest to them, who should remember that without men, there would be no cats, but without cats, there might well be no men. Do you understand?"

"No." I had been a kitten then, sullen and full of pride at my own potential. I had been a fool.

Uncle Tybalt, though . . . if ever he had been a fool, it had been long before I came into his life. He had looked at me with understanding and said, "There were cats in the world before there were Cait Sidhe. We exist to help them when we can, and to be honored to have the opportunity; we are kings and queens among our kin. But we do not exist to command them. We do not exist to make their lives more difficult. Death follows them all the days of their lives, and it needs only catch them once. The very hands that feed and stroke them are too often raised against them. They are temporary, and we are not. We owe them our respect."

I hadn't fully understood, not then. Now, as I looked at the empty cage, with no way of knowing whether its occupant had been released to their loving owners or whether their body was in a box nearby, consigned to the grave, I thought I finally did.

I closed my eyes and willed myself to sleep again. I needed to get stronger. I needed to heal. If I didn't . . .

An empty cage, and silence, could be a fate that waited for anyone.

You were wrong, Uncle, I thought, the words petulant and small, like the crying of a lost child. *We're temporary, too. We always have been. We can go. We can disappear.*

I slept.

FIVE

Helen's face peered out at me from a tangle of thorny vines. They had wrapped themselves around her so tightly that they pierced her skin, thorns driving their way down toward her bones. When they struck, I knew, they would root there, growing into her body and becoming a part of her. She would unravel into a new briar, girl-shaped at first, but losing its form as it forgot what it had been, forgot that it was anything other than a predator designed by a monster.

"Run," she whispered, voice ragged with agony and hoarse from screaming. She had stopped screaming several minutes before, when the pain had reached the point of becoming numbness. Her body was shutting down to protect her. Her mind was refusing to let go. Whether that was an intentional part of Michael's cruelty or her own will shining through, I didn't know, but she was still lucid, still *Helen*, and I couldn't leave her. "Run, please, run. I don't want you to see this."

I tried to reach for her. The vines slithered, cradling her tighter, preventing me from touching her. They had their prey. Until she was digested, until she was transformed, they didn't need or want me.

"Raj, please."

No. This was—this was wrong. This was *wrong*. She was too young, her face too soft, her eyes not shadowed by the sleepless days she'd been enduring since our escape from Blind Michael. Since our *escape*. If we escaped, how were we back here on this endless, foggy plain?

None of this had happened. I'd seen another child taken by the vines, but not Helen. She'd been too slow. That was the terrible

truth of Blind Michael's lands. The faster you were, the better prepared for their dangers, the more likely you were to be taken,
transformed, and consumed. It was the slow ones who stood half
a chance of getting away, because the fast ones triggered all
the traps.

I have always, always been fast. If not for Helen grabbing my
hand and asking me not to leave her—if she had grabbed for someone else, if I had shaken her away, commanding her imperiously to
keep her hands off of me—I would have been at the front of the
mob. I would have been dead long before October could have
come to bring me home.

None of this happened.

The thought shattered the dream. I opened my eyes and found
myself back in the brightly lit room, back in the cage. I felt better
after my nap, however unpleasant my dreams had been. Not
enough to feel like *myself*, but enough that when I tried to sit up,
my body obeyed me. I was still weak, and my legs were still unsteady; standing was out of the question. That didn't matter. Sitting
up was a start.

The cage across from me remained empty. Another human was
there, wiping it down with a cloth. He was dressed like the woman
had been, in soft pastel scrubs. I decided to take a risk and meowed as loudly as I could, attracting the human's attention. He
turned to look quizzically at me. Then he smiled, apparently delighted by what he saw.

"Hey, little guy, you're awake," he said, approaching slowly, like
he didn't want to frighten me. That was silly. I was in a cage. He
was outside the cage, and had thumbs. He was clearly in the supe-
rior position here. "You're a lucky fellow, you know that? If that
car had been going just a little faster, or if it had hit you a few
inches to the right, you wouldn't be here with us now."

I forced my ears to stay up and my whiskers to stay forward, trying to project an air of curious friendliness. The tube still taped to
my arm made it difficult. I wanted to bite it. I wanted to bite it so
badly, to bite and bite until it dropped away and I was free. But the
shadows were still outside my reach, and while my thoughts remained somewhat fuzzy, they were clear enough for me to understand that my painkillers were contained in the tube. If I removed
it, the agonies it was keeping at bay would quickly overcome me.

No, the tube would remain until I was ready to make my escape.

That was the sensible choice, the choice that led to a clean exit. I could collapse once I was somewhere safe, whether that be the Court of Cats or back in Helen's bedroom. The thought of her hands stroking my ears was almost enough to chase the last, lingering traces of pain away.

"A handsome boy like you must have an owner," said the man, holding his fingertips up to the cage bars for me to sniff. I did so obligingly and then, knowing what was expected of me, I rubbed my cheek against them, marking him as my own. "They're probably worried sick about you, huh? I hope they show up soon. I need to ask them why you don't have a microchip."

I meowed at him.

"Don't be a baby. Microchipping doesn't hurt. We just pop it under all that loose skin at the back of your neck and then you don't have to worry about getting out and getting lost. We'd already have your people on their way to see you if you had a microchip." His expression turned sober. "Of course, maybe it's better for you that we haven't found them yet. Once we know who they are, they can refuse further care. You're an expensive little guy, my friend, and your treatment isn't finished. I see a lot of good cats die because people don't think they're worth what it costs to heal them."

That couldn't be right, could it? People who kept cats as pets took care of them, loved them, made sure they had everything they needed to be healthy and hale. I understood enough about human concepts of money to know that sometimes they would run out of it—October was forever complaining that Quentin and I needed to get jobs if we were going to continue to devour her bank account— but the idea that someone could simply refuse to pay for medical care was baffling.

"So as long as they're not here, we can treat you, and if they can't pay your bill, I guess we have a new foster." He held his fingers up to the bars again. "I'll be honest, I expect you're going to go home with whoever owns you. You don't seem like a long-term resident of a place like this. You seem more like the kind of cat who knows he's in charge, and doesn't understand why anyone would argue."

You have no idea, I thought, and meowed at him again.

"I'm going to go tell Dr. Bailey you're awake," said the man. "Try to stay that way until I come back, all right?" He pulled his hand away from the bars and walked away, leaving me alone.

"He has you fooled," said a new voice.

I looked down. There, on the floor, was a fluffy black-and-white cat with yellow eyes, looking disdainfully up at me.

"I know what *you* are," she said. "Cait Sidhe. Shapeshifter. Too good for the likes of us. Slumming, shapeshifter? Or did you really go and get yourself hit by a car by accident?" She flattened her whiskers, telegraphing amusement.

I bristled, or tried to, anyway. I was too tired to do more than flick one ear in irritation. "If you must know, I am a Prince of Cats, and I was struck in the process of saving one of my subjects. They would have been killed if they'd been hit in my place. I am a hero."

It felt good to refer to myself that way. October's heroism is recognized by the Queen in the Mists. Mine might be smaller and more contained, but that doesn't negate it. I saved Cal's life. I saved Helen's, too, back in Blind Michael's lands, and she saved mine, more than once.

We're all heroes. We all do what we have to, when we have to.

The cat below me curled her lips back and made a disgusted sound. "Are you enjoying your cage, *hero*? Do you intend to fill your stomach with crunchy biscuits and then run away into the shadows, the way your kind always does?"

"Why are you talking to me like this? The Court of Cats is always open to any of our kin who have need. If you're angry because you want for something, you could have come to us. We would have done our best to help you. If you simply wish to taunt me because my magic is insufficient to get me out of here, please, continue. I'll remember you later."

The cat swished her tail. "They treat too many of us poorly. They let too many of us die."

I thought of Uncle Tybalt in the shelter, opening cages, sweeping kittens away, and a sinking feeling grew in my stomach. He was only one man, and he had never been able to spend *every* night doing rescue work. The humans would have noticed. And those were only the cats who were captured or surrendered by their people. It wasn't the cats shivering in alleys, the strays fighting for scraps to stay alive.

It wasn't the cats whose humans could choose to discontinue care.

"I am sorry," I said. "Once I go home, I'll talk to my regent. Perhaps we can find a way to make things better."

"There's no 'better' when there are humans involved," sneered the cat, and got up, and sashayed away, her tail a banner held high behind her, her posture telling me without any further words between us that she had no use for me or my Court.

I tucked my paws underneath myself and watched her go. When she was out of sight, I closed my eyes and thought about what she'd said. Yes, we tried to help the mortal cats around us, and yes, there were some of them who made the Court of Cats their home, but there was so much more we could have been doing. Had we done exactly what we accused the Divided Courts of doing, withdrawing so far into ourselves that we could no longer see how much our subjects needed us?

A new woman approached my cage, a fresh clipboard in her hands. "You're awake," she said, with evident delight. "Let me get a look at you, handsome boy. Oh, you're a nice one, aren't you?" Her voice had dropped, taking on the honeyed sweetness of a human who truly enjoyed the company of felines.

I decided to grace her with a purr.

"Aren't you a sweetheart? I wish you could talk, handsome boy. I want to know where your owners are. I want to give them a piece of my mind. You're too old to be running around the city unaltered, and if you're a breeder, you should never have been able to escape. I almost hope you came from a kitten mill. Then we can be responsible with you before we help you find a new home. A handsome fellow like you, you won't have any trouble."

Were all humans this obsessed with the testicles of others? I couldn't plant my butt any more firmly on the floor of my cage, so I settled for flattening my whiskers and giving her my most imperious glare. Uncle Tybalt's subjects have been known to fall over themselves trying to get away from me when I look at them that way, as if the force of my disdain might be sufficient to do them physical harm.

The woman laughed.

"You're a charmer, aren't you? Well, you're a lucky little charmer because you didn't break any bones, and you don't have any internal bleeding. It's just bad bruises and a little concussion. We've been giving you painkillers and space to recover, but you should be right as rain in a few days."

It was fascinating, the way she spoke to me, like she expected me to understand. I meowed at her again. She nodded.

"Yes, you're a good boy." She produced a syringe from her pocket.

Damn. I'd hoped they were done adding things to the IV bag. My head was finally starting to clear, and I was going to need my wits about me if I was going to break out of here.

"Don't you worry about a thing. This will help you stay nice and calm, and I'll examine you again in a few hours, when I'm sure you've been here long enough that we would have noticed any additional complications."

I meowed again, or tried to, anyway. The world opened up and swallowed me whole, and I fell back into the darkness.

SIX

We were running, running through Blind Michael's lands, Helen and I hand-in-hand. We had tried running separately, but she was too afraid; she kept losing her balance, unable to focus on where she was going and look over her shoulder at the same time. This way I could guide and protect us both, could keep her heading for the safety of the trees.

I'd known her less than a day, and I already knew that if I could only keep her safe, if I could only see her to the trees, I would die knowing I'd accomplished *something*. I had been someone's hero.

It wouldn't be enough to make my father proud of me. Nothing short of a throne and a crown and the willingness to let him speak through me, like a king was merely a puppet for another's will, would ever make him proud of me. But it would make my mother proud, I thought. It would make her curl her tail in sorrowful pleasure, because her son had been brave before he died, had been something other than a useless and weak-willed princeling without the sense to save anyone else.

And then there was Helen. She spoke to me kindly but without reverence, like I was anyone, like I was no one, like everyone deserved to be spoken to that way. I wasn't sure she knew what the

Court of Cats *was*, much less that she ought to be respectful of my place in it. I knew almost nothing about her, but I knew that she was clever and kind and deserved to survive this. *I* wanted to survive this.

I wanted us both to survive.

We ran, and the rocks bit at our feet and the thorns whipped at our heels, and behind us I could hear the pounding of hooves and the sounding of horns, and then it wasn't Helen holding my hand at all, it was Quentin, and I had lost her, and I was going to lose him as well, sacrificing them both to this dark and terrible place, and all for the sake of getting away, alone again, Prince of Cats, Prince of Nothing—

I sat up with a yowl, eyes open, and had never been so relieved to find myself inside a cage. And then I fell over, the drugs in my system robbing me of balance and stability. I meowed petulantly, tail lashing, and forced myself to sit up. It was a slow, difficult process. My legs were clumsy as a kitten's, and my paws felt like they were five times too big for my body. I looked down, suddenly afraid that I had regressed in age while I was drugged into slumber. My body was as I expected it to be, save for the bandage wrapped around my paw and the tube that slithered beneath it.

Once again, I considered the virtues of biting at the tube until it came free. This time, my head, while still fuzzy, was clear enough for me to reason against it. If I bit at the tube, they would replace it, possibly with something sturdier or fastened to a part of my body I couldn't reach. This place would have to close eventually. The humans would have to go home to eat, and sleep, and do whatever else humans did behind closed doors. I could wait until they were gone before I freed myself.

The drugs that kept the pain at bay were in the tube—the same drugs that kept my head too fuzzy for me to reach the Shadow Roads. Once I removed the tube, my head would clear and I would be able to escape.

I hoped. There were several flaws in my plan, including the fact that I had no idea how much pain I would actually be in once I stopped my medication. If I was too badly hurt, the shadows might not come at my command, or worse, might come and then refuse to carry me all the way home, dropping me into some limitless void from which I would never be freed.

Cait Sidhe have been lost on the Shadow Roads before. Not

Princes, not usually, but the weaker ones who can't control their magic well enough to control their destinations. Their bodies litter the hidden tunnels and dead ends of the darkness, and it can be centuries before they're found and brought back into the light, exactly as they were before they fell. No: the risk was too great. If I couldn't be sure of controlling my passage through the shadows, I couldn't take the chance of being lost. Quentin, Chelsea . . . Helen. None of them would ever know what had become of me.

That wasn't entirely true. Uncle Tybalt would know, would smell my magic and my fear hanging in the frozen air the next time he stepped onto the Shadow Roads. Even if he couldn't find my body, he'd carry word of my loss home to the ones who loved me—and then what? Without an heir, he couldn't step aside. He'd be forced to remain King until a challenger appeared, and Princes and Princesses of Cats are rare. So rare. He could be King for years yet, delaying his marriage to October, stranding them both in lives they no longer wanted.

I could ruin everything by allowing myself to be lost. For the first time, I let myself reflect on how foolish it had been of me to intercede when Cal was endangered . . . and how little choice I'd had. Yes, I needed to take care of myself, needed to remain a viable heir for my uncle and a viable protector for the Court—but if I'd been willing to stand by and watch Cal die because I was too concerned with myself to move, I would have been no fit King.

I made a small, aggravated sound. There was no winning at this game, no perfect answer that made everything easy and gave everyone exactly what they wanted. There were only different sets of complications. There were only different ways to fail.

I'd never been in feline form for this long before. I thought uneasily of the trouble Uncle Tybalt had had with shapeshifting after the Liar—I wouldn't even dignify that woman, or her place among the Firstborn, with her name—had been forced to release him. His imprisonment had lasted days. Mine had been hours. Surely the same thing wouldn't happen to me. Surely I wouldn't lose myself. Would I?

Mother never stood on two legs, not once. She was born in feline form and had died the same way. Her magic had simply refused to turn inward the way it needed to in order to accomplish transformation. But she had never lost herself. She had known her name and her place, always. She had known me. She had *loved* me. She had cared for my father, enough not to leave him when it became apparent how much he privileged power, but she had *loved* me.

I loved Helen. I loved Helen, and Quentin, and even my uncle and October. Surely that would be enough to keep me from slipping away or forgetting who I was supposed to be.

But my uncle loved October, loved her more than I thought I would ever be capable of loving anyone. I couldn't imagine giving that much of my heart to someone else to hold. Even if I tried, I couldn't imagine giving it to someone like October, who seemed bound and determined to make some unnamed date with death. Loving her would be like loving a natural disaster. Pleasant enough from a distance; all but guaranteed to break your heart.

I made another aggravated sound and tried to stand. My hind legs refused to obey me. That would be alarming, had I not been able to feel them; they were being stubborn due to bruising and drugs, not because of any permanent damage. I lashed my tail just to be sure. My stomach rumbled. That was new. If I was feeling well enough to be hungry, I must be recovering.

Not that there was anything in this cage worth eating. There was a small bowl of brown, crispy things, the likes of which I had seen in the shelters and occasionally on back porches in the mortal city. They smelled like they had once been part of some sort of animal, although what kind was less than clear; they had been ground and dried and processed until they became an unimpressively uniform color. I sniffed again. There were *things* in there that I was nowhere near hungry enough to eat.

I would be eventually. I knew that. Hunger is more than an annoyance; it's a reminder to keep one's strength up, to be prepared to run. But until I removed the tube, I wasn't going to be running anywhere, and I'd already decided the tube could stay where it was until night fell.

I tucked my paws under myself and wrapped my tail around my body, intending to take another nap. They're restorative, and it wasn't as if I had anything else to do with my time, since no one had seen fit to provide me with an Internet connection.

"—please, I know it's irregular, but I really think you have my cat."

I cracked one eye open. The voice was familiar, even through the haze of pain, drugs, and ongoing exhaustion. But who in the world did I know who might be here?

"All right." This voice belonged to the man from before. "He's right through here."

A door opened in the distance, and then she came around the corner, resplendent in her beauty: Helen, my Helen, her hair pulled into a bushy ponytail, her body swallowed by one of her father's sweaters. Her father was right behind her—and behind him, back in human form, wearing overalls and a white shirt with mud stains on the sleeves, was Cal.

I jumped to my feet, or tried to. Once again, my legs refused to obey me, and I collapsed to the bottom of my cage. I didn't let that stop me from meowing frantically, my eyes fixed on Helen.

"There you are," she said, clasping her hands against her chest. There were tears standing in her eyes. "I was so scared."

I meowed again, louder. I had never in my life wished so dearly that she were Cait Sidhe. She would have been able to understand me, if she had been.

Helen unclasped her hands so she could press her fingertips to the bars, then looked pleadingly at the man who'd been at least partially responsible for my care. "He wants out," she said. "You have to let him out."

"Is that how he wound up on the street, throwing himself in front of a car?"

"That was me," blurted Cal, then flushed, cheeks going red as they realized what they were saying. "I mean, I'm the one who let him out. It was an accident, honest. I thought my sister was going to *kill* me."

Cal and Helen look nothing alike, but two kittens from the same litter won't always resemble one another. The man looked at Cal, somewhat dubious, before glancing to Willis, who nodded.

"Well, young lady, it was very irresponsible of you to let the cat out," began the man. "He could have been killed, and—"

"I'm not a young lady," said Cal.

The man blinked. "Excuse me?"

"I said, I'm not a young lady. I'm not a young man, either. I'm a young me, and I don't like it when people use the wrong pronouns." Cal's cheeks flared an even deeper red. "That's all."

The man blinked a second time before nodding and saying, with what sounded like genuine apology, "I'm sorry. That was rude of me, and I should have known better. But so should you. It's not safe to let cats run around outside. There are cars, and coyotes, and people with dogs that haven't been trained properly. Something very bad could have happened. Something worse than being hit by a car."

"I understand," said Cal, voice small.

"If you don't mind, we'd like to pay his bill and take him home," said Willis.

"While we settle up, I want to talk to you about having him neutered," said the man. "You need to consider how much easier it would be to keep him inside, and how much better it would be for his mental health. If he's not going to breed, he doesn't need to be intact."

"Oh," said Willis, shooting me an amused, faintly pointed glance, "I'm very concerned with his ability to breed."

Wisely, I was silent.

I didn't want to give him any ideas.

SEVEN

It wasn't safe for me to transform anywhere I might be seen, and with the painkillers still lingering in my system, I couldn't reach for the shadows. Helen removed me from the carrier as soon as we were in the car, and I curled in her lap, tail tip over my nose, for the short drive to her place.

Cal sat with us in the backseat, bubbling over with nervous energy. "You're not mad at me, are you?" they asked, hands fluttering like they wanted to reach for me but didn't quite dare. "I didn't *mean* for you to get hit by that car, I swear by Oberon's eyes, I didn't even know it was there, it was so early in the morning the sun hadn't even come up yet, but then there it was, and I thought I was going to die, and you pushed me out of the way. You're a hero. You're the reason I'm still *here*."

I made a small grumbling sound rather than answering them directly. It seemed rude to carry on an actual conversation when Helen wouldn't be able to understand my side of it.

"I didn't know humans would get out of their cars and *take* cats who'd been injured, I swear I didn't," said Cal hurriedly. "If I'd known, I would have jumped out of the bushes and bit and scratched them until they left you there."

That painted a picture of the incident that made a dismaying amount of sense. The driver, upon hitting me, must have gotten out to see whether I was still alive—and upon finding I was, had loaded me into their car and driven to the nearest twenty-four-hour veterinary hospital. Cal wouldn't have been able to keep up. *I* wouldn't have been able to keep up, and my magic made me both faster and more durable than they were.

My magic was probably the only reason I had survived the impact. That was a daunting thought.

"How did you find me?" I asked, breaking my own determination to stay quiet until Helen could understand me.

Cal looked infinitely relieved. They must have been afraid I was intending never to speak to them again. That was silly. They were going to be one of my subjects. I had to be willing to speak to them, even if it was only so I could give them orders.

"He wants to know how we found him," said Cal, translating for Helen before looking back to me. "I know you didn't want me to talk to your girlfriend, but it was an emergency. I knocked until her father let me in, and then I told him what had happened, and he started making calls. It took a while for anyone to recognize his description of you."

I must have been a mess when they brought me in, and intake and initial treatment would have taken time. Still, I didn't care for the delay. I nestled deeper into Helen's lap, grumbling at the pain beginning to radiate through my body. The medication was passing through my system. I'd listened as the vet explained the realities of my situation to Willis—how could I have done anything else, when I was in a cardboard carrier right next to their conversation? The second woman turned out to have been my doctor. That was fine. She had good hands.

According to her, I was likely to ache for several days, and would need to be checked again in a week or so. I was sorry for the regret she'd probably feel when Willis and Helen failed to reappear with me, but the people in that building were far too interested in the state of my testicles, and I didn't want to give them any opportunities to threaten them. I *liked* my testicles. I liked them exactly where they were, either between my legs or beneath my tail, depending on the form I was in, and a part of me I had no interest in losing either way.

Willis pulled up in the driveway of the small house he shared with Helen. "All right. Helen, you need to hold onto your boyfriend like you're concerned about losing him; Raj, please don't run away. I know you're a smart boy who generally makes good decisions, or I wouldn't trust you in my house, but you're probably still a little stoned, and I have no interest in going through the last twenty-four hours again."

My heart sank. I knew I'd been gone longer than I'd promised Ginevra, but I hadn't realized it had been a full day. She was going to kill me when I finally made it back to the Court of Cats. I meowed plaintively.

Cal shot me a sympathetic look. "It's worse than that," they said. "Don't worry, though, it'll all be over soon."

"Be nice," scolded Helen.

"I am being nice! You would never have found him if not for me!"

Helen huffed as she got out of the car. I didn't make a sound, wrapped as I was in contemplation of Cal's words. They were right. If they hadn't been there—if they had run a little faster when I'd knocked them out of the way, or if they hadn't woken up when I slipped by them, or if they'd gotten tired of waiting for me and decided to go home—I could have been lost forever, or at least for a very long time. And yes, there was every chance I wouldn't have been hit if I hadn't been trying to rescue Cal, but that wasn't the only time I'd had a close call with a car, was it? Cars were everywhere, and while most humans tried to avoid hitting supposedly stray cats, not all of them were that kind. Some might even steer *toward* a stray, seeing it as an opportunity to avenge a fallen songbird.

I could have died. I could have died, and no one would ever have known for sure what had happened to me, only that I was gone.

Maybe Ginevra was right for wanting me to have someone with me when I went out into the city. Not when I took the Shadow Roads to October's—anything that wanted to attack me *there* could enjoy contending with the occupants of her house—but otherwise, an escort, and some additional care, couldn't go amiss. I was a Prince of Cats. I had responsibilities. One of those responsibilities was to not disappear without a trace.

Willis unlocked the door and Helen carried me into the cool, dim confines of the living room. The fire in the hearth roared back to life as soon as Willis followed her in, reacting to his pureblood presence as it would never react to hers. I'd never considered her in any way lesser because of her human blood, but I saw the way the skin around her eyes tensed at the reminder that the fire loved her father more than it loved her. She was outside parts of her own world, removed from them by blood and the circumstances of her birth. It had to be hard.

I meowed for Helen to put me down. She walked over to the couch, bending to set me gently on a cushion. I rubbed my cheek against her hand as a gesture of thanks, then closed my eyes and reached deep into myself, into the simmering wellspring of my magic, looking for the switch that would allow me to change forms.

It had never been this difficult before, not even when I was on the cusp of leaving kittenhood. Kittens often lack control over their transformations, instinctively choosing the form that was best suited for the situation. With control comes the risk of getting stuck. I'd been feline for almost a week when I was nine, unable to convince my magic that I'd be better off having thumbs and attending my lessons. Father had been furious. Mother had been amused, and washed me so thoroughly that I kept expecting to find myself entirely without fur.

I reached deeper, fighting through the pain and the lingering effects of the human painkillers until abruptly, I was naked and standing on the couch. I immediately fell over, reverting to feline form on the impact. Willis roared with laughter. Helen blushed. Cal sighed.

"I wish I'd had a camera ready," they said. "Can you do that again?"

I looked at them imperiously. This time when I transformed, my clothing came with me, and I found myself seated, not standing. I sniffed, nose in the air. Unfortunately, that meant I missed it when Helen flung herself at me, knocking us both into the couch cushions and awakening a whole new degree of pain in my injured side.

"Helen, *please*," I managed to wheeze.

"I'm going to go make some scrambled eggs and toast," said Willis. "Raj, you're going to eat what I put in front of you, without complaining. Understand?"

"Yes, sir," I said.

"Good boy." He walked out of the living room, leaving me, Helen, and Cal to our own devices.

Helen's devices seemed to consist entirely of trying to squeeze the life out of me. I raised one hand, awkwardly patting her on the shoulder. She responded by making a muffled sound and burying her face against my chest. I glanced at Cal. They shrugged.

"She was pretty scared," they said. "We'd never met before. I guess having a strange Cait Sidhe wake you up and tell you that your boyfriend's been hit by a car is freaky and not so much fun. Maybe you should introduce her to more of your friends. Only we're not friends, really, so maybe just introduce her to more people, period? That way if this happens again, she won't be so scared."

Helen pulled back enough to twist around and glare at Cal. If looks could kill, as the old song goes, her expression would have struck them dead on the spot. "Don't you even say that," she snapped. "Raj isn't going to get hit by any more cars."

"I could, though," I said uncomfortably. She turned her face back toward me, eyes going wide and wounded. I swallowed the impulse to flinch, forcing myself to look levelly at her as I said, "The world doesn't stop being dangerous because we tell it to. If it did, my Uncle Tybalt would fret less."

"Something has to be safe," said Helen stubbornly. "We can't be afraid all the time."

I hesitated. "Helen . . . we shouldn't have to be safe to not be scared. We should just stop being scared."

She looked at me like I'd slapped her. To be honest, I felt sort of like I had.

"Please, Helen," I said, trying again. "The world is big and wild and dangerous and wonderful, and even though it's never completely safe, it mostly doesn't hurt us. I go outside every day, and this is the first time I've been hit by a car. I had to save Cal."

"I appreciated being saved," said Cal.

I ignored them. Helen, and that look on her face, was infinitely more important. "We can't take the danger away. Not entirely. We can just learn how to live with it."

"What if I don't *want* to learn how to live with it?" Helen shoved herself off me, pushing me deeper into the couch and knocking the wind out of me when her hands pressed down on my bruises. "What if I don't *want* the world to be dangerous? Huh? What then?"

"Helen—"

"You could have *died*," she spat, and ran out of the room, her footsteps thundering up the stairs.

Slowly, I pushed myself out of the couch, groaning as my bruises complained. "I should go after her," I said uncertainly. "That would be the correct thing to do. Wouldn't it?"

"I'm not getting in the middle of this," said Cal, putting their hands up in proactive self-defense. "I just met her and she already scares me. Maybe I'm glad I'm not your friend. All of your friends are scary. Like, super scary. I think your *least* scary friend is that Daoine Sidhe kid, and there's something about the way he looks at me that makes me think he's scarier than he wants anybody to realize he is. Like he's secretly scary. Secret scary isn't un-scary. It's actually sort of worse."

Quentin would probably laugh to hear himself described that way. I still looked at Cal in dismay. "I'm your *Prince*. One day I'll be your *King*. You don't get to tell me you won't get in the middle of something. If I want you in the middle, the middle's where you're going to be."

"Yeah, but you're my Prince with a sitting regent, and she said to keep an eye on you, which means not getting myself murdered by your scary changeling girlfriend. I know what my job is right now. My job is *you*."

I glared at them. They shrugged, unrepentant.

"If you don't want someone else telling me what to do, hurry up and take the throne. Until then, you aren't the one in charge."

I started to object, then stopped, sighed, and stood. "Stay here," I said. "As you said, you're staying out of this." I turned, not for the stairs, but for the kitchen.

Willis was at the stove when I stepped into the room, his attention primarily focused on the skillet of eggs sizzling away in front of him. He had a little bowl of grated cheese that he was sprinkling over the top of the pan. The burner wasn't lit. Hob magic has its uses.

I frowned. "That looks like cast iron," I said. "It isn't, right?"

"Since I don't want to poison myself or my daughter, or even you—not really—no, it's not cast iron," said Willis. "It's granite."

I didn't know how cookware could be made of stone, and I had the feeling that if I asked, he would tell me, so I didn't ask. "Oh."

"I heard Helen's door slam. She's pretty mad at you right now. I expected you to be upstairs trying to apologize to her."

"I can't."

"And why's that, son? Keep in mind, she's my beloved baby girl and the only thing I have left of her mother, and you're the boy I sometimes allow into my home. Answer carefully."

"Because . . ." I stopped, sorting through my tangled thoughts, and finally said, "I didn't mean to get hit by that car. It hurt and I didn't like it and I'll try really hard not to let it happen again. But if I had to make the choice to save Cal or not right now, I'd still save them. I'm faster than they are. I'm stronger. I can survive it, and they probably wouldn't have."

"You're willing to break my daughter's heart over 'probably'?" Willis gave the eggs a stir.

I sighed. "If this is enough to break your daughter's heart, I may have to break it even worse because this isn't going to change, and I can't hurt her on purpose."

Willis glanced over his shoulder at me, and for the first time in our acquaintanceship, I thought I actually saw respect in his eyes. "I didn't realize you understood that."

"I'm a Prince of Cats. I have been since I was born. It was never . . ." I paused, looking for the right words, and finally said, "It was never *optional*. I could run away tomorrow, tell my Uncle Tybalt I won't take his throne, trap him in a position he's no longer suited to hold, and I'd still be a Prince of Cats. It's not about being someone's heir. It's about having the kind of power the Court of Cats requires to survive. It doesn't matter what I want. People will always need me to be an anchor for them. If I ran, someone would eventually challenge me for the crime of being in their territory, and I'd only have to win once to wind up King somewhere else. Somewhere that isn't here and isn't home. I'd rather stay here and keep my word and be someplace familiar when I have to be King. But I *do* have to be King. I can't say no."

"And that means you're going to have to put yourself in danger," said Willis.

"It means we're going to have to break up."

I wasn't sure what I'd been expecting his reaction to be. Anger, maybe, or relief that I was finally going to get away from his daughter. He just nodded, though, and turned his attention back to the eggs.

"You're young, you know," he said. "Honestly, if I've ever had an objection to the two of you being . . . involved . . . it's that you're young, and I remember being young. I didn't always make the best choices. It's hard for human kids, or kids like Helen, to understand that something they do today can impact them in five years, or ten, or twenty. For kids like you, like the one I was, it's even harder, because we're looking at a scale of centuries. When we screw up, it can haunt us for hundreds and hundreds of years. That's not easy. That's not fun. So yeah, I haven't always totally approved of how close you two are, or how much time you spend together, but it's not because I don't approve of you. I just . . . I don't want her to do something she's going to regret later."

"That sounds like I'm something she's going to regret," I said, voice as neutral as I could make it.

"That's not what I meant."

I took a deep breath, forcing my fingernails to stay the way they were, rather than extending into claws. "I know Helen's your daughter, and you don't want her getting hurt. But she *did* get hurt. Blind Michael hurt her. He didn't do it by mistake, and he didn't do it because he loved her and thought it would be okay. He did it because he was a monster. Monsters hurt people. October killed him, and I guess if you asked him, he'd say that made her a monster, too, and maybe I'm a monster because I'm glad he's dead. I'd kill him every day while Helen watched if I thought it would help her. Lots of things can hurt her. I don't want to be one of them. I'm afraid I'm going to be because I'm always going to be what I am. But it's not because we're *young*. It's because the world sucks."

"I understand." Willis lifted the pan off the stove and began portioning the eggs onto the waiting plates. "Let me guess: you either expected relief at the idea that you'd be getting away from my daughter, or anger, because why wouldn't you be planning to spend the rest of your life with her? She's smart and funny and beautiful and good. You'd be lucky to have her."

He was right, which made my stomach curl. "I guess this is where us being young makes a difference, huh?" I couldn't imagine marrying Helen, even if the throne weren't going to get in the way. I liked her a lot. I probably loved her. But Willis was right when he said the choices we made today could last for centuries, and I wasn't ready yet to decide which choices were the right ones.

"I guess so," he agreed.

"How old were you when you met Helen's mother?"

He laughed mirthlessly. "Four hundred and nine. Still a young man, by the standards of the Hobs I was living with. When I started stepping out with a human woman, they called me a hothead and a fool, said she'd just die and break my heart. They were right about that part. They were wrong about the rest. My Tina was the smartest choice I ever made. She didn't mean to leave me. She didn't mean to leave *us*. I made my choices, and I stand by them. As long as you treat Helen with respect and can say the same thing about your own choices, I'm all right with them."

Willis picked up two plates of scrambled eggs and held them out to me.

"Take them upstairs," he said, almost gently. "She's probably waiting for you to follow her. I'll feed Cal."

"Okay," I said, and took the plates, and left the kitchen.

EIGHT

Climbing the stairs with bruises that felt like they ran all the way down to my bones was an experience I wasn't planning to repeat any time soon. Once I was recovered enough to return to the Court of Cats, we'd find me a healer and make all of this go away. Yes. We'd make all of this go away, and then Quentin and I would go to a spa and sit in hot water until my body forgot what it even was to ache.

Helen's bedroom door was closed. I looked at it and sighed.

"I have your eggs," I called. "I don't have any free hands, and I don't trust myself on the Shadow Roads yet. Can you come open the door? Please?"

Silence answered me. I sighed again, louder this time.

"Come on, Helen. This isn't fair. I just want to talk to you, okay?"

Footsteps from the other side of the door heralded her approach. Then it opened—not far. Just enough for her to scowl out at me.

"You won't promise not to put yourself in danger, but you'll bring me eggs."

"Well, yeah." I shrugged helplessly. "I'm a Prince of Cats. Danger is always going to be part of my life, even when I wish it wasn't. You know I'd rather be watching movies on the couch with you than getting hit by cars." Movies on the couch, or other things in her bedroom. I could try for dignity as much as I wanted. I was still a teenager.

Although, if Uncle Tybalt and October were anything to judge by, adults liked to blame everything teenagers did on their hormones while still being more than half-ruled by their *own* hormones. It was another case of "do as I say, not as I do," and the fact that it was funny didn't make it less annoying.

"Really? Because you just told me you weren't going to stop."

I held up the plates. "Eggs. Eggs for eating." My stomach grumbled. "I need to eat them. Can we sit down and talk about this? Please?"

Helen looked at me sullenly for a moment before she turned and walked back over to her bed, leaving the door open for me. I sagged with relief and followed her into the room. I closed the door before I moved to sit beside her on the mattress, handing one of the plates over.

"They're not cold yet," I said, before driving my fork into my own plate of fluffy scramble. The eggs were excellently well-prepared—hearth magic tends to lend itself to excellent outcomes, regardless of the cook's actual skill—and I took several quick bites before glancing at Helen and lowering my fork.

She was pale, trembling slightly as she stared down at her plate. A tear ran down the slope of her nose and fell onto the eggs, vanishing.

"You're going to leave me," she whispered. "I always knew . . . I always guessed you would, but it was always later. Like 'later' was a different country and I didn't have to worry about what happened there. Only later isn't far away anymore, is it? Later is right around the corner."

"Helen . . ." I set my plate aside before taking hers out of her lap. Then I moved, slowly and achingly, to kneel in front of her. She looked at me gravely. I took her hands in mine, holding them as tightly as I dared.

I took a deep breath.

"I love you," I said. She flinched. I didn't let go. "You're brave and smart and loyal and beautiful, and I guess I'd love you even if you weren't all of those things, but it makes it easier that you are. You're perfect. You're better than I deserve."

"So why can't you choose me?" Her voice was a whisper, aching and broken.

I sighed. "Because I don't have a choice. I was born a Prince of Cats. That's what I *am*. It's what I have to be, whether I like it or not—and I do like it, Helen. I really, really do. I'm powerful and I'm well-taught and I'm going to keep my people safe from monsters like the one who hurt us. I love you. I love my people, too. I'm not going to turn my back on them because I'd rather be with you."

"That's what your Uncle's doing," she snapped, and everything suddenly made sense.

"Helen . . ." I stopped, catching myself before I said anything I wouldn't be able to take back. When I tried again, I kept my voice softer, kept my eyes steady on hers. "My uncle has been King of Cats in San Francisco for more than a hundred years. He's earned a break. He's earned a chance to heal from everything that's been done to him. I don't want to be King yet. I want to be a teenager. I want to kiss you and tell you you're beautiful, and let things go wrong without feeling like I have to take care of them. But I can't do that if it means forcing my uncle to stay and become a bad King."

"He's losing his throne because he loves Toby," said Helen.

I nodded.

"You'll leave me because you have to put your people over me."

I hesitated before I nodded again. "If I have to. I don't want to. Helen, I want to stay with you more than anything. But I think . . . I think you need someone to talk to. Someone who isn't me or your father. You're not getting better. You're still scared all the time. That's not good for you. It's not *healthy*."

She laughed unsteadily. "Who do you want me to talk to? I can't exactly go down to the local urgent care and ask for a therapist with experience dealing with fae issues."

"Why not?"

She blinked at me. "Did you hit your head against that car? You *know* why not."

"I really mean it. Why not?" I stood, still holding her hands. "Your Queen in the Mists lived in the human world for like, a hundred years, and her Chatelaine's a changeling, and my regent used to be a changeling. Toby knows all the halfbloods and thinbloods and everybody. I bet *someone* out there knows a fae therapist. Someone you could talk to without betraying any secrets, because they already know them!"

Helen scoffed, turning her face away. "Therapy is for humans."

"Therapy is for people who need to talk about their problems so they can get better. I mean, honestly, most of the purebloods I know would *really* benefit from some professional help. They get so messed up, and then they never talk about it, until one day they wander off into the nearest forest, or go evil and try to kill everyone, or decide they'd be better off as monsters. Can you imagine how much easier everything would be if people made better choices? Or at least choices that involved less knives?"

There was a long, long silence before Helen asked, in a small voice, "Do you really think there's someone out there who helps people like us? Who'd be willing to talk to me? I'm just a changeling."

The urge to scratch everyone who'd ever made her feel that way—including, at times, myself—rose in my breast, the way it always did when she talked about herself that way. Like she didn't matter. "If there's one thing I can be absolutely sure of after spending the last several years following October around, it's that there's no such thing as 'just' a changeling. Everyone's different. Everyone's important. You matter so much, and it . . . it scares me sometimes, thinking about the way you're shutting yourself away in here. I won't always be able to come make sure the world hasn't forgotten about you."

She looked back to me, eyes abruptly distant. "You're going to break up with me, aren't you? As soon as you become King, you're going to break up with me."

"Maybe." I didn't see the point in lying to her now, not when she was already upset. It would just make things worse later. "I might have to. I don't know. Or maybe I won't have to. Uncle Tybalt was dating October for a while before anyone started talking about abdication. She gets into a *lot* more trouble than you do. We could probably be a couple for a long time before you wanted to, I don't know, go off to culinary school somewhere else, or met somebody you liked better than you like me."

"I'm never going to meet anyone I like better," she whispered.

"Not if you stay locked up in your house, you won't, but maybe.

You'll get help and you'll feel better and you'll go to Trader Joe's to buy cheese and trail mix and meet some nice Hob working at the free samples station, and you'll realize you never wanted to be with a Cait Sidhe who forgets what time he's supposed to be places." I shrugged. "The future's really big. It has a lot of stuff in it. Why don't we worry about right now first, and see what that gets us? I'll try not to jump in front of any more cars. You'll look for someone to talk to. We'll both get better. That's what matters, right? We'll both get better."

"Together," said Helen, and squeezed my hand.

I smiled. My stomach grumbled, and she laughed. I ducked my head, sheepish but pleased.

"Right now, maybe what matters most is our eggs," I said.

"Maybe," Helen agreed.

They were still delicious, even though they were cold. I sat on the bed next to Helen, our shoulders touching, and I ate every single bite.

NINE

When I came downstairs carrying our empty plates, Helen following close behind me, Cal was standing at the base of the stairs, nervously shifting their weight from foot to foot. Willis was leaning in the doorway. I swallowed my sudden panic and looked past him to where Ginevra was waiting for me, sitting on the couch like she had all the time in the world. Her clothing was mortal—jeans and a sweatshirt—and completely at odds with her fae, faintly feline appearance. I shot Willis a panicked look.

"I didn't want to interrupt, but I think you're grounded, kiddo," he said, and took the plates out of my suddenly nerveless hands. "Don't worry. It was a first offense. I'm sure she'll go easy on you."

"I'm not," said Ginevra. I winced, focusing on her face. Then I blinked.

She didn't look angry, or cold, or imperious; none of the things I had expected from her. She looked . . . exhausted, like she'd been awake all day, and wasn't sure how much longer she could keep it up. Her hair was frizzy and her sweatshirt was baggy and shapeless, not at all befitting a Princess of Cats.

This was bad.

"Do you understand what you've put me through?" she asked, standing and moving toward me. "You didn't come back when you said you would. You gave me your word and then you didn't come *back*. I thought . . . I thought you'd run away to make the point that I didn't get to tell you what to do. I thought you were dead in the Bay. I thought you'd been kidnapped. I thought a *lot* of things, and somehow, none of them was worse than you getting hit by a car and taken to a mortal veterinarian! That was the worst thing I could possibly have imagined happening, and it happened! Do you understand what you've done?"

"Um," I said. "I got hit by a car?"

Ginevra stared at me.

"In my defense, I didn't do it on purpose," I said. "I was saving Cal. They're going to be one of my subjects someday. I couldn't stand there and let them die."

Cal grimaced, but said, "He really did save me. I couldn't move."

"I'm sorry," I said. "I would have come and told you I was all right, but you don't have a phone that works in the Summerlands, and I didn't trust myself on the Shadow Roads after getting all those painkillers pumped into me."

Ginevra opened her mouth like she was going to object. Then she stopped, and took a deep breath, and said, "You're right."

Now it was my turn to stare at her.

"You couldn't have stood there and watched Cal die. If you'd been able to, I would have needed to tell your uncle that my regency wasn't going to end with you on the throne, because you'd be completely unsuited to the position. You acted like a Prince of Cats. You acted like a *good man*. So you didn't do anything wrong, and your punishment, such as it is, is going to be getting me a phone so that this never happens again. All right?"

I looked at Ginevra, my Regent, the woman who was making it possible for my uncle to move on and remember how to be happy. I looked at Cal, my subject-to-be, who would follow me to the ends of the earth for what I'd done for them. And then I looked over my shoulder at Helen, my girlfriend, who I loved, who was finally going to get the help she needed.

When I returned my attention to Ginevra, I was smiling.

"All right," I said. "That seems fair."

I can be a Prince of Cats—I can be a King, someday—and still be a good man. Somehow, if I can manage that, I feel like I can manage anything. I feel like I can save the world.

In my own way, I feel like I can be a hero.